THE FAT MAN

IN AMERICA

by

"DANIEL"

First Published 1993 by :

YELLOW BRICK PUBLISHERS. 2, LONSDALE ROAD, QUEENS PARK, LONDON. NW6 6RD.

British Library Cataloguing in Publication Data :
A catalogue record for this book is available from the British Library.

ISBN : 0-9520560-7-0

For Stella, Ray,
and of course, for
Delia

PREFACE

Why are the F.B.I. and the Mafia both in a race to find Daniel?

Why does the beautiful Dee Stone stay with him in the face of certain death?

Why do the C.I.A. want them dead and why are the Nicaraguans so willing to help assassinate them?

How can one little robbery make one fat Englishman so many high powered enemies?

How can one broke unarmed overweight conman on the run threaten the stability of the United States?

What is the secret of the little store in Miami?

When the Government is partners with the mob - there's no hiding place for the Fat Man in America.

From the headquaters of the C.I.A. to the banking halls of Europe, the word is out - Bury the Fat Man.

This book is based on fact, although certain names, locations and factual details have been changed in order to protect the individuals concerned.

"Tell him I can't screw. Tell him anything. Tell him I'm gay! Say all that stuff about you being happy and satisfied was just bullshit bravado. He'll believe it."

Dee concentrated on her crossword puzzle.

Anyone would believe anything of her in that crimson negligee. Draped across the sofa she made a dramatic splash of colour against the bland nothingness of the rented apartment. I paced back and forth, puffing my last cigar.

Melted butterscotch masquerading as sunlight streamed from the balcony, adding fire to her golden hair. I tried to blow a smoke ring. My smoke rings always break early. I never know why.

"Dee, imagine youre the star and I'm your director. Play the scene right, you get paid in gold like Sarah Bernhardt."

Dee lasered me with a pale blue stare.

"You're directing? It'll be a disaster movie." She turned back to the puzzle.

I blew cigar smoke in her general direction. "Please don't aggravate Mr. DeMille when he's giving guidance," I said.

She assumed a beatific expression. A nurse humouring the chronically insane. I continued:

"We have no money. He has the gold. He wants

you. String him along. Tell him life with me is... too insecure."

"It bloody well is," she said, picking up her cigarettes and lighter.

I knelt down beside her and growled softly in my best Edward G. "The greatest production of your life and you won't listen to my stage directions?"

The gold lighter flashed. Dee exhaled half a cigarette over my face.

"Listen, Toulouse. You want total attention, use animals. They jump up and down for a biscuit. You haven't even fixed me any Rocket Fuel!" She waved the empty glass.

I stood up, my right knee creaking. At the cabinet I mixed her cocktail. Equal gin, tonic, ice and lemon juice.

I took a sip. Awful.

I passed her the drink......

Once we had made the essential decision, the rest was easy.

Like making love.

I took one of those cardboard sheets that the laundry puts inside my shirts (I've always been a back-of-an-envelope man).

The thing to do is make a plan. Write everything down in sequence. Tick it off as it happens. I saw Steve McQueen do that once in The Thomas Crown Affair. At the end of the movie he was in a jet with the readies whilst his girlfriend was still waiting for him in a graveyard. Dee would never stand for that.

Those last few days in Miami, she followed her

usual routine; asleep till three in the afternoon, a little swim, a little lounging around the apartment wearing a couple of postage stamps, screwing up my concentration.

I was frequently ordered out to buy a copy of 'Pravda' as she called the London Daily Mail. Give Dee enough gin, newspapers, cigarettes, and crossword puzzles and she would sit out World War III.

Occasionally I managed to fire her up to perform in the cuisine department. She made an amazing toasted cheese sandwich. Amazing because I must have eaten a thousand of them and they all tasted different.

Starting from the end of the rainbow, from the dream moment when I would have the pot of gold free and clear, I worked backwards, writing everything down point by point on the laundry card. Wipe the apartment, burn all papers, photos. We needed air schedules, hotels, transport, cash and an emergency contact point in case anything went wrong.

For the contact point, I reckoned Benny the Bookie was the best bet. He was out of jail now and firing on 12 cylinders. Benny was ideal, firstly because he was in England, beyond the reach of the FBI, the U.S. Marines and anybody else Uncle Sam could sling after us. Secondly, Benny was perfect for the 'magic' spiel.

With open disdain Dee watched me grafting with the laundry card.

"Efficiency, my girl," I said picking up the phone

and calling the airport.

"Efficiency is all right if you're Rockefeller," she replied. "Otherwise you want the world to be inefficient. Sloppy. You want..." Dee raised her gin and tonic proposing a toast. "a pathetic police and negligent border guards." The ice clinked in her glass as she drank. "Where are we going anyhow?"

I covered the mouthpiece. "Somewhere we can't be extradited back to the States from," I said. "Rio is wonderful, they tell me."

Dee leapt up onto the sofa, holding a pineapple from the fruit bowl on top of her head in an impromptu Carmen Miranda. Her flimsy negligee fell open, revealing that young body. Pale outlines told where her bikini had been. She began to warble about Brazillian coffee beans. I couldn't hear what the airport were saying. I motioned for quiet.

No such luck.

Dee became a stern voiced G-Man. "The search is on for the fat man and the ice-cool blonde. Last seen wearing a million dollars' worth of gold coins and a pair of maraccas."

I flicked a cushion at her with my free hand. While it was still in the air, she jumped over the back of the sofa. She had always been athletic at school. The cushion landed on the sofa with a plump. I thanked the airline operator and hung up.

"The amazing thing," said Dee, popping her head up over the back of the sofa, "is he really thinks he's got you. You're his mug. Working all hours and cleaning coins in the toilet for a lousy one fifty a week. He's incredibly mean and stupid." She climbed over the sofa and squatted on the floor, cradling her drink. "He doesn't know who you are."

"Who am I then?"

"You're a kosher genius, dear."

"Are you sure you can make him fix the date?" I looked at her.

"Is the Chief Rabbi a Jew?" she replied, hands on hips. "is Paris a city? Does a ten cent soda cost a dime?"

"Not in Paris, darling . Nothing under a hundred francs. We have to be certain." I needed reassurance. "He must believe that you're dying to spend the weekend with him."

"Darling," she said, her head bowed in concentration. "I wasn't the star of Moseley Village Amateur Dramatic Society for nothing. Not only do we have a weekend booked on the yacht, but the moment he drops you at the airport, he's going to pick up food, wine, cocaine, kinky clothes and my mystery present."

"Not less than 5 carats." Her frown vanished. The pencil flew across the puzzle page.

"I'll tell you what," I said stubbing out my cigar. "You steal the gold shipment and I'll spend the weekend on the yacht with Stuart."

MIAMI SHORES
APRIL

"Are the wrinkles still in the pool, Daniel?"

Dee always woke up that fraction of a second before I did. I had never once beaten her to either consciousness or unconsciousness.

I touched her briefly with my fingertip, to make sure she really was in bed with me and that I wasn't hallucinating. Her skin was smooth and warm. I think I found a buttock; she's so curvy it's hard to tell. If I had left my hand there longer I would have known for sure. But then I wouldn't have been able to leave the bed.

I crawled out into the usual Siberian blackness. Dee insisted on keeping the air-conditioning blasting away all night, and the blinds tightly drawn.

My throat felt as if someone had performed a tracheotomy whilst I'd slept. I certainly hadn't done it myself: I don't have the same courage as the Frog, after that Viet Cong landmine blew half his face away. Anybody who can prop themselves up against a tree and open their own windpipe with a bayonet, could handle a bit of a sore throat from the air conditioning.

Three months in the apartment had given me a rough idea where the curtains were. Tapping blindly around the bed, I launched myself shivering across the icy room, arms stretched out in front of me, feet stumbling over the various silk and crocodile items which I had stripped off Dee the night before.

My hand found the curtain pulley and I closed

my eyes. There was a rolling rattle as I pulled downward and the colour level beyond my eyelids brightened.

With all the caution that only serious vodka drinkers have, I risked opening my right eye. A sharp burst of light exploded in the back of my skull. In the split second before reflex snapped my eyelid shut again, my brain photographed a shining turquoise rectangle, framed with palms.

As usual by three in the afternoon, the swimming pool was devoid of our elderly neighbours, 'the wrinklies'.

Dee had to be sure of that, before emerging from bed. She once told me that the sight of all those wizened New Yorkers airing their retired pale corpses in the Florida sunlight was enough to send her straight for the gin, bypassing breakfast.

Holding a curtain across my stomach, no mean feat for one of my girth, I slid the balcony door open. Ovenfuls of hot, moist air swept over me, triggering memories of my father. The humidity in Miami always releases deeply buried childhood recollections of the Humidor rooms in elegant London cigar emporiums where frock-coated gentlemen would reverently profer Havanas. My father would pass them under his nose, hold them to his ear, and roll each cigar between thumb and forefinger. Dad had the game of life sorted out. Nowadays, when I buy a cigar, I'm lucky if I don't get a parking ticket whilst running to the tobacco stand. Whenever my father encountered traffic police, he declined to converse with them on the grounds that they hadn't been introduced socially.

I opened my eyes. Beautiful. A child's painting of a day. Below me in brilliant sunshine yachts scudded across the Gulf, their sails startlingly white, as they cruised aquamarine oceans beneath designer skies the colour of lapis lazuli.

Duplicate horizons glittered on the crystal canyons of Collins Avenue and palm fronds whispered in warm Gulf stream breezes.

It would have been a wonderful day if Scotland Yard, Interpol and the FBI hadn't been looking for me.

I stepped back into the apartment to make my report.

"Pool area clear of wrinklies, ma'am."

A sound somewhere between a grunt and the cry of a hungry heron emerged from the pillow where Dee's face was buried.

Padding into the kitchen, I fumbled about with kettles, taps and coffee cups. There were some tapes scattered near the stereo, I chose John Williams as a musician who understood hangovers.

Soft guitar notes drifted through the apartment as I staggered to the bathroom. Uneasily, I registered white shapes pushed under the door.

In the shower stall I leant against cold tiles while power jets fired hot water over me. Letters, I reasoned, wouldn't be from the FBI, who send more bullets than mail. My head was in no state to play guessing games. I stood on the scales. Two hundred and ninety one pounds. It had been two ninety three yesterday.

Must be the worry. I wrapped my bathrobe about me and went to pick up the mail.

The first white shape was a postcard in the thin spidery hand of Juliette Dahl, my mother's elderly friend. The one I should have seen by now but kept putting off. I turned the card over. It was one of those fifties colorchromes of Hialeah County where the palm trees are too green, the sky too blue and the swamps just out of camera range.

I squeezed the other two letters.

Not good news, for sure.

The kettle had boiled. I fixed Dee's coffee impossibly strong, just the way she liked it, sliced and squeezed a couple of local oranges into a glass for myself and juggled my way out. As I crossed the lounge I took in the empty bed and shower sounds from the bathroom.

Out on the balcony, I lit up the first Jamaican Corona of the day and settled myself more comfortably into the cane armchair, gazed out over Biscayne Bay and tasted the salt on the breezes.

I'd been feeding some seagulls, and they usually arrived when they spotted me up here. How they do it, I don't know. They came, God's creatures circling for a late breakfast.

I felt a world away from cops, lawyers, handcuffs and grimy jails. I certainly was a world away from having any money.

Seabirds wheeled above me as I opened the first letter.

It was from the management of our condominium.

Predictably, but with discretion, they reminded me that this month's rent should have been paid two days ago and under the terms etcetera.

Par for the course.

It was a polite 'pay up or piss off'. I knew precisely how much cash I had left.

A thousand dollars. The month's rent.

Money to me is always food. I see steaks and fruit in every banknote.

If I pay the rent, what then? Of course we still have our jewellery.

But we need that. Props in the play.

Dee without diamonds wouldn't be Dee.

We have to look the part.

Front is part of our stock in trade. In our game, the true artist exudes wealth and confidence. Silk shirts and tinted windows, crocodile and chrome.

The rich only want to be robbed by the rich.

Look rich and you'll soon be rich.

Oh well, something will turn up.

Mr. Micawber rides again.

I picked up the second letter. Expensive stationery. Cream coloured.

Certainly not FBI issue.

Someone with an electric typewriter had printed the word 'Daniel' on the envelope. Nothing else.

Now how had that arrived under my door?

Below me, two old men sat on the dock, trailing lines into the green water.

Dee would pawn her jewels if she had to. She was top class about things like that. She was top class about everything.

Two dinghies sailed by in tandem, about thirty yards apart. A boy in one, girl in the other, young, healthy, carefree.

A sip of orange juice and open the cream envelope.

A hundred dollar bill flutters out.

Bingo! Your starter for 10, Oxford University!

I shake the envelope to see if there are any more bright surprises. But no. Simply a sheet of matching cream, typed on one side.

The initials didn't register at first.

Then I remembered.

The man with the gold shop.

It was the kind of letter someone had spent a great deal of trouble over to make it look casual.

Dear Daniel, I should be delighted if you and your lady would join me for drinks and supper on the yacht, My Paradise. We will be berthed alongside Le Joint on Miamarina tomorrow evening for 7 p.m. I enclose $100 being a practical 'thank you' for your kind advice regarding the English five pound note.

Yours faithfully

S.F.

Destiny's gears began to grind. I leaned back in the easy chair, and blew cigar smoke skywards, trying for a ring.

The gold man.

Now he could come in handy.

There was a rustle as Dee materialised behind me, her hands lightly on my shoulders. I caught her scent. What was it? Private Collection.

She leaned down and kissed me as she spoke.

"Mail with money in it, darling! Are you doing postal porn?"

"Your next boyfriend, dear." I passed her the letter.

Dee glanced at the text and fingered the banknote. "The punter you told me about. I like his style, darling."

"I don't think he's got much style."

"Ooh, cranky this morning."

"Well, I woke up five million dollars short."

"So what's new?"

11

Dee moved around me and lay on a sunlounger, stretching out, a sexy animal in a bikini bottom.

Sunlight dappled her breasts and the waters of Biscayne Bay. A light breeze ruffled the letters.

"You're jealous," Dee decided and made a move. She's so attractive when she pulls faces.

"Me? Jealous of a few million dollars, a yacht and a man whose style you admire before you've met him?"

"You *are* jealous."

"Of course!" I said.

Dee sat up and kissed me. "I feel sorry for him already."

I handed her the hundred. "Here you are, Princess, the first of his money. Buy yourself those shoes." Dee had seen some multicoloured sandals in Dade which she had only mentioned twice.

"We can't afford them, Daniel."

"We can't afford to think that we can't afford things."

"But I don't need shoes, darling. Besides which that's the first American money you've earned. Was it for making him buy the five pound note?"

"It was for telling him how rare it was."

"We'll tell him how rare I am, darling. Maybe he'll send a thousand!"

Dee folded the note and slipped it into the top pocket of my robe, then leaned forward again and kissed my cheek. A child's kiss, a brush with rose petals.

"Hang onto the readies, darling. I've got more shoes than hundred dollar bills." Dee shook a cigarette from a pack and her gold lighter sparkled briefly in the afternoon sunshine.

Down on the dock the fishermen had become

excited. One was reeling in his line rapidly. The two dinghies were moving toward Broad Causeway now.

"Any money in the other one?"

I handed her the landlord's letter. She read it then put down her coffee cup decisively and climbed off the lounger. I was treated to flashes of creamy gold as her thighs scissored. There really was nothing much to her bathing costume. I wondered why she bothered to wear it.

"Just a moment." Dee disappeared into the apartment, whistling Happy Days Are Here Again.

I watched the fisherman land a fish. Probably a leatherjacket. It's mostly leatherjackets that you can catch from the dock, although I've seen sea bass and nurse sharks taken there.

Dee re-emerged holding the rent letter, and another thicker envelope.

"Close your eyes and put your hand out," she said.

I obeyed. "Cross my palm with pussy please."

"Later."

"Promises, promises."

I found something in my hand. Not pussy. Paper. It felt like banknotes. I rubbed. It was banknotes.

"Right on," I yelled, eyes still closed. "How much?"

"Two thousand dollars Australian," Dee said quietly.

I opened my eyes. There he was. Forty smiles from Kingsford Smith. Big yellow Aussie fifties. I looked at the money and Dee.

"Did I ever tell you that I love you?"

"Only when I pay cash," my girl grinned.

I propped the money onto the table and reached

for Dee. Pulling her down onto my knees I said, "You are really good, do you know that?" I nuzzled her ear. A breeze ruffled through papers on the table. Dee put my empty glass on top of the cash as a paperweight.

"Any more little reserves?" I asked as John Williams crescendoed in the apartment. "Swedish kroner? Yen? Hofman Laroche Bearer Bonds?"

"No dear, that really is it." Dee looked down at the fisherman below, proudly holding up his catch on a short twine. The other man, our neighbour, gathered up the equipment. Dee stretched over the balcony edge. I held her hips lightly, feeling her taut body through the thin gown.

"You could get fucked like this," I whispered.

"Show off," muttered Dee and then in a louder voice she called to the fishermen.

"What did you catch?"

"Leatherjacket." The old man grinned up at her and held the fish high for her inspection. "Want to come round for supper?"

"Yes please," called out Dee.

"Anytime, ma'am." The fisherman waved and walked on.

I pushed against her, pinning her body over the railing. I was growing hard. I gave her a thrust as I said, "You're just a flirt. He must be a hundred years of age. "

Dee put on a heavy Cornish accent. "Anything for a bit o'fish, moi dear." Then lapsing into her normal voice, "Besides he's got two million in Dade County Bonds. He told me so in the pool."

"Ouch," I said. "but he can't do for you what I can do."

"No, but I'll be comfortable and have my memories." I stepped back and held my hands up in surrender.

"Okay, wiseguy." Dee turned and poked me in the chest. "So what are you going to do about Mr. Gold Shop?"

"He's moving up rapidly in the placings, Princess. I'm thinking about it every little minute of the day." I sat down.

"That's my clever boy." Dee dropped into my lap and wriggled around, angelic and irresistible, golden locks framing a startingly pretty face. I kissed her pink, moist lips. She returned the kiss and then jumped up. She swayed to the music as she moved across the balcony, and her negligee swirled open, revealing that firm petite body. I was given a glimpse of perky breasts, and smooth belly tapering into a light blonde triangle. Rhythmically she turned, the gown closed and the vision vanished. Just as well. I was exhausted. Being on the run is a powerful aphrodisiac for Dee. She had woken me twice during the night.

She faced me, hands on hips, tantalizing. Her nightdress parted and I couldn't take my eyes off her.

"Can you think in the pool?" she asked.

"Not if you keeping wafting about like that." She grinned and danced away. "I'll get my cossie." I ogled her as she rhumba'd out of the living room, only to reappear a moment later, slim and magnetic in a new black bikini, black towel slung across one shoulder, a good advert for youth, sex and sunshine. "Coming?" she invited. "In a minute, Dee. Someone's got to do some thinking on the firm." "Flash bastard—I love you." "I love you too. Go ahead, excite the voyeurs, I'll join you down there."

Back on the balcony I pocket the Australian cash and watch Dee bounce toward the pool. My regular seabirds call out, chastising me for delaying their breakfast and I toss some bread into the air. Two birds swoop and catch crumbs, then wheel away. The day feels better. I fix myself a fresh glass of orange, add a shot of Stolichnaya Vodka and return to the balcony, the birds and the breadcrumbs. I sip breakfast, pull on the cigar, watch Dee float below and the seagulls dive above. Thanks to my Baby we have rent for a couple of months and money for food. Below me, Dee backstrokes in the pool, a little blond dolphin who cares for me. Trusts me. Time for a move on the chessboard. Time to bring my queen into play.

MIAMI SHORES
APRIL

I fingered the letter from the gold man.

My mind wandered back to last Tuesday, the argument about dinner. Where to eat, in or out?

I remembered how I had wanted to take her to the North shore.

"I'm hungry," I had said. "Starving. Let's go to Tony Roma's. Spare-ribs, juicy sauce, piano music, visiting Mafiosi. What do you say, kid?"

Dee gave me a motherly look. "I'd love to go out as much as you, Daniel, but the gelt is running out. The Uncle Teddy is slipping away. De Nelsons are sinking. The red light is winking on ze old cashome-ter."

I suppose my face must have fallen. "Okay." I gave her Robert Mitchum. "So we're losing height and belching black smoke, but I hate to think that we can't go out for a nosh-up. We might meet a punter and I'll sign him up for a donation. No one's going to knock on the door or chuck gelt through the window."

"You never know," said Dee. "I say save the readies. But Tony Roma's will leave you no change from a century and you don't a wanna rob de Mafia—not in Miami."

"When in Roma's?"

"Save the cash, Daniel. We're short."

Thoughts like that only put pressure on my head. Dee jumped up and bounded in front of me, then knelt and reached her hands up to cradle my face.

I dived into her eyes and the pain began to fade.

"Look," she said brightly. "You go to the supermarket and buy steaks and ice-cream. I'll make a salad, we'll stay in and watch TV. Take it easy. What do you say? Go with the flow."

What could I say? Dee cooking was rarer than icebergs in Biscayne Bay. Go with the flow. Don't fight the programme.

"Okay, baby. We dine at 'Homa's'. Don't drop a diamond down the kitchen sink. You know it's not your scene."

"Do try and find a blue rinse in the supermarket, Daniel. Old General Motor's widow or someone like that."

"All the rich widows are out eating on the North Shore," I grinned wryly.

It was late afternoon as I stepped out into Florida; a pleasant shock after Siberia upstairs.

I manoeuvred our rented Ford past the Jaguars, Cadillacs and Porsches of my wealthy neighbours. I always enjoy driving American cars: effortless power, automatic gears, bundles of gadgets.

I eased the big car onto the six lane Venetian Causeway which links North Bay Village and mainland Miami. Heading across Biscayne Boulevard to Miami Avenue I decided to aim for the Pantry Pride supermarket about a mile away where we sometimes shop. Around me, insulated inside their glittering robots, Floridians race homeward to their mortgages and divorces, talking into carphones and stoking up the blood pressure. The freeway was packed, the sidewalk deserted. Only Dee walked in Miami. A Cadillac burst past me, phone aerial swaying, its solitary occupant deep in conversation to his mistress, coke dealer or book-

18

maker.

Or all three.

I thought again about earning some money from cars. I had already decided to bring over a used Rolls Royce or Bentley from Britain. Americans are crazy for them. Importing isn't difficult. Steam clean the car in England, eight days shipping to Florida, a few forms at customs, a bit of duty and In Like Flint.

A trial advert in the Miami Herald had already brought me a great response. I do love an ad. The phone never stopped, with punters from all over the States offering thousands of dollars more than the car cost in Britain. I looked like I had found a clue to earn a good living. If Benny kept his promise to buy me a Rolls and ship it over.

I need to be careful with the customs people in case their computers were linked to the FBI. I was, after all, a well-wanted illegal immigrant by now. I wonder if the guy at the car rental place knows about Customs computers. He seems to be a bit of a mover.

Leaving the Ford in the carpark, I strolled through the surreal evening sunlight into the supermarket.

I enjoy shopping in America. The variety is so wide. I bought thick fillet steaks, Iceberg lettuce, and cellophane wrapped tomatoes, celery and kohlrabi. A jar of olives and some onions completed the salad. Buying food always makes me hungry, and I began to think about a snack.

The checkout girl's syrupy Southern "Thank you for shopping Pantry Pride," was still ringing in my ears as I decided on a hamburger. A big one with relish. It would only take a minute to pick up, and Dee wouldn't have supper ready for ages.

There was a MacDonald's further along the freeway. You couldn't miss it. The golden arches of its M sign dwarfed the palms.

Out on the waters of the bay magnificent yachts cruised. The open ostentation of America frustrated me. Survival in the States means money. Money takes time.

Money and time were running out for me. One smart cop to check my driver's licence and I'll be in jail, then my worries about money will be over; that's when the time will start to be the problem.

I pulled up at the MacDonald's.

In the empty restaurant the helpful staff pushed computer buttons and took my cash. The smell of burger assailed my nostrils as I waited for my order to be filled.

I glanced out of the window and encountered Nemesis.

Across the freeway, dignified and imposing, stood a white Rolls Royce Silver Cloud III with British number plates.

An import? How much did the owner pay for it? I decided to go over and find out.

I picked up my Big Mac and munching on it, jaywalked over to the Rolls.

I wasn't thinking about robbing anyone at all.

MIAMI
APRIL

When I was younger, I used to get a sexual thrill from Rolls Royces.

Not even money does it for me now.

As I ran my eye over the Silver Cloud, I could tell that it was not a straight car. At some stage in its elegant life it had been bashed and the bodywork professionally sprayed. The red leather interior was _too_ clean for its age. It was a 'punter's' car, 'well spoodled up' as we used to say. I squatted and ran a hand underneath the sill, just like my old guvnor at Lincoln Street had taught me. No rust. Someone must have been busy with the filler bucket if this had recently arrived from Britain. The salt we spray on the roads in winter murders the underneath of Rollers. I stood up scanning the area.

Miami Avenue was silent in a rare still moment. An evening breeze offset the closeness and rustled the palms along the highway.

The Rolls stood beside an elegant white building set back from the roadway in luxurious contrast to the garish gas stations and strident car lots.

It was above the door that I saw the sign; gleaming gold on white, a message from the Gods sending shivers of ESP down my spine.

THE ROLLS INVESTMENT COMPANY, COIN-DEALERS.

A small window sunk into the marble beside the door displayed a single gold coin, nestling in red velvet.

My kind of touch.

The open door spoke of 'defences down', of an arrogance that said it couldn't be robbed, of challenge, a glint of gold like the first rays of a Las Vegas dawn, of a jackpot tantalizingly glimpsed on the tumblers of the machine, not quite lined up but only a good pull on the handle away.

I push through the door and step inside. It's pitch black after the sunlit street and my eyes take a moment to adjust. I realise what I'm looking at and stop breathing. My heart trip-hammers against my ribs.

Maybe this is where Farouk docked after he fled Egypt with a yacht full of goodies from the Cairo Museum. I've never seen anything like it. Well, not in my waking moments. The whole place is a Floridian Aladdin's Cave. A floor to ceiling treasure house.

Behind glass panels glow stacks of gold coins, racked in unbelievable rows. But they are real. Objets d'art in precious metal and stones tumble in a display that would make an eastern potentate's heart sing. Yellow chalices, gleaming candlesticks, and burnished shields are piled on red velvet, surrounded with white ropes. Boxing rings crammed with golden antiquities. Shelves lined with statues and necklaces fill the walls. Artful leather chests overflow with gold coins like Bluebeard's Treasure, rubies and diamonds burn tantalisingly amongst the seashells. Glass cabinets heaped high with Hapsburg Thalers vie with cases of dandelion-size Doubloons and amber sovereigns. The jewels throb and twinkle beneath the neon.

At once a premonition possessed me, this gold was like sharks' teeth, either it would devour me or I would wear it about my neck or both.

I have found the end of the rainbow.

At once I am nervous and embarrassed. There must be powerful alarms in this place. "The gaff will be well-belled up", as my pal from London, Kim the Burglar, would say.

Not that I'm any good with sophisticated security devices. Not being electrical, practical, digital, logical or clinical, I usually have trouble with my own front door key.

Blowing vaults and burglary have never been my style.

You'll never find me dressed up in a black ninja suit. I'm too heavy, too clumsy, too much the klutz. If I tried to suspend myself from some rope I would fall crashing through the exhibits. Cracking computer codes is not my scene. If I need a cracksman, I'll hire one.

I glance around me. The shop appears an expensively fitted, unoccupied temptation. I could reach my hand over the rope and touch the gold, but I bet a fire station full of bells would ring. Red carpet, oak-panelling and the carefree chandelier create an ambience suitable for well-heeled Florida retirees to write rows of sweet zeros on the cheques.

The cash registers in my mind tintinabulate until I feel the urge to press my hands to my ears.

The display captures me. But there's something wrong. It's too good.

There is a latent power here, an absurd arrogance in a city as full of sharks with submachine guns as Miami. In this town Heckler & Koch are the practicing attorneys. In Miami, Smith & Wesson ride the high streets in cocaine plated Cadillacs. An open door to a treasure house like this speaks of protection. Mob money.

Robbing the mob won't bother me. I'm the little Jewish boy whose daydreams are swindling the PLO out of their bomb fund or ripping the IRA off in some fantasy coup, so milking the Mafia is just my scene.

The shop is not empty. A pair of glasses and a moustache turn towards me. A blue shirted figure pecks on a telex in the back of the room. A tanned hand waves, gold bracelet helioing with the movement of the wrist.

"Be right with you," calls the man who stays hunched over his machine.

I wander around blowing Partagas smoke into the conditioned air, giving off rich punter vibes. A heat motivated camera tracks me, red light blinking. I spot a one-way mirror set back into the wall, and wonder who is concealed behind it. The air-conditioning hums and telltale bumps beneath the carpet indicate hidden alarm triggers. I don't look at the ceiling. No point in being obvious.

I am impressed. Any desperado-on-the-run, not-really-a-thief would be. I marshal my thoughts and focus on the moustache at the telex. What's his clue? He's working late, therefore he must be the governor, therefore it's his Rolls outside.

People are my game. I'm a one-on-one specialist. People are the key to treasure and people are my long suit. I'm at my best with reasoned arguments, brilliant points, firm handshakes, well-answered questions and of course, the unbeatable deals.

So far the whole scene is very me. The Rolls, the man on the telex, the gold.

24

On my mental cashometer the needle is rising. My mind is crackling. Now come on, son. Try to fight the impulses down. You're not here to rob. Do yourself a favour. Just get the price of the Rolls. Haven't you got enough problems already? You want more trouble? But I can't help it. I'm hooked. I know I've struck. I've had the message. It's too late for me. I just signed up for the dream. I'm the commander-in-chief of the doomed battalion yelling CHARGE!

I've made enough deals in my life to know the meaning of physical gold. Possess gold and you are immediately rich. Gold is exchangeable anywhere on this planet. From the high Andes to Zurich. From the Transvaal to the Paris Bourse. Humble peasants in mud huts will bite on a gold coin and shelter, feed or transport you.

Swiss bankers rip open the cognac bottles and push Havanas across their desks.

Gold.

The stuff of dreams.

My dreams.

Champagne at the end of the rainbow. Gold bars in Nazi lakes. Bullion stacked up in Fort Knox.

Gold in vaults, treasuries, teeth.

Settled people often misunderstand the reality of money. Refugees and thieves know it in their blood.

If you steal a painting what have you got? A bit of oily canvas. You move it, you ruin it. Try to sell it, and they want a letter from the Pope before they'll talk to you.

Walk down the street with the Mona Lisa tucked under your arm and a dozen Picassos up your shirt and you're still poor. You can't cleanly steal cars, houses or ships; at the end of the day they're still there. Jewels can be fake and overvalued.

Deal or steal drugs and you're holding twenty years in jail and a load of aggravation. Currency - they'll take the serial numbers. Try changing your stolen yen in Burkina Faso and see what happens!

But walk down any street with a bag of gold and you are rich. You are also a target for robbery, like the jeweller in the blue shirt.

One little gold coin will perform for you everywhere on this planet and this guy has them stacked to the ceiling and piled up on the floor. Behind glass and white rope.

My aunt used to do much the same with tins of food in case there was another war. Except she stuffed her hoard in the cupboard. I wondered what motivates this man? My good intentions evaporate. I know I am going to rob him, or burst into the attempt. Time for me to get out my weapon.

Conversation.

The telex stops chattering and I hear the beep as the man switches off the machine. He's walking towards me now, a Jewish professional with a smile on his face.

"May I help you?"

He is courteous, American, middle forties, sun-tanned and goes to an expensive dentist. I see my own twin reflections, distorted in his glasses.

"Is that your Rolls Royce outside?" I ask.

No reply.

He appraises me like a horse dealer at the Kentucky Sales. My hair isn't grey enough to excite him, but my silk, jewellery and crocodile accessories are encouraging.

"Why do you want to know?" Slick. Question a

question. Typically Jewish.

"I'm thinking of importing them." Tell the truth, it's easy.

"You're English?"

"Yes. I've come back to claim the colony."

He decides I'm rich enough to touch and sticks out a hand.

"Stuart Falkman."

I introduce myself. As I touch him a nervous thrill runs through me, the mists part and I see trouble ahead. There will come a time when we'll both wish he'd thrown me out then and there. He is staring at my wrist. He's going to ask to look at my watch.

"May I see your watch?"

I unclip my fifteen thousand dollar Beaume & Mercier. It's an unusual piece. The face is a TV shaped black opal inset with a circular plate of diamonds. The strap a crazy paving in gold links.

The jeweller screws in an eyeglass and examines it. Dee and I believe in maintaining a front. It's okay for billionaires to walk about barefoot in jeans, the rest of us need costumes and props in our movie. I had bought the watch one night in Hawaii together with a diamond cluster ring of similar value for Dee. The shop in Waikiki had just been robbed (not by us) and whilst strolling around sipping Mai Tais we found the owner clearing up. Seizing the moment, I had made a brutal offer in cash. The owner had accepted, no questions, no receipts given. I bought pieces in his window the thieves had missed.

The shopkeeper in Hawaii had been like most people, greedy and ready to swindle his own insurance company.

I study this jeweller as he turns my watch over in his hands. Beaume & Mercier don't cut them out of cardboard. He removes his glass, his greedy beady eyes gleam; a frog spotting a tasty dragon-fly.

"Do you want to sell it?"

"Straight swap for the Rolls, Stuart."

He laughs. A mechanical little sound calculated to let me know he's seen the joke. He lays the watch delicately between us. I leave it there. A psychological move to show him both that I don't care and that it's still a bargaining point.

"Care for a drink, Daniel?" He gestures at an array of crystal decanters.

"Thank you, Stuart. Whisky, please." Go with the flow.

He deftly unplugs a decanter and makes crystal and glugging sounds, then returns carrying two tumblers generously filled and hands one to me. We clink glasses and say, "l'chaim". To life. I sip my drink. Chivas.

"You still haven't told me how much you paid for the Rolls."

"I'm not sure I want to. I've a feeling you'll buy it off me and make a profit selling it again."

My turn to laugh politely.

My wrist watch floats on top of the glass cabinet between us, drifting above his treasures like a diamond and opal magic carpet. My mind is racing. I've already intrigued and fascinated him and established a rapport. How can I turn this to cash?

That's the way my mind works. Cash, food and sex.

The conversation roams. Stuart tells me how he started fifteen years ago with a thousand dollars and a partner called Skill who now runs the even bigger New York operation.

I make 'what-a-wonderful-Jewish-success-story' noises.

Now the jeweller puts out feelers, probing me like a surgeon.

"What do you think of Dade County Bonds, Daniel?"

"Not too much, Stuart, my walls at home are lined with defunct bond issues."

"But Dade County is triple A rated."

"Yes, Stuart. And half the local administration are under indictment for corruption."

"You have a point," concedes the jeweller.

"Yes, but don't tell anybody. I'll get run out of Dade if I keep rubbishing their bonds. You're open late, Stuart."

"A lot of my customers like to come in after work and choose their pieces."

It's true. Places that take chunks of money off punters don't close at five. The heat activated camera locks onto us recording the scene. I wondered just who is behind the one-way mirror.

"Your shop is very discreet. I wouldn't have known it was here."

"My customers prefer it that way."

"Everyone else in Miami seems to want to vacuum people off the streets," I said.

"We have all the trade we can handle."

"I know the feeling," I replied.

He asks me what I'm doing in America and I give him a suitably edited version. He's curious. Englishmen in silk shirts and fifteen thousand dollar watches don't stumble in on him every day of the week. I try not to be specific. The rich avoid specifics.

The gold gleams around us, tantalizing back-drop to the conversation. I'm alert whilst being casual. I have to play this by ear. The whole setup has the word 'clue' written all over it. But what the clue is, I can't tell. I'm not going to come out of here with any money tonight. It's not that sort of clue and I'm not that kind of operator.

Slow and big, that's me.

Books line the glass and brass shelf next to us. There are titles on coins, currency, bonds, antiques and banking. As he refills my glass I have one of my crazy inspirations. Bingo! I don't know why I know I'm right, but I'm a gambler betting on a card in a game that hasn't started. Among the titles on the shelf I spot Franz Pick On Currency.

"Stuart, I bet I can tell you your favourite book in the whole world."

His eyes dart to the books. He knows the title isn't there. He grins.

"Go ahead. This'll be interesting."

Deep breath. The moment is liquid crystal. I can see everything clearly. I'm at the top of the diving board, the wind and water are still, the audience is craning upwards. A surge of excitement runs through me as I speak, another shiver of cold ESP down my spine.

"The Man Who Stole Portugal: The Story of Artur Alves Reis."

It's the first time in my life I've ever actually <u>seen</u> someone's jaw drop open. He stares at me dumb-founded. I could stuff a telephone directory between his chops. A flicker of fear crosses his eyes. He's frightened of something. I've always been too hot with the ESP. I've overdone it. He's much more disturbed than he should be. He recovers his composure quickly, however.

"How in the hell did you know that?"

His eyes asking, who are you?

"An educated guess. I'm brilliant like that," I say. Now this is really interesting. I have freaked him. One mention of the story of forged currency in Portugal and the guy goes pale. He turns away to hide his discomfort, busying himself with the decanters. I look around the room. I've definitely got the horn. There must be a couple of million dollars in here and presumably more in New York. I wonder what the source is of all this wealth. My little fat Jewish antennas are quivering. The old cashometer needle in my brain rises like a high speed lift.

The jeweller is speaking now, his composure regained.

"Since you're British you might know something about English five pound notes."

"Well," I concede. "I've handled one or two on their way through." Modest bastard I am. He smiles and shuffles papers, finding a handwritten letter to which a blue crisp five pound note is attached.

"Would you look at this one, Daniel?" He hands me the banknote. I examine it carefully knowing I'm being tested. The front of the note seems perfectly normal. There is Her Majesty, happy as ever, reigning along. I guess I'd be happy if my face was on the money. I'm getting plenty of vibes from the jeweller. He's scrutinizing me. I've disturbed him. I turn the note over. There is Her Majesty again.

I pronounce my verdict.

"The note is a rare misprint with the Queen's face on both sides, and valuable, Stuart." I hand back the fiver.

"How valuable?" There's that little greedy look again in his eyes.

"A few hundred dollars, I suppose. I've never seen one before. The Bank of England are normally meticulous in not allowing errors to slip through. Besides, some alert cashier should have spotted it and kept it for himself, swapping it for a normal one. They do that a lot in British banks, so not many errors find their way into circulation. It's certainly rare."

"Thank you, Daniel. You're quite an expert."

"Not really." Time to be Modest Mo, the coin-dealer's friend.

"Where are you staying in Miami, Daniel?"

His eyebrows rise appreciatively as I give him our address.

"That's a beautiful condominium. Do you live there alone?"

A real prober this one. He wants to know if I'm gay, married or into tropical fish.

"I have my fiance with me. When both our divorces come through, we hope to be married."

Falkman laughs. I pick up my watch.

"I have a yacht at Miamarina, Daniel. Perhaps you and your fiance would care to join me for supper one evening?"

"I'd be delighted, Stuart. I have to go now. I have a hungry woman waiting for steaks."

"When they're hungry, Daniel, feed them."

"It depends what they're hungry for, Stuart."

Now, I haven't got the faintest idea what I'm talking about, so it's time to leave. I sense that he wants me to stay. He seems lonely for intelligent company. Who isn't? But I go.

Always leave them wanting more.

In the apartment, I tell Dee the story. She is thrilled.

"The book guess was brilliant! Absolute magic. You've found a clue, darling," she enthuses. "Gold piled to the ceiling and an invitation to supper on a yacht. You didn't do too badly popping out to the supermarket."

"I didn't discover the price of the Rolls."

"But you found a punter, Daniel. A clue!"

After the meal I stacked the dirty supper dishes in the sink.

"I bet he was impressed with the book guess," said Dee for the fifth time. "I would have been."

We sipped white wine. Stan Getz doing his thing quietly on the stereo.

"What was the book about, Daniel?"

"In the 1920's Artur Alves Reis had persuaded the British printers, Waterlows, to run him off a few billion 100 escudo notes by the simple pretence of pretending he was a government man with a secret banknote contract. He said the government wanted the deal kept quiet because of inflation."

Dee nodded, her eyes glazing slightly.

"Since Waterlows already printed Portugal's currency, this was no problem. Reis took delivery of the notes himself and by the time the fraud was discovered he had become one of the richest men in Portugal on the proceeds. I saw the books on currency, Dee, and guessed the gold dealer's favourite story. But his reaction was odd."

Dee yawned. "Yes, darling. A puzzle."

By the time I came out of the kitchen, she was already in the bedroom with the lights out.

Dee liked to make love in the dark. She adored

touching and feeling. She said darkness helped her to lose herself. I often wondered if she found me repulsive with the lights on. Dark was the way she wanted it. I would have preferred to be able to see her beautiful body. Dee was the original platinum blonde all the way, with naturally creamy skin, white thighs tanned to gold, and the blonde pussy of a Swedish dream queen. I took off my shirt in the blackness.

Dee was already in bed lying on her belly, her arched back illuminated by the red and green stereo dial, like a painted nude in a Paris floor show. Anonymous jazz framed the moment, and she moved her body, rythmically thrusting her buttocks upward in provocative invitation.

I tremble in anticipation like I always do when we have sex. It's a gift, a privilege that might be withdrawn at any moment. There is a threat in our impermanent relationship. We are two kids on the run together never knowing when the knock on the door will come. The danger gives our lovemaking spice and poignancy. We can be arrested at any moment. Dee's world of soft sheets and diamonds can vanish into iron bars and hardfaced wardresses. I might exchange her perfume for filthy bunks in damp cells. I brought myself back to the moment to enjoy her. She wriggled erotically, stimulating me. I was already erect as I climbed onto the bed, crazy to fuck her.

My eyes grew accustomed to the darkness. I reached out and touched her skin. Cool and electric. I stroked her lightly, touching her soft neck and slowly tracing my fingers over her fine shoulders, feeling her skin come alive. I found her arm and ran down its slimness, encircling her wrist in

34

a gesture of capture. Awkwardly I moved nearer now, my leg against hers. I buried my face in her hair and pressed my body against her back, kissing the nape of her neck passionately. My cock stiff along the crevice of her soft buttocks. Dee stirred beneath me. I move my head downwards raining kisses on her shoulders and back. Lying half on top of her I slid one hand under her belly and eased my hand around her pussy. She was hot and excited, a living furry animal. I ran my tongue over her bottom and licked the top of her thighs, burying my mouth in the back of her legs.

My hand is around her front now playing with her pussy. The back of her ankle is against my cock. I can feel her high heeled shoes. Suddenly she rolls over and slithers beneath me, eel-like. I am on top of her, rubbing my cock against her taut belly. In the stereo glow her green lips are parted, her red eyes glazed; a sci-fi goddess psyching me out. She spits into her hand then reaches down and grips my cock. Ecstacy shudders through me and I almost come from the touch of her slippery fingers, cool and slim. Sharply her fingernails grip my balls in a vice of iron and I feel real pain. Instantly she releases the pressure and guides my swollen hardness down into her. She is a furnace, hot and dry. Dee is always like this. I began to screw her crazily, jerking us back and forth. She stops me, pushes me back and slides away. She slips down and begins to kiss my stomach, burying her face between my legs. Her teeth gently biting my erection. Now she's driving me crazy. I feel her tongue slavering over me. Now I am lubricated and she pushes me onto my back and straddles me. I'm dying to be inside her as she hovers above me, athletic nipples erect on her proud breasts. She eases herself onto the tip of my cock, one hand on my chest, the other lightly guiding me to her.

I am on fire.

"Ooh, you are an idle bastard," she says as she eases her fur over me.

"Where's his fat nose darling? Does he want to come to mummy?" I groan as she slides onto me and begins to ride me rhythmically. She's moving faster and faster now and suddenly there's a slap. She has hit me. I have a pain in my eye and I can taste blood at the corner of my mouth. Dee loves to slap me but sometimes she goes over the top when she's coming. This time her big diamond must have caught me. She rides me furiously now, shouting and slapping me as my hands guide her hips. I daren't come before her or I will be in real trouble. Now she's jumping up and down on top of me, a girlchild screaming and shouting as she climaxes.

She crumpled in a wet blond sweating heap and I held her like that for a moment, bent double over me, senseless, breathing hard, sweat pouring off her. Then I hoisted her up and spun her on her back, never losing the connection as I rolled her over. Now I lay on top of her and forced myself into her. She resisted, but I jerked her leg roughly to the side. Now I thrust up and down on top of her, taking delight in being a large unfit beast ravishing my slim athlete. Limply she lay underneath me becoming aroused again just as I climaxed. I came into her in great thrusts and then collapsed exhausted. Gently she pushed me off and we lay there side by side breathing heavily, shattered by our passion.

"You're turn to make the tea," I said. "Ooh, I do

love a bit of romance," said Dee in a pure Manches-
ter accent.

MIAMI
APRIL

Malvin Berg wiped a handkerchief around his neck. It was hot in the car rental office. The Jaconelli brothers were too mean to fit air-conditioning, and Malvin was too deep in debt to them to complain.

Easing his three hundred pound bulk out from behind the desk, Berg waddled across the room to the refrigerator. The machine, like the rest of the room, dated from the fifties. Save It was a well-established company renting budget cars at prices the customers couldn't refuse.

There was one Doctor Pepper left in the fridge. Expertly, Berg cranked the top off the bottle using the opener fixed to the wall. The metal cap tumbled into the bin, joining a hundred others.

Some of the sticky sweet fluid dribbled onto his Van Dyke beard as he tilted his head back to drink.

He glanced at the cheap watch on his wrist. His 'drop' should be here soon. The man was late. Puerto Ricans never seemed to be on time. He would never have dealt with them in New York, but Miami was different.

Malvin Berg hated Miami.

Malvin had originally been employed as a collector for a New York 'Family'. After disgracing himself by gambling away a large sum of his bosses' money, Berg had avoided meeting his Maker only because he was married to a niece of one of the

Capos. Now he was under pressure to repay what he had stolen.

He had been sent to Florida to run the car rental operation which acted as a front for the Family's main business in Miami.

Cocaine.

MIAMI SHORES
APRIL

"Give the gold man a good flash. Let him see a bit of quality gear."

"You want me to come naked?"

I took her in my arms, Rhett Butler in an XL size dressing gown.

"I always want you to come naked, my darling. Meantime wear the Patek Phillipe and the Blue Whites."

"But he's in the game, he's seen it all before, Daniel."

"Jewellers love jewels more than the people who wear them," I replied. Using her for bait was a risk. I'd never done this before.

"Remember what I told you?"

"You mean what we agreed?" asked Dee.

"Your instructions, dear," I said. "You can do what you bloody well like but don't sleep with him. You'll ruin the plot."

"So there *is* a plot."

"Well, not exactly a plot, but while I'm working out what plot there isn't, don't sleep with him."

"I don't want to sleep with him," pouted Dee.

"Well then, that suits both of us perfectly," I replied.

"I'm only THIX!" screamed Dee, leaping around the room. "And I don't want nasty old men pawing over me." She was standing on the sofa, her knees knocked together in a Little Orphan Annie pose, sucking her thumb and scratching herself on the behind with different hands.

"How old are you, then?" lisped Dee.

"Four," I said confidently.

"Well, you're NO BLOODY GOOD TO ME, MATE!" she yelled as she leapt toward me. I caught her, but lost my balance and we collapsed backwards, laughing, into the potted palm in the corner.

"Would Myrna Loy have done this to Darryl F. Zanuck?" I yelled, brushing potted earth off my shirt.

Dee raised her wedgewood blue eyes to the ceiling. "Wrong era, darling," she said. "Different studios."

"Hah!" I said. "All of a sudden I got a cinema buff on my hands. Don't be too easy with Stuart. Drive him crazy." I paused, searching for the right nuance. "With your near availability."

"Und vhat should I do vit mine pussy?" she said in her best Yiddish accent.

"Drive him crazy with it, like you do me. Tell him that you don't want to hurt me."

"But I do!" yelled Dee scissoring her legs. "I want to walk all over you in my high heels." She started to unbutton her dress.

I surrendered.

No wonder E.T. was the biggest grossing movie of all time. It must be easier to work with a dwarf in a rubber suit.

STRAITS OF FLORIDA
APRIL

"It's exhilarating to do the unexpected."

Dee grinned up at me impishly. A teenage Jean Harlow framed in sky, clouds, and rushing sea.

I was in a trance. Beating up the Straits of Florida on a tangible floating lump of this man's money. I congratulated myself on breaking through. One moment hamburgers and conversation, the next on the yacht. The ocean spray was a salty blizzard, the whipping ropes and bucking hull a symphony in cash.

Reality had moved into another waveband.

Dee planted herself six inches away, one hand clutching the rail, the other cradling a gin and tonic, high on the moment, face flushed, eyes bright.

I put on my sternest Scots voice. "Would you find it so exhilarating if ye fell in the Loch, madam?"

"Here?" She did a Dame Edith Evans and swung the gin and tonic in an imperious gesture to the ocean. "Here in Loch Miami?"

"Aye," I replied. "Have ye not heard of the Loch Miami Monster?"

Dee became Welsh. "I've a feeling I live with him, boyo." Laughing, at home afloat in sneakers, jeans and diamonds, she moved toward Stuart at the helm.

The yacht was a fifty foot Gulf Star 'Motor Sailer', the kind that may be used with engine or sail and handled easily by one person.

She was white, she was named My Paradise and

we were aboard her in the deepening dusk. The moment when the waves turn from green to grey, and the pink Florida sky devolves into indigo. On the distant shore, twinkling lights are either cocktail bars or police cars.

Out on the ocean a thousand luminous fibreglass lemmings had come out to play. Snatches of music and voices drifted to us, second-hand encounters with parallel lives.

Dee turned to me in all seriousness. "Do they have sharks in these waters?"

I gestured at the flotilla of luxury yachts twinkling in the twilight.

"Yes, and they're all driving Chris-Crafts and Moonrakers.

"A hundred and fifty thousand dollars she cost me," said Stuart. For a moment I thought he meant the blind date, Carol.

He was dressed for 'yachting' by Neimann Marcus. Silk shirt, chamois jacket, canvas slacks and zips everywhere. On his head he wore a camp little cap that I'd seen on the parcel shelf of the Rolls. The clothes sat uneasily on him. The jaunty peak at odds with his glasses and moustache, Himmler goes to sea.

"Good value," I returned.

I'm all at sea with boats, but owners love talking about them. So talk about his boat. This is the part I hate. This is real work. Showing interest when you're not interested.

"How far will she go on the engines?"

"Around twelve hundred miles: after that, as far as the wind will take you - free."

"No charge after the first hundred and fifty grand, eh, Stuart?" I couldn't resist it. He was such a pompous ponderous pontificating bastard.

He was trying too hard, a National Geographic Magazine man, doing everything in just the right style, full colour spread. Still I had to admit the yacht and the Rolls were choice items. He handled the boat with skill, on fingertip control.

"There's not enough wind today to push the boat to its limits," said the jeweller. I was pleased. Round Weymouth harbour for half a crown an hour was my nautical track record.

A shoreline of upended credit cards slipped by. The sun a white orb, a shining disc held between the thumbs and forefingers of gigantic clouds.

I sipped white wine and listened to Falkman listing his possessions. The man exuded heavy middle-aged caution, but my little Welsh dolphin was eroding that.

Stuart was falling in love with Dee. Her looks and sparkling flippancy were gently driving him crazy.

Beautiful.

Right on the money.

"There's Boca Raton," the jeweller told us.

"Mouth of the rat," said Dee

"Pardon?" from Carol.

"Spanish. Boca Raton means mouth of the rat," Dee stated.

"Where they charge like wounded bulls for condominium living," I said.

Stuart laughed. The blind date pulled a sour face - or maybe it was the wind. It's a pleasure to watch Dee work. She makes the whole game look easy. Like Lester Piggot winning the Arc de Triomphe.

Dee is a natural. She doesn't do anything and they're hooked. We drifted with the evening, passing smokes and filling each other's wine glasses, cruising off Broward County.

"That's Fort Lauderdale and Ocean Mile," said the jeweller.

"Looks like a kid's model," commented Dee, indicating the distant condominiums ablaze with light. Pinpoints blinked between them where the headlights from the freeway could be seen from the ocean, which at current real estate prices wasn't often. The illuminations vanished for a moment as Stuart brought the boat about for the return trip to Miami.

Dee gracefully navigated the stairwell down to the cabin, the jeweller's eyes following her every inch of the way.

"She's some lady," he said to me.

"Some handful," I replied, accepting a joint from him.

I eased my bulk up from the deck and swung down the companionway after her.

In the cabin Dee raised her wine glass in a toast: "Onassis and Churchill."

"In concert," I responded. "Millionaires for a minute."

"The Monte Carlo Kids make it in America," said Dee. "How do you feel, Daniel?"

"I've got the vibes, Dolphin. The mythical magical magnet of money. I'm going to rob him. I've got that roulette ball in the number feeling. Do you know what I mean?"

"The last card dealt is the one you needed, Daniel."

"It's a gold card," I said, passing her the joint.

She closed her eyes and took in a big puff, then opened them and stared at me, exhaling smoke.

"You're a genius, dear. What a punter," she said gesturing at the rich surroundings. "He's a burk."

"I'm not so sure, but he likes you, Dee."

"They all do, dear. They all do." She passed me back the joint.

He wanted her all right. But then they always did.

I've seen it happen before. Rich, poor, old, young. Men generally go bananas over her. It gives me a charge, a thrill. So far she's bounced them all back and stayed faithful to me.

So far.

I passed her the joint back. She smoked like a little girl being naughty behind the bicycle sheds, sucking exaggeratedly on the joint and then blowing smoke machinegun style into my mouth.

"Logic and greed, Daniel, sex appeal. Not bullets. Feed the man with his own expectations."

"Which include you, Dee."

"What do you expect, my genius man?"

I struck a Nelson pose. "England expects you to do your duty, but stay out of his bed."

"No big problem, darling, I assure you." She patted me on the cheek.

"Go gently, kid. I am fond of you. As much as we need the money, I don't want to risk you."

"You're in charge, Daniel."

"The secret is to convince Stuart that this is his game, his script. As long as he thinks that he's calling the shots—we'll win. You and I will become his puppets, his victims. He'll employ me and want to sleep with you."

"He probably snores," Dee eased out of her seat, kissing me lightly. "Mustn't leave them alone for too long," she said as she skipped up the companionway.

What we do has to be exact, no slips. No second takes, there's no script either.

In a movie, the star can come through a door seventeen times until he gets it right. A bank robber can rehearse again and again; entrances, exits, getaways.

But the confidence trickster is on real time. Every nuance, gesture, and response counts. One mistake, one note that jars and as the veneer peels away, the game is lost. You constantly judge the atmosphere for radioactivity. You respond and shepherd each moment.

Front is essential and knowledge. Clothes, homes, attitudes, facts. You're a mug only when you want to be. You slip below their net, wire-walking through casual conversation. It only becomes a minefield if you fall off the wire.

We have to insinuate ourselves into the tapestry of the jeweller's life until we are part of his reality. When we go we'll leave behind only images.

Dee mustn't get woven in too tightly. I'll have to watch that. I stubbed the joint out into a little brass ashtray. The motion in the cabin was making me queasy, so I clambered up on deck for the fresh air.

Carol, Stuart's blind date, was showing Dee the little plastic bag that kept the walkie-talkie dry.

"Very useful if you're drowning," said Dee. With the blind date she was disarming and all-girls-together, holding Carol spellbound with small talk of clothes, Paris and beauty creams.

Stuart demonstrated the stereo.

"What? No orchestra?" asked Dee selecting a T-Bone Walker tape.

"Ah, we dine at the Captain's table," laughed

Dee when the deli sandwiches were opened.

On the shoreline the hotels and apartment blocks became a pointillist painting in electric light. On the stereo, T-Bone sang:

"It's great to be rich and it's a doggone shame to be poor."

"And the street bands of New Orleans," Dee was saying.

"At funerals," said the jeweller.

"It's a dog dirty deal when your woman don't want you no more," sang T-Bone.

"Pardon?" This was the blind date.

"They played at funerals and in their churches. That was how jazz began." Stuart was at his most educative. "This country was lucky enough to have the musical influence of the black Africans, who had been forcibly brought here."

"Jazz was happening in North and South America at the same time," said Dee. "In different ways and neither place realised it until much later. Nineteenth century communications. Twentieth century music."

"They had the phonograph," said Stuart.

"But no radio," joined in Carol.

"Right," said Dee. "And no TV."

It was obvious to everybody that Stuart had been smitten in a bad way. He invited us to come to lunch the following day. I hoped that it would turn out to be a better nosh-up than the so-called 'dinner', which had consisted of take-away sandwiches from Wolfie's Diner.

The blind date was not interested in me, nor me in her. Dee's interest in Stuart was whatever I wanted it to be. We all wanted the gold man but for different reasons. It was a great evening.

MIAMARINA
APRIL

At the end of the yacht evening, we returned with Stuart and the blind date to the Miamarina.

Stuart insisted on taking us all for a drink. He was already well sloshed so I drove the Rolls.

The familiar interior of the car, its green instruments glowing onto the walnut, made me think of London. Stuart sat in the back like the King of Lampedusa, an arm around each girl as he directed me around the harbour to Le Joint nightclub.

Le Joint turned out to be a crowded, crazy glass walled cafeteria brilliantly lit and set on the edge of the ocean.

The name was apt. In America 'joint' means prison, amongst other things.

Stuart and the girls went ahead of me whilst I parked the Rolls. No flunky carhops here.

Inside, a bank of jungle music and exotic smoke enveloped me. I pushed my way through the pack of suntanned bodies in bright multicoloured shirts. A melange of scents filled the air. Forests of bronzed arms clutched frosted glasses. Ears rattled beneath the weight of gold and not so gold jewellery.

I find it impossible in America to tell who anyone is or what they want. The crush was oppressive. I caught up with Stuart and the girls.

"People come here for fun?" I asked. The shot went over Stuart's head. Latin music and polygot conversations battered my eardrums. A waiter, indistinguishable from a customer in his gold bracelets and Hawaiian shirt took our drinks order. Very quickly, oversized glasses stuffed with flora arrived.

"What are we drinking?" Dee whispered to me.

"Kew Gardens on ice, dear."

"I asked what we were drinking, not where we were."

Lush plants abounded; they overgrew the tables, sprouted from the floors, hung from the ceilings and lurked in the liquor. Stuart was impersonating a drunken octopus, arms all over Dee, who was obviously not enjoying herself. His hand strayed a few times to her knee, she firmly removed it.

"Having fun?" I asked.

She lashed me with a look that would have intercepted missiles.

Carol, the blind date, had become colder than the drinks, but the jeweller was by now oblivious to all of us.

I didn't fancy his chances of getting laid that night.

My own were good, provided I could keep awake long enough.

There was a clue in his drinking, I stored it away.

Dee was making 'home' signs. Time to make a move. I wanted to go. I was exhausted and bored and didn't care about gold, sex or even food right now. All I wanted to do was sleep. I still had the keys to the Rolls in my pocket. First rule of escape.

Stuart said something to Dee. He leant over red-faced and spluttering in her ear. She looked bored. It was probably just as well I couldn't hear what he was saying, because I was reaching the point of no return with him.

I whispered to Dee. "This creep is mauling the

love of my life."

She sipped her drink. "He hasn't touched your stomach once, Daniel."

"Balls," I growled.

"Remember the millions, darling," she whispered back smiling.

Stuart stopped pawing Carol and pushed me aside with his arm to maul Dee.

I moved behind her and whispering into her ear, "Millions or no millions. I'm probably going to belt him on the nose."

"Calm down, Rover," hissed Dee. "You can take me home in a minute."

Dee finished her drink and slipped gracefully out of his tentacles in a fluid movement that was over before it had begun.

"Beddy-byes, please," she said brightly to me in a six year old voice. "Homie-womie now, PLEATH."

"Come on Stuart," I said.

The jeweller grunted.

Carol stood up as Dee gathered her handbag and moved away from the table.

Stuart was still seated, lower lip trembling, eyes blurred, glasses smudged and hanging off his nose, looking like Hardy after a fight with Laurel. If this guy gets this drunk, I thought, all I need are the keys and where's the alarm button?

"C'mon old son, I'll drive us all home," I said. The jeweller stared up at me through cocktail olive eyes.

Dee was wriggling through the crowd, who didn't want to let her go.

"Okay," muttered Stuart. "I'm okay to drive." He lurched up from the table, threw an arm around Carol and staggered toward the door, following

Dee's sexy retreating back.

As I made to leave, my way was barred by a giant black man holding a pencil torch and a piece of paper.

I paid the sixty dollars. I was sure I had bought a garden instead of just a few drinks.

Another night out with the rich. If a millionaire takes you out to dinner, bring plenty of money and eat first.

MIAMI SHORES
APRIL

When I was younger I never seemed to suffer from hangovers. Mind you, I didn't drink when I was younger.

I awoke in the freezing darkness that I had come to know and love as our apartment. I reached out and touched Dee, just to make sure she was still living with me, and then sank back onto the bed swamped with waves of pain and nausea.

I opened my eyes and tried to sit up. Same waves.

I flopped down again. More pain.

I have been poisoned.

I'm never going to touch another drop.

I always know when I have been poisoned.

Who has done this to me?

This is enemy action.

I leant over gently toward Dee to see if she was breathing.

Soft Dee snuffles of breath.

More pain, now of the chain-around-the-head variety. Thank God, Dee was alive. I have this horror of waking up and finding the person I went to bed with the night before dead next to me. Or worse, someone I don't know. Just my little horror house fantasy fear.

But the pain I had was real enough.

I managed, with heroic effort, to sit upright.

I felt suddenly like I wanted to vomit.

I made it to the bathroom just in time and spent several minutes examining the ceramic bowl from a very close angle indeed.

I seem to have spent an unreasonable proportion of my life studying toilet bowls all over the world, and their names Dauntless, Shanks, Dolphin, Splendid or the gamely entitled The Shark, have never ceased to intrigue me.

I'm a compulsive reader. Even when I'm being sick.

I felt bad. The yacht, the deli sandwiches. I didn't know if it was the cocktails or all three.

So Stuart's two million dollars, Rolls Royce, yacht and bullshit conversation aren't enough. He wants to poison me with cheap cocktails.

Unless he slipped me a Mickey Finn?

No - too heavy for him.

These days everyone is sleeping with everyone else, (so the Atlanta Centre for Disease Control say in glossy pamphlets), so one hardly needs to poison a lady's companion in order to secure the prize.

I realised that I was naked on the bathroom floor, with my head in the bowl, on my hands and knees, all twenty stone of me.

I'm never going to touch another drop.

"Not a pretty sight," said Dee's voice from the bathroom door.

She was right.

MIAMI
MAY

Malvin Berg watched the Puerto Rican courier climb into his car and drive away. The car rental man put the two sacks in the store cupboard and glanced at his watch. One of Jaconelli's 'button men' would be here soon to relieve him of the burden.

Malvin never liked having drugs around the place, despite the strong protection that the Jaconelli family enjoyed.

The fat man collected bags of powder from couriers and passed them onto family members. He never handled cash, he didn't take cocaine.

Malvin had one or two other little hustles going on the side. For money, he would find you a girl, or a boy if that were your preference. He didn't care as long as you paid.

Berg also supplied fake documents, driver's licences, social security cards and the like.

Save It had one other big attraction as a car rental agency. Many of the mob-connected guys leased their cars from the agency. If you were 'connected', Malvin would file your rental under a fictitious name and address, very useful if you were under investigation.

Save It didn't attract tourist business, which was why Malvin was surprised when the English couple had rented a car.

Malvin rarely allowed himself the luxury of liking people, but the big Englishman intrigued him.

**He was up to something.
Malvin wondered what.**

MIAMI SHORES
MAY

"Where do we go after we die, Daniel?"

"Lou's Burger Bar on 169th. They're always open late."

"At least we'll eat, darling." She turned a newspaper page.

"Stuart called, inviting us to lunch," I said. "We have to meet him at the gold store."

"Ze conducted tour perhaps?" asked Dee in a mock French accent.

"I think he wants to be flash and show you his gold."

"He probably hasn't much else, darling," said Dee. I blew another smoke ring toward the ceiling.

It had been five days since the yacht ride and Stuart had offered me a chance to learn the coin business with pay. It wasn't really much of a job. But I was going to take it anyway. "Just until my deals overseas come together," I told Stuart. "Learning the coin trade should be interesting."

It would give me the entree into Stuart's business. Easier to rob from the inside. The job offer had suddenly crystallized over a smoke in the back room of the office.

I can't really clarify the moment it happened. I convinced Stuart that I had money coming and could be a potential investor.

Sex and greed, the unbeatable combination!

Stuart imagined having me around would get him nearer to Dee's panties, or rather their contents.

I could see Stuart's little brain computing that bright, articulate, well-spoken English Jews with bored blond girlfriends and a few quid in the offing, who were prepared to work for peanuts, were not being given away in Cornflakes packets. I grafted double hard to get him to trust me.

I'm hot when I hustle.

My only danger is generally overkill, I oversell myself. Especially when I'm stoned, broke and surrounded by gold.

But this time I must have been on the button.

After all, I landed the job.

Dee put the Daily Mail down, jumped up onto all fours in the bed. Her negligee parted, and two pink cones pointed downwards.

"Are you selling those puppies?" I asked.

"Woof!" barked Dee.

"Woof yourself," I barked. "I don't really know if I want to go and work for him."

"You're right, Daniel. You'll only finish up robbing him. And then we'll have to leave this wonderful life."

"I don't like him, but someone's got to suffer and he's it, our kid. You tease him, I'll take the gold."

The joint was finished now, and I leaned across her naked body and stubbed it out into the ashtray. Outside the light was fading, shadows filled the corners the room.

"You mean," she said, "He'll have to part with some of his old gold?"

"No gold is old," I said, switching out the light.

MIAMI SHORES
MAY

"You've offered him a job?" asked Kathy.

"Why not?" said Stuart. "The Agency lets me run the business how I want. It's perfect cover to have people who are not associated with us."

"I'd hardly call it perfect cover." The girl looked up at the winking light.

Someone had set off a pressure pad out in the shop.

"Marquez is here," Kathy said. "You've got the hots for the little English girl, haven't you?"

Stuart flushed. "Is that against regulations?"

Through the one-way mirror they watched the Cuban in the shop.

"No," said Kathy. "But it's dangerous. Her boyfriend is crazy about her."

"I'll deal with him," said Stuart. "Marquez is early."

Stuart spun the dial on the safe and unlocked the heavy door. From within the safe he extracted a black code book.

"I can't remember what today's code is," said Stuart.

"But we know Marquez," said Kathy impatiently. "You don't need the code. Just get him out of here as quickly as possible."

"Okay. How much does he have to collect?" the jeweller asked.

"Langley said sixty thousand dollars," Kathy replied.

"You could start a revolution with that kind of money," laughed Stuart.

The girl turned to him, "Isn't that what the Agency is trying to do?"

MIAMI SHORES
MAY

Dee laughed. "What time is Benny supposed to ring?"

"Between 11:00 and 12:00 English time, that's between 4:00 and 5:00 our time, princess."

Dee angled the Patek round close to her face and squinted at it. In a stage American accent she said, "We're in the time zone now."

As if on cue, the telephone jarred the stillness. Dee grabbed at the phone.

"Fort Knox Bullion Counting Division."

A pause. Then, "Certainly, sir. How many bars and where do you want them sent?"

I wrestled the receiver from her grasp and pressed it to my ear in time to hear Benny say, "Will you take a cheque?"

"Benny, my boy," I said. "How are things in the Old Country?"

"Which Old Country?" Benny's voice seemed surprisingly close.

"Any old country," I responded. The gag was an old one.

"Do you want the good news, the bad news or the worse news?" stormed the bookmaker.

"It's a very clear line," I said. "Give me the good news first."

"The good news is that I'm in Miami." Benny sounded as if he thought he was still on the race-course shouting the odds.

I turned round to Dee and said, "Benny's here in

61

Miami."

"Whoopee!" yelled Dee. "There'll be a steer roasting on the old primus tonight."

Into the phone I said, "Where are you?"

"I'm at a little hostelry called the Fontainebleau, Room 1208. Got time to see me?"

"Are you kidding?" I said. "I'll come now. What's the bad news?"

"I'll tell you when you get here. How long will you be?"

"About half an hour."

"Meet me in the lobby," said Benny hanging up.

"So what do you think the bad news could be?" asked Dee for the fifth time, peering into her compact, as if the answer were there.

I manoeuvred the Ford through the late afternoon traffic. "I don't know," I said, for the sixth time. "Maybe they can extradite us."

"But the lawyer said there was no extradition for fraud." Dee patted her nose with a powderpuff.

"Lawyers will say anything for money."

Dee pursed her lips, examining her immaculate make-up.

I followed the big green signs for Collins Avenue.

On the radio, the announcer was extolling the virtues of something called 'Total Living' in a secure environment at Boca Raton.

"So if they extradite us," said Dee brightly, snapping the compact shut, "We'll be experiencing total living in a secure environment."

"It'll be all right for you," I said. "You can plead the secretary's act."

"You mean I vos only obeying orders." Dee went

mock German. She lowered the sun blind and eyed herself in the vanity mirror. I gave her some Bogart.

"Listen kid. If that defence was good enough for Nuremberg it should go down okay at Knightsbridge Crown Court." Dee applied more lipstick.

"That defence failed at Nuremburg." She pursed her mouth again.

A Cadillac whose occupants had been to Disney World and had the stickers to prove it cut in front of me. I leant on the horn, to no appreciable effect. Moments later I swung the Mustang onto the pink concrete of the hotel forecourt.

The Fontainebleau Hotel was erected in the 1950s as a monument to bad taste and boom money. The grandchildren of the immigrants who had fled pogroms were now refugees from the rigours of New York winters. For years the annual sundance to Miami meant Fontainebleau. The hotel was enthroned like a wedding cake between squeaky clean Collins Avenue and the blue green Atlantic rollers.

As the vacation habits of New Yorkers evolved, second homes became de rigeur and condominiums had mushroomed along the Florida coast. The Fontainebleau had become unsure of itself. No longer fashionable. A stateless relic of a bygone age. A twenty-five million dollar face-lift still left the uncomfortable feeling of an elderly dowager squeezed into designer jeans.

I drove in past a sign telling me this was a total resort with constant action and a half acre freeform pool complete with waterfalls.

Everything's so total in America.

I wrapped the keys in a dollar bill and gave them to a Ruritanian general who turned out to be the car jockey. I received a sneer that encompassed the dollar and my rented Ford.

As Dee emerged, flashing her legs, sneer turned to leer.

At the top of the steps an overdressed walk-on from the Student Prince broke his back opening the door for Dee, leaving me to shuffle awkwardly around him.

In the gloomy lobby a familiar figure bounced towards me. Benny the bookie advanced like Patton with plenty of fuel, larger than life and at better odds, lurid in florid shirt and Brylcreemed "Barnet-Fair" as he would call his own hair in Cockney rhyming slang.

Benny pumped my hand. He was not the embracing kind of Mafioso.

"You're losing weight, young man," he said.

"It's the cocaine and salad diet," I replied.

Benny grinned. At five foot two inches, the bookmaker was an irrepressible bundle of action. A man who had forgotten how to relax. His mind a calculator fixed permanently in his own favour.

Two years older than me, he had no real business calling me 'young man'. Benny cuddled Dee who kissed him extravagantly.

"What a movie star," said Benny. "I don't know how she hangs around a bum like you."

"I'm a terrific lay," I said.

"Where're my gold bars?" said Benny to Dee.

"They're outside in the car," said Dee. "Do you want me to send them up to your room?"

"No. Leave them on the beach. I'll pick them up later in my submarine."

We laughed.

Benny handed Dee a duty free perfume bottle.

"Bought at 26,000 feet." I felt Dee was overdoing the 'thank you kisses'.

"Come have a drink in the Poodle Room." Benny linked arms with Dee, and spoke back over his shoulder to me as he swept her away. "You're going to need one, Daniel - the plod in London want to talk to you about a murder or two."

"Murder?" I said, my thoughts roulette wheeling. "But I haven't murdered anybody." Herb Alpert and the Tijuana Brass drifted invisibly around the near empty lounge.

Dee stopped staring at the cocktail menu and stared at me. Benny blinked.

"Well, so far the police have been around to me, your mother, your ex-wife and your solicitor. Apparently two people were murdered and officially they want to eliminate you from their enquiries."

My stomach dropped a few hundred feet. I had a weak feeling of surrender. I ran my finger through the red velvet pile of the banquette seat. Dee opened her mouth as if to speak and then closed it again. Absent-mindedly, she fiddled with the perfume bottle. I looked at her.

"What do you think?" I asked.

"Pussyfoot, Nursery Fizz, Jersey Lily." Dee tapped the cocktail list.

"Those don't have any alcohol," said Benny, pointing to the card. "You've gone quite pale, Danny Boy."

"Kahlua Kiss, Grasshopper or an Acapulco?" asked Dee.

Two men in dark suits filled the doorway, paused and raked the lounge with searchlight eyes.

"A Harvey Wallbanger. It's got vodka, orange

and Galliano." She frowned at the menu.

"Not Galliano," I said.

The waitresses ignored us, striding by in short skirts, their high heels clicking as they crossed the dance floor. One, a tall redhead, would have been a good stand-in for Cher, the singer.

"I've never murdered anybody in my life." I looked at the bookie.

"I believe you," said Benny. "But nonetheless the blue pointed-head mob are making enquiries."

"Bloody Mary. Vodka, tomato, Tabasco, Worcester sauce and ice." Dee read the cocktail menu aloud.

I fought down the impulse to tell her to shut up.

"But they must know I'm not a killer."

"I'm sure they do," said Benny. "It's a get-up. They want to talk to you about the money. They can't extradite you for that."

The two men began to move towards us. Dee tried to catch Cher's eye.

"They know that you haven't murdered anybody," said Benny. "If they can lean on you this way, the Americans will return you to England."

"Is absolutely everything here vodka based?" I asked Dee. "Then tell me, Benny, do they know I'm in America?"

"My man says they do." Benny's 'man' was a high ranking police commander at Scotland Yard.

"Whisky Sour, Tom Collins, John Collins," said Dee.

"All those Collins - no whisky," I said. Benny touched my arm.

"The FBI *are* looking for you." I glanced around the room uneasily. The men in dark suits had found a table.

A waitress with a blond rinse and fingernails that would have been the envy of a Peking Mandarin was taking their order.

"You'll just have to lie low," said Benny.

"We came in before them," Dee complained.

"What are you doing in Miami, Benny?" I asked. "You didn't cross the Atlantic just to tell me this." Dee began waving her arm. The waitresses ignored her.

"It's a long story," said the bookie. "I met a man in a car park in London and sold him a share in a pornography business for a quarter of million pounds. There was some confusion about whether the business actually existed. He complained to the police. I've been arrested, charged and bailed."

Dee caught the tall waitress's eye.

"I've flown over to Miami because he has a house here. I'm going to get him to try and change his statement."

The redhaired waitress stood by our table. Close up, she didn't look so much like Cher at all.

"Well, I wish you luck. Can I help you in any way?"

"Three Harvey Wallbangers," ordered Dee.

"I don't like Galliano." Does she never listen to me?

"There's not much you can do about it," said Benny.

"Two Harvey Wallbangers and one Bloody Mary, please," said Dee.

The waitress moved away.

"You said there was worse news."

"You mean apart from you being wanted for murder?" I nodded. "My accounts are frozen and I can't ship any Rolls Royces over to you," said

Benny.

I felt Destiny's gears grinding again. Now I would have to do something with the gold shop.

"Well, it's nice to see you anyway," I said.

"We'll have dinner together tonight," said Benny. "Have you got any moves?"

I started to tell him about the gold shop. "What's the bloke like?" asked Benny. Dee interrupted. "Old, rich and too mean to die."

MIAMI
MAY

Time. The golden Swiss franc of life is running out, and while it does, it's no fun sweating in a fume filled toilet cleaning coins, while your boss squires your girl around Miami by Rolls.

The chemicals I was using made me feel sick.

The gold and silver coins contrasted tantalisingly with the bare and scruffy toilet.

I have to rob him.

Instead of murmuring sweet zeros over floodlit velvet he's got me cleaning coins. Me, the genius salesman. And where's he? On his fucking yacht with Dee. The whole staff here are laughing at me cleaning and studying coin books while he's out and about.

Where are they now? In some restaurant? Screwing in his apartment?

Besides which, there is something weird about the whole setup here. The gold company doesn't seem to be doing much business, yet they have unlimited cash and stock. Security trucks arrive with heavy boxes which don't appear to contain coins at all. These are stored at a garage at the back, completely separate from the gold shop. Once or twice I've seen other trucks arrive, usually driven by Hispanic men, all moustachioed, bright shirts, bangles. They load up boxes and drive away. Never coming near the store.

The only people to know what's going on are Stuart and Kathy. He sees a steady stream of visitors in his soundproofed booth. I've seen him handing over packages and money. Once, watching Miami television, I saw some Cuban exiles at a demonstration. I recognized one of Stuart's visitors amongst the agitators.

Politics?

I thought at first he might be coke dealing. But I've never seen any evidence of the drug. There's plenty of money here. That's all I care about.

One evening I managed to get access. I had spotted where Stuart kept his keys to the back store. As far as I could see, the only alarm was a bell, which you had thirty seconds' worth of buzzer time to switch off. None of the cameras was trained on the store.

Stuart and I were working late, and he had to go to meet some people on Flagler. The soundproof booth door was open, and the storeroom keys were on their hook. All the other staff had gone home, and with trepidation, fear or sheer nerves trembling inside me, I lifted the keys down.

The smallest one was the burglar alarm key. A couple of times during my coin cleaning stints in the toilet I had seen Stuart and Kathy entering the store. I had watched them carefully through the toilet window. Each time they had entered the store, there had been the buzzing of an alarm, and they had turned to the right of the door to switch it off.

The shop was quiet and I slipped out of the back exit into the little courtyard connecting the shop with the storeroom. I paused. This was definitely not my scene. If I got this one wrong, I would have blown it with the coin business for good.

I realised suddenly as I stood at the store entrance that there would be no light inside, and I ran back into the shop to pick up a plastic cigarette lighter, no time to buy a torch and I don't own one. I told you, burglary is not my game.

The store was quiet. I peered up and down the boulevard through the office window, no sign of the Rolls. I closed the front door and walked back through the shop. As soon as I was off camera, I ran through to the courtyard, selected the key that I had seen Stuart single out, and opened the door. The alarm buzzer sounded immediately. I turned to the right in the darkness, and flicked the lighter.

The buzzing emanated from a black box set at waist height. I moved over to it and stopped dead in my tracks.

A luminous panel of numbered buttons glowed at me.

The damn alarm required a combination to be punched into it, as well as inserting the key. The buzzer sounded as if it could be heard all over Florida.

My heart raced and did cartwheels.

Now I was done for.

In desperation I punched in the phone number of the store.

No joy. The word ERROR flashed up on the tiny screen.

The woodyard saw noise kept screaming.

Think. Think. I punched in the number of the Rolls and then the store street number.

ERROR.

With a flash of manic ESP I punched in the number of Stuart's private line.

The buzzer shrilled louder than ever.

I tried punching the number in backwards.

The silence was deafening.

Sometimes I don't deserve my luck.

I ran around the stacked boxes, drums and cartons.

There were guns all right. M16 rifles, Uzis, handguns and ammunition.

Those I understood. Drug dealers or political messers, both occupations need guns.

But what did Rolls Investments want with drums of Gelatin, and high pressure roller presses?

MIAMI
MAY

The more time Dee and Stuart spend together, the more pain and nervousness I feel. I'm using Dee to get inside Stuart's mind, but it's a dangerous manoeuvre. When I was younger, I thought that people could be shuffled around like packs of cards. As I get older I find that they are irreplaceable. I love Dee. She makes me feel human, worthwhile.

Stuart has become quite blatant about finding me hot, heavy work to do or sending me on small errands across Florida. Which take all day to complete.

Sometimes I come home and find the apartment empty. A note propped up on the coffee table tells me 'Gone to dinner with Stuart'. Well, isn't that what I wanted?

Dee reports faithfully back to me about how Stuart is trying to seduce her, urging her to leave me and move in with him. I am burning up inside and getting broker by the minute. At work I begin to examine ways of robbing the gold business.

For a time I contemplate using the company's credit facilities and dealing accounts to set up a fake deal for myself. I examine the ways which customers were paid. The problem with that is that my moves would be discovered before I get my hands on the money. I prefer games where the cash comes first, the scream afterwards.

But the jeweller is cautious and there is no time

when I am left alone with any appreciable sum of money or gold. Except at coin shows.

"We're going to a show in Tampa," said Stuart. "I want you to come with and see how a coin fair works. I think you'd be good selling and dealing."

"Well," I reply. "I'd like to try. I don't know the values of all the coins."

"Have you been studying the book?"

"Yes. But there's about a million different types of everything."

"Don't worry. I'll be with you. I'll book the tickets." We are sitting in the office. Bullion gleams. Stuart passes a joint.

"Can Dee come with us?"

"I'm not paying the expenses for her."

"I'll pay," I say. "She wants to see America."

"But I thought you wanted to save money. You told me yourself how short of funds you were." Cunning bastard.

"Dee and I hate to be separated. It's not really much extra and she wants to see more of the States." Stuart frowns. He doesn't like it.

When wages time came that week, instead of a hundred and fifty dollars, Stuart handed me a ten dollar bill, explaining that he'd deducted Dee's travelling expenses.

Back in the toilet I cleaned more coins angrily, my mind tumbling.

You can't even get a bit of grass in Miami these days for ten dollars. I have an apartment, car and two people to feed. He says he has to deduct Dee's expenses. Hell, he's going to pay by credit card sixty days later, so why on earth deduct the money from me now?

Pressure, that's why. The bastard is putting

pressure on me.

Two can play pressure.

I told Dee to drop him a few hints like how she's unhappy with me, there's no future. I want this guy hot for Dee. Cool for me.

I have to convince Stuart that I am settled in the coin trade. It's plain that the jeweller is not going to let me earn any real money doing any real deals. I have painted myself into this corner. It's time to make the quantum leap back out.

Preferably with a large amount of gold.

CORAL GABLES
MAY

"Why do you stay with him?" Stuart had his back toward Dee while he poured the drinks. She couldn't see his expression. The apartment was small and not what she expected of a millionaire. The furniture was plain and cheap. She had imagined expensive rugs, exquisite art, space. Not this cramped rented anonymity.

Stuart turned and handed her a gin and tonic.

Raising an eyebrow quizzically, he stood for a moment. The question lay unanswered between them.

"He's exciting," she said.

"Sexually?"

Cheeky bastard, thought Dee. "Amongst other things."

"And what will your future be?" asked the jeweller.

"Does anyone know the future?" Dee parried. "You could choke to death on a bristle whilst cleaning your teeth." And I hope you do, she said under her breath. Middle-aged, pompous boring old lecher. Heavy. That was the word for Stuart.

Heavy. Manners and mannerisms.

The American settled into an armchair and eyed her. This is some good-looking lady. A Goldie Hawn type. Beautiful but wacky.

What does she want in life? Not poverty, judging by the clothes and jewellery. Someone has been taking good care of her.

"So what do you want from life?"

There he was again, she thought, the heavy question. To rob you, you fool, and to stay with Daniel.

"Adventure and security," said Dee. What will you say to that, dumbo?

"The best of both worlds?"

"I'll settle for the best of one."

They were due for dinner. She knew what the jeweller wanted for dessert. He was playing the potential sugar daddy. She could have had dozens of those, better than him.

She knew the breed. Promise you the moon and you're lucky if you finish up in a cage with a slice of green cheese.

Still, she was enjoying the game.

Daniel was right, the jeweller *was* mean.

That was one trait she depised - meanness.

He deserved to be robbed.

And Daniel was just the lad to do it.

MIAMI
MAY

Malvin Berg was so sharp he could cut himself. He was a fine judge of who to rip off and who to merely shave. The Englishman didn't look like a sucker to him. He could see that the man was a hustler. He encountered a lot of people at the car rental shop and prided himself on being able to sum up most folks at a glance. He knew who would return the car on time and who would disappear with the vehicle.

He watched as the English couple drove away. The girl was a dream. He could see right away she was a hustler. Berg figured that Dee and Daniel had a few secrets. But then who didn't?

Each week when the couple came in to pay their rental they would exchanged pleasantries and light conversation. Malvin sold Daniel a little cocaine. He wondered if they were on the run from something. Whatever it was, it hadn't worked. You could tell they'd been high flyers from the clothes and jewellery. But they were short of money now. High flyers didn't rent last year's Ford.

The Englishman had startled him though, asking about driving licences. What on earth did the man want with false papers?

Nothing surprised him anymore.

Malvin Berg shrugged, stuffed the Englishman's car rental papers in the filing cabinet and settled himself down with the Miami Herald. There looked like one or two good things racing at Gulfstream this afternoon.

MIAMI SHORES
JUNE

Dee was dressing for a night out with Stuart. Across from the bed I watched her, pangs of jealousy stabbing me. Her black silk slip clinging to her hips and breasts, enhancing her lightly tanned body. A Neapolitan ice cream, in pink, white, brown.

Dee sprayed Estee Lauder's Private Collection on her breasts and thighs. For someone who wasn't sleeping with her date, she was making a thorough job of smelling nice. That's *my* private collection, I thought. Just for a moment I wanted to call the whole thing off. I hoped she wasn't screwing him.

Watching her own reflection, she slid her feet into the stiletto-heel crocodile shoes that I adore. She caught sight of me in the mirror.

"You were just the same in London, Daniel. Arrogant, yet insecure. A soft centred chocolate with a quick mind."

"I seem to be banging my quick mind against the wall lately."

"Then I hope you find a soft brick."

Around one slim ankle a gold chain glinted. She hoisted the slip up to spray scent on her upper thigh. I saw two Dees, the one in the mirror revealed more; a golden triangle bursting from a tiny G-string.

"Don't sleep with him."

"That sounds like a plea."

"The puppet master has stopped giving instructions, Dee. The game has gone too far for that."

"Don't worry dear, I find Stuart repulsive, just hurry up and rob him." The golden vision vanished as she turned and straddled the little Louis Quatorze dressing stool. She began to highlight her face. I took a last drag on the joint of Columbian grass and slid naked out of bed. Falling to all fours on the floor I crawled towards her.

"NO!" cried Dee sharply. I reached the small stool and prostrated myself on the floor underneath her. Her ankles erotic in the sharp crocodile shoes. I began kissing the front of her foot.

"Stop that at once," said Dee imperiously. She knew I liked to be shouted at.

I began licking her foot, her shoe, her ankle, I kissed her leg.

"I told you to stop that! You won't listen. You are a wicked impudent slave," cried Dee.

Above me I saw her reach for the slim crocodile belt she was going to wear tonight, so I licked her legs frenziedly. The belt whipped smooth across my back. I felt the stings but they only goaded me. I like a bit of domination now and then. I began to kiss her thighs.

"STOP IT!" she screamed.

I grabbed hold of her, but she pirouetted away from me and stood hands on hips, eyes blazing. Sometimes I think she's genuinely angry. It's hard to tell. I was still on all fours, my erection painful. I crawled over to her. She cracked me across the back again with the belt.

I love all this.

"No, no, NO!" she screams. I bury my face in her thighs, tongue under the skimpy slip, around her panties and I began to kiss her passionately between the legs.

Dee was still screaming as I began jerking off, licking her at the same time. Still she beat me with the belt. I had driven her back against the wardrobe door now and my head was buried, my tongue reaching into her warm and secret places, my eyes closed. I felt repeated blows across my buttocks. More urgently now I played with myself. She lifted her leg and pushed between my legs with the tip of her shoe. The crocodile skin was cold on my balls. I ejaculated over her leg and the carpet just as my tongue made her come, shuddering.

Dimly her voice penetrated my ecstasy.

"You've made me late, Daniel."

"That's not all I've made you. Now you can go out and wind him up."

I just rolled out of the way in time to miss the belt.

WASHINGTON D.C.
JUNE

The grey uniform at the gate hardly glanced at my exhibitor's pass. The tinted glass door sprang open as the elderly guard pressed a concealed button. I humped the heavy coin cases into the hall where rows of vulnerable glass cabinets displayed the dealers' wares. Some cabinets had been draped over like mirrors at a Jewish funeral. The guard shuffled back to his stool and newspaper.

The restaurants and bars of the hotel were crammed with dealers from all over the States. The Washington Fair was a big event and the dealers had set up their cabinets earlier in the day. Now the vast hall full of gold belonged to the elderly guard and me.

A well organised room clearing would net twenty million dollars

Isolate the room. Gently hold the guard. Move everything through the exits into the underground car park. No one would see you loading up. Do it at night when everyone is asleep.

I doubted that the hall had sophisticated alarms. This was a hotel. Not a diamond bourse. I brushed the thoughts to one side.

I was fantasizing. You needed weeks of organization for such a coup. The coins would only be here tonight.

By our allocated display case I fumbled through my pockets for the keys Skill had given me. Finding them I opened the cabinet, then closed it again.

I wasn't leaving anything here tonight. Just checking. I would set up in the morning. The old guard never even looked up as I picked up the coin cases and left. I kept on with my fantasy.

The door opens easily from the inside. No problem leaving. It's getting in that's difficult, unless you are an exhibitor.

"Of course, I run the New York end of the business," said Skill.

Dee smiled and tried to look suitably impressed. I knew that she was bored sitting in the hotel room, on our first night in Washington. But with four cases of gold to babysit, it was room service and TV this evening.

"I started with Stuart fifteen years ago. We didn't have a thousand dollars between us." The bearded little man tossed back his fourth bourbon. He'd ploughed steadily through half a bottle and his speech was becoming slurred. Everybody drinks too much on this firm, I thought.

I pushed the remains of my steak aside and stood up. I'd undone my trousers whilst eating and now I shuffled awkwardly, hands in pockets, over to the window. I must lose weight.

Raindrops trickled down the pane like glass worms. I wanted to be alone with Dee and in bed. Reluctantly, I accepted another glass of bourbon from Skill.

The bearded little man had been rip-roaring drunk but was tamer now. Dee had long departed down the corridor to our bedroom.

The late night film was flickering and Gene Hackman chased the heroin dealers of Marseilles across the screen for the millionth time. A loud snort startled me. Skill was slumped in oblivion on the sofa.

Gently I loosened his tie and eased off his shoes. He never stirred. The empty bourbon bottle lay in testimony on the table beside him.

Cautiously, I crossed the room, bent down and tried to unlock Skill's boxes. They opened. I stole a glance at the sleeping jeweller, my heart was pounding like a machine pump. I was perfectly entitled to be examining the coins we were to deal with tomorrow, but I didn't want him to wake up and challenge me. Skill's Smith & Wesson revolver lay on top of the coins; a mute guard in a sheepskin case. I slipped the gun into my pocket and called Skill's name out softly, then a little louder. No response. Leaning over the sofa I rolled one of the New Yorker's eyelids back gently.

The gold dealer was dead to the world.

My heart was in my mouth as I picked up Skill's cases and placed them by the door, followed by my two

A nervous thrill electrified me. Watching Skill all the time, I gingerly opened the door. One by one I lifted the four cases and placed them in the empty corridor, then gently eased the door shut behind me.

"I didn't want to be here when you took it," complained Dee.

I was disappointed that she wasn't as excited as I was.

"Listen Dee. The man is lying in his room, blind drunk, dead to the world, we've got his gold, our gold and both the guns. This is it!"

Dee looked at the carpet.

"We agreed you would take it on your own when I was a long way away," she said sullenly.

"Look. Forget all that. This is a big result - there's twice as much, we've DONE IT!" I can't believe what's happening. I've scored the winning goal, but the home team has gone sour on me.

"We were supposed to have an agreement, remember?"

"Let's take the gold now and have the agreement later.

"I'm not supposed to be part of it." She shook her head, crossed to the armchair and plonked decisively into it. A little dolphin going nowhere, her face said.

Wearily, I lay on the bed, the guns beside me, and loosened my collar.

"Our agreement wasn't an immutable pillar of the universe," I said. "I took the opportunity that arose."

She stayed silent as I continued.

"They know you're part of it," I said, absent-mindedly playing with the safety catch of the Smith & Wesson.

"What are you going to do, shoot me?" asked Dee.

I put the gun down.

"This is ludicrous!" I raised my voice. "Now I've got the gold, I've got to fight you, Dee." I tried to reason with her. "We're already wanted. If they catch us for being illegal immigrants we'll finish up in jail."

She lit a cigarette, the flare illuminating her unhappy and determined face. She stared out of the window.

Across the square, a Washington policeman, rain glistening on his cape, was rocking back and forth on his heels, slapping a night stick in his hand.

I needed him there like a third nostril.

The rain-slicked roadway mirrored the changing traffic lights. I tried to marshal my arguments. I felt more like screaming. Instead I said:

"We don't have money. You can't travel far on your own." She wouldn't look at me. I persisted. "If you vanish, the authorities will assume you are with me anyway. If you stay, they'll grill you about everything under the sun and hold you for Interpol and the Yard. The gold must be worth the best part of a million dollars. We've got a five hour start. What more do you want?" I asked. I bit the end of a fresh cigar and held my hand out.

"Diplomatic immunity," smiled Dee, passing me her lighter. My cheeks bulged as I lit the cigar.

"If I take the gold with you, I've committed a major crime in the States," she said.

This was crazy. "We're broke. For months we've been scheming. We might not get this shot again!"

She stayed silent.

Dee had proved herself very loyal to me following the collapse of our investment business in London. She could easily have stayed, fronted the investigation and pleaded the 'I vos only obeying orders' act.

I'd told her to, in fact. She'd chosen to come on the run with me.

A sudden gust of wind sprayed more rain onto the window. I watched Dee stroke the radiator, her ghost reflected in the rain dottled glass. Below her, a yellow taxi crossed the square, tail lights glowing as the driver braked for the corner by the policeman.

Dee lit a fresh cigarette as she spoke.

"I don't want to blot my copybook in America. I

told you that all along."

"The truth is you're not as desperate as me! I've got the 'moody' murder charges. My track record means that I will be arrested and banged up in Brixton for a year. The fat city cats I fronted for will keep the money and I'll do the time!"

The ghost in the window glass spoke to me. "Oh, Daniel. I just can't handle it."

So now it comes to it. I'll order a cab, pick up the gold and head for the airport. I'll be in Brazil before Skill wakes up.

She was still married to a wealthy man.

I could read Dee's thoughts. If she took the gold tonight, she could be in a women's prison tomorrow. I picked up the telephone and began dialling the airport. Dee turned to me earnestly.

"I've got good lawyers in England. My husband will help me with anything I might have committed so far. But this is much more serious, darling. I want to stay with you. I want to see you pull off your coup. But I don't want to be with you while you're taking the gear. It's too final. It's too big a step over the line."

"Buenos Aires," I said. For a moment Dee thought I was speaking to her. "What time does that depart?"

Dee looked round the room. I followed her gaze to the white towel on the orange marble bathroom floor. She'd been showering when I had come in with the boxes. It was all happening too quickly for her.

"It's too dangerous," she said. "It wasn't how we planned it. I won't do it."

"Okay, Dee." I kept my voice tight and cold.

"What will you do, Daniel?"

"And how much is the fare?" I said into the mouthpiece.

"The boxes," she muttered. "They're sitting there, great dead weights. Golden ball and chains. Gold bars can become prison bars." She could wax quite poetic at times.

"I don't want to be here when you take the gold," she said.

I hung up the phone. "Are you coming with me?"

Dee closed her eyes and shook her head.

"My God. Where is your head, Dee? Are you coming with me?"

"No," said Dee simply. "But you go. I'll tell them I didn't want any part of it. I'll get out of it."

I moved closer and wrapped my arms around her. She nuzzled into my shoulder, her voice muffled.

"I can smell the eau de cologne I bought you from Trumpers, Daniel. It seems so long ago." She smiled up at me brightly, tears brimming in her eyes. Women are strange in times of crisis. I could think of nothing to say.

"Go on, Daniel. Take your gold, go to Argentina, think of me in Sing Sing where they put the naughty women.

"They'll ask why you didn't raise the alarm."

"You could have done it when I was asleep," she said. "I might not have known anything about it. I'll help you."

I sat back on the bed and started to undo my shoelace. It was raining harder outside now.

"What are you doing, Daniel?" She thought I wanted to tiptoe barefoot away. "Oh, you silly sausage," I said. "you think that I would leave you to face all the crap?" She jumped on the bed and nuzzled me. I picked up the remains of the cigar and did a Groucho. "What's a million dollars anyhow?"

"I'll do anything for you," she murmured. "Well, there's one little thing." "Name it," said Dee. I pulled her up on top of me. "Well since we're not going to be running about, shclepping lumps of stolen gold in the rain with half the police forces of the Western world chasing us...." Dee interrupted, "You want to get laid, M'sieu?"

WASHINGTON D.C.
JUNE

Waking up hung over was Skill's usual state. The night on the sofa had left him cramped and aching. Somewhere a road crew were using jackhammers.

It took him a few moments to remember where he was, then he sat bolt upright. The jackhammers went stereo. He recognised the grey dawn as belonging to Washington. He urgently needed to use the toilet. Something was wrong. As he stumbled across the room he realised what it was.

No gun. No boxes of gold.

Forgetting the toilet, he lifted the housephone. Oh Jesus, he thought. Stuart will kill me.

The operator answered. For a moment Skill forgot Daniel's surname. He fought down panic as he remembered.

Chill gnawed at the gold dealer's stomach as he waited for the connection. More than a million dollars, with what the Englishman had carried. He squinted at his watch. The man had at least five hours' start. He could be in China now. This'll be the end of the dealership and worse. He was startled to hear Dee's voice in his ear.

"Hello."

Skill blurted the words out. "Could I speak to Daniel please?"

"Just a moment," said the girl. Then a wave of relief swept over him as the Englishman's voice came along the line.

"Good morning, sir," chuckled Daniel. "How are

you this morning?"

"Fine," said Skill. "I'm coming to your room."

"Come on then," said the Englishman.

WASHINGTON D.C.
JUNE

I replaced the receiver and hugged Dee under the bedclothes.

Then I lifted the phone and dialled room service. There was a knock on the door.

Dee dived naked into the bathroom. I hung up the phone, swung out of bed and picked up a towel from the chair to wrap around my waist. Then I unclipped the sheepskin case and took out Skill's revolver. Crossing the room in two strides, I peered through the spyhole in the door.

I saw a distorted Skill, clothes askew, haggard, a vignette from some hall of mirrors. I reached forward and unclipped the security lock, pointing the gun at the doorway.

"It's open," I called. Skill blew into the room like a tramp in a hurricane, then came to a halt as the steel eye transfixed him.

"Thank God you've come," I said, lowering the revolver. Skill's eyes darted past me, searching for the boxes.

"I've hardly slept all night with the responsibility." I turned my back to Skill and picked up the telephone to re-dial room service.

Skill sat down. I knew he was dying to ask where the gold was.

Dee came out of the bathroom in her robe, a towel wrapped turban-like around her head. Through the open door Skill caught sight of the boxes on the floor and relaxed visibly.

"Thank you," stammered Skill. Still with my back to the American, I winked at Dee.

"Orange juice, scrambled eggs? Hashbrownies? A few waffles with syrup? What do you fancy for breakfast, Skill?"

The gold dealer buried his face in his hands. "Just some black coffee for me," he muttered. "I must have passed out last night."

I gave the breakfast order into the phone.

"Were we caning the old Jack Daniels last night?" asked Dee.

Skill groaned. I slipped the Smith & Wesson back into the sheepskin and proffered it to him.

"I shouldn't really give you this, the way you feel."

Skill kept glancing at the boxes.

"Here, old chap," I said, very Oxford now. "You know we don't use those things in England."

Skill grinned. "I really tied one on last night."

There was a knock on the door.

"Careful," I said. "That's the fastest bloody room service I've ever heard of."

"It's all right," said Dee glancing through the peephole. "It's the same waiter as last night."

She opened the door and a man in a white jacket wheeled in a trolley.

I still had the gun in my hand. The waiter never batted an eyelid. He behaved as if twenty stone men brandishing revolvers while wrapped in a towel were par for the course in downtown Washington. Which they probably were. I suppose that there were hundreds of men in this hotel today with gold and guns in their rooms. The Washington Coin Fair was internationally famous. The waiter began lifting up table flaps and setting out dishes. There was hot toast, orange juice, scrambled eggs.

The man reached under the table. He was bringing up something large, black and heavy. I stiffened.

"Oh good," Dee said as the waiter flourished champagne.

"The James Bond Breakfast," she said, tipping the man, who murmured his thanks and bowed out of the door. Skill closed his eyes.

Suddenly, a noise like pistol shot made us all jump.

I poured champagne. Skill looked sheepish.

MIAMI
JULY

This is the big one.

This is the crime I would go on a diet for - after the event. Let the world look for the fat man. I'll be the slim guy with the cash. This is the will o' the wisp that I've been chasing.

Move over Goldfinger.

The scene with the coin shop had gone too far. Every day I worked surrounded by millions of dollars worth of gold. Deals took place, cash was exchanged, Stuart earned money.

The staff earned money. They chattered and parked their sports cars with the carelessness that only valid credit cards and high salaries can bring.

It all drove me bonkers. I was wound up like an eight-day clock. Here I am the fastest tongue slinger in the West and I've become Desperate Dan. I am broke and working harder than anyone else in the whole place. Life has begun to imitate art. My relationship with Dee really is strained. The Washington business hasn't helped. I believe her when she says that she isn't sleeping with Stuart, but there are times when I have my doubts.

I had had enough of cleaning for the day. The fumes were making me ill. I racked the coins back into their slots, rinsed out the sink and splashed water on my face. The tiny room was not air-conditioned and I felt queasy. Picking up the coins and book I stumbled out of the toilet. As I walked out into the bleak corridor my mind raced.

Events had taken on an inexorable motion towards the 'parting point'. The point at which the punter parts. The best conmen do not measure their success in money but in mesmerism. All of us have the conman inside us; nurses tease elderly cripples out of millions, wives convince husbands that they're faithful, children con everyone around them.

The conman doesn't necessarily need sincerity. The victim may recognise the swindle but he becomes bound by invisible mesmeric threads, usually of his own making. This was the case with Stuart. The con was already there. It was up to me to pick it up.

The impromptu edge of uncertainty, the atmosphere, fascination, the hypnotic effect, the people; these are the intangibles.

I wondered where Dee was.

Maybe she's at the beach on her own. That's just as bad. She lies about in high heels and a bikini, with all the young guys on the beach ogling her. Sure and they talk to her too. She'll be screwing in some lifeguard shed if she's not fucking Stuart. People will drown. Or maybe I think too badly of her. Then maybe I don't. What has she got to lose?

In the shop, I turned in the coins to Kathy, who checked them and slotted them into the safe.

"I'm going home," I said to her. "The chemicals have made me feel ill."

It was true.

Kathy nodded. She didn't like me being there for some reason.

There were a couple of desultory goodbyes from the staff.

If anything they were nervous of me. Was I there

to steal their jobs? I smiled to myself.

In the bright sunlight I strolled across the car park.

This week Malvin had changed the car. I eased another Mustang into the Miami bound traffic for the short ride across the ocean to North Bay Village.

I glanced at the fuel gauge. There was enough for a little run around. I would head north to Dade and pick up some of those fine cigars, made in Florida by Cuban exiles. Then perhaps a saltbeef sandwich. The dashboard clock told me that Dee would be a good two hours yet.

I can't have a company cheque mailed to myself, too complicated. I drove on autopilot. I'd be better off taking a parcel of gold physically. But where from? Not from the shop. Too many alarms.

The only logical place will be a coin fair. Stuart has to entrust me with a parcel. But will he send me on my own? Will the parcel be big enough? I slotted Bob Dylan's Desire into the car stereo and cruised down Ocean Boulevard, one hand on the wheel, another underpaid worker killing time.

How will I get away? What about Dee? I've got to devise some scheme where I'm sent away with a parcel and Stuart stays behind funking for a dirty weekend with her. That's it, I thought.

She's out with him a lot. I hope she hasn't started sleeping with him. I need him chalishing, hungry for her. His judgement has to be affected. He's already telling her how much of a has-been I am and how much money he's got.

She has to drop more hints about being fed up with me and wanting to leave. How we're not making love anymore. Just enough to whet his appetite. Make him think that all he needs is a little time alone with her.

He can have a lot of time with her. If I get another chance I'm going to do it whether she wants to come or stay.

MIAMI
JULY

Stuart had been muttering on for days about the Milwaukee coin fair. It was the best part of three thousand miles away from Miami, and involved a four day weekend. The jeweller planned to send me and stay behind himself. The cunning rat knew I couldn't afford to take Dee with me. This was his big chance.

The jeweller was so hot for Dee that he would have given me the key to the store. I told her to arrange to meet him late Friday in downtown Miami and to make sure she had a plausible excuse to go on the missing list until night-time.

I didn't want him creeping around to the apartment and finding it empty. If he found her absent, the balloon might go up whilst I was still airborne.

Dee told him she was going to the movies.

I'd made a big study of the airline schedules. I could have quoted them by heart. There was only one non-stop Miami-Milwaukee flight. All the coin dealers would be on that one.

I knew how Stuart's mind worked now. He would pack me off on the plane, ask the other dealers to keep an eye on me and have Skill meet me at the arrival gate in Milwaukee.

Somehow I had to make Stuart miss putting me on the non-stop plane. The next sensible Milwaukee flight stopped over in Atlanta for twenty minutes. There, I planned to switch planes and catch a connecting flight to New York.

I'd timed everything exactly. The Atlanta-New York plane touched down at JFK 6 minutes before the Atlanta-Milwaukee flight. I'd be more than two and a half thousand miles distant when the scream went up in Milwaukee.

A continent away.

I should be rubbing Dee's tits with gold coins while Skill was watching passengers file off the Milwaukee flight, well almost.

Dee would have to leave Miami early to catch the Red Eye to the Big Apple. I told her to rent an inconspicuous room and car and pick me up at JFK. From there we would drive direct to the Canadian border.

We wouldn't be staying long amongst moose and maple leaf. The Canadians are too pally with the Yanks for my taste. By the time the law gets its act together, we should be winging our way southward to Brazil, Tahiti, Fiji.

A print shop had made me letterheadings and cards proclaiming me an English coin dealer, which when you think about it, exactly what I was.

Dee and I were aware that we were moving into the danger zone. This was G-Day. G for gold. Once started, there'd be no stopping, no turning back. I didn't like to split from Dee. Who knew when or where we would meet again?

Benny agreed to be message centre and promised any help we needed, from long distance, of course. And Benny would make the 'genius move' to delay Stuart.

This was our last day in the North Bay Village apartment and probably our last in Miami.

"There's a clue," said Dee, tapping her book. She held up a puzzle solution. I could see the word

Durban. "Perfect place to sell gold coins. South Africa."

I shook my head. "They grow their own and they're linked to Interpol."

"We're running out of world, Daniel."

"You'd think you'd be welcome <u>anywhere</u> with a bag of gold these days," I said.

We roasted round the clock in the apartment, planning, scheming and bouncing moves off each other. I made sure Dee and Benny knew the schedule by heart.

It would have to be right. There was neither room for error nor funds for back up.

I thought of my old mentor Bobby, eighty-six and worth millions. "Do it right the first time," he would say. "You may not get a second chance."

I ran my eye down the shirt stiffener... apartment cleaned, flights booked, tickets bought, papers collected.

The ticks were piling up on the card. Readies.

We must have cash. I ordered Dee to the pawnshop with her ring and necklace. We needed the money for airline tickets, car hire, hotel rooms and all the rest of it. She never murmured.

We cleaned all kinds of junk from under the bed. I didn't want to leave any phone numbers, clues or notes. I pulled out the back of every drawer from every wardrobe in case there was a photograph or something.

Draining the last of her gin, she stood at the apartment door, dressed for the street in the tropical silk suit I had bought her in Hong Kong.

"Time for the three golden balls, Daniel, my lad."

"Will they give you any hassle at the pawnbrokers?"

"Are you kidding?" said Dee. "The street outside Rod Steiger's is bumper to bumper with poor little rich girls in Porsches, hocking rocks to support their skiing habit. They'll just think I'm another blizzard baby."

Dee always referred to the Miami passion for cocaine in 'snow' terms. I had tried to give her a line of coke once on a train in Switzerland and had received a gale force nine rebuttal. After hours of persuasion she sniffed up half of it, like Royalty tasting the pensioner's gruel. When I asked her how her first line felt, she had wrinkled up her nose.

"It'll never replace gin and tonic for me, dear," she said.

It was a good thing really. I couldn't afford blizzards for both of us.

We worked and worried late into the night. A Marx Brothers movie on the TV flickered over open suitcases and plastic dustbin bags. Dee and I kissed and touched a lot, more than ever aware of the pending parting. The danger. We both could be captured. For Dee this was the leap into the shark infested depths of criminality that she had so much wanted to avoid in Washington, the night Skill got lost in the Jack Daniels bottle.

Around four a.m. there was no more to do in North Bay Village. It was all systems go. Short of torching the apartment we'd done everything. Dee's cab would be here soon. My eyes roved around the little flat that had been our home these past few months. There'd be no more cushion fights, screwing in the kitchen, fishing from the dock or floating in the pool. No more take-aways from Wolfie's to be devoured at dawn, while George C. Scott replayed World War II.

Miami days were ending. Who knew the next act in our little play? If I'd had any idea what was coming, I would have unpacked my suitcases and stayed. I'd have unpacked the rubbish too.

Dee lay naked in my arms, balancing a champagne glass on her breast, magnifying the nipple. I removed the glass and licked the little cherry. With a quick wriggle she sat bolt upright in the bed. I proposed a toast.

"Sleepy border guards." "Unmanned crossings" she responded. "Diplomatic immunity," said I. "Secret accounts," settled Dee, draining the champagne.

MIAMI
JULY

Everybody has gone crazy this morning, including me. I felt inordinately pleased with myself. The office had booked me on the non-stop. Another tick on my shirt card. Those hours poring over the airline schedules have paid off. Now all I have to do is be too late for the non-stop. They will have to re-book me on the Atlanta stopover.

I had a couple of moves lined up to help slow things down.

Telephones rang, telexes chattered and staff constantly had to deal with couriers and customers in the shop. That suited me. The more aggravation and slow-ups, the better my chances were of making him make me miss the plane. I had inspired one or two of those couriers myself.

The big boxes in the middle of the office were slowly filling up as Stuart, Kathy and I selected choice items. I dutifully noted everything down on the manifest. Well, not quite everything. Once, miraculously in the confusion, I managed to weed two small but heavy parcels out of the safe. I rammed the sealed packages into my pocket. I didn't have any idea what they contained. The fact that they were in the safe was good enough for me.

He was sending me to the Milwaukee Show, the biggest coin fair in the States, and I wanted plenty of stock. Whether I made it to Milwaukee or not.

I enjoyed packing the boxes. Things are more fun when you've a personal stake. If I'd had a third arm I would have volunteered to take another case. The staff were hustling so that I wouldn't miss the plane. I was stalling like a mule so that I would. Stuart was well occupied. Most of the morning he alternated between the telex and the 'phone. My genius move was working. I'd realised early in the plot that missing that non-stop meant gold or death. Slowing Stuart himself down was the key.

The gold dealer had found a new customer from Switzerland, a Herr Zeigelbruner.

That morning the Swiss had been on the phone with a fabulous deal for Herr Falkman. What the jeweller didn't know was that Herr Zeigelbruner was my pal Benny the bookie, who'd opened an account at the gold shop only two weeks earlier, using a Zurich accommodation address and plenty of complicated spiel. No one was better than Benny at pretending to be a difficult rich customer who drove people mad. Every point of every transaction required telex confirmation.

Stuart was on the 'phone to him now. I almost felt sorry for the jeweller. He was torn between this mysterious deal involving cheap Nazi gold, getting rid of me onto the plane, and slithering between Dee's legs.

If things worked out according to my cardboard shirt stiffener he'd blow out on all three.

A big stand had been taken at the Fair. The cream of the coin world would be there. Apart from yours truly, of course.

The 'phone lines between New York and Florida were open. While Skill and Stuart thrashed out what stock to send, I kept quietly packing and writing the manifest, repeatedly stopping for checks, bringing the whole process to a halt as I did so. I managed to get on the 'phone a few times and take part in the stock discussions.

The office clock rewarded me with a steady drip of minutes. I'd learned their routine by now. Rolls Investment Inc. kept duplicate stock in both cities. So whatever I packed, Skill wouldn't bring. Like the wisest king would say, "You go on ahead with the frankincense and the myrrh, I'll catch you up later with the gold."

The staff thought it unusual that Stuart wasn't attending Milwaukee himself. I'm sure one or two of them suspected that it was Dee he wanted to give the work experience to. The jeweller was really in an excellent mood. A rat about to steal the trap cheese, with the whole game going to his plan. I was a nice helpful shmuck. A nice, helpful, slow shmuck.

Joints were being passed around the back office. That was a big help. Dope slows everything down immensely. Once or twice I took lesser items back out of the cases and after ponderous discussions with Skill in New York, replaced them with high value stock. This needed to be unlocked from the safe. As each item went into the big boxes I noted it down on the manifest. Every time I knelt by those bags I felt like kissing them and praying.

Be cool, son, cool.

Stuart hovered around the safe like Dracula at a graveside, becoming more harassed with each passing moment. Herr Zeigelbruner the world famous Nazi bookmaker was keeping him pretty busy. Up on the wall clock those beautiful luminous digits kept on keeping on.

I chose a long stack of St. Gaudens 'Libertys' for my lovely black bags. These twenty dollar gold pieces commanded two thousand bucks apiece all day long. Sought after enough to be valuable but not so rare as to be impossible to sell.

Gold coins are as good as cash in the hand. Which I suppose is what the U.S. Government intended in the first place. On my knees I added them to the list, all forty of them. For eighty thousand dollars they didn't take up a lot of room.

I wondered how Dee was doing. She had been stoking Stuart up for the past week, with the 'personal problem scenario'. How we were having arguments, short of money, she was thinking of leaving me to live with him.

He was one happy punter.

One of the office girls passed me a joint. It was a laid back place. I was sorry to be leaving. I thought about Dee again. She was due to 'phone Benny in England once she had the car and hotel organized in New York.

The clock marched loyally onward like a mechanical soldier. Soon we would reach a point where I couldn't make the non-stop. According to my calculations the next sensible flight to Milwaukee was the one with that darling little twenty minute stopover in Atlanta.

Those twenty minutes could make a million dollar difference to my week.

I'd given Dee most of our cash. In my back pocket I had a hundred dollars and my Atlanta-New York ticket in some moody name.

My beautiful black bags were nearly full now. I was beginning to feel rich.

I tried to be as cool as possible.

I glanced up at the clock. It had happened. The fatal moment had passed. We were in magic time.

Even Emerson Fittipaldi couldn't have made Miami International from Biscayne Boulevard in time for the non-stop.

Stuart was still heavily involved on the 'phone with Herr Zeigelbruner. I'd have donated blood to have heard what Benny was saying. Stuart's head bobbed up and down, nodding dog fashion. The man was so secretive. The staff weren't supposed to know about his funny deals. It was all rattling telexes and locked code books to them.

I'd racked my brains for days trying to figure out how to keep Stuart preoccupied on the crucial morning. My baby hit the heart of the matter, as usual.

It had been Dee who had suggested having a fake Swiss, offering cut price gold.

"Greed, dear," she'd said. "Offer him cheap gold. He's such a shmuck punter he can't resist it."

Now I realised how spot-on she'd been.

Inside his Eichmann style glass cage, Stuart's head was still on 'nod', totally entranced by Herr Zeigelbruner. How disappointed the jeweller would be when he tumbled to the fact that his mysterious Nazi was really fat Benny the Jewish bookmaker, sitting in Brighton making Zurich noises.

Kathy, Stuart's overburdened assistant, crossed the room and tapped on the glass booth. As Stuart motioned her to wait, the girl turned to me and I saw what looked like an airline booklet in her hand.

"I think you've missed that plane," she said.

I tried to be suitably shocked, making a show of looking at my watch. "Oh NO," I boomed, clapping a hand to my forehead. I hoped I wasn't overdoing all this. "Are you sure Kathy?"

"Yes, Daniel. You should have left for the airport twenty minutes ago. You'll never make it now."

"What do we do?" I put on my best puzzled grammar school expression.

Always make the punters think they're running the show.

I could see her bursting to tell me about the next flight. But she was too well programmed.

"I have to ask Mr. Falkman."

She tapped on the glass booth again. Stuart motioned her to enter, holding the 'phone to his chest while she spoke.

I busied myself on the floor with my treasure chests, pretending to arrange coins while my heart did the Eygptian sand dance. This was the moment. The point of no return. Would he go for it? I squinted up from the floor ostensibly checking the manifest. The jeweller and the girl were hunched over the airline schedule. I could see her pointing something out to him.

Yes yes, come on, I thought. There's the next plane. I saw Stuart frown. He appeared to be asking about other flights. This time Kathy's head shook.

That must be the Atlanta stopover. A chill thought exploded. Supposing he sent somebody to accompany me on the journey? Then I'd be boxed in! Jesus Christ, why hadn't I thought of that? I must have been blind. I busied myself with the coins. There was the great big flaw in my plan. I thought I was so damn smart. He had six staff here. What was to stop him sending one of them to ride 'shotgun' on me?

The boxes were bulging and nearly too heavy to lift. There must be close on a million dollars' worth of coins here. Come on, come on, what's happening?

Stuart was shrugging his shoulders. He appeared to ask the girl a question. He didn't seem happy with Kathy's answer. What on earth are they talking about? He raised the 'phone to his mouth, spoke briefly then returned it to his chest.

Kathy speaks. The gold dealer shakes his head. What is happening? I have visions of everything draining away. We had pawned our jewellery, spent all the money, and burnt more boats than a football stadium full of dead Vikings. And me on my knees, the two-bob genius who had overlooked the simplest stumbling block .

Kathy emerged from the booth. Leaning down to me she spoke.

"You're going on a later flight, but you have to be ready in ten minutes. I'll call the airport now."

"Yes ma'am," I said, my mind whirling. That had been a very negative shake of Stuart's head. Had she asked him if it was all right for me to travel alone? Had he said no? Damn that soundproof booth. Had he decided to come himself? Could he abandon the tempting charms of the best bit of crumpet in Florida to keep tabs on me? Did he think the stopover was too much of a risk? Would he send one of the staff with me?

In the booth Stuart was on the 'phone again, mining deep into Herr Zeigelbruner's gold mountains. At least Benny's doing a good job. I hope it isn't in vain. I closed the boxes. There was more gear in those cases than in the rest of the shop. I had creamed the stock.

Kathy was seated at her desk now dialling the airport.

110

I had to hear how many reservations she was making.

If somebody else was coming with me I might have to abandon the whole scheme. Dee would have to be told. How much time would I have to make the call? I felt sick. I needed very badly to hear what Kathy was saying.

I picked up the bags and hauled them across the office. They weighed about a million dollars. I leant over the desk and placed the manifest in front of Kathy. She was talking to the airline now. Who would he send with me? Could I pretend to be taken seriously ill when the plane stopped in Atlanta? I've never had to hit anybody over the head to get money in my life. I didn't want to have to start now.

"Yes, that's right," said Kathy into the phone, "and the passenger will pick the ticket up at the desk.

Passenger ticket. The words each have a singular sound, rich and delicious. My heart does a helicopter lift-off as the truth dawns.

Of course! I should have realised! Stuart was far too cheap to spend hotel and ticket money sending somebody else with me. I nearly burst out laughing. I had been paranoid to think that Stuart would part with a dollar more than he had to.

That's my punter!

Stuart emerged from the booth.

"Put those bags in the Rolls, Daniel." Stuart addressed me as if I was the butler. "I'll run you to the airport. You're going to Milwaukee, pal."

That's what you think, I thought as I picked up the heavy cases. I could hardly stand upright. None of the staff offered to help me. I backed awkwardly out through the side door. Behind me Stuart was examining the manifest and giving Kathy instructions. She would have to phone Skill in Milwaukee and tell him about the new flight time.

Come on, you cheap bastard, I thought as I put the bags in the back of the car. I don't want to miss this flight as well.

NEW YORK CITY
JULY

Fifteen hundred miles north, on 8th Avenue, Dee craned her neck up at the Howard Johnson Motor Inn, marvelling at the gall of New Yorkers who could call a forty-story skyscraper an 'inn'.

Daniel's instructions had been simple and efficient.

Keep yourself to yourself on the plane.

Two taxis. One from JFK to the Waldorf.

One from the Waldorf to 8th Avenue.

Walk to the hotel.

Check in, rent the car.

Wait.

She loved efficiency and hated sloppiness.

Now then, girl, she thought. You're Mrs. Susan Webster and you're gonna use your best Texan accent, and you're awl gonna have a nice day now, ya hear?

Jauntily she bounced up the hotel steps, crocodile satchel swinging from a silken shoulder screaming old Houston money. Okay, girl, this is the bit you enjoy. Bundles of front and ready for anything.

Checking in proved to be absurdly easy. Daniel had provided her with a false driver's licence from Malvin and an address gleaned from Houston Chronicle. The young desk clerk filled out the registration card. She passed over a hundred dollar bill and treated the young man to a thousand dollar smile.

113

"Credit this to my room, please. I'll just be here the one night." She'd practiced the line fifty times on the plane under her breath.

Dismissing a hovering bellboy, the desk clerk himself showed her to her room; he couldn't get enough of her. In the elevator, Frank Sinatra wanted to be flown to the moon. Dee smiled up at the ceiling hoping that this jerk clerk wouldn't make conversation. She'd culled her Texas voice from old episodes of Dallas. It was one thing to play up as a pretend Texan in Britain but another game entirely here in New York with God knows who looking for her. She was on the stage for real today.

In the room the clerk snapped on lights, opened the curtains and showed her how to operate the mini bar. Amazingly he declined her tip, before pirouetting out through the door, his eyes soaking her up throughout.

Well, there's another fan.

In the mini bar she found all the ingredients for a large gin and tonic. She felt drained by the flight and tension. Dee sipped her drink while the tub filled. She'd been up all night wiping the apartment. Throwing out fabulous memories of four adventurous years around the world together. How sorry she'd been to burn the photos but Daniel insisted, pointing out that their liberty depended on such details.

As the girl luxuriated in the bath, exhaustion came up on her. Dee glanced at her watch. The diamond studded one Daniel had bought her in Cannes the previous year. She remembered Daniel's sheepish grin as he returned to their suite in the Carlton.

"Only popped out for a pair of socks," he had

said. "Saw this in the window. Made a mistake with the 'frog' money. Thought there were less zeros." She smiled at the recollection.

The diamonds on the watch face sparkled under the bathroom lighting as she read the time. Daniel would be leaving Miami. If he'd caught the Atlanta flight, then Dee had six hours before she was due to collect him from JFK. She decided to rest while she could.

A little shluff would do her the world of good. She dialled reception and asked for a six p.m. call.

Dreamland beckoned as she sank back on the bed and closed her eyes. Distant traffic noise from 8th Avenue drifted up to stroke at the windows.

God in heaven! She'd forgotten to rent the bloody car! The little shluff would have to wait. She bounced off the bed.

Less than thirty minutes later, Dee was back in her room, cradling the phone. The car was tucked away below the hotel. Earlier she had tried to call Benny but kept getting the busy signal. She remembered Fridays were busy for the bookmaker. Lots of racing.

Dee was having trouble with a Puerto Rican voice in room service.

"Medium rare. With lots of mustard on rye bread, please. Mustard, you know? Hot, yellow?"

She replaced the receiver and pressed TV buttons. American television fascinated her. This was her first and perhaps last chance to watch the New York stations.

Where would they be next week? What language did they speak in Rio?

The car rental people had been very helpful. She spread out the large scale map of North America on the bed and traced the route to Canada with an elegant fingernail. On the television a black lady with a hairstyle that could house a swarm of bees urged her to turn to Jesus for help.

The telephone rang.

Dee stared at the instrument as if it were an uncoiling cobra.

She looked at her watch. No calls due yet.

Maybe it's Jesus. This must be bad news. Paralysis gripped her.

The cobra jangled again.

Have to answer. Don't panic. Come on, girl. Front. Only one way to deal with a ringing phone. Stick it in your ear.

The snake shrilled once more.

Remember, Texas accent, breathe deep, pick up the receiver.

"Howdy!" she said.

"Howdy yourself." Benny's voice crackled across thousands of Atlantic and satellite miles. "You made it then. What's the weather like?" His voice reminded her of nights at the River Club, days at Ascot.

"Oh, Benny." Dee laughed with relief as she glanced out of the window. It was beginning to rain.

"It's raining."

"It's raining here too," said Benny. "Your man's caught the kosher flight."

"Thank God," said Dee.

"No, thank Herr Zeigelbrunner and his Nazi gold mountains. I must have spent a monkey on the blower this morning."

"Oh, you're a star Benny."

"I should say I am. What time's your date on the

116

yacht?"

"Ooooh Benny." Dee did her stage Welsh. "I don't think I'm going to make it on the yacht this weekend. I must have taken a wrong turning. You know how difficult it is for a young girl to find her way about America."

"You seem to be doing okay, my love," said Benny. "I'll speak to you later. I've knocked out enough on transatlantic calls for one day with your plots and schemes."

"It'll all end in tears, Benny."

She hung up and gazed at the screen. The woman with the beehive hairdo said, "Jesus loves you."

"Thank goodness somebody does." Dee Stone realised she had spoken aloud.

MIAMI INTERNATIONAL AIRPORT JULY

I pick up the two cases and walk through to the passenger area. I've done it. Plenty of gold—no Stuart. I look around. No one is taking the slightest bit of notice of me. I cross to the departure area and read the information board.

Little electronic lights wink at me. According to the board the Milwaukee flight is due to leave in twenty minutes. I have just enough time. A thought crosses my mind. If I had realised that Stuart wasn't going to wait to see me on the plane, I needn't have caught the Milwaukee flight at all.

But the plan is in place. I look around for my office, spot the sign for the gent's toilet and head towards it.

The men's room is empty. There was a row of cubicles with a space underneath. I bend down to look. No feet. I have the place to myself. Swinging the heavy cases in ahead of me I slip gratefully into the end cubicle and lock the door.

I check my watch. Eighteen minutes to take-off. I have a line of cocaine left. Taking my little silver cigarette case out of my pocket, I open it, balance it on my knee then empty the packet onto it. I find a crisp ten dollar bill, roll it into a cylinder and whoof the coke up my nose.

A warm burst of colour hits my head as I slip the case back into my pocket, sniffing sharply. Daniel my boy, here we go.

Fourteen minutes to take-off.

I open the two cases. As usual all the coins are packed in protective boxes. Taking great handfuls I stack them up behind the toilet seat until I have completely emptied the case. I pray that no toilet user would come in, glance under the partitions and find me shuffling jewel boxes on the lavatory floor.

Rapidly I break open boxes and tip loose coins into the empty case. The broken packs I pile up on the floor.

The coke makes me speed. By a miracle no one comes in the men's room.

At the end of six minutes I have one case full of broken display boxes and the other crammed full of gold. I glance at my watch. Eight minutes to take-off.

I remember the packages I filched from the safe. They are still in my pocket. I take them out. There are two of them, one light, uneven and lumpy, the other flat and very heavy. They are both wrapped in brown paper and sealed, with a crest stamped in wax. Squinting in the toilet gloom, I slowly decipher the words on the seal around the American eagle.

CENTRAL INTELLIGENCE AGENCY.

A chill of fear sweeps through me.

Too late to worry now.

Now I understand where the gold shop's money comes from. I crack the first package open. Inside I find a little chamois leather bag. I gently open the drawstring.

Lots of little brown rocks. It took me a moment to realise what they were. Uncut diamonds never look like much.

Christmas just came early.

I sit there numb.

It makes sense.

I put the wrapping and wax seal inside the chamois bag, closed the drawstring, and slip the bag into my pocket. Turning my attention to the second parcel, I take out my Swiss army knife and slit the paper. Carefully, to preserve the seal.

I ease out the contents. Two flat metal objects, about eight inches long and five inches deep.

It takes me a moment to realise what they are.

It is a good thing that the men's room is empty. Any customers would have wondered why someone was laughing so loudly in the end cubicle.

I pull myself together.

Now I know why the gold shop has such a preponderance of Cuban customers.

I am in serious danger now. I've robbed the bloody CIA. I knew the game had been too good.

No one has come into the toilet. Time to march. A mellow 'ding-dong' comes over the loudspeaker.

A syrupy voice announced a delay on a flight to Syracuse. I opened the toilet door and pushed out the boxes. I caught sight of myself in the mirror. Sloppy me. There was a white streak of cocaine on my face that went with the dash of devilment in my eyes. I washed the cocaine off in the sink. The devilment would have to stay.

Another ding-dong delay on a San Francisco flight. I should worry.

There is no turning back now. The broken display boxes are mute testimony to my theft. I am no longer a legal courier. I feel happy and hyped up. Visions of tropic islands and lazy days waft across my mind. I hump the bags out of the toilet. As I cross towards the Delta Airline departure gate the public address system ding-dongs again.

The syrupy voice says: "Passengers on Delta Airline flight 508 to Milwaukee are advised that there will be a ten minute delay."

My flight. Good, the delay gives me time to dump the box of boxes.

Something is bothering me. I cross the concourse to the Left Luggage lockers, and search my pockets for a quarter.

The airline announcements. That was it. Since I had come into the airport, there had only been delay announcements. Flights to New York, Los Angeles, Washington all delayed. Could there be fog all over America? I wondered. Come on son, don't be paranoid. This isn't England. They have sunshine here. At the departure desk a small knot of passengers were being reassured by the pretty Delta stewardess.

Maybe the CIA are blocking all the flights!

At Left Luggage, I selected a large locker. Pop in a quarter, turn the key, open the door, place the box inside, re-lock the door, take out the key. Bending down to pick up the big case I scanned the area discreetly. No one appeared to be taking any special interest in me.

Good.

Those packages are burning a hole in my pocket. Uncut diamonds for God's sake. Who would have thought it!

I walked back to the departure lounge trying not to lean over from the weight of the gold. As I passed a litter bin I dropped the Left Luggage key into it. I knew that the locker would not be opened for at least twenty-four hours.

At the departure gate I was pleased to put the heavy case down on the floor, and ease myself into one of the small plastic chairs. I stole another glance around. Businessmen, old ladies, harrassed families with children. I didn't recognize any other coin dealer going to the fair, most of them would have travelled on the earlier non-stop, but I knew that Stuart had planned to ask somebody to keep a discreet eye on me.

I spotted no eyes, discreet or otherwise. I couldn't relax. I felt no special elation and the cocaine was wearing off. I was on my way. I had the gold, but I wasn't home and dry yet.

The loudspeaker was ding-donging again. All the departure lounges seemed full and no flights were leaving. I listened to the announcement.

"...on the flight to Chicago we regret to inform you that there has been a cancellation due to industrial action by ground crew in Chicago. Passengers are advised to contact their ticket office."

Some of the travellers around me began to show signs of restlessness.

I hope the strike is local, I thought. Chicago is pretty near Milwaukee.

The speaker donged again. "Passengers on Eastern Airlines 101 to New York, are advised that there has been a cancellation due to industrial action by ground crews."

A strange chill swept over me. This couldn't be happening. Not now. Maybe it wouldn't apply to Milwaukee.

More ding-dong sounds.

Ding-dong. "Passengers on National Airlines... "
Ding-dong. "Passengers to Seattle..."
Ding-dong. "Passengers to Atlanta-Milwaukee

are advised that the flight has been cancelled..."
The rest of the announcement was lost as my fellow passengers burst into a volley of groans. I went numb.

Around me the whole airport erupted into American chaos as travellers stormed the airline desks. I put my head in my hands. The words of Robbie Burns echoed through my mind:

"The best laid schemes o' mice and men gang aft agley."

And then my muse assisted me, another quote (W.E. Hickson) sprang to mind:

"If at first you don't succeed, try, try again."

Well, Mr. Hickson, I thought. You may be dead but I have to be quick.

My mind was racing. I knew that I couldn't hang around here. Stuart was still motoring towards Miami. He could hear about the strikes on the radio newsflash and turn round and come back for me. I could think of no comprehensive believable explanations as to why all his delicate gold coins were crushed together in one bag, that I'd ripped open and dumped the packages in a luggage locker, the key to which I had thrown away.

Also there are the packets I filched from the safe. Maybe they've been discovered missing by now. I've broken the seals on two packages I wasn't supposed to have. It would be about two million dollars better for me not to meet Stuart.

Plus my life.

And Dee's.

I just couldn't believe this was happening to me. Just at the moment when I've got my hands on the loot, fate intervenes. I have never felt the hand of the Lord so heavily upon me in all my days. I don't mind the hand of the Lord. It's the long arm of the law that bothers me.

I had to get out of Miami International Airport. Fast.

On the concourse, passengers mobbed the telephones. The airline desks were besieged with people complaining and reclaiming luggage. Distraught travellers wandered dazed looking for friends and relatives. I must use this precious confusion time to get out of the airport and out of Florida.

I picked up the case and pounded rapidly towards the exit. By the time I reached the doors my heart was doing an upbeat version of the night they shelled Tobruk.

Outside I was surprised to find forty or fifty taxis waiting and no passengers. Most people were still <u>inside</u> trying to get their luggage back.

I had the only bag I would ever need right here and I was out ahead of the crowd.

I took the first taxi, putting the case inside the car with me.

"Where to, buddy?" asked the cabbie. I had to think fast. If Stuart had heard the announcement he would be bowling back down the expressway at this moment.

"Snapper Creek." The name had stuck in my mind. It was to the south of the airport on the Dixie Highway. If Stuart was coming back he'd be heading down from the north. I couldn't risk him catching a glimpse of me in the back of a taxi.

I felt naked and conspicuous as we headed out.

Once we were travelling south, I spoke to the driver.

"I've changed my mind. Take me to the Eden Roc Hotel, please."

I caught an odd look in the mirror. To hell with him.

I needed a phone and transport. Think. Think.

The driver turned onto Flagler Street. Hiring a car would be out of the question. I only had my British driving license and in Florida every rental car has a distinctive 1-E number plate. I knew from Malvin that the police had a fast phone-round system. No, I wouldn't be renting a car. Malvin. Now there was a thought. But I didn't trust him.

I needed help. It wouldn't just be the police after me, not when the owners of the packages found them missing.

We crossed Highway 95. The most important moves were to get off the streets and out of Florida.

I was trapped in the United States. Crossing borders was a non-starter now.

When the scream went up on the robbery a lot of people would be looking for a fat Englishman and a box of gold. I stuck out like Santa Claus throwing firecrackers on the Fourth of July.

I was half the country away from Dee. I had useless airline tickets and less than a hundred dollars in cash.

I did, of course, have a million dollars in gold, plus one or two other negotiables in the packages.

Think.

I thunk.

Trains. I didn't know when they ran, but then trains are traps. You can't stop them and get off. And all those stations with prying eyes.

So no train.

Think.

It's four hundred miles out of Florida on Highway 1. Fifteen hundred miles to New York. I studied the traffic from the back of the cab as we turned left onto Biscayne Boulevard.

Stuart's office was on Biscayne. This was the most dangerous part of the journey. Stuart <u>must</u> have returned to Miami International by now.

When he doesn't find me there, what will he do? He will check the apartment, and then what? Return to his office and wait? How long would he wait for Dee?

It was growing dark now. I hunched down in the back of the cab as we swept past the shuttered office. No white Rolls Royce.

About forty minutes had elapsed since the strike announcement. I hoped I was still smothered by the cloud of confusion.

The taxi turned right onto Venetian Causeway and drove towards Collins Avenue. This is crazy. I have to contact Dee and tell her what's going on. When was the punter due to meet her? I hadn't phoned him and Dee wouldn't be at the apartment. He must know something was amiss.

About a million dollars. That's what was amiss.

I have to get out of the state. As we crossed the causeway and passed North Bay Village, I ducked down again. I hadn't planned on seeing our old home quite so soon. No white Rolls in the carpark there either.

At the Eden Roc I paid off the driver. When the FBI quizzed the cabbies later this guy was bound to recall the big fat Englishman with the heavy case. I made as if to walk up the steps of the Eden Roc and go into the hotel, but the moment the cab's tail lights disappeared, I picked up the bag and left the hotel area.

Night had fallen now and as I tilted and sweated

along Collins Avenue, headlights from oncoming cars floodlit and dazzled me. My mouth was dry, my feet hurt, my clothes shifted uncomfortably about me and my arm ached.

I was illuminated by each car, like an actor on a spotlit stage. Nobody walks in Miami. Especially if they weigh the best part of four hundred pounds, including the gold.

I reached the Fontainebleau Hotel. The sign outside still boasted that this was a total resort with constant action. Nothing had changed. I still had a choice of restaurants, bars and a half acre free-form pool complete with waterfalls.

I just hoped the 'phones worked.

MIAMI BEACH
JULY

A figure sprang towards me as I pushed through the door. In the lobby of any big hotel you'll run the gauntlet of house detectives, nosy receptionists, spies, thieves, hookers, pimps and lounge-lizards. The Miami Fontainebleau is no exception. I waved the helpful bellhop away with my free hand and crossed the foyer to the 'phone booth.

I didn't intend to take up residence, just the 'phone. If I didn't get off the streets soon I'd be taken off.

I didn't want to waste any money on transatlantic calls. But it was important that I contact Benny and tell him what had happened. I placed a collect call to the bookmaker's number and was rewarded with a variety of bleeps, crackles and echoes, part and parcel of our modern electronic age. Every international call is taped by somebody. Those from the United States are monitored by the National Security Agency's Surveillance System. What they do with all those taped calls, God only knows.

God, the NSA, CIA, FBI, DEA and anyone else with access to the information.

Deep in the heart of Kansas, stored on microchips in massive bunkers, billions of conversations are waiting to be replayed in another millenia.

I heard the distinctive double ring of the British phone system and then Benny's cocaine and whisky voice accepting the call. "Hello Jew," he said. "You got problems?"

Benny knew that I was supposed to be in the air right now and not 'phoning. He was quick. I was pleased that I had chosen him as our emergency contact point.

"Only one," I said. "There's been a national airline strike."

"That's handy. Still got the gear?"

"Yes, I thought it better to hold onto it."

"Quite right," said Benny. "You never know when it might come in useful. Where are you now?"

"In shtuk."

"I know it well. I go there every year for my holidays. I just called the girl to tell her you were okay. Now what do you want me to do?"

No names on the telephone - we both knew the drill.

"Please 'phone her and tell her to stay where she is. I'll try and make my way to her. But I'm very short of readies."

"So what's new?" said the bookmaker.

I laughed. "Not a lot. I'm on the move. Speak to you later."

I hung up. Then I picked up the bag and walked straight out of the hotel. There were several taxis waiting out in front of the Fontainebleau, but I certainly wasn't going to take one from there.

Back on the street again, me and the gold. This is ridiculous, I thought hysterically. If I don't get arrested or die of a heart attack I'll probably become flavour of the month for a mugger. If I do, he'd have the best result of his life.

My poor feet, carrying nearly four hundred pounds up Collins Avenue. I was so exhausted I'd have probably been relieved if somebody had taken the case off me.

But at least the phone call had given my arm a rest. It's amazing how staggering up the road with freshly stolen heavy swag concentrates the mind.

About a thousand yards along Collins Avenue there was a bank of 'phone booths. Gratefully I slipped inside one and plonked the case down. My arm nearly falling off and my back aching from the strain of trying to walk upright to disguise the load.

On the wall of the phone booth there was a simple tourist map of Florida with happy golfers and dolphins. Although trains are traps, I decided to dial Amtrak.

I got the busy signal. The tourist map told of the delights of The Serpenterium where visitors can come face to face with some of the world's deadliest and most exotic snakes. Visitors needn't have wasted the fare out of Miami from what I knew. I redialled Amtrak. Still busy.

I realised that Ghengis Khan and his brother Don would be trying to catch trains out of here tonight.

I tried the next number on my list. The Greyhound Bus Company. This time I was lucky. The 'phone rang.

And rang.

And bloody well rang. The tourist map urged me to visit Monkey Jungle. I'd have been delighted to move in for keeps.

Still no reply from Greyhound. Benny would have said that I was "well out of form".

The map assured me there was lots of excitement in Florida. How true.

As I glanced out of the phone booth it looked as I were in for some now. The kind not mentioned on the tourist map.

Two black men walked past the 'phone booth. Dudes with leather pants, gold chains and faces that would have gained them officer rank in the Tontons Macoutes. One of them gave me the kind of stare that tigers normally reserve for tethered goats. Starer touched his pal on the arm.

Collins Avenue was deserted but well lit. Too well lit. I felt on show like Sunday Night at the London Palladium. Inside the booth I began to sweat. My paranoia level soared. The box of gold took up most of the floor space and made it awkward to stand. It seemed to glow radioactively.

The black men had stopped about twenty yards away and were having an energetic conversation. One of them kept glancing in my direction.

I can tell a hungry look when I see one. I saw two now.

For the first time in my life I wished I had had a loaded gun in my pocket.

I did the next best thing. I glared straight at them and put my hand deliberately inside my jacket and kept it there. My hand touched the cold metal of my propelling pencil. I gave them my best 'if you're looking for trouble you've come to the right place' vibes.

The Tontons moved on. First result I'd had all day.

Greyhound answered. I asked the times of the buses to New York. I took my propelling pencil out of my jacket pocket and noted the details. On impulse I asked for the bus times from Orlando and Jacksonville. Names I spotted on the tourist map. I thanked the girl and hung up. As I did, I realized I had forgotten to ask how much the ticket to New York cost. But I figured it must be less than a hundred dollars.

I certainly didn't fancy hanging around the bus terminal in downtown Miami. The map was out of scale but it looked about two hundred miles north to Jacksonville. Ideally I wanted to get hold of a car and drive to New York. But if that were not possible and I could only get transport to Jacksonville, I could catch the New York bound Greyhound bus from there. Surely only a few people with a million dollars about them travel by bus. My case shouldn't attract any attention.

How to drive to New York?

An inspiration hit me.

The lurid map reminded me of something.

What was it?

I dredged my memory, something else over-coloured.

The postcard from Juliette in Hialeah County! The old lady didn't live in a shoe but in a bungalow on the edge of the Everglades. My father had served with her husband in World War II. I had been there once for dinner when I first came to America. They must have cars. Everybody else in America did.

I found the number from enquiries and called her up. After exchanging the usual pleasantries I explained to her how my motor had broken down and I had to get down to the Keys tonight. Could I borrow her car?

"It's pretty old, Daniel, like me." Americans think that any model other than this year's is ancient.

"Juliette, darling," I said. "I've always considered you at the top end of young."

The old lady laughed. "Well, come on over whenever you like."

"I'll be with you in about an hour, Juliette. Thanks a million."

And I meant it.

NEW YORK CITY
JULY

Dee put the phone down, stunned by Benny's news. Her mind went out to Daniel. How must he feel? Where was he? How was he going to get to New York? How long would she have to stay in the hotel room? A thousand questions tumbled through her mind and no answers. Well, she had to stay cool.

Benny had told her to remain in her room and leave as little as possible. She wouldn't go out at all. She had a TV, bathroom, room service and puzzle books.

Daniel always used to say she could sit out World War III as long as she had a bottle of gin, plenty of cigarettes and a few puzzle books. Well, she'd sit this out.

There was over a thousand dollars left from the pawn money. She was thrilled that Daniel had captured the parcel. She had faith in him. He was a survivor. He'd make it to New York.

They'd have a right laugh when he got here.

When he got here.

First thing was to extend the room and car.

She picked up the phone.

DADE COUNTY
FLORIDA
JULY

Residents of the Dade County suburbs find stray alligators a nuisance.

Many a morning Juliette Dahl awoke to find one or two of the beasts basking on her back lawn.

"They crawl up from the canal, you know," she complained.

I sipped my bourbon and nodded politely.

There wasn't much I could do about the alligator problem. The Dahl's lived on the fringe of Florida's Everglades. Thousands of square miles of primeval marsh. Millions of years and a forty minute ride away from civilization.

I had paid my taxi off in pitch darkness some distance from the Dahl's secluded house-on-stilts.

The cabbie had looked at me quizzically. I guess he didn't get many passengers asking to be set down in the Palaeozoic Age.

"Are you sure this is the right place, buddy? There ain't nothing out here but swamp and quicksand."

"I'm on a survival course," I told him. He didn't seem reassured. Overweight Englishmen who insisted on carrying their own cases and on being set down at midnight in alligator country were obviously not a dime a dozen in his book. I pushed two twenties into his hand. He scrutinized them with a pencil torch like a man reading the instructions on a firecracker. After deciding that they weren't going to explode on him, he gave me one last look of disbelief and disappeared into the night.

I took a deep breath and stood for a moment and let my eyes adjust to the velvet darkness. The air was tropic, perfumed and warm. My senses were heightened. Stars punctuated the black sky. For the first time I was alone with my golden million. If you didn't count a few thousand cicadas.

Who counts cicadas?

I hauled the case in what I hoped was the general direction of Juliette's home. After five minutes of staggering through the blackness I was cursing myself for not buying the pencil torch off the taxi driver.

A distant lamp lit the entrance to the Dahl property.

Ten yards down their drive I thrust the case deep into the foliage and then presented myself at Juliette's door.

Fortunately, husband Chuck was away on business and I sat alone with this old lady who had dangled me on her knee in England thirty years before.

Juliette Dahl had once been a great beauty. My mother kept 1940s photos of the athletic Dahls. I was pleased that Chuck wasn't here tonight. He'd have been far more inquisitive than the arthritic woman with the alcohol washed eyes who sat opposite me.

I didn't feel particularly good about what I was doing to her.

I needed to borrow her car to drive to New York. I certainly wasn't going to be able to return it. My intention was to mail her the keys and a couple of thousand dollars. Overcompensation for the trouble of having to collect it from fifteen hundred miles away.

The Dahl's *were* friends of my parents after all.

After a social lobster dance of the 'how is everyone back home' variety, the old lady, glass in hand, led me to the garage at the side of the bungalow. She handed me her drink and fumbled with the lock. The door came open and Juliette disappeared inside. I followed her into the Stygian gloom. Suddenly the lights snapped on.

"Here's my Chevy." She grinned lopsidedly.

My heart sank.

Juliette's Chevy wouldn't be going to New York.

Benny the bookmaker would have given me long odds about it getting out of the driveway.

The nineteen-sixty model Chevrolet Impala had undoubtedly seen better days.

Too many of them.

Its ugly finned body had a coating of dust that would have done justice to a vintage wine cellar.

Once, when Richard Nixon was only a twinkle in Eisenhower's eye, this car had been painted green. The windshield looked like something bootleggers had used for target practice.

The tires would have made Kojak feel like a Beatle.

I rubbed grime away from the window and peered in. It wouldn't have surprised me to find the Lost Ark in there with Moses himself slumped over the wheel.

I pulled the door handle.

It fell off into my hand.

"The driver's door opens," Juliette said brightly.

"Jolly good," I replied.

I walked sadly around the car and returned the

bourbon and soda to Juliette. The driver's door did open and I eased myself tiredly into the interior.

I found the key in the ignition. Like a gambler who tosses his last coin into a fruit machine after losing his life's-savings at the casino, I turned the key.

Noises emanated from under the hood reminiscent of Canadian lumberjacks sawing through giant redwood trees.

To my astonishment the engine fired.

"Chuck keeps it going in case of emergencies," piped Juliette happily, as she slid open the garage doors.

"I'll bet it's an emergency driving it!" I laughed, fighting back hysteria.

So far this is one bastard of a night. If I ever make it through all this, I'll write a book.

The old lady showed me the controls.

Those that were working.

I cautioned Juliette to stand aside and selected reverse gear.

The elderly vehicle leapt violently backwards like a Scotsman presented with the bill for the Last Supper.

If I hadn't stamped my foot on the brake I would have overtaken the taxi I came in. I jerked the shift into neutral and hauled myself out leaving the engine running at revs more suited to a bomber awaiting take-off.

Magnificent clouds of grey smoke belched around us as I helped Juliette close the garage doors. I just hoped I could find the car again through what was developing into a Sherlock Holmes type fog.

I helped Juliette back to the house and thanked her profusely.

138

She had been my only chance for transport. On the steps I declined another drink, refused supper, promised to give my mother her fondest regards, assured her I'd return the Chevy as soon as possible, kissed her goodnight and finally eased the door closed.

I groped my way down the drive in conditions that would have kept the Murmansk convoy in harbour. Past the roaring beast I began to search the bushes for the leather.

For the second time that night I cursed myself for not obtaining a torch. If I didn't find the bag soon and get the hell out of there, Juliette would be floating out to ask why I hadn't left.

By now my face and clothes were soaking from the foliage. I scratched my face and hysteria turned to fury.

My fingers touched the cold handle sending a wave of relief through me. I hauled my treasure chest out of the undergrowth and lugged it down the drive to the car.

Do you think the trunk would open? Frantically I jiggled the button. The trunk stayed stubbornly shut. Finally I shoved the case onto the back seat of the car and settled myself in behind the wheel.

This time I was prepared for the violent leap backwards.

DADE COUNTY
FLORIDA
JULY

Alligator Alley dissects the Everglades for three hundred miles, linking Florida to the rest of the States.

As I rocketed down the deserted night highway, my headlights revealed only empty scrubland.

Even the alligators were home in bed.

I hoped that the local highway patrol had taken the same sensible course of action.

I wished I had.

Glancing in the rearview mirror I noticed a trail of thick black smoke billowing out behind me. I was more likely to be arrested for polluting Everglades National Park than for stealing gold.

By now I was lightheaded with the whole ludicrous nightmare. Here I am in a land crammed fender to fender with powerful automobiles, jockeying this reject from a Laurel and Hardy short.

I have a hundred dollars in cash and a million dollars' worth of what will by morning become the most famous gold coins in North America, carried by the most sought after portly Englishman.

I am filthy, dishevelled, paranoid and hyperactive. Apart from that I feel fine.

This isn't really happening to me.

I checked the instrument panel. The gas gauge registered half full. The temperature was hitting the dangerous mark. I needed water.

Now.

Alligator Alley crosses thousands of square miles of deserted swamps, not a place to break down at any time, let alone at three in the morning.

The Chevrolet was not what my old pals in the motor trade would have referred to as a good 'driver'.

The steering shook uncontrollably.

The springing would have defeated a rodeo rider. The shock absorbers didn't.

Long loud groans emanated from deep in the bowels of the beast, like foghorns out on Nantucket Sound.

I switched on the radio.

A loud scream assaulted my ears and continued to do so whichever way I span the dial.

Of all the cars to cross America in I have to be stuck with this one.

In all the best gangster movies people always listen to the radio news bulletins about themselves and the chase.

Reality can be SO different!

You put your foot down and push on into the night.

By day Alligator Alley is overburdened with traffic between Miami and Disneyland. But the gas stations that serve this artery are closed at night. I urged the decrepit Impala northward. The water gauge stuck on red. Delirium now replaced my earlier exhaustion.

The car and I were running on nerves alone.

Suddenly white scalding smoke streamed from under the bonnet, smothering the windshield, blinding me.

I hit the wiper button—you've guessed it!

I put my hand outside and rub a patch clean.

A gout of brown muck sprays the windscreen and the back of my arm.

I laugh madly.

After a few moments, the spraying muck stops.

Goodbye radiator.

I push the car faster in the vague hope that the in-rushing air will help cool the engine.

I'm not a scientist.

My eyes strain through the murk into the head-light tunnel. Endless scrub and shuttered isolated gas stations.

Once or twice I twiddle radio knobs.

Still The Scream. I castigate myself for not keeping a hired car in Miami as a fallback. But who could have forseen a nationwide airline strike?

This kind of thing never happens to Steve McQueen.

But I have the gold.

I wondered how Dee was getting on in New York.

The speedo needle couldn't make up its mind whether we were doing eighty or a hundred. I kept my foot down. I wanted to put as much distance between myself and the Miami police as possible. My headlights picked out gas station after gas station.

All closed.

I dreaded meeting a police car. I could just imagine the conversation. "Whaddya have in the case, son?"

I passed a sign.

Still over a hundred miles to Jacksonville. My watch said twenty past one.

I glanced again at the instruments.

Astonishingly the temperature gauge had fallen.

I cruised at eighty. There was a Greyhound to New York that left Jacksonville at four thirty and I was beginning to think that I might make it.

That's when the front tire blew.

The loud bang startled me and the steering began gyrating wildly. Instinctively I began to slow down, laughing deliriously. Then I realised that there was no point in stopping. Juliette had told me that the spare was flat.

Anyway, I've never been able to change a tire to save my life let alone for a million dollars. I know my limitations.

I chomped on my cigar and drove on like Ghengis Khan.

The steering wheel juddered as the tire shredded. Grimly, my arms screaming with pain I battled forward on the rim.

This is the most ridiculous situation of my life.

I sang California Here I Come.

I was going raving mad. I didn't care anymore. The whole fucking night was a conspiracy against me. The airline strike, the Chevvy, the tire. All of it.

I was torn between despair and euphoria. As the speed dropped it became impossible to hold the car in a straight line.

Then I saw the gas station. I was so surprised, I nearly drove straight past.

Thar she blows! The white whale of Alligator Alley. Lit up and smiling in the night. The answer to a gold robber's prayer.

The attendant hardly raised an eyebrow as I ground the Chevy onto the forecourt and killed the engine. Steam belched from under the hood and I caught an acrid stench of burnt rubber and ground metal from the rim.

The mechanic ambled out from his little booth wiping his hands with a rag. He raised a polite eyebrow as if all his clients arrived in this condition. I remembered my Americanisms.

"Can you fix a flat?" I asked.

He stared at the bare rim. "Sure Mister. Where is it?"

I had to laugh. "Somewhere back on the highway."

"What you need is a new tire."

"Go right ahead," I said. "And thanks."

I went off to find the toilet, pleased as punch.

A sign directed me around the back of the building.

I was relieving myself when I suddenly remembered that I'd left a million dollars on the back seat in an unlocked case.

I no longer cared.

I began to care as I came around to the front. The attendant was a problem either way. If he hadn't vanished with the gold he'd be able to pinpoint me, my route and vehicle when the scream went up tomorrow.

I hoped I'd make it to Jacksonville. I worried about how much the new tire would cost.

The mechanic hadn't vanished with the gold. He had opened the trunk and was worrying about the tire.

"You need a new spare,"

"Just the front wheel, please," I felt guilty at suspecting him and not giving him more custom.

With a shrug he ambled to his workshop.

"Can I use your 'phone?" I asked.

"Be my guest," he called out.

In the office I found a payphone and dialled the

operator.

While I was waiting for my collect call to Benny, I helped myself to a cold Coke from the fridge and a couple of Hershey bars. I realised I hadn't eaten all day. My head ached. My arms felt like jelly.

Now I could hear the sound of Benny's phone ringing in England.

And ringing.

"There's no reply," the operator warbled inanely.

"Keep trying please." Telephone operators sitting blindly at switchboards connecting ten second slices of other peoples lives.

Suddenly Benny's voice came on the line with his usual non-committal "Haloo?"

"Hello," I said. The operator cut me off while she went through her rigmarole.

"Jew," he said. "Where are you now?" It was an old telephone joke. We're both Jewish.

"In slightly deeper shtuk. I've had a puncture."

"You're not doing too well tonight, are you? First an airline strike and now a puncture. I've heard better excuses from horse trainers."

I smiled. It was good to hear his voice, and his comments.

"Listen, can you give a message to her?" I didn't want to phone Dee myself. The call from the gas station would be traced. Any investigator could summon up Ma Bell's computer and the long distance records. To contact Dee direct from this phone would blow her location.

I told Benny what I wanted him to do.

"Anything else you need?" asked the bookmaker.

"A helicopter would do for starters," I said. "I'll have my man take care of it," said Benny in the reassuring confident voice he used when he wasn't going to pay someone.

"Still got the gear?" Benny asked.

"I put it all on a horse at Gulfstream. It runs in the three o'clock tomorrow."

"What's it called?"

"Midas Touch," I shouted and hung up the phone.

The mechanic had changed the tire, gassed up the tank, inflated the spare somehow and topped up the radiator with water and sealant. People like that embarrass me. I paid him, tipped him, thanked him and roared the Impala bomber gingerly back out onto the highway. I hoped to reach Orlando in time for the New York Greyhound.

I wondered how many alligators Juliette would find on her lawn in the morning.

JACKSONVILLE
FLORIDA
ONWARD
JULY

Four o'clock in the morning at Jacksonville bus terminal is not a good time or place to be inconspicuous. Especially if you roll up in a twenty year old Chevrolet wreathed in clouds of steam and belching black smoke.

And you are white.

The United States of America has the world's most mobile population. A good proportion of them crowded the terminal as I arrived.

During the night the poor are on the move; the rich travel in daylight by plane, train and automobile.

The hungry, dispossessed, rootless and desperate travel on buses.

Tonight I joined them.

I cruised into Jacksonville on streets glistening from a brief tropical shower, the old Chevrolet steaming like Stevenson's Rocket.

Like a pin-table on 'tilt', the Chevvy's instrument panel had lit up and the old car died on me on a patch of ground right next to the terminal. I hauled the bag out of the back and patted the old Impala on the nose. If I'd had a flower I would have laid it on its hood.

I arrived just as the four-thirty Flyer for New York was loading its cargo. Mostly human, mostly black.

The airline strike had increased the crowds. Inside the terminal I struggled with the heavy case through restless knots of people, all of us unsettled, floating and bewildered. Mothers calming screaming children rubbed shoulders with gangling black youths. Patient, tired old men wrapped up against the rainy night, soft bags resting by their feet, waited for buses to nowhere.

I felt homeless, yet at home.

Another footless vagabond moving his problems by night.

Pushing through the crowd I spotted a free ticket window and thrust my face in, dumping the case down, and resting my knee on it.

"A single to New York, please, straight through."

"Fifty-seven dollars," said the clerk without looking up.

I winced and handed over my last three twenties.

"You'd better hurry." The clerk handed me the ticket. "Flyer leaves from Stand Five."

Stuffing the change in my pocket I grabbed my Old Man of the Sea and hauled him out into the terminal. The angular case banging painfully against my leg as I barged my way through the mass.

At Stand Five my heart plummeted. Another problem; a long line of agitated people milling about, the bus already full. Two huge black men were shouting at each other by the coach door. Women screamed as the driver started up the Greyhound's engine.

Fuck it! I thought.

Hoisting the gold in front of me I did a rugby run past the line to the door, pushing my way between the astonished arguers, I hurled the case into the bus and sprang up after it.

There are some advantages to weighing three hundred pounds.

The door closed with a hiss behind me as the Greyhound pulled away.

Barging my way as gently as possible down the aisle, I found a seat at the back next to two old black ladies and fell thankfully into it, resting the case at my feet.

It's a lovely feeling when you just make a bus.

We slid past the line of angry, open-mouthed non-travellers. One of the black men banged the window near me.

My need is greater.

Out of the station. The underbelly of Jacksonville crawled by. Soon we were on US 1 through hamlets with names like Yulee, Gross and Woodbine.

It's easy to be depressed, when travelling long distances by night in a strange land, tired, broke and on the run. Add a fortune at your feet that you must stay awake to protect, and which you could be stabbed for, or robbed of, and you add a new dimension.

Paranoia.

You don't dare sleep.

And you can't the leave the boodle behind you when you go to the toilet.

Supposing someone opens the box?

Most of the other passengers sleep. Me, I gauch. Dee's word for dozing whilst awake. My legs across the loot. Everytime I get up to answer a call of nature I haul the case with me into the toilet.

This does not go unnoticed by some of my fellow passengers.

They were a pretty rough looking crowd. I've seen tamer crews in pirate movies. There were three black men travelling together playing cards. One of them possessed a scar that ran from hairline to jaw, past the blank ugly socket of a missing eye. His companions were wild Rastafarians, their dreadlocks swinging as they played and quarrelled.

Another was a strange Charles Manson lookalike, a pale jittery-looking young man with wisps of beard, wearing a jacket emblazened with Rock-Satanic symbols. Two words were tattooed on his right cheek.

Across the aisle lay a grizzled individual who looked as if he hacksawed children into pieces for a hobby. I could savour the aroma of his rags from four seats away.

I ran this happy little gauntlet everytime I used the john.

Ill, nervous and exhausted, my head felt like Dresden on firebomb night. I had sweated and re-dried in these clothes ever since dawn yesterday. My underwear itched and twisted up around me. I had a stomach ache and felt thirsty. Most of all I needed to close my eyes and sleep.

Sleep.

Sleep and someone will relieve me of my burden.

I dozed from time to time and shook myself awake, feeling worse each time.

I wished for cocaine, cognac or some stimulant. Anything to assuage the pain.

The jittery man walked past me to use the toilet. I read the words on his cheek. Helter Skelter. You can't get much more heavily into Manson.

I had never been on a Greyhound bus before. I had no idea where this one stopped or how they worked. In the dingy toilet a tap reluctantly parted with trickles of a stale brackish fluid that I hoped was water.

I developed quite an art in drinking this. There were no plastic cups available and I have seen teaspoons bigger than the sink. I had to crane my head around at an angle, twist my body down and then poke my tongue out under the filthy tap.

A few sour driblets in my mouth and substantial blows to the head were my reward from the jolting bus as I carried out this exercise.

There was nothing for sale on board. No sweets, colas, chewing gum. I was of the opinion that Greyhound ought to be prosecuted for un-American activities. A sandwich or a coffee from my remaining three dollars would have gone down well.

Mine was a waking delirium.

In my paranoia I began to imagine that several of the passengers were taking an unhealthy interest in me.

They were.

As dawn broke and we edged towards Savannah my unease grew. Eye-Socket and Child Chopper had stayed awake with me. As we pulled into Savannah the black lady in the next seat told me we would be stopping here for thirty minutes. I thanked her.

I needed coffee, food and a phone.

At the bus station everyone got off the bus to stretch their legs.

Only one man carried a bag off with him.

Me.

Inside the brightly lit terminal I spent a twelfth of my capital on a Left Luggage locker.

Manson, Child Chopper and Eye-Socket watched me do it, along with the other passengers queuing for self-service food.

Balancing scalding coffee on the pay 'phone I waited while the operator went through her 'twenty questions' with Benny.

I imagine the bookmaker. It's two in the morning in Brighton. He'll be sitting in his pyjamas and dressing gown watching old pornographic and racing videos. His antique snuff box of cocaine at his side, the wife and children asleep upstairs. Three 'phones receiving calls; from me, from his private police commander and his man in the police computer room who tells Benny whether the commander is lying.

"Jew," booms Benny's voice. "Where are you now?"

"I'm on a bus. We've stopped in Savannah."

"I've got my kid's school atlas here. We're all following the journey with great interest."

"I'll put on a lecture with slides if I get back. What odds do you give me?"

"You're odds-on to win, Jewboy. You'll make it." "How's my girl?" "She says she loves you and she's putting on weight from room service." "Give her my love. Tell her I'll cuddle her however big she is." "Still got the gear?" "Just." "The people over there are in touch with the other people here." The 'other people' is how Benny refers to the police. "Can you find out anything for me?" I asked. "I just did."

"Thank you. I'll call you later."

"If they haven't cut my phone off." I hung up and I glanced at the Beaume & Mercier. Stopped. I should have pawned the bloody thing. The terminal clock told me I had about five minutes to get back on the bus or be stuck in Savannah with two dollars. I trudge back to the luggage lockers. Child Chopper evinces intense interest in the Left Luggage regulations but he can't help glancing at me. I can't work out how to do the hand in the jacket trick, open the locker and take the case simultaneously. But I do my jacket number anyway. I make sure he's looking when I do. I hesitate and stare at him. He avoids my gaze and shuffles out towards the bus. I'm getting quite good at the jacket job now. I look around. No sign of the other Hitchcock rejects. In America everyone thinks everyone else carries guns, which is very useful. I hefted out the case and lumped back onto the Greyhound. Hardeeville and Greenpond slipped by us on US 17 as we crossed the Combahee River heading for Charleston. Rich tobacco fields rolled by my window, interspersed with architecture ranging from ruined Palladian to corrugated shack. Hoardings scarred the countryside extolling the virtues of identical toothpaste, petrol, and cigarettes. The day grew hotter. The bus was not air conditioned. Motel signs taunted me, offering beds, colour TV, swimming pools and hot food. There were some good bargains but nothing my two dollars could have handled. I wanted to get off that bus and sleep for a year. I daydreamed of showers, clean shirts, cool gardens, iced champagne, soft beds.

Most of the other passengers dozed or slept. Manson had nodded off now. Child Chopper's chin was on his chest. Eye Socket and the two Rastamen still played cards. Occasionally Eye Socket swept a cyclopian glare in my direction.

Was he keeping an eye on me or what?

By now the octopus machine of American law enforcement, State, Federal, and local is slithering into action.

Computerised tentacles flickering out, looking for me.

I make a nice target for some trigger-happy cop who could claim he found me and not the gold.

At Charleston, another thirty minute stopover. We all troop off the bus again. I do my number with the locker. The Rastamen study my antics as they line up for coffee.

I wonder whether to call Benny again but decide against it.

I could call Dee though.

But not with only a dollar left.

I find out that the bus stops for an hour in Raleigh. I decide to leave my phoning till then.

I hope to find a dealer in Raleigh who isn't in a drug recovery programme.

Maybe I can cash some coins.

Back on the Greyhound many of the passengers are eating. I watch morosely as a woman across the aisle feeds her little girl an apple. The little black child smiles at me and holds up a piece.

"Appuh," she says.

I smile back hoping the kid will give me the slice.

She pops it into her mouth.

It is going to be that kind of day.

MILWAUKEE
JULY

Skill had arrived early at Milwaukee Airport and had eaten a wonderful dinner with Frenchie the coin dealer from Chicago. They had talked about old times and sunk a fair amount of liquor. Skill could handle a fair amount.

Frenchie was off whoring. Skill would have joined him, but the Englishman was flying in. The little man figured that if he drove to the airport early he could get nicely mellow.

Now Skill had drunk alone at the airport bar for two hours. He found the place unusually quiet. He hated barmen and never spoke to them, preferring to plow his way steadily and silently through the Jack Daniels.

At 11:06 p.m.,the flight's arrival time, he rolled down to the strangely deserted concourse. At the ticket desk he enquired of the Miami flight and learned of the nationwide strike by ground crews.

No one could tell him how long the strike would last, or when the Miami plane might arrive.

Skill did the thing he always did when faced with an unforseen problem. He weaved back to the bar and sank a big one. Then he found a phone and tried to call Stuart in Florida. Frustrated with busy signals, Skill decided to return to his hotel. He saw no point in taking a cab, his car was at the airport and he would only have to collect it in the morning.

He felt okay to drive. He had driven in worse states than this, ferchrissake.

At 11:53 p.m. he was stopped by the highway patrol for erratic driving.

At 11:55 p.m. he was breathalysed.

By a quarter to one in the morning he was charged, photographed, fingerprinted and fast asleep in the drunk tank at Milwaukee Public Safety Unit.

MIAMARINA
MIAMI
JULY

The Rolls Investment office was a blaze of light
in the pre-dawn darkness of Biscayne Boulevard.

Stuart had waited forlornly on the yacht until
nearly two o'clock in the morning. He kept no
'phone or television there and had known nothing
of the airline strike.

At midnight the jeweller had walked to the 'phone
booth at the end of the Miamarina and called Skill
in Milwaukee to check that Daniel had arrived
safely. He was sure that there would be no problem
with the Englishman.

The receptionist in the Milwaukee Hotel had
told him that Skill hadn't returned from the airport. Daniel had not checked in. Stuart figured that
maybe they'd gone for a meal after Skill had met
the Englishman off the plane shortly after eleven
p.m.

He dialled the couple's apartment. No reply. He
called his own home, activating the remote control
answerphone for messages. Negative. Likewise the
office. So Stuart had hurried back to the My Paradise.

The 'Popped out for a minute' note that he had
left for Dee was undisturbed.

The jeweller wondered where the girl could be.
Had she changed her mind? Falkman couldn't
imagine she had. Who could offer her more? And it

wasn't as if he was bad looking. Alright, so he was myopic and bald, but lots of powerful men wore thick glasses and wigs. Some girls found it attractive. He fixed himself another drink and dozed in the cabin.

He was awoken by a thump and the motion of the rocking boat. His spirits lifted. The girl had arrived.

Poking his head on deck he discovered the cause of the motion. It was the Rogerson family, his neighbours at the Miamarina. Rogerson was a dentist.

"Hi. Good morning," called Stuart.

"Hello, Falkman. Sorry we woke you. Bet you're surprised to see us."

Stuart tried to remember why he should be surprised. "Oh, yes. Weren't you flying up to Annapolis tonight for some naval function?"

That's how Stuart learned of the airstrike. The Rogersons didn't know of course, whether this applied to Milwaukee.

From the phone booth at the end of the dock, the jeweller called Miami International, receiving the busy signal for his pains. He tried the apartment and the shop. Still no messages. He dialled the operator, gave her his credit card number (he had every credit card possible) and was put through to the hotel in Milwaukee.

No Skill. No Daniel.

He learned that the Miami flight had not departed Florida.

So where the hell was the Englishman?

Where was Skill?

Where was Dee?

Where was his gold?

Stuart Falkman, jeweller, incompetent CIA operative and jilted suitor, decided to return to his office. He had a sickening feeling that something downward was about to happen to his career. Falkman called Kathy and told her to meet him at the gold store with her safe key.

Stuart Falkman was a meticulous man. Closing the boat took him over half an hour.

From the office at four a.m. while Kathy was checking the safe, he connected to Miami International.

As Falkman talked to the airport, Kathy told him about the missing packages.

Stuart dropped the telephone and ran to the safe to see for himself.

"This will have to be reported at once," said Kathy. "Will you do it or shall I?"

"I have to," said Stuart. "I'm the senior officer, after all."

Kathy gave him a look that was somewhere between pity and contempt. Not for much longer, she thought.

Stuart Falkman's hands were trembling as he dialled the memorised number that he had been told to use only in extreme emergencies.

Langley would go ape.

RALEIGH
NORTH CAROLINA
JULY

Sunshine in Raleigh highlighting the green leaves, white buildings and black faces. The broad tree lined avenues bathed in morning gold.

The Greyhound pulled into another clone terminal. The cafeteria, a rhapsody in formica and shining cracked plastic seating. In the waiting area, luggage locker banks, scribbled with graffiti, provided a backdrop for milling passengers.

On the journey from Charleston I had taken my Siamese twin into the toilet and extracted a handful of gold twenty dollar pieces. The everyday kind worth about three hundred dollars each. I had torn the page relating to Raleigh from the coindealers guide, and this was now in my pocket along with the locker key and my remaining seventy-five cents.

I planned to use the stopover in Raleigh to sell some coins. I needed cash for food, 'phone calls and maybe a motel.

I found what I was looking for in a seedy district about five minutes walk from the bus station. Amongst the abandoned cars, empty lots and clapboard houses, a sign proclaimed Wintermans to be dealers in guns, coins and stamps. They were not on the 'Recovery' list and I was about to take my risks with them.

I paused at the iron-trellised door and squinted through the dusty windows. Old television sets, transistor radios and guns jostled for room with cameras, junk jewellery and bric-a-brac - the un-claimed pledges of Raleigh.

As I walked through the door a buzzer sounded, triggered off by a photo-cell. At the rear of the shop an iron grille backed with glass ran from ceiling down to counter. A cashier's window was set into it, for passing objects through.

Despite the warmth of the day, the old man behind the grille wore a thick grey cardigan. His bare, blue, fanatical eyes bored into me through spectacles, like the reception officer at Auschwitz. His gaze took in my dishevelled clothes, dark hair and two days growth of beard. He's probably a grand wizard in the local Ku Klux Klan. On the wall I saw militaria, Nazi Regalia, the Confederate Flag.

Wonderful.

My confidence belched black smoke and lost height rapidly.

"Morning," I said brightly. "Do you buy gold coins?"

"Would they be U.S. coins?" he rasped.

A dry Southern accent. The polite kind that doffs its hat to ladies before going to a lynching.

His question about U.S. coins woke me up.

This guy was sharp. "Sure," I said. "Twenty dollar gold pieces."

"I'll take a look." He parted with each word grudgingly, as if he lost blood speaking.

I slid two coins under the grille. They were worth three hundred dollars a piece anywhere in the world.

Except here.

The old klansman examined them through a magnifying glass as if they were insects that he'd found in his mint julep. A lizard tongue flickering dryly across his thin lips.

"Fifty dollars."

"Each?" I said astonished.

The fanatic eyes glittered. "The pair."

As broke as I was I wasn't going to let this Jew hating, slave whipping bastard rip me off five hundred and fifty dollars, on a six hundred dollar deal. No matter what I had back in the bus station.

"Give me three hundred dollars the pair and they're yours. There's still a nice profit in it for you."

"Seventy-five dollars." His lizard tongue flashed again. I was glad I wasn't selling him linen for the hoods and robes.

"Two hundred and fifty," I said.

"Seventy five dollars is my final offer, Sir."

Fuck you, I thought. I shook my head and wordlessly held out my hands for the coins.

As I walked down the street with my seventy-five cents in my pocket I wondered if I was crazy. Those few dollars would have bought me food, drink and phone calls. I dearly wanted to leave the bus and take a room for the night. Sleep that knits the travelled sleeve of care.

But I just couldn't let that old lizard take me. In Raleigh the Ku Klux Klan have got enough money in the linen fund as it is.

BRANDYWINE
VIRGINIA
JULY

Deep in the Virginia countryside, in his carefully refurbished colonial mansion that was so convenient for the office at Langley, the Deputy Director (Intelligence) of the Central Intelligence Agency of the United States of America was awake, despite the hour. James Benedict Ampleforth II was working at the elegant Carlton House writing desk; his wife's twenty-fifth wedding anniversary gift to him from Sotheby-Parke-Bernet.

A light sleeper and a career intelligence officer, he relished this part of his day above all. The house was quiet, his wife was asleep and in the early dawn his soundtracks were the wild birds of Virginia, and the panting breath of the Rotweilers as they enthusiastically tugged the bleary-eyed armed guards across the lawn beneath his study windows.

Spread out before him were the latest satellite photos from the National Reconnaisance Office, the joint CIA/USAF operation, and intelligence digests from around the world. Libya, Iraq, Iran, Poland, Nicaragua, the Philippines, Haiti; the DDI scanned the digests rapidly. Nothing especially dramatic in this morning's reports.

Perhaps he would be able to manage nine holes after the National Security Council meeting scheduled for later today.

That was when the little red light on his telephone console began to wink.

As he listened to the duty officer relaying to him the news from Miami, his dreams of nine holes at the club disintegrated. The duty officer finished his report.

"Tell them to report the theft to the FBI and State Police as normal, but to make no mention of our goods, or the Agency."

The Deputy Director paused, that much was standard procedure. Operations were not his field, but the Miami business was special. He wondered what kind of idiots they were using down in Florida. This could turn into a mess. The earlier he passed the buck upward, the better.

"And I want a chopper on the pad and fuelled for Washington, NOW!"

Such was the vehemence with which he pronounced the last word that his wife woke up.

MIAMI
JULY

Stuart Falkman replaced the receiver and looked at Kathy.

"They said report the theft in the ordinary manner. Who first, Kathy?"

"Local police. They'll call the FBI." My God, thought Kathy. This man is a CIA paymaster and involved in de-stabilising programmes, and he doesn't even know how to call the police. It's no wonder the Agency gets such a bad name everywhere. The Soviets don't need Boris Ponomarev and his disinformation committee while we've got agents like Stuart Falkman, she thought.

By five a.m. the Dade County Public Safety Unit had run the details that the jeweller had given them through the National Crime Information computer.

By five thirty, Federal Bureau of Investigation had called Stuart and told him to stay put.

By five forty-five, the Dade County Police had located Skill in the drunk tank in Milwaukee.

By six a.m. the FBI man was seated opposite Stuart, holding the photos which had been telexed from Scotland Yard.

For the first time, Stuart learned who Dee and Daniel were.

The jeweller washed the four aspirins down with lukewarm Coca Cola.

"This isn't going to be such a wonderful weekend," he said to the FBI man

Special Agent Dexter Pendleton nodded. British police photos of Dee and Daniel lay on the desk between the two men.

"Trusting women is like swallowing knives," said Stuart Falkman.

RALEIGH
NORTH CAROLINA
JULY

They were waiting for me at the Raleigh Greyhound terminal. Eye Socket and the Rastamen taking a coffee together. Child Chopper hunched over a glass of beer at the bar. All within sight of the locker. No sign of Manson. The station clock told me I had ten minutes in which to call Benny. "Where are you now?" It was a pleasure to hear his English accent. "Raleigh."

"I thought that was a bicycle. Hang on. Let me look at the atlas."

"Never mind the bloody atlas. How is she?" "Fine. She did what you told her and the other fellow is waiting up there too." I could hear racing details coming over the loudspeaker in Benny's office. They were betting odds on about Goodwood. "Thank you." "Still holding?" "No. I slung it in a river. I got fed up with it." "Best thing, really," said Benny. "Travel light."

"Put me a monkey double on the first two favourites at Ascot."

"Your credit is no good," said Benny. "Tell me when it ever was?" I said hanging up the phone.

On the US 1 now past Henderson, Dinwiddy and Colonial Heights into Richmond; tobacco country names I'd known only from cigarette ads. Manson had disembarked in Raleigh and new passengers had boarded. There was a different kind of crowd now. Some backpackers, a few soldiers and more white faces. I didn't bother to get off the bus in Richmond. I was the only passenger who stayed on board. I was saving my seventy-five cents for the nation's capital.

THE WHITE HOUSE
WASHINGTON D.C.
JULY

The President of the United States of America gazed through the green tint of the Oval Office window.

Beyond the bulletproof glass, the Rose Garden blossomed in summer glory.

Across the room the Director and Deputy Director of the CIA awaited The Word.

Turning back toward the men, the President affixed them with a gimlet eye.

"Why is it that I never hear of these damn fool ideas until they go wrong?"

The question did not require an answer, and both the Intelligence Officers examined the shiny tips of their shoes with diligent attention as their Commander-in-Chief continued.

"I know we've done some funny things to fund the Contras but I'd sooner be caught fornicating with Gadaffi than have the Agency exposed as being involved in this. How long has it been going on?"

The CIA Director was about to speak when the President held up a warning finger.

"No, don't tell me, I don't want to know. The First Lady would have a fit. She's running a huge anti-drug programme, and here are we, the United States Government, smuggling cocaine onto the streets of America." The old man shook his head sadly. "This is a real canyon of worms."

The soft whisper of the air conditioning was the Oval Office's' only sound as the President began to doodle on a pad. He had too many secrets. This really was the hot seat. The media often derided him as a fool but that was disinformation. The old man knew too much and unlike some of his predecessors, did not relish knowing more. Ampleforth saw that the doodle was a horse and coughed politely as he broke the silence.

"Mr. President, would you think it better if this Englishman were to be...." The Deputy Director's voice trailed away. The three men knew that there were more microphones now in the White House than had ever existed in the days of 'the plumbers'.

The old Californian doodled on. He wasn't worried about tapes. Since the Watergate disaster all Presidential recordings were scramble-coded and stored by the Central Security Service. A little known arm of clandestine government, the CSS erased anything the moment it became hot and that included people.

The President of the United States shuddered. He was staring into the abyss of eternal disgrace. Drug smuggling, for God's sake. Is that what it took to support his beloved Contras? Didn't he have enough problems on his plate without this? Now they wanted him to authorise the murder of British citizens. And what would that nice lady Prime Minister say?

The Director and Deputy Director watched the Chief as his tanned hand reached into the spotless glass jar on the Presidential desk and extracted a jelly baby .

"Hell," said the old man, bouncing the little blue sweet in in his palm. "You'll only make an embarrassing situation worse. You've got an operation to overthrow Castro linked to cocaine smuggling. I congratulate you. Everyone from the KGB through Jane Fonda will have a clambake with this one, boys."

Ampleforth tried one more time.

"The Englishman might get shot resisting arrest, Sir."

The President sighed and tapped his wristwatch, an indication that the meeting was coming to a close.

"Try and recover your goods without such drastic measures," he said.

The CIA men exchanged glances. The ball had been cunningly tossed back into their court.

The President of the United States of America popped the jelly baby into his mouth and sucked hard.

GREYHOUND BUS TERMINAL
WASHINGTON D.C.
JULY

The first thing that struck me was how many black people there were. Statistically over fifty percent of the population of Washington is black. My fears about Eye Socket and his companions proved groundless. They left in an elderly Cadillac driven by a startlingly pretty girl, who resembled Diana Ross in her Supremes days.

I sat nursing a coffee, the heavy bag at my feet, my last fifty cents recklessly thrown away on a beef burger and French fries. Whatever beef had once graced this sticky grey composition had long since galloped away across the prairie. Now I knew what they did with the Capital's old police horses. This troubled mess lurked between two slices of a stale substance that I could only assume was a recycled copy of the Washington Post.

The Greyhound bus terminal canteen was not likely to feature in Fodor's Guide To America.

I saw Child Chopper at the window, buying an onward ticket.

The last stages of my haul through Baltimore, Wilmington and Philadelphia were uneventful. Child Chopper left at the bus station in Trenton. I heaved a sigh of relief.

From there I called Benny, just to check that everything was okay with Dee in New York.

He would pass her the time of my arrival and she would be at the bus station to meet me, together

with the man who had flown up from Florida at my
suggestion.

NEW YORK CITY
JULY

Unseasonal rain was falling along with the dusk
as the Greyhound rolled off the New Jersey Turnpike to join a billion dollars' worth of machinery
crawling down JFK Boulevard. Names I dimly
recalled from childhood movies; Jersey City, Ho-
boken, Weehawken flashed by as we looped into
the Lincoln Tunnel to dive under Manhattan.

New Yorkers scurried for shelter, their plastic
raincoats flying distress signals. Yellow taxis, red
tail lights, and neon signs were reflected in the
shimmering strets, painting Picasso mobiles in every
gutter.

I understood the expression 'rubber necking' as
I craned up in my window seat at the artificial
Alps.

With a final sigh of airbrakes, the silver Greyhound pulled into its stand. There was a still moment
of thanksgiving, before everyone burst into noise
and grabbed their bags. I spotted Dee anxiously
scanning the disembarkers. Next to her stood a
bulky figure.

Malvin Berg's Van Dyke beard surrounded into
a grin as he reached up to take the case from me at
the bus door.

I passed down the bag and lost sight of him
immediately. The blur of Dee's embrace enveloped
me, her cheeks wet and scented. I felt conscious of
my stink and stubble.

Malvin was putting the case into the trunk of a

Ford compact parked on the bus stand.

"Come on," he said, "or we'll be in trouble."

"You really smell awful," said Dee as people streamed around us in a wall of greeting, a sea of moving noise.

"You mean we aren't in trouble already?" I asked.

"Listen, pal." Mal growled in Brooklynese. "You're a crime star, wanted coast to coast, bulletins on thirteen TV channels and your photo in every paper, OK? But a parking ticket in the bus terminal... that's serious."

Somewhere a siren wailed. The American slammed the trunk shut and I clambered into the back. Dee cuddled me as Mal started the car.

"So what do you want to see in New York?" asked Mal. "The Empire State? The UN?" As we pulled away I glimpsed his eyes in the mirror, colder than his cheery voice.

"I want to see Umberto's Clam House. Where Joey Gallo got his."

"You want to eat or get shot?" The New Yorker laughed.

"He goes under a shower first," Dee wrinkled up her nose.

I nuzzled Dee and murmured, "Stay with me and we'll shower all night or do anything else you want to do." And then quietly whispered, "I don't want us to part again. I missed you."

"I missed you too, Daniel." She lay her head on my shoulder.

At the Howard Johnson we had adjoining rooms.

Washed and draped in a bathrobe, I pushed the remains of my steak and salad to one side. Around me coins were spread out. Gold sparkled around me on the bed, the dressing tables and the floor.

Okay. Time to work.

"How much cash do we have?"

Dee and Mal looked at each other.

"Around five hundred bucks," stated Malvin.

"It's not really enough," said Dee.

"What are you talking about, kid?" I gave Dee a playful shove. "The Indians sold Manhattan for a string of beads. We should be able to buy a few skyscrapers with this lot." I gestured at the treasure and then jerked my thumb at a million squares of light beyond the windows.

"Not at today's real estate prices." Dee shoved me back. "Besides, the Indians weren't on the run from the FBI, darling".

I pressed a coin into her hand as I turned to Malvin.

"Do you have a connection we can sell to?"

"This stuff is hot, man." The beard wobbled as Berg flung pudgy arms about. "I already made some enquiries. Every coin dealer and jeweller knows about you and the heist. This parcel will have to be buried for a long time."

Malvin doesn't want to be helpful, it seems. He'll have to go.

Crossing to the window I gazed at the twinkling towerscape. The rain had passed now. Far below me, dinky toys driven by ants edged down Eighth Avenue, moving in a miniature necklace of firefly lamps. From the 20th floor the city appeared bearable.

"What about the ordinary coins?" I queried. "The gold twenties, the common stuff. They can be sold as scrap surely." The gold gleamed frustratingly around us. I tried to open the window but it wouldn't budge. Howard Johnson doesn't want you to make

176

unscheduled flights from his skyscrapers.

"Listen, Daniel," said Malvin. "The Feds, The Mob, the people you robbed, everyone is looking for the fat Englishman. Your photo's been on the TV ferchrissakes." Malvin stuck a cigarette in his mouth and patted his pockets, enjoying our discomfort. I regretted calling him. He wants to make himself the big shot or set us up to be robbed.

"So I'll diet and grow a beard." I looked at my girl.

Dee leaned forward and flicked her lighter.

"I could sell some," she piped brightly.

Instinct told me no. I shook my head.

Malvin puffed out his cheeks as he accepted her light.

"Are you kidding?" he said. "You're a bigger star than Monroe right now." Smoke billowed around his beard. "The papers and TV have your picture as well and they're showing it hourly. You're a photogenic little lady, you know."

Dee fluttered eyelids.

"There must be some other crimes going on," I said.

"Sure," replied the American. "But yours is the game the whole nation can play. No violence, a pretty lady, a three hundred pound Englishman, missing millions in gold. I could probably get you on the Johnny Carson Show right now." The room had become stuffy. I found the air-conditioning and turned the knob.

"We'll have to find some other way of raising cash," I said.

Loud clattering noises heralded cold air. I banged the top of the machine.

"We'll sort out the ordinary coins and work out

a way to sell them. Then I'll figure out where to keep the rest." Malvin shrugged, eyes flickering over the gold. The sooner I got rid of him the better.

"It's stash and cash time in the old home town tonight," said Dee.

I watched the big man pick up a St. Gauden's Liberty and roll it over in his hand.

The air conditioner rattle was driving me mad. I turned the knob to 'off'.

There was a knock from the adjoining room and the car rental man moved swiftly to deal with it, closing the door between the apartments as he did so. Dee and I started to put the coins back into the bag. I left a chunk out for Berg to sell. I noticed he'd kept the St. Gaudens.

I needed sleep. Through the door I could hear Malvin dealing with room service. I climbed onto the bed.

"Don't leave Malvin alone with the gear," I whispered.

"No fear. I'll stay awake."

"Want a cuddle?"

For an answer, Dee began unbuttoning her blouse, then paused as the New Yorker returned with the drinks from room service.

"I guess we could all use some rest," he said.

I passed him the chunk.

"Could you stay awake long enough to cash these? There's about 10,000 dollars worth."

"I guess so," grinned Malvin. "See you later. Sweet dreams." The door closed behind him.

Alone, Dee and I lay in each others arms.

"Don't trust that slob further than you can throw him," I murmured.

"The only person I want to throw is you," said

Dee.

I kissed her gently. It was wonderful to be back with my girl.

"Ready when you are."

NEW YORK CITY
JULY

As soon as I was sure that Malvin had left the hotel I got out of bed and started dressing. Dee looked up at me.

"Where are you going?"

"Out, my darling," I said. "I'm sticking this gear in a twenty-four hour safe tonight. Tomorrow it's going into the bank. I don't trust Malvin and if he walked in here now with a gun, what could we do about it?"

Dee rolled across to slide open the bedside drawer. She produced a sheepskin pistol case, unclipped the flap and extracted a shiny black automatic which she then waved carelessly in my direction.

"We could shoot him!" she said brightly.

I was already prone on the carpet.

"Put that fucking thing away before you do yourself a mischief!" I muttered into the deep pile, then I risked a peek.

Dee was stark naked on the bed, her nipples erect, in the classic marksman position, arms out front, both hands clasping the weapon. Her abdomen was taut all the way down to her little golden triangle. She was the best looking item in the world.

"FREEZE, MOTHERFUCKER!" she yelled. "I'm a New York Peace Officer! Freeze or I'll blow your fucking head off!"

"Please stop waving that gun around."

Dee lowered the pistol. "You want to argue with the arresting officer?"

Wearily I pushed myself off the floor. "When I come back from the all night safe, darling," I said.

NEW YORK CITY
JULY

Malvin Berg stood out on the street with the ten thousand dollars' worth of gold coins that Daniel had given him. In his pocket he had a few more that he had helped himself to. Normally they would have been easy to sell. This week a fat man selling parcels like this would come under heavy scrutiny.

He wondered whether to call one of his Miami contacts or go back up to the room now with guns and rob the English couple. He decided not to. There was nobody he could really trust in New York.

Malvin Berg didn't trust anybody anymore.

The English couple wouldn't last long. The best thing for him to do was stash these coins away now and tell the Englishman he'd been robbed, so he'd have to give him more.

Malvin Berg headed for Grand Central Station.

NEW YORK CITY
JULY

Stuart Falkman was furious. His twenty year career lay in ruins. He'd always been a desk man and this was his first field operation. The gold shop had been established both to fund Cuban exile groups operating out of Florida and to provide logistical support for the Agency's anti-Castro plots.

Enter stage right, the Nicaraguan Contras who needed funds which Congress didn't want to give.

But the President and some of the young Attillas at Langley did.

Suddenly Miami was in fashion, and the old connections between the Agency and the Mafia had been revived.

"Hell, the stuff came from South America," the argument ran. "Let some of the money stay down there and shaft the Communists."

Garrity had been his immediate superior, and it was Garrity who dreamed up the idea of grafting the money-changing side of the drugs business on to Falkman's gold shop.

Falkman had been given more authority, more power. Suddenly the sun was shining on him: It had seemed as if he could walk on molten gold. Until he had fallen for the English girl. Now he was neck deep in CIA inspectors carrying out damage assessments.

The Englishman had made a fool of him. Through his negligence over the fat man, Falkman had lost over two million dollars of the Agency's money.

Plus the keys to Operation Reis.

And what else had the Englishman learned? He must have been crazy to employ him.

If it became public knowledge that the US Government was running drugs into its own country, the political consequences were unthinkable. The words had come down from on high. Insulate. Eliminate. Already activity at Biscayne Boulevard had been wound down.

Garrity had pulled out all the stops and Falkman had been sent to New York with one last chance to redeem himself. Falkman mobilized CIA staffers coast to coast. Using photographs that he had extracted from the gold shop's video security system, he produced his own 'flyer'. The notice offered ten thousand dollars reward to anyone who assisted in the recapture of Dee or Daniel.

Low key but enough to create interest.

He printed hundreds of thousands of these and mailed them in batches across the United States. In each of the major cities, teams of Agency personnel distributed these to every luxury hotel, coin shop, bank and outsize mens' clothing store. This activity was in direct contravention of the wishes of the people and Congress of the United States of America: that the CIA should never operate on domestic soil.

The flyer went out as if it were a private reward offer from the coin store. In addition, over twelve thousand coin and jewellery dealers belonging to National Recovery Network had been circulated by telex.

Falkman himself had flown to the city to direct the teams of people placing flyers there. His whole life was on the line. But somehow he began to enjoy the chase. He had a hunch that the Englishman was somewhere in New York.

There were others seeking the fat con man. Garrity and his mob friends. If they found the Englishman, no trace would remain of the man or the gold and that meant disgrace for Falkman. Or perhaps erasure. The Agency would want to shut and seal all the doors, so what was one Jewish jeweller more or less? Falkman shuddered and picked up the batch of possible sightings that had filtered through to him from across America. Every lead had to be followed and checked out. The jeweller gritted his teeth.

Stuart Falkman was determined to find the golden worm in the Big Apple.

NEW YORK CITY
JULY

A knock on the door. Dee and I exchanged glances. I leapt off the bed and jumped to the door. Through the spyhole I saw Malvin's fat face.

I knew something was wrong.

The New Yorker came into the room, hands shaking, body jerking up and down. I felt immediately sick. I knew what he was going to tell me. His hands shook again like an old time revival preacher.

"What's the matter?" Dee was genuinely alarmed.

"I - I - I was," Berg stuttered.

"Take it easy now," said Dee. "Get him a drink, Daniel."

I crossed wearily to the mini bar, took two miniature whiskys and tumbled them into a tumbler. What a faker, I thought. What a cheap bastard.

"I - I - was in the s - s - station."

"Take it easy," Dee repeated, taking the whisky from me and putting the glass to his lips. I pinched her backside. She turned and stared at me, her eyes widening in comprehension.

"There was some black guys," Stutter, stutter. More gasps for breath.

"I - I - I'd been to a couple of places to sell the coins. I decided to put them a locker at the station instead of walking around like a Christmas tree." The fat man paused and shook again. He was certainly in line for today's Thieves' Oscar.

"I - I - took a locker," Malvin gripped the whisky in both hands and drank. "Some guys must have seen me taking coins out. I came back to the locker. I - I was robbed. These guys," Malvin started shaking again. "Black guys. They had knives. They were serious."

I walked to the window tiredly and stared down into the kaleidoscope twenty stories below me. How I hate this town, I thought. The people. My whole scheme went wrong from start to finish. We should have been long gone out of America by now. Why did it have to happen this way? I call this creep up to help me, because I needed a connection. Now he rips me off and I have to 'believe' his story in order to part good friend, and give him more gold so that he shouldn't go away empty handed.

Wonderful.

I turned. The fat man was still shaking. Dee had her hand on his shoulder. Berg's glass was empty. I reached into the minibar and took out four more miniatures.

"Take it easy, Malvin, have some more whisky." I picked up another glass. "In fact I think I'll join you."

KEY LARGO
FLORIDA
AUGUST

Arturo Jaconelli, Crime Lord, bent over the marble, fixed the white crystals with his cold dark eyes and snorted the cocaine, the muscles under his silk shirt bunching as he did so.

The mafioso sniffed the drug from a table, bejewelled and Sicilian like himself, but some two hundred years older.

Jaconelli's white arched villa on Key Largo enjoyed uninterrupted views of the peacock blue waters of Florida Bay, and the palm fringed Keys beyond.

Uninterrupted, apart from the armed guards patrolling both sides of the discreet electrified fencing.

Out on the trim jetty, his hundred and fifty foot yacht the ATAHUALLPA rested immaculate and dazzling on the azure ocean.

The cocaine made the handsome Italian feel extrinsic. In charge, detached from, at yet at one with the world.

The real world.

His world.

Jaconelli was a corporate boss no less than the men who ran the great industries. Like them he held board meetings, paid dividends, discussed diversification, asset management and the competition.

Arturo Jaconelli's business was cocaine.

He felt himself a worthy successor to the gore and guts Capos of bygone days. He had inherited his father's lucrative operations in loan sharking, garbage handling and numbers, but had swiftly realised that cocaine was the Prohibition of the eighties, and it was here that the millions were to be made by young men of vision and courage.

And so it had been.

Today, his international empire encompassed partnerships with the coke barons of Bolivia, Columbia and Peru.

Crop growers, lawyers, accountants, pilots, marine captains and assassins would all play their part in ensuring that turnover for the current year would exceed the three hundred and fifty million dollars that his computers projected. Business was booming, thanks to "crack", converted reduced cocaine which the nation's addicts were smoking in glass pipes, in their expensive search for higher highs.

Jaconelli's youngest brother Michaelangelo had a three thousand dollar a day crack habit, and had been in and out of the family's luxury clinic at Coral Gables.

The running of the day to day business of the empire had devolved upon Arturo.

Rightly so, he was a strong man, a *leone,* a lion. At thirty seven years of age, he had survived the bloody cocaine wars, when Miami had become a charnel house as rival gangs of Puerto Ricans, Columbians and the Mafia slaughtered each other for a share of the drug boom.

Each day, six cocaine-dealing related corpses found their way into the morgues of South Florida, as natural frictions of the trade took their toll.

But these were small time deaths, street hustlers. A truce had been made between the big distributors, brought about by pressure from the Bolivians and the Mafia themselves.

"A little death is good for business," Arturo had told the meeting. "There is enough profit for everyone, but if we continue quarreling, there will be enough death for everyone too."

Currently, with payoffs to politicians and customs men in both American continents, Jaconelli could land a kilo of 91 per cent pure cocaine in the United States for less than four thousand US dollars.

This he then wholesaled for twenty four thousand dollars a 'key' to his 'soldiers', who passed it on to their distributors for twenty-eight thousand.

Jaconelli had a sound business.

He held real estate across North America, he owned private health clinics and retirement homes for the aged. His stockmarket holdings were strategically placed in defence industries, manufacturing and mining.

Dummy corporations, managed by trusted accountants and lawyers, ran the shipping fleets, aircraft charter and car rental operations which had proved intelligent and profitable fronts for transporting and distributing the deadly but profitable snowstorm.

Now, since the unofficial partnership with the Central Intelligence Agency, business was booming.

The Contras received the funds denied to them by Congress and Jaconelli enjoyed a protection and immunity known to few criminals in the modern world.

With CIA planes making his drops, costs had plummeted. No transport to pay on the bulk of his shipments, no customs officers to bribe. Just neat, anonymous vans plying between Homestead Airforce base and the car rental operation in downtown Miami.

His niece's husband, the Jew Berg, took delivery of the powder and the CIA's coin dealing office paid out the money. Berg had no knowledge of Jaconelli's link with the Agency.

Then, by one of those strange coincidences, the paymaster had been robbed, and Berg was involved in the heist. A fortune of gold and diamonds and 'vital equipment' that Garrity wouldn't specify.

Now the CIA friends had come to Jaconelli for help. And help them he would. If the information held by the Englishman became public, the cloak of death would be upon them all.

And Berg was involved!

The fat bum was already in disgrace from his gambling debts and he, Arturo, had let him off the hook out of weakness. But had the Jew thanked Arturo?

Had he let his Don wet his beak?

No. The greedy slob had kept the deal to himself.

This was unforgivable.

NEW YORK STATE
AUGUST

Malvin Berg sat hunched on the New York - Florida train possessively clutching the bag of coins.

He had gotten away with it.

He wondered whether the English couple had believed him. The shaking act had been convincing. Anyhow, what choice did they have? They were over a barrel and knew it.

His man in Miami would cash the coins in for him and Malvin would clear better than ten thousand dollars on the deal. He always believed in striking first. Berg reasoned that Dee and Daniel didn't trust him, so what the hell. The English were out of their depth in America. Their arrest was only a matter of ticking clocks.

Malvin felt he had got out in time. He'd called his wife and told her to meet him off the train.

He was okay. He couldn't be implicated. He had never met the coin man. It would only make things worse for the the English couple if they tried to involve him. He had the coins that he had pretended were stolen and the stuff that Daniel had given him for his trouble. Mal laughed to himself.

It was beautiful.

A hot August morning, mercury in the high eighties. New Yorkers hustled around me looting, raping and burning. Vikings of the New World, selling smack and stolen razor blades. Mafiosos demanding protection money; modern Danegeld. I rode across Queens in Mickey the Buyer's orange Cadillac. The brownstone Thirties apartment blocks were giant Lego sets for people to live in. Queens was a cliché; spurting fire hydrants, bare-chested Puerto Ricans fanning themselves on steps, Seven-Eleven stores, used car lots. The windows of the shops wore overcoats of wire grill. Mickey the Buyer had a towel around his neck.

"I don't care what Anthony says. The vigorish is due, it has to be paid."

Mickey spoke into his car phone. He was Benny's connection. A small sweaty Jew bulging out of his track suit, the white running shoes on his feet stamping up and down on the Cadillac's pedals as he jerked the limousine through the morning traffic.

"I don't care *whose* fucking cousin he is!" Mickey slammed the phone down. "Everybody goes to the movies now and comes out thinking they're Al Pacino."

"As Don Corleone Junior?" I asked.

Mickey's hands were hairy-backed but delicate. He spun the white wheel of the big Caddy easily.

"As Scarface."

The buyer had the air of a man who spent a lot of time with masseurs and manicurists.

"I been up all night playing poker. At one stage I was down sixty thousand dollars. SCREW YOU!" Mickey yelled.

I realised he was addressing a motorcyclist who had cut in front of us.

"I had to work all night to break even. Then I went to the Turkish bath for a sitz and a massage. You like a massage?"

"Only from young girls, Mickey," I said.

"Girls is no good. They don't have the strength in their arms. You see this pack of cards?" He passed me a deck.

"I was sixty grand down and hurting. I told them to change the cards. This was the pack I broke even with. This deck won me sixty grand."

I didn't like to ask if he kept the losing decks. I placed the cards on the seat between us.

Mickey stopped next to a fire hydrant. We had parked outside a store bearing the legend 'Goldfarb Pawnbrokers'. A sign said 'Loans, Jewellery Wanted For Cash.'

Goldfarb's seemed long on money, short on syntax.

Three dusty gold balls swung above me as I clambered out of the Cadillac, satchel over my shoulder. The building was clad in even more wire and bars than its neighbours. The door was a studded sheet of iron, galvanized metal covered the windows.

"Are you expecting a bomb attack, Mickey?"

"Are you kidding?" shot back the little New Yorker as he pressed the buzzer. "Last week some jerks tied railroad sleepers to the front of a Mack truck and drove clean through the front of a jewellery store not two blocks from here."

A small panel in the door opened at eye level, revealing a grille.

"People will do anything for a bargain, Mickey," I said.

A young face wearing a black skull cap and pebble glasses peered at us through the grille. Mickey looked around. The street behind us was empty, he nodded at the face and the door opened to admit us.

"Your stuff is hot," the little man said. "You're on the TV. The Feds want you, your own people want you, the guy you robbed wants you." The room was surprisingly quiet. Through soundproofed windows I watched the traffic beyond golden balls. On Mickey's desk closed circuit TV screens monitored his pawnbroking operation below. The staff were white, and, I surmised, Jewish. The customers appeared to be mostly black or Chicano. Armoured glass separated client from broker in the private booths. One TV screen showed the street outside. From the angle of the picture I guessed the camera was sited on a building opposite.

"Was the Miami man connected, Mickey?" I asked.

"No, but he's getting attention. The word is he's government."

"Your government I can handle, Mickey. It's the mob that worries me." The phone on the desk between us rang. On TV screen a fearsome black man gesticulating at the counter.

"Yes, yes," said Mickey. "But I lent *him* the money,

195

not his cousin." A well manicured hand covered the mouthpiece and the pawnbroker looked at me.

"Have you seen the reward notice?"

I shook my head.

The buyer rummaged around in his desk drawer. "I looked at it the other day. I never thought I'd be handling the stuff. Goods like this usually get taken to order."

A desk mounted console displayed the world's precious metal prices. I was pleased to see gold was up a couple of points.

"Listen. The money everyone spends calling me up, you could have paid the kid's debt," said Mickey into the telephone.

Somewhere a telex chattered sporadically.

Mickey's hand came out of the desk drawer holding a long white roll of paper which he passed to me.

"He sent this out to twelve thousand dealers. The Government should have saved the postage."

I glanced at the paper and then focused my full attention. It bore the imprint of the 'RECOVERY' anti-theft network to which Stuart belonged and announced:

'MEMBER THEFT ALERT'

Followed by a lot of 'URGENTS', 'STOLENS', descriptions of Dee and me, lists of coins and reward details - money for the goods back, money for our necks.

I noticed Stuart had made me lose weight.

So they were offering personal bounties for our arrest too, were they?

I would have to be more careful. It's not clever to underestimate your enemies. These people were too powerful and active for comfort.

"I'll be here," said Mickey, hanging up the phone. He raised a quizzical eyebrow. I carried on reading.

I wondered how much the pawnbroker really knew.

What surprised me was the list of missing coins.

Twice as many as I had taken. The checky bastard! Maybe Stuart was screwing the insurance people as well as the CIA.

The list showed a large number of untraceable twenty dollar gold pieces, more than I had. Also lots of mythical Feuchtwangler cents, Lincoln pennies and other valuable but common items. There was no mention of uncut diamonds or the other objects.

The jeweller had inflated the claim of two million. No wonder we were on coast to coast television!

The additional twist meant that now I would be hung for a sheep, while having stolen only the lamb.

"This is bullshit, Mickey."

The little man grinned. "So he's claiming big?"

His humour was infectious. "Yes, he is."

"Well, you can't blame him, Daniel. Everyone does it. So what have you got for me?"

I took the buyer down my list. The real one. Eventually he spoke.

"You have a hot lot of rarities, Daniel. Every dealer in the States is on the look out for them." I glanced at my watch. It was nearly noon.

"I should make a move," I said.

"Leave with me what you have, Daniel." Mickey had a wonderful New York Jewish way with him.

"There's about fifty thousand cash value here." I

tapped the satchel I'd brought from the safe deposit. "Twenty dollar gold pieces mostly. All ordinary untraceable coins."

"I can get you most of your money for those," Mickey acknowledged. "But the rare pieces make only fifty percent in good times. In this case ..." Mickey's voice trailed away.

On screen, the young man with the skull cap was paying out the money to the black guy. Fences always give you this spiel about how your stuff is too hot, it's the wrong time of the year for what you've stolen or the market is weak right now.

But I had to deal with someone. At least in Mickey I had a straight runner. Benny had okayed him through a mutual 'rabbi'. I was lost and at risk in America and thankful for the connection. Anybody could stick a Saturday Night Special in my ear and become a million dollars richer. The wrong dealer might call the Feds and claim Stuart's reward. Mickey knew all this as well as I did.

On another monitor I watched the big man walk out on the street, still counting money.

"Could you let me have some cash now, Mickey? I have a lot to do."

I opened the satchel. Gold coins spilled over the polished desk. Always give them a flash!

The pawnbroker's eyes lit up.

"I'll advance you fifteen thousand, Daniel. We'll work it all out later." Mickey picked up the intercom and spoke into it.

Idly, I turned a coin over. At least I would get my hands on some reddies. I was fed up with having no cash.

The buyer looked up as the office door opened. An attractive, dark haired woman in her thirties entered, smiled at me and placed two styrofoam cups and a paper package on the desk. As silently as came, she withdrew.

"My sister Miriam," said Mickey, passing me a cup.

A smell of coffee came from the styrofoam. I took a sip, it tasted surprisingly good.

I watched Mickey unwrap the parcel.

The pawnbroker's plump hands extracted two thick sandwiches.

"Salt beef on rye," he said passing me one. He then produced a key, swivelled round in his chair and addressed himself to a small, fierce looking safe. I had to trust someone. Mickey was sound. Years of mixing with faces in casinos had given me a feel for people. The buyer swivelled back and stacked up packets of hundred dollar bills.

This is what the game is all about.

Gelt.

He pushed the wad over to me.

"Thank you," I said, leaving the money untouched, my hands full of saltbeef sandwich.

"A pleasure," Mickey smiled, reaching out to shuffle coins back into the satchel.

"Eat, Daniel, eat."

I ate.

KEY LARGO
AUGUST

Jaconelli put the phone gently back in its cradle. Crazy Tommy would take care of this.

'Crazy' had earned his nickname when, after serving ten years of a fourteen year sentence of torture, Tommy had dashed his chances of parole by refusing to say that he was sorry to the Parole Board.

"I'm not fucking sorry," Tommy had told them. "I don't want your fucking parole. Just leave me in peace to finish my sentence."

Jaconelli smiled as he opened his Garrards' silver box and tipped out cocaine.

NEW YORK CITY
AUGUST

Mickey had wanted to drive me back uptown, but I had insisted on taking a cab.

As I pulled away from the pawnbrokers in the back of the yellow taxi I felt better. I had cash and things were happening with Mickey.

There was a chance that he could move the entire parcel. New York looked better, but not much.

At Eighth Avenue I paid off the cab, and walked until I found a paybooth.

In the hot plastic box I dialled our new hotel and asked for our room.

Dee answered at the first ring.

"Mrs. Webster," I said. "How nice to hear your voice."

"Likewise I'm sure," Dee giggled.

"See you tonight at the theatre."

"I look forward to it." She hung up.

Everything okay.

This nonsense meant that Dee would meet me in the MacDonalds opposite in fifteen minutes.

The fast food cafe had entrances from two streets.

As I queued for food, remembering the last MacDonalds I had visited, the one in Miami where all this had started, a shiver ran through me, and not just at the prospect of having to eat here. I found a seat where I could watch the hotel entrance. I tasted my cheeseburger.

That was a mistake.

I was reminded of a survey Playboy magazine

201

carried out once. They had a nutrition expert ana-
lyse a Big Mac. Playboy alleged that there was
more protein in the cardboard wrapping than there
was in the burger. MacDonalds replied there was
even less protein in a copy of Playboy.

I concentrated on the hotel lobby across the road.
Dee would allow ten minutes after the call. Then
leave the hotel. If she had grown a tail, I would
spot it.

Around me the hubbub of fast food staff yelling
orders. Punters munching, talking. Beyond the plate
glass, New York bickered by. I pushed the awful
burger away from me and sipped hot bitter coffee.

Foul.

A glass door flashed across the street and there
she was, my little dolphin. Her blonde curls brilliant in the pale sunlight. No tail. Dee skipped
across the road in her funny way, neatly dodging
the chariot thrusts of the traffic. New Yorkers drive
as if they are in a mechanised remake of Ben Hur.

She burst into the MacDonalds, in her crisp
Burberry, pink cheeks glowing, eyes shining with
excitement, loving every second.

Ignoring me, she bustled through the restaurant,
her prettiness turning the odd head.

I continued to watch the street. No one hurried
after her. She appeared to be clean.

I eased my legs from under the cramped table
and followed her out the back.

On the street I caught up with her after fifty
yards. I gripped her arm.

"FBI," I said. "Sexual Harassment Squad, ma'am."

"You come to boast or investigate?"

"Neither, ma'am, we need you in our training
course."

"Anytime."

"This will do." I pulled her sharply to my left and we ran down a small alleyway onto Sixth Avenue.

One more left down a side street, into a back alley, we ran for a few hundred yards until I could handle it no more. Lumps of my internal anatomy always find their way into my throat and prevent me breathing. I am built for style rather than speed. I glanced over my shoulder again and again. We were on our own. Emerging onto a crowded street. I felt naked. New York was hostile territory to me. If I wasn't lugging bags of gold around then I had pockets full of money. Fat and conspicuous and a mugger's bonanza. I didn't even feel safe in my hotel. Dee and I had no private secure place to meet.

I steered her up the steps of a cinema.

"Fancy the pictures?" I asked.

"Movies," corrected Dee. "In America they call it movies."

"So who's in America?"

The film was Jaws.

"But I've seen it," she protested as I hustled her inside.

In the lobby I bought two tickets with a hundred dollar bill. The smallest I had. The bored clerk scanned the note under an ultraviolet machine.

For a moment my heart froze. Mickey wouldn't have given me false money?

The cashier made change. I let out an inner sigh of relief.

Dee bought chocolate, popcorn and a soft drink.

"It makes a change from room service."

"You'll get fat."

"I'll borrow your trousers, Daniel."

Inside we sat down. The cinema at midday was deserted and dark. "Very inconspicuous," whispered Dee. "Hundred dollar bills and the only punters in the picturehouse - very cool."

I squeezed her arm playfully. We kissed and sat with our heads close together. We had so little time, so few relaxing moments.

Carefree holidaymakers romped on a beach. Heavy tense music accompanied the prancing children and dozing adults. In the water swimmers splashed happily. In the darkness I pulled out the wad of cash Mickey had given me.

"If you're going to moan about hundred dollar bills, I'd better throw these away," I whispered.

Dee's attention was on the screen. She turned to me.

"Throw what away?"

"These." I flapped the cash in the gloom. "Fifteen Grand in readies."

Dee looked back at the film and held out her hand.

"Give them to me, dear," she said with a sigh. "You'll only lose them or get mugged. "

"They have muggers in New York?"

I counted off thirty notes in the dark. On screen a rubber shark was being shoved about unconvincingly by a stage hand off camera.

Small children screamed happily on the cinematic beach. I handed Dee the rest of the money.

"There's twelve thousand dollars there," I breathed into Dee's ear.

"Thank you, kind sir." Colours flickered on Dee's face.

"You have to go New Orleans," I said.

Dee popped popcorn into her mouth, eyes transfixed by the rubber shark.

"When?" she munched.

"Tonight," I said. "You have to rent a flat and a
car and wait for me. It's going to take more time to
sell up the stuff."

"When will you come?" asked Dee.

"This afternoon, when I get you in bed."

Dee absentmindedly squeezed my knee. The
rubber shark was devouring a swimmer. Clouds of
tomato sauce floated in the water. The music reached
a crescendo.

"I'll be down as soon as possible."

I put my arm round Dee, deeply in love with her.
Her head rested on my shoulder. I like it when she
does that.

"Must we split, darling?" she murmured.

"It's safer," I whispered. "You can rent an apartment more easily alone. I'll have a chunk of money
in two or three days, then I can fly down to join
you. Mickey will sell up the rest for me. I'll pay Mal
off. I don't think I'll tell him where we're going."

I handed her the packages. Dee balanced them in
her hand.

"Heavy," she said, squeezing the pouch like a
scrotum. "What's in them?"

I told her, then watched as she slipped them into
her handbag.

"What do you want me to do with them?"

I told her that too.

Dee nodded, sipping her drink. The townspeople
were berating the police chief and the mayor was
urging them to do something.

There was no sign of the rubber shark.

NEW YORK CITY
AUGUST

A million dollars richer and I'm still in these bloody nylon trousers.

Once I had seen Dee safely onto the New Orleans plane, I decided to go shopping. When you weigh twenty stone, comfortable smart clothes are a problem .

In fact, at my size all clothes are a problem. I had about three thousand dollars in my pocket and was still dressed in the same green T-shirt and nylon slacks in which I had left Florida, eight days and two thousand miles ago. Such are the sartorial difficulties of the overweight thief.

I had asked Mickey the Buyer where I might pick up some readymade clothes.

"Try Barney's," the pawnbroker had told me.

Barney's Store in New York is an old fashioned modernised emporium. All things to all shoppers. The feature which attracted me was the outsize men's clothing section.

Barney's was a benison. Acres of shirts arrayed in a dazzling variety of colours and sizes. Banks of suits, trouser arenas, jacket boutiques, tie bazaars; Barney's was a wonderland for the fat dresser.

I could relax for a while. Before long I had three assistants on the go. They were measuring suits and jackets, boxing shoes, altering trousers, racking up socks and ties.

I handed over a thousand dollars cash for starters and, leaving my now empty satchel on a chair,

I wandered down the broad staircase into the shirt section.

Down among the silks and voiles, I began to get very strange vibes indeed.

Something was wrong. A well-dressed tall man approached, fit looking, dark-haired.

"Can I help you, Sir?" The 'Sir' should have put me off immediately. But I was tired, and relaxed, my mind on clothes.

"I'm looking for shirts in my size," I said.

"This way, Sir, follow me." I followed. We seemed to be passing all the shirts. My nerve ends tingled. I became uneasy. Paranoia, old son, I told myself. Calm down, shmucko.

The man drops back next to me. There is a faint smell of mint. We turn into a corridor. I don't like it. There are no shirts, no goods on display here. Memos pinned to the wall and rubbish on the floor tell me this is the staff area. Now I'm in trouble.

I turn back. What a nuisance. I'm not going to get my new clothes now.

"This way," says the guy, grabbing my arm.

I burst free and yell, "NO!" and run back down the corridor into the open sales area, where there are people about.

I have to get out of Barney's fast.

"SHOPLIFTER," yells the man. A few startled customers turn their heads. I decide to follow my mentor Sid's maxim, "When in doubt, shout." Give them the How Dare You Treatment. Plenty of verbal.

I hoot:

"HOW DARE YOU! I'm an English tourist. I've spent THOUSANDS of dollars in your shop today. Is this how you TREAT people?"

Customers stop shopping and stare. Frantically I looked for the exit. But I am too late. The tall man has summoned security guards. Two grey uniformed men appear, and stand smack in front of me, not touching, but menacing.

"This is a MISTAKE!" I shout. "I'm NOT a shoplifter. I've spent THOUSANDS upstairs."

The onlookers start muttering to each other. The security guards seem uneasy and shift about from one foot to the other.

Quite a crowd is gathering now. A happy interlude in their humdrum day. I wonder what the security guards will do. One of them has his hand on his holster.

"Do you have any identification?" asks the tall man. I give him some more stick .

"IDENTIFICATION?! Your assistants didn't ask for any identification when they took a thousand dollars off me as a deposit five minutes ago. Where's the manager? You'll hear from my attorneys. And it won't be a singing telegram."

The tall man smiles. I don't like that smile. He knows something. I know when it's 'on me' and it was on me now. He tries to calm the shoppers who are staring with open mouthed interest. I'm a lot better than breakfast television.

The tall man addresses the gathering crowd:

"It's alright folks."

"It's NOT all right, folks," I yelled. "I am a customer just like you. I've spent thousands of dollars in this store, and this clown has mistaken me for a shoplifter."

The crowd mutter further to each other. I'm doing as well as Mark Anthony in Julius Caesar. The tall man looks flustered.

"Hold him there," he orders the guards and crosses the store.

I watch him approach the counter, as he does so a small dapper man emerges from a concealed door marked 'Private', set in the elegant wood panelling. The tall man speaks earnestly with Dapper Dan. I HOW-DARE-YOU again.

"I am a CUSTOMER here. I have spent THOUSANDS of dollars in this store this morning. This is a case of mistaken identity. My attorneys use Exocet missiles not writs. You'll be holding a bankruptcy sale by the time I've finished with you!"

I turn to the guards. "I want your names," I say.

They looked uncomfortable. In the United States of America, when Jews sue, everyone ducks.

The dapper man shake his head. I address the customers. "I want everybody's names and addresses as witnesses. I'll pay all the expenses."

The tall man is pleading with the Dapper Dan.

"This is an OUTRAGE!" I yell. "Give me your names and addresses, folks. It's Barney's Bonanza.

The whole store has come to a standstill; assistants, shoppers. Dapper Dan shakes his noddle once more, the tall man's face falls.

Dapper Dan calls over to the guards. "Let the man go, this is none of our business."

A few people start fumbling in their wallets for pens and papers.

I bolt for the door.

Bursting out of Barney's, I spot a free cab. Oblivious of the traffic I ran across the street shouting, "TAXI!" dodging death beneath the wheels of a huge truck.

I leapt into the cab. "Twenty dollars for you. Get me to the Essex house on Park Avenue, NOW."

I fall back into the seat as the taxi pulls away. The airhorns of the truck still screaming in my ears. My hands tremble. I grasp for breath. What a gevalt!

Good old Sid. The How Dare You Treatment works every time.

I gather my scattered wits, and try to work out what has happened. My heart gradually slows from Ferrari to lawn mower.

I realised that I had left my satchel in Barney's. Inside the satchel was a book of matches from the Essex House, where I am staying. In the strong room at that hotel was ten thousand dollars cash, some of the coins, my passport and the safe deposit key to the Chemical Bank. Back to the Essex and clear out fast.

Stuart must have circularised the outsize clothing stores.

Never underestimate your enemies!

I am still dressed in the damn nylon trousers and T-shirt.

NSA STATION
HOMESTEAD AIRFORCE BASE
FLORIDA
AUGUST

"Fortune doesn't smile, she grins, with a thousand razor sharp teeth." James Benedict Ampleforth II was in a jovial mood. "This is the first real break we've had, Patrick."

The DDI tapped the photocopy FBI report, his words drowned by the scream of a flight of F18 bombers as they bucketed overhead on a training exercise. The CIA Chief paused to watch the planes and Senior Co-ordinator Patrick Garrity followed his eyes. The DDI slapped the younger man on the shoulder.

"Magnificent. Never forget that the skies over the Caribbean are but one frontier of our nation. Excellent work, Patrick. You did well to follow up the car rental clue. The human brain will beat a computer every time."

The younger man was embarrassed. Praise from Ampleforth was a rare and heady wine. Garrity felt he ought to say something.

"I recognised the name Save It, sir, and realized that it was one of the operations owned by our friends in the Family." Garrity paused and the Deputy Director smiled at his assistant's use of the euphemism for the Mafia.

"Go on, Patrick."

"Well, sir, it appears that the Englishman became friendly with one of their car rental operatives." Garrity consulted the paper in his hand. "A Malvin Berg."

"Do we know him?" queried the DDI.

"I've run Berg through our own computers, plus those of the NSA, DEA and the National Crime Information Centre."

"Any results?" Ampleforth raised a Patrician eyebrow.

"Nothing from the National Security Agency, sir, no political involvement, Berg is listed with the Drug Enforcement Agency as a small time operative with the Jaconelli people and is on NCIC's computer with immoral earning convictions."

"Where is he now, Patrick?"

"He told his wife he was going to New York, and Jaconelli's people are trying to find him. They have a man at his home and people are on the streets."

"Good work, Patrick. Find him and you may find the English couple. But if you get to this Berg first keep the Agency out of it." The Deputy Director of the CIA studied his fingernails. "I'm sure he'll talk to his Italian friends."

James Benedict Ampleforth II permitted himself a wintry smile.

NEW YORK CITY
AUGUST

I left the Essex House in brilliant sunshine. A freshly purchased bag in my hand contained the things from the safe. I was still a bundle of nerves from the business in Barney's. I was hot, tired, paranoid and back on the street again. The nark in Barney's must have had a photograph of me. How many more snapshots of me are there floating around the streets of New York?

Every face seemed hostile. I thumped along the crowded pavements. I had felt bad ever since kissing Dee goodbye at JFK. She had looked into my eyes, tears in the corner of hers.

I remembered her parting words. "Get out of New York, Daniel. I've got bad vibes."

How perceptive!

I wandered along the sidewalks not knowing where I was. Exhaust fumes assaulting my nose and throat. Sirens wailed, traffic roared, hostile crowds pushed around me. My shirt clinging to me, wretched nylon trousers sticking and irritating, head aching.

Well, pull yourself together. You've got cash in your pocket, get off the streets. Then I saw the sign.

I crossed the road against a battery of car horns, squealing brakes and shaking fists. Outside the hotel I paused. The heat and filth of the Big Rotten Apple oppressed me.

Beyond the tinted windows the lobby was cool and inviting. Like the grave.

My appointment in Samarra.

The Sheraton Hotel in New York is an anonymous glass and concrete pile where the management don't care what you do as long as your credit card is valid.

I checked into the Sheraton using my right name and paying a cash deposit, planning to stay but a few hours. The receptionist handed the bellhop a key and I followed the little man into the elevator.

We rode eleven floors in silence unless you count the ersatz orchestra in the lift. Emerging into a deserted corridor, the piped music followed us out of the elevator. My headache was more intense now. Fluorescent lights buzzed and flickered as I followed the bellhop in his ridiculous uniform.

He opened a door and showed me into a room. The window gave onto a brick wall. The curtains bore a jarring flower pattern. The air conditioning gave off the death rattle of a parched python. The room was as spacious as a coffin full of sand. I gave the bellhop two dollars.

"I don't like the room. Can you get me something with a view, please."

"Sure. Stay here," he said.

A little ginger haired man with a freckled face. A lifetime of humping luggage and showing other people into grotty accommodation had made him bow-legged and blank-eyed.

"I'll come back down to reception with you," I said.

If ever I'd seen a room to commit suicide in, that was it.

Back down the corridor ubiquitous canned music written and played by robots swirled around me. My shoulder strap biting in from the weight of the coins.

At the elevator door, little opaque buttons flashed in slow motion. The bellhop rocked on his feet humming along to the Muzak. The doors opened with a rattlesnake hiss. I caught sight of myself in the elevator mirror.

I looked like a ninety year old Billy Bunter. Gucci designer bags under eyes. Blotchy face, spots. A gross gorilla beside the midget bellhop. I felt dizzy.

In the reception area men in three piece suits stared at me across the potted palms seeming to follow my every move, while the bellhop changed keys. I could have cornered the paranoid market today. Back in the elevator up with the Muzak. Out on the seventeenth floor, down another corridor. This one in blue sported sand filled chromium ashtrays and long numbers on every door. Spyhole after spyhole revealing nothing. The bellhop led me into a room with a view this time. I tipped him again. And slipped the chain behind him as he left.

I flung the satchel on the bed and stripped. In the bathroom I soaked myself gratefully under the shower and thought of Dee. At the airport we had felt a strange sadness. About everything. I had hugged her, and relieved her of the automatic.

Airports are hot spots. Lots of law, cameras and one-way glass. I didn't want to be out in public with her in case someone recognised us from the TV broadcasts. There's always a fink; New Yorkers invented the term. In the cab back to the city, I had planned my shopping expedition. Now I still had to sell the rest of the gold. Mickey the Buyer told me to call in two days. There was no point in going through all the hassle of withdrawing the parcel from the Chemical Bank until then. The gold was secure enough where it was.

The safe deposit box wasn't going anywhere. I dried myself and slid back into my nylon trousers. They had a life of their own now. I lay down on the bed. I felt nervous. The incident in Barney's had disturbed me. New York was too hot. And not just from the August temperatures. Despite the crowds, I sensed a hostile emptiness from the city. New York's hidden violence and anonymity oppressed me. My scheme had gone wrong from the moment of the airline strike. I should have been sitting somewhere warm with Dee out of America. The empty ceiling gave no information or comfort. Thirsty, I called room service, and ordered ginger ale. Ice. Deep in my mind I realised I was a target in the middle of an enemy city. Stuart must have moved fast with his circulars to the clothing stores. He was cunning.

Wasn't it enough to be on the run? To be wanted by half the police forces in the States without having Stuart's cowboy moves slung at me as well? Private individuals with a grudge are more dangerous than the police. Stuart had plenty of money, a big staff, lots of energy. This was his home town. I needed him on my tail like a bullet in the brain. I wished Dee was there to talk to. Being alone made me feel thoroughly depressed. I was sick of the sight of my green shirt and nylon trousers. I couldn't even buy a damn change of clothes!

But I had been lucky in Barney's. Thank you, Dapper Dan.

The hum of the air conditioning bored me. The wallpaper was tedious Everything in that damn room bored me. For lack of something better to do I hauled myself off the bed, crossed to the window and stared down seventeen stories below me.

Insects and Cadillacs.

A knock at the door startled me. A muffled voice call out, "Room service."

Cautiously I approached the door and peered through the spyhole. I saw the expected. A fish-bowl vision of a Phillipino waiter holding up the tray of ginger ale and ice.

I unrattled the chain and stepped back. The door burst open. Suddenly the room was filled with men in three piece suits. Two of them pointing guns at my head, yelling.

"FREEZE! FBI!"

I should have realised that Sheraton room service is never this fast.

EN TRAIN
NORTH CAROLINA
AUGUST

Malvin Berg looked up as the compartment door slid open. The fat man's jaw dropped as he recognised 'Crazy Tommy', the feared enforcer for the Jaconelli family who now closed the door of the compartment.

Malvin Berg felt dampness spreading across his trousers.

"Why fatso," laughed Crazy Tommy. "You pissed yourself."

NEW YORK CITY
AUGUST

"You can put those guns away, gentlemen. We don't use them in England." I give them my best Oxford. Front. The only way to deal with agents of the law.

The man who yelled 'freeze', a tall, well scrubbed youngster, was himself frozen in a pose, gun in one hand, FBI wallet in the other. I knew at least half a dozen forgers who could produce those.

There were five of them smart, clean cut, efficient. It was the haircuts that convinced me. I wondered if they all went to an FBI barber. Despite my reassurances guns were still pointed at my face. Another agent squatted behind frisking me expertly. A third agent in a grey suit went into the bathroom, the fourth began opening drawers and wardrobes. The fifth muttered into his walkie-talkie. He was probably the accountant.

Grey Suit came out of the bathroom holding the bag of coins. The frisker asked me to empty my pockets.

"They're empty," I said.

"Where's Dee?" asked the tall man.

"Please put the guns down. You're making me nervous."

"Where's your girlfriend?" asked Grey Suit.

There was a silence you could have cut with a credit card.

I stared out of the window as Frisker handcuffed me.

This wasn't going to be my day.

We left the Sheraton by a side entrance, the one the public never sees. Reserved for staff and arrested guests. Two brown anonymous saloons were parked amongst the garbage cans and empty cartons.

"Can I get my deposit back on the room gentlemen?" I asked, as they shoved me into the back seat of one of the cars.

Nobody answered me.

"Your Manhattan Seven is clear," said the radio. Four of the agents climbed in with me. The expenses man was left to ride alone.

The streets of New York drifted by us, polluted and unsafe. I rode crushed between two agents. Both very fresh and sanitised.

On the FBI radio the dispatcher was trying to find Bronx 12. Bronx 12 didn't appear to want to know.

We blew down side alleys where the cast-off of New York lives. Orange peel, broken TV's, bag ladies. The rags and bones of metropolis.

Questions tumble through my mind. How have they found me? I'd escaped the fiasco in Barney's and changed hotels twice. No one had known my new location. They must have circularized the big hotels. Stuart knew me too well. The Sheraton had been my Samarra. The 33rd waveband of reality had happened. I'd been arrested. I felt sad for Dee - I'd let her down. The handcuffs bit into my wrist. Freedom would be a long, long way off now.

The gold was no use to me. Scotland Yard and Interpol would be in the queue behind these people. I faced a Chinese puzzle of courts and jails.

We emerged from side alley into back street. The

despatcher had given up now on Bronx 12. Our driver spoke into the the mike as we turned onto a ramp and descended underground.

We halted outside a steel roller door, in an area of concrete and brick. A sign said, 'Water Supply 8' 6"'. I hadn't got the faintest idea where we were. I hoped these men actually were the FBI.

A crackle of static came over the radio. "Delta Seven, Delta Seven," said the driver into the transceiver. He was rewarded with more static.

"Damn," said the agent in the front seat. The driver honked the horn. The big steel door stayed stubbornly shut.

The man on my left said, "that's twice this has happened this week."

"Delta Seven, we have an admission," said the driver.

The agent on my right unwrapped a stick of chewing gum and popped it carefully into his mouth.

"Jerry's asleep on the door," said the man in the front seat. Somebody laughed. The driver sounded the horn again. The agent on my right placed the gum wrapper in his top pocket.

The driver clambered out and banged twice on the roller shutters. "Alright already," said a voice from beyond the door. The driver climbed back into the car.

There was a squeal as the rollers rattled upwards.

WASHINGTON D.C.
AUGUST

James Benedict Ampleforth II replaced the telephone onto the console. Beyond the darkened windows of the bombproof Fleetwood Cadillac, the Potomac's tree lined banks drifted by. Ampleforth still felt twinges between the shoulder blades that his club masseur hadn't entirely eradicated. He never should have agreed to a third squash match.

That State Department analyst was a vigorous player, and 20 years younger than him. Everyone was 20 years younger than him.

So the FBI had caught the Englishman. Now he would have to send someone to see the man, to talk to him, and recover the Agency's property. It would have to be done discreetly. It wouldn't do to have the Bureau get wind of what was going on. The scandal would be immense if the details ever emerged. There was no love lost between the CIA and the FBI.

Ampleforth wondered what kind of character the Britisher was. Still, the man should want to play ball, he was facing ten years in prison.

The FBI had neither found the bulk of the gold, the girl or the Agency's packages. Perhaps it would be more prudent to locate the girl before rushing into bargains with criminals.

The Deputy Director of the CIA wriggled his shoulders into the soft leather seating of the limousine and picked up the telephone. The twinge stabbed him again. His bet was that the Agency's goods were with the little English lady.

Now it was a case of cherchez la femme.

FBI DISTRICT OFFICE
MANHATTAN
AUGUST

Of all the forces of law and order operating in the United States of America, the Federal Bureau of Investigation commands the most respect. Their officers have high standards of discipline, education and conduct. The FBI like to do things by the book. The rough stuff is left for the local boys.

Their treatment of me was classic. After making me sign an inventory of my possessions they left me to stew in a bare green painted cell. The only furniture, an iron bench bolted to the wall. The door was studded steel, set with a small peephole. No window. Light came from a flourescent tube recessed into the ceiling and protected by thick steel mesh.

After what must have been an hour the eye-panel slid open and then closed. Keys rattled in the lock and Frisker appeared bearing a cellophane wrapped sandwich and a plastic cup. Wordlessly he placed these on the bench and left the cell, while Grey Suit kept watch from the doorway.

Was the food so bad that they expected violence?

The sandwich consisted of two stale slices of white bread and a thin disc of what I presumed to be some kind of salami. Everyone in the world must have rejected it for it to wind up as my supper.

After what I judged to be another hour the celldoor opened again and I was motioned out. We trooped past a succession of vacant, gloomy offices. It was night now, and Manhattan's lights winked at me from beyond the wired windows.

They were all waiting for me in a brightly lit room at the end of the corridor. Through the chicken wire mesh I watched New Yorkers hustling by three floors below. The skyscrapers outside a blaze of electric diamonds, cars crawling between them, like glow worms in a petrified forest.

"Sit down," said Frisker. I sat. Maybe I'd get a biscuit. I looked at the desk in front of me. A large perfectly rolled joint lay in an ashtray! They must have found the grass in my suitcase. How funny to be offered a joint in FBI headquarters!

Grey Suit smiled, trying to be friendly. A wasted effort.

"Go on, it's okay," he said. "Smoke."

"No thanks," I said. "I only like cigars."

"Are you Daniel Mordecai Liebermann?" the tall man asked.

"You're the FBI," I said. "You work it out."

"Who do you think you are? Humphrey Bogart?" said Grey Suit.

"Eighteen," I said.

"Pardon?" said the tall man.

"Seventeen," I repeated.

Puzzled looks multiplied.

"You've had three questions out of twenty. You've got seventeen left."

"Listen, wiseguy. You're in a lot of trouble."

"Why? What did I do?" I asked.

Grey Suit kept his smile. "Where's Dee?" Where's your girlfriend?" They all looked at me. Did they seriously expect me to tell?

"Look. You're wasting your time and mine," I

said. "Just send me to bed. Show me a room where I can get a bit of sleep for the night."

The Special Agents stared at each other. The phone rang. Frisker picked it up.

He said, "Oh, that's good." Then paused and looked at me. "I'll be right out." He put the phone down. "I think I can tell you all about yourself in a moment," he wagged a finger at me as he left the room.

I glanced at the joint. I would have liked to smoke it. But I needed the control. I didn't want them to think they were dealing with a junkie.

"You can make things a lot easier for yourself," said the tall man.

"I didn't know they were hard," I said. Beyond the chicken-wired windows, New Yorkers were going home or to the movies. Going home to make love to each other, commit murder, shoot up drugs or have their supper. Whatever I did or said, I wasn't going to be out there joining in tonight.

The permanent Christmas lights of Manhattan and freedom teased me.

"You think you're real smart don't you? You always got to have a con running. Where's the gold?" asked Grey Suit.

"Where's Dee?" said the tall man. "You wouldn't want her arrested in a rough manner, would you?"

"Tell us where she is?" pressed Grey Suit. "Then we can pick her up nice and easy."

"She's not going to be arrested by you or anybody else," I said. "Now can I get some sleep? I don't have to put up with this nonsense."

"Where's the rest of the gold? Where's Dee?" they droned.

I shut out the questions. Such a limited repertoire. I sought comfort from the walls. Bare, except for last year's calendar. The joint still in the ashtray unlit, a box of matches nearby. I really wanted it. I stared out of the window. An Agent stood up and pulled the blind. Manhattan disappeared.

I wondered why they had last year's calendar on the wall. Frisker came back holding a long telex that flapped against his knees.

"I think we know who you are now," he crowed. "Scotland Yard seem to have a lot of information on you. They want to talk to you."

"Wonderful. I'll pop off to London now, shall I?" I said.

Scotland Yard wanting me was a good thing as far as I was concerned. There was nothing the FBI could do to me or promise me. And when they finished with me they would have to hand me over to the British Police. I was sure that with their famed technology, the FBI would be able to trace the gold soon.

After all, it was in my real name, in a bank vault not two blocks away from here. The safe deposit key had been on me when I was arrested. They had it in a little polythene bag, together with my watch, papers and personal items. Surely the FBI can tell a safe deposit key when they see one. I was almost tempted to tell. Fuck 'em, I thought. Why do their work for them?

Suddenly the tall Agent spoke. "We're going to charge you with interstate transportation of stolen goods. Upon conviction this carries a maximum penalty of ten thousand dollars' fine and ten years' imprisonment. You have the right to call an attorney. You have the right to remain silent...."

They read my rights out. I like my rights. I think

rights for people in custody and accused of crimes are damn good things. I don't hold them in contempt.

"I'd like to call England."

"Sure. Go ahead." The tall man pushed the phone toward me.

"Who are you calling?" asked Grey Suit.

"Benjamin Rodriguez, my cousin." I pressed buttons as the Agents feigned indifference. We all knew their computers would identify the number. Benny was out of their reach. He had committed no crime. Grey Suit rolled the window blinds back up again. The tall man was reading the telex from London over Frisker's shoulder.

Beyond the chicken wire winked Manhattan's untouchable lights. Benny's phone rang, far away in Sussex. Somewhere in this building a tape machine was whirling. In my mind's eye I could see the waves breaking against the shingle of Brighton beach. The town's Regency facade mysterious in the evening mist.

Benny will be snug in his flat, clad in dressing gown, sipping a cup of tea, flicking the remote control of his video as he watches films of that day's racing. Freezing a frame here, analysing a jockey's riding there and munching endless pieces of well buttered toast.

I gazed out of the window at Manhattan with the phone to my ear. There was a click then I heard Benny's voice.

"Jew," I said.

"Jew," said Benny. "Where are you now?"

"I'm calling you from FBI Headquarters in New York. There's been a slight misunderstanding here. They've arrested me. They want to charge me."

228

"How much do they want to charge you?" said Benny. "Do you want me to speak to them, explain who you are? That you should have a room for nothing?"

"That's very kind of you. But they've been spending their money on telexes. They appear to have a pretty good idea who I am." The Agents were hanging onto my every word.

"How are they treating you?" asked the bookie.

"Fine," I replied. "They've been absolute gentlemen and most hospitable." The FBI were opened mouthed. "I need a lawyer," I said.

"No problem," replied Benny. "Give me the details where you are and the names of the arresting officers."

I gave Benny the details.

"I'll get on to it right away. Let me speak to the officer in charge."

I handed the phone to the tall Agent who took it gingerly from me. I leant back smiling inwardly. Benny will drive them crazy. He'll be telling them how important I am and that a top lawyer will be summoned forthwith. Normally this kind of bullshit may not impress the FBI men, but coming transatlantic from Benny in stentorian tones it should be enough to ensure that I wouldn't be abused.

Not for the first time, I was pleased I had chosen the bookmaker as our contact point. Dee would phone him soon. She had to remain free at all costs. Benny would have to get her out of America. Slip her across the Mexican border or something like that. But for me it wouldn't be so easy. It looked like I'd be staying a while.

They say the streets of America are paved with

gold, but rip up a paving slab and they get very
upset over it.

BROWNSVILLE
TEXAS
AUGUST

Dee Stone looked up from the sink. The face that greeted her in the mirror was hers, but the brunette hair certainly wasn't. the English girl peeled off the rubber gloves. The instructions on the bottle said allow one hour.

Okay, she would.

There was still one whole puzzle book untouched.

The Camaro outside was gassed up, her suitcase packed. She would cross the border at Matamoros just as Daniel had instructed. From there the drive to Mexico City where an airticket would be waiting.

Benny was puzzled at her choice of destination, but Daniel had been explicit in the movie house, outlining exactly what she must do if things went wrong.

Well, things had gone wrong, but she hadn't lost faith in Daniel. He would get them out of this.

She would follow his instructions to the letter.

Resting on the bed, Dee lit a cigarette and blew smoke at the flyblown ceiling.

Poor Daniel, she thought. I wonder how he's getting on. He'd want her to keep on trucking.

Now then. How to cross the border. Dark glasses, chewing gum, and a cheery wave. Just another day tripper.

Wanted by just about every law enforcement agency there was. Oh, well.

She flipped over to a new puzzle and picked up
her pencil.

WINSTON SALEM
NORTH CAROLINA
AUGUST

As the Amtrak train pulled into Winston Salem station, Berg recognised some of the people waiting on the platform, more of Arturo's 'problem solvers'. Obviously he was not going to be killed, as he had at first thought. Crazy Tommy could have done that at any time in the compartment.

The enforcer hooked an arm under Malvin's sweat-soaked shirt. The fat man stood up, his trousers a mess.

"Jeez, Berg. You stink."

Crazy Tommy helped Malvin down onto the platform solicitously, and shepherded him toward the station exit where a dust covered Fleetwood Cadillac waited.

"The boss wants to talk you," grinned Tommy. "He really likes you, Malvin. He's sent his helicopter all the way up from Miami. The boys are going to drive us out to the airfield right now."

FEDERAL HOLDING FACILITY
NEW YORK CITY
AUGUST

> "If you should go skating
> On the thin ice of modern life
> Don't be surprised
> If a crack in the ice should appear."
> Pink Floyd

To wake up in the morning in one of the world's most exciting cities, with a million dollars at your command and to go to bed the same night stripped, in a cage and facing ten years in prison, is a long drop.

I lay on the floor. Around me, the smell and noise of a thousand men. A vegetable soup of languages assaulted my ears as Blacks, Chicanos, Italians, Hispanics, and Asians harrassed themselves. The cage was one of the hundreds which comprised the federal holding tank deep in the bowels of New York City.

Once the FBI decided that they weren't going to get any more out of me than flip answers, they formally charged, fingerprinted and photographed me. I was delivered by Grey Suit and Frisker at midnight to a door in a wall. My clothes were taken from me and I was given a pair of khaki pants and an undershirt, several sizes too small. To be truthful I was pleased to get out of the nylon trousers.

All my possessions were taken from me. Around

my neck I now had a piece of string holding my gold Star of David. A poor replacement for the twenty-four carat gold chain that had held it there for the past ten years. The man at reception had peered at my Beaume & Mercier, holding it up delicately from one end, squinting at the diamond watch face.

"Does this thing work, buddy?"

"No," I replied. "What do you expect for fifteen thousand dollars?"

He dropped the watch into the little plastic bag that contained my world. The key to the safe deposit at the Chemical Bank grinned and gleamed at me through the polythene.

The FBI hadn't noticed it. With all their training and four billion dollar budget you'd have thought they would have recognized a safe deposit key.

So I still had the gold.

A couple of city blocks, a few dozen bars, locks, guns and prison guards were all that stood between me and it.

The reception man gave me a dirty foam rubber mattress, a clean pillow slip, two clean sheets and a contemptuous look.

From reception I was led through an airlock of steel doors into a vast enclosed prison.

Dante's Inferno - New York Branch.

Inside a vast hangar a thousand men were held captive. Iron staircases ran up to steel boxes of all shapes and sizes on different levels. I followed the reception man down the street of a thousand tragedies. It was a human zoo with the cages arranged in long alleys. I shuffled past exhibit after exhibit. Prisoners squatting in conditions of unbelievable squalor, squashed together by fate.

235

The heat would have baked bread. The stench of unwashed bodies and fleabag bedding rose up to meet me.

If I wanted to film A Bad Day In Kabul Jail, this would have been my location.

I was shown to my new accommodation; a very desirable central Manhattan residence within easy reach of Wall Street and Fifth Avenue, full-time security guards and fully furnished.

If you can call an open toilet in a cage you share with thirty people fully furnished.

I stood blinking as the reception man rattled keys. In the flickering half light from a black and white television I made out dozens of sleeping shapes. Every bunk full. Men were stretched out on foam-rubber blocks on the floor, tables, and benches.

"Hey hey, man. What's happening?"

The speaker was a black shape, half propped up on one elbow, smoking and watching TV.

"Say, man," I said. "Where can I lay my mattress?"

The black inmate looked at me. From a long bony face and glittering eyes.

"Put it right there," he pointed to the floor at the edge of the bars.

I struggled across sleeping bodies and flopped the foam piece down, threw the sheet on top of it, collapsed.

"Say, man." It was Glitter Eyes. "You got any smack, man?"

I knew that pupils like his came from heroin.

"No, man. I don't."

I lay on my side staring through the bars. I heard the junkie coming as he crossed the cage.

"Where you from?" He crouched over me. Scarred like a Zulu tribesman. Broken, blackened teeth hovered inches from my throat. I moved my head back.

"London, man," I said.

"Who's your running partner, man?"

"I don't have one," I replied.

The knife was at my throat, almost before I saw its blade gleaming in the television light.

I froze.

A bony hand with dirty fingernails crawled across my chest like a black tarantula and delicately lifted the string holding my Mogen Dovid. The blade flashed, spliced the string and my gold star was in his hand.

This was the final straw in a haystack of a week.

I went beserk.

"Fuck YOU!" I yelled at the top of my voice. And screaming "bastard!" I jumped for him, oblivious of the knife. My fists smashed into the side of his head and he went reeling backwards onto another prisoner. I jumped after him, punching, kicking and beating.

The whole jail awoke in uproar. Glitter Eyes dropped his knife and screamed. I smashed his hand against the iron stanchion of a bench. The tarantula opened and my gold star fell to the floor. I felt blows to the back of my neck and shoulders as I grabbed the Mogen Dovid.

That was the start of my first night as a guest of the United States Government.

SIERRA MADRE DESERT
AUGUST

The guard at the U.S. border had waved her through without a second glance. Why not? It was wetbacks coming the other way that they were on the lookout for, wasn't it?

The packages lay under the seat of the Camaro. She had quite a drive ahead of her. Past the Laguna Madre, the Mother Lake, across the mountains to Ciudad Victoria.

Buy another gun in New Orleans, stay on the main road, Daniel had told her, and learn how to change the tire on your car before you set out. She had spare fuel and water, food and cigarettes.

Dee hoped that she wouldn't have to use the gun. She'd probably shoot her foot off.

The day grew hotter. The Englishwoman was pleased that she had selected an air conditioned car.

Choosing the southerly route to Mexico City, the girl skirted the fearsome desert of the Sierra Madre. She didn't want to finish up like Humphrey Bogart in that film; robbed, dead or dying of thirst.

Dee was in high spirits. This was true adventure, this was what she had 'joined up' for.

As she passed signs for villages with impossible names like Xicohtencatl and Magiscatzin, she felt high, relaxed, happy. She was out of the United States. She was performing.

Dee Stone pushed the powerful car forward.

Daniel would be proud of her.

OLD RHODES KEY
FLORIDA
AUGUST

The silver Allouette helicopter fluttered like a dragonfly above the skyscraper's roof before settling itself delicately and with precision on the white painted 'H'.

The wind from Biscayne Bay and from the beating rotor blades whipped at Malvin Berg's clothes as he was shoved unceremoniously out of the cabin by Crazy Tommy, who jumped down behind him.

The fat man's garments flapped and billowed around his body as he was pushed across the roof to where a hard faced guard held open the door.

Four hundred feet above the ocean, Malvin felt his stomach lurch, and not just from the helicopter ride.

He was in the worst kind of trouble.

Jaconelli trouble.

The penthouse apartment resided on the top of the twenty story building. Only the top three floors were occupied, the lower seventeen remained empty.

The elevators had been ripped out long ago.

The building was sealed off from the ground.

The only access was through the roof by helicopter.

This was the headquarters of Jaconelli's cocaine empire. Oerlikon anti-aircraft guns, purchased from a Latin American dictatorship, swivelled in their well oiled base atop the skyscraper, a deterrent to uninvited aircraft, such as those from the Drug Enforcement Agency.

The guns reminded the fat man how little the Jaconellis tolerated interference.

Or disloyalty.

Or family members who kept juicy gold heists to themselves.

FEDERAL HOLDING FACILITY
NEW YORK CITY
AUGUST

Still clutching my Star of David in my hand, and feeling lucky to have escaped a stabbing, I was escorted by three guards to the punishment wing.

My feet hardly touched the ground. as I was dragged along the rows of cages. The whole jail seemed to have woken up, and were blaming me.

The hacks threw me into the segregation tank.

"Get in there, troublemaker. You're on a report."

I fell backwards into the cell, noting thankfully that I was the only occupant.

The following morning I gave my version of what had happened to the Captain of Guards. He grunted, and told me that they were allocating me to another cell.

I stayed in segregation for about half a day. I wasn't sorry to be there, at least I managed to get some sleep.

At one point a priest came around, and offered me a crucifix from a bunch he held in his hand. I told him what had happened, and he very kindly removed one of the crucifixes from its metal chain, and gave me the chain.

About three o'clock in the afternoon, one of the hacks unlocked me.

"Someone wants to talk to you," he said.

I leapt off the bunk, ready for my big chance, and

241

followed the hack down the corridor. He unlocked the gate and we stepped through into what appeared to be an office area, with deep pile carpets and air conditioning. Outside a door we stopped and the hack tapped gently on it.

"Mr. Heim," he called out.

A muffled voice bade us, "Come in."

I took a deep breath.

This must be the CIA come to negotiate.

They weren't in a position to threaten, after all.

OLD RHODES KEY
FLORIDA
AUGUST

The football sized rock of cocaine rested on the smooth marble block.

Arturo Jaconelli picked up the silver hammer as the Allouette helicopter whirled above the penthouse windows to land on the roof above.

The diamond bracelet on Jaconelli's wrist twinkled in the sunshine as the hammer flashed downward into the cocaine. Crystals that men had died for burst and sprayed across the marble.

"What comes off is what you pay for," said Jaconelli to his guest.

"That's why I wanted you to smash the rock," grinned the other man. "I would have been too delicate. After all, it's not my money."

"The Agency can afford it," stated Jaconelli. "We're paying you people enough down there in South America." The mafioso began to crush one of the shattered rocks with an antique silver spoon. His guest removed a slim crocodile billfold from his pocket, extracted a hundred dollar note, rolled it into a cylinder, which he waved at Jaconelli as he spoke.

"We need the income, we can't support the Contras on what Congress votes us."

"I just hope that your Contras never come to power," Jaconelli concentrated on pushing the crushed powder into two heaps with the back of the spoon. "Right now they're a useful irritant to our people, they keep them in line." The young mafioso laughed dryly at his own pun.

His guest leant forward, eyes hard. "It's not a joke to our people. If the Communists take over in the Caribbean basin and the South, they'll soon be marching up Collins Avenue with Kalashnikovs."

"Not while the Jews own all the real estate, they won't," laughed the Italian, as he gestured for his guest to take the first snort.

Patrick Xavier Garrity, Senior Co-ordinator (Intelligence) for the CIA bent down and sniffed sharply at the snowy crystals.

FEDERAL HOLDING FACILITY
NEW YORK CITY
AUGUST

"A lousy nine million dollars, Daniel," said Jack Heim. "That's how much tax they're claiming from me. And they gave me four years in prison."

Jack Heim wasn't the CIA man after all, but I doubted if any mere Intelligence Agent could have organised himself in that cagehouse the way this Jewish godfather had.

To see him now, clad in his silk dressing gown, and pouring me out Blue Mountain coffee, I could have mistaken Jack for just another retired New Yorker living on a pension. I swiftly realised that here was a man whose writ still ran from Little Italy to Las Vegas, from distilleries in Scotland to government officials or gangsters. A word from Jack Heim and attention would be paid.

Attention and respect.

Jack had heard of the incident down in the cage the night before, how an English Jew had woken the whole jail in a fight for a Star of David, and he had asked for me to be sent up to him.

I told him my story.

All of it.

The old Godfather questioned me closely and at length, nodding when I told him of the Miami operation and the contents of the packages.

"This is a very dangerous thing you've gotten mixed up in, Daniel. These Intelligence Agencies influence all our lives today. This is not the Old

America that Meyer and I used to ship whisky into. Our country has taken a strange turn, ever since the killing of the students on Kent State University. Nothing is what it seems anymore. I'll try to find out what I can for you, Daniel. I promise you nothing."

"Thank you, Jack."

We sat now in Jack's pleasant little room. Unlike the other cells in the jail, there was no lock on the door. The old man gestured towards a suit of clothes, hanging neat in its polythene wrapper behind the door.

"I have to go out every so often. I'm subpoenaed before congressional committees and I only have a few months of time to serve. They allow me a great deal of latitude." The godfather smiled. "Because of my age." Jack sat on a divan bed, preparing coffee in the percolator which stood on the small table between us. "And because of my relatives."

I relaxed in the comfortable armchair, certainly not prison issue, and Jack told me briefly of his early life as a young boy in Poland. How he escaped the pogroms, walked overland, and finally sailed steerage sleeping on deck under the stars with his cousin Meyer until they arrived in America with hardly a word of English between them.

Some of the beans were unsatisfactory, and Jack tossed them into the waste bin. Two elegant bone china cups nestled in matching saucers.

"So what happened then, Jack?"

"Well, Daniel. At Ellis Island they couldn't pronounce Suchowlansky, so my cousin became Meyer Lansky. He made quite an impression then."

I recalled the headlines, HEAD OF THE MAFIA EXPELLED FROM ISRAEL, THE MOST WANTED

MAN IN AMERICA. I remembered the pictures of Lanksy. A shrivelled old figure in a raincoat, clutching a million grubby dollars in a crumpled bag, a lonely old man on board a jet to nowhere, deported from Israel, wanted by the United States. Meyer Lansky was a billionaire refugee. A forerunner of the Shah, Vesco and Marcos. Modern Dutchmen flying in Boeings.

"But Jack. Wasn't Lansky the only Jew ever to be refused the right of return by Israel?"

"That's true too, Daniel. The U.S. told Israel that if they kept Lansky, they wouldn't get the F15 Fighter." The coffee had percolated now, and Jack filled the china cups, offering me cream and sugar. "They chose the F15."

"Well, Jack, they could hardly fire your cousin Meyer at the Syrians. The Israelis needed those aircraft. They had to expel Lansky."

Jack ran a hand through his silver hair before he spoke.

"It was a bad precedent for the Jews." The old man looked sad.

"What happened to him?" I asked.

"No country would take him and all that schlepping killed poor Meyer. He should have been left in peace on Collins Avenue. He did a lot of good for this country." We sipped coffee peaceably.

On the cream walls hung a picture that looked suspiciously like a Mondrian.

It must be a reproduction. A steel filing cabinet stood in the corner. On the bedside table, today's Wall Street Journal and Financial Times lay beneath a Tiffany lamp alongside a silver framed photograph. I wouldn't have been surprised to see a telephone. I peered forward at the photo.

A younger Jack in U.S. Army Sergeant's uniform stood alongside General MacArthur.

"I was one of the first hundred American soldiers on Japan after the surrender," said Jack as he handed me a sharp knife and gestured towards the fridge.

"You'll find some Gravad Lax in there, Daniel. I much prefer it to plain smoked salmon." I glanced again at the Mondrian painting. It looked original.

"My job was to set up the British-made telecommunications equipment which our military had shipped to Tokyo."

I reached into the refrigerator and found the Gravad Lax.

"When we were shown into the Japanese communications room, we found identical equipment. The Japs had been using British radio since 1937." The old man chuckled. I peeled slices of salmon onto my plate. Jack passed me a cup and saucer. I balanced all this crockery with difficulty.

"So they charged you with tax evasion, Jack?"

"They didn't get the nine million, Daniel." The American poured coffee into my cup. "There was no point in paying them. I didn't owe it. I went to a hearing."

"There were cameras and one of those congressional appointed tax committees looking into the running of Las Vegas. Of course when I took over The Silver Slipper, the skimming had already been severe. They called this big tax enquiry and started looking into my finances. They still had to allow me seventy-seven thousand dollars a year when they froze everything."

"So they sat up there at this hearing, the chairman says to me 'Heim, two years ago you declared personal income of one million dollars, you paid half a million dollars taxes. Last year you declared a personal income of one million. You paid six hundred thousand dollars taxes. This year you only declared half a million dollars income. This hearing wants to know why.'"

Jack paused and munched on a piece of the salmon. "Do you know what I told them?"

I didn't.

"I looked around the room, all these congressmen, lawyers, TV cameras, everyone waiting for me to speak. I looked at the chairman and said, 'What is it with you people? I am sixty-eight years of age. You think I earn a million dollars every year?'"

"I've told you everything I know," Berg sobbed.

"You're an asshole, Malvin." Crazy Tommy jerked the fat man's head round, gesturing to the huge machine in the corner. "Do you know what that is?"

Berg knew. He didn't need to look.

It was the furnace.

The top floors of the skyscraper were well equipped to conceal evidence of drug dealing. Although the defences had never been tested, Malvin knew that whilst the Oerlikons on the roof would keep unwanted helicopters at bay, any cocaine and drug paraphernalia could be burnt in the two thousand degree centigrade incinerator that the Jaconelli brothers had installed on the seventeenth floor.

The fat man knew that drugs weren't the only thing to disappear in that oven. It was not by accident that interrogations were held in this chamber. Handcuffed to the iron table, Malvin slumped forward, sweat pouring down his bare chest. His upper torso had become a mess of blood and charred flesh. Across the room, Tommy the Torturer grinned and revved up the oxy-acetaline torch in his hand. The flame glowed in an incandescent rainbow of hellfire. Malvin's eye-sockets were pools of blood and the iron table had become slippery.

"Where's the girl, Malvin?" Berg dimly heard the words through a pain-racked mind.

"The Feds have caught the fucking Limey. Where was the girl going, Malvin?"

A glottal croak came from the quivering bulk.

Arturo Jaconelli nodded at Crazy Tommy. The burner hissed and flared as the torturer advanced.

Behind the darkened one-way mirror, Patrick Xavier Garrity snorted another line of cocaine.

FEDERAL CORRECTIONAL

INSTITUTION
MANHATTAN
SEPTEMBER

In my orange jump suit, I stood at the tinted plastic window.

I wasn't going to jump. Not from the eleventh floor. It made sense to put the prisons in towers. This one was brand new. A designer jail. That's America for you. Slums or skyscrapers.

My cell was white and pristine, and I was the first prisoner ever to be held there. The cell was equipped with a single bunk in Swedish teak, a drawer underneath holding new bedclothes, and a spare jumpsuit in a plastic wrapper. The cell also boasted a sink, and a toilet bowl in sparkling stainless steel. It was miles better than the Sheraton.

The door opened from the inside and I was free to let myself out into the communal area. Jail facilities included a well equipped kitchen, ping pong tables, a colour television, exercise mats and weights.

A knock on my cell door made me turn from the narrow window. I seemed to have seen New York mostly through windows. Buses, cars, hotels, prison cells. I crossed the cell and peeped curiously through the spyhole. My visitor was Murphy, an inmate who ran the phone timetable. I opened up.

"It's your phone time. There's a guy who says he'll buy it for two packs of cigarettes."

"Suits me," I said. I didn't need my fifteen minutes during the day. I was allowed out of my cell at midnight to call England because of the time difference.

The previous morning, amid conditions of enormous security, the old federal holding facility had been closed down, and we were transferred here to Manhattan.

We had been taken from the overcrowded cages, handcuffed, belly and ankle chained, then loaded into coaches.

Battalions of police, U.S. marshals and FBI men accompanied the last wagon train across the city. New York came to a standstill around us. Traffic lights were set in our favour and police helicopters rode shotgun high overhead. The move passed without event.

The cavalcade had swept us underground to the steel doors of FCI Manhattan, where we were met by induction teams. We were stripped and showered. No articles of clothing or bedding from the old slum jail were to be allowed into the clinical tower.

I was given a perfunctory medical examination. The doctor asked me if I had any problems. I told him I was in jail. A man checked my head for lice and then gave me a paper housecoat like hospital surgeons wear. It wasn't big enough. I was made to stand naked for a while and then someone handed me a brand new pair of shorts and a large T-shirt. I felt clean for the first time in a week. The bag with my possessions reappeared and I was made to check and sign for them.

The safe deposit key beamed at me.

An elevator ride to the eleventh floor. Maximum Security Wing. I owed my status to the size of the crime and the warrants from Scotland Yard.

And presumably the packages.

I had become fatalistic toward my lot.

The million dollars' worth of gold still lay in the vaults at the Chemical Bank on Columbus Circle, a couple of blocks away.

Or ten years in time.

Someone from the CIA must contact me soon.

If only with a poisoned cigar.

ARLINGTON NATIONAL CEMETERY WASHINGTON D.C. SEPTEMBER

The funeral cortège sleepwalked through Arlington Cemetery. As James Benedict Ampleforth II bowed his head, the warm breeze ruffled his grey hair and Patrick Garrity watched the wind reveal the Deputy Director's bald patch.

Ampleforth turned to his Senior Co-ordinator. "MacKenzie was a great man, a dedicated officer and a patriotic American, who gave his life to the Agency. We shall not see his like again."

The Deputy Director turned back to gaze at the flag-draped coffin. Garrity recalled wryly that only last week, Ampleforth had described the man they'd come to bury as the most obstinate, meddlesome, time-wasting bastard he had ever encountered. Perhaps becoming a corpse was the one sure way of getting in the DDI's good books.

The younger man shuffled his feet impatiently. He was a dynamic individual and the rows of sepulchral tombstones unsettled him.

The two men stood in silence whilst Marines, immaculate and white-belted, dead-marched past to the solemn beat of a muffled drum, their brass regalia shimmering in the September sunshine.

"Where is the Englishman now?"

Garrity had to strain to hear the DDI's whisper above the elegiac notes of the Last Post.

"He's in maximum security at Manhattan, Sir."

The Marine Captain stepped smartly up to the bier and commenced folding the Stars and Stripes.

"I want you to monitor every word he breathes, Patrick. Even in his sleep. I want to see transcripts of every call he makes. I want to know who he's mixing with, and what he does. I want to know how many times a day he goes to the can!"

A solitary Scottish bagpiper, resplendently kilted in the MacKenzie tartan, began to skirl a wailing epitaph.

"Yes, Sir. May I make a suggestion, sir?"

"That's what Uncle Sam pays you for, Garrity."

"Well, Sir. Why don't we question him?"

"What makes you think he'll answer? He's already hostile, and questioning will only alert him to the true significance of the packages. Locate the girl first, Patrick."

The priest was reading the oration now.

Shielded from the blazing sun, beneath a royal blue canopy bearing the seal of the Central Intelligence Agency, women in black veils were weeping. Amongst the mourners under the privileged tentwork, Garrity recognised senior State Department officials and at least four generals from the Pentagon. He wondered if MacKenzie had been moonlighting for Army Intelligence or State or both.

Maybe the fat cats had come to Arlington just to make sure that Mackenzie was dead.

"The President wants this matter resolved, Patrick."

"Perhaps we should try hallucinogenic drugs on him."

"On the President?" Ampleforth wheeled round,

256

shocked.

"Oh no, sir! On the Englishman. We could feed him some LSD."

"Have you read his record, Garrity? He'd probably enjoy it. No, softly softly until we have our goods."

The young man opened his mouth to respond, but the Deputy Director motioned for silence. The Marine Captain gave his men an order. Reflected sunlight flashed as the soldiers raised their carbines, and twenty-one gunbolts rattled in unison.

"The Cubans and the Soviets will have a field day if they learn of Operation Reis. The American public wouldn't understand about the way we've funding the Contras," whispered Ampleforth. "Don't approach the Englishman directly, but keep him under the closest observation."

A flock of birds startled skyward as the twenty-one gun salute shattered the afternoon calm. Garrity's ears were stunned for a second and he almost missed the DDI's parting words.

"Find the girl, Patrick."

FCI
MANHATTAN
SEPTEMBER

I looked up expectantly as the visiting room door opened and a plump prosperously dressed man entered. The guard glanced at me over the visitor's shoulder then closed the door locking us in alone, save for the FBI microphones.

The stranger glanced around the room, his eyes taking in the green and cream paint, the bare table, the two iron chairs. He stared at me as if I was personally responsible for the decor. I gestured toward the vacant seat. Carefully, my visitor examined the chair, removed a handkerchief from his top pocket and wiped the seat before gingerly lowering his expensively tailored bottom into it.

He appeared to be Jewish, in his mid-fifties, and wishing he had some other way to earn his money.

Was this the CIA man? I had been on tenterhooks ever since they had told me that I had a visitor.

"I'm afraid I can't offer you coffee." I smiled.

His gold rimmed glasses flashed as he nodded. My first spy, just like in the movies, I thought. I bet he'll write everything down and not speak. I watched as he delicately inserted a thumb and forefinger into his top pocket and extracted a heavily embossed cream card which he laid on the table between us. He seemed to want me to read it. So far he hadn't uttered a word. Not wishing to upset the flow of this pantomime, I leaned forward and swivelled the card around.

WEINSTOCK SMITHERS AND GOLDBERG, the legend. Fifth Avenue address.

My heart sank. I realised that this must be the lawyer that Benny had promised. Now I thought about it, he looked like one of the Benny's lawyers; an expensive shark.

"I'm Goldberg." The man spoke for the first time. His voice surprisingly quiet, a sandpaper rasp. Maybe for more money he speaks louder. I gestured towards the card.

"How did a guy like Smithers get stuck between two Jews?"

The attorney smiled bleakly.

"Your Mr. Rodriguez said you had ah... a sense of humour."

The lawyer made it sound like an affliction, perhaps something contagious. I felt annoyed with this pompous rich bastard. The New York sky had turned grey beyond the barred window.

"Did my friend send you any money?"

Goldberg extracted a small gold toothpick from his pocket. I wondered what else he kept in there. He carried no briefcase or papers. Opening out a blade he began to worry at his teeth.

"Er.. yes," he replied. "I believe we have received four thousand dollars." The information was reluctantly uttered, as if under examination from a tax inspector. Perhaps the microphones worried him. The FBI must know Fifth Avenue lawyers' rates. Half of the Agents prayed they could leave the Bureau and join such a team of shysters. The man made the four grand sound like a mere bagatelle.

"Have you been briefed as the facts of the case?" I asked.

"Your Mr. Rodriguez provided us with a very comprehensive account, and I have seen the preliminary reports from the FBI." The lawyer paused and stared around the room. It seemed time for me to take the initiative.

"They want to extradite me to Miami. What do you suggest?"

My visitor looked at me for a few seconds and then nodded, his head moving downward as if he had no control over it. Suddenly he rose as if to leave. I was startled. Goldberg crossed the room and pressed the bell on the wall. He was leaving.

"But what is your advice?" I burst out.

There was a rattle of keys. The blank faced guard expectantly held the door ajar. The lawyer made as if to step through, then paused and turned to me, toothpick still in his mouth as he spoke.

"Go to Florida, son."

I stared astonished at his retreating back as the hack closed the door, leaving me alone in the room.

"Go to Florida, son?" That was this high priced fatso's advice?

"Go to Florida, son!" Jesus, that was a thousand dollars a word. I'd heard about American lawyers, but this was ridiculous. I burst out laughing, remembering the FBI microphones. I wondered what they would make of it all.

Then I said aloud, "And FUCK YOU, TOO!" It looks like Florida for the winter. I gazed through the bars at the distant Manhattan skyline beyond. Surely the CIA knew that we had their packages? I would have to stir things up, and that would be dangerous.

AIRWAVES BETWEEN LANGLEY AND SHIP TO SHORE
FLORIDA BAY
SEPTEMBER

"The Mafia, the Mafia. Everyone blames the Mafia."

The hurt in Jaconelli's voice crackled over the radiophone link.

"And the CIA, Arturo."

"That's true, Pat. They blame you people as well."

"What do you have for me?"

"No news on the lady. I'm afraid my niece became a widow this morning."

"I'm sorry to hear that, Arturo."

"You'll have to speak with the Englishman direct."

"My boss has forbidden me to." There was a tinge of regret in Garrity's voice.

"No problem, Pat," stated Jaconelli. "I have people in Manhattan right where your man is. I could have one of them have a little talk to him."

"Let me think about that one for a while, Arturo. After all, he's not going anywhere."

FCI
MANHATTAN
SEPTEMBER

There were some weird characters in maximum security at Manhattan Correctional. I moved amazed between the plastic walls. Villains, gangsters and desperadoes of every stripe swam in these waters, high above New York. Plague men, hothouse exotics, tanked together by a Federal Government who held them as dangerous enemies of Society and State. It was not your run of the mill jail with its normal motley band of wifebeaters and auto thieves.

Here was a Mafioso, daily in the news, treated with reverence by staff and fellow sufferers alike. There was a mad doctor who had helped young men avoid the draft to Vietnam. For a fee, naturally.

In the cell opposite, Frankie Catania, a broody Sicilian who told me of his artificial cocaine factory and taught me how to make a silencer from wire wool.

All I needed now was a gun.

There was Marino, a self-confessed assassin, who had given himself up on the steps of the United Nations building in Caracas, to ensure publicity and avoid premature liquidation. Most of the other inmates stayed away from him, but I took coffee and biscuits with him and Red the Razor Blade, the hijacker, in the afternoons. I liked to listen to everyone's stories, especially Maurie the bookmaker, whose coast to coast racing operations had been frowned upon by the Government. I told him how racing worked in Britain, how everyone could have a bet in shops on the street, and how racing information was transmitted legally by wire, radio and television. He turned to me.

"But that's what I was trying to do here," he said. "I'm a fucking pioneer and they give me twenty years in jail!"

I refrained from pointing out that bookmakers in Britain try to avoid murdering their punters, even the slow payers.

It wouldn't have been sporting of me.

FEDERAL COURT
MANHATTAN
SEPTEMBER

Manhattan District Federal Court was straight out of Alice in Wonderland. They whipped me out of Maximum and into the FBI car faster than you can say Clarence Darrow. Another underground tunnel, agents flanking, walkie talkies everywhere, up a flight of steps, through a door and into this brilliantly lit little room.

There's a U.S. marshal who takes me by the hand. I'm still blinking blindly when I hear a voice say:

"All rise."

As my eyes clear, there he is, His Honour; black robe, blackrimmed glasses, black looks. The room is packed. If you can call a room with eight people in it packed. The place has the dusty little-used air of an antechamber. In one corner stands the Stars and Stripes. In the other, Goldberg, Benny's thousand dollar a word attorney.

Up pops a joker in a grey suit. Goldberg crosses the room to me, bowing his head at the judge as he does so.

"I'm going to apply for bond."

"Good. Maybe he'll get me out of here."

"Who?" says Goldberg.

"Bond. James Bond," says I.

Goldberg doesn't think it's funny.

The grey suited attorney is on his feet. "This is

the United States of America versus Daniel Mordecai Lieberman," says the prosecutor.

It seems like a mismatch to me.

Goldberg stands up.

"I represent the defendant."

Everybody sits down.

Except me; thoughtfully there's no chair provided for the star of the show, who's fighting the United States.

"The defendant is charged with interstate transportation of stolen gods," Laughter in the court. "I'm sorry. I mean goods. The sums involved are substantial, and have not been recovered." Everybody looks at me except Goldberg the Lawyer who has his back to me.

"One of the alleged perpetrators is still at large."

Dee, he means. I wonder where she is now. I hope that she's at large in Europe. Making those magic little moves with the packages. The prosecutor reads out details. Everybody knows the whole story. The prosecutor calls a witness from the Federal Bureau of Investigation.

Everyone waits while Frisker takes the stand, and is sworn in. He puts a yarmulke, a little Jewish skullcap on his head. That's funny, he doesn't look Jewish.

Well, whaddya know. Jewish FBI men. Only in America.

Frisker is giving details of how Scotland Yard and Interpol want me. Everyone wants me. I'm flavour of the month. I hope someone springs me clean underwear soon.

Goldberg is on his feet, mouthing a little piece about my statutory rights to bail. I perk up. The judge pretends to consider all this. Then he speaks for the first time, a little raucus horse players' voice. I can see him over a gin game, crowing as he calls up rummy.

He calls up rummy now:

"Bond is set at two hundred and fifty thousand dollars."

The judge raps his gavel and rises. Everybody rises. Tumult breaks out. The judge disappears through a secret panel like an heretic fleeing the Spanish Inquisition.

Goldberg the Lawyer looks at me:

"Can you make the bond?"

"Yes," I say.

"Where will the funds come from?"

"I have my own resources."

"Well Mr. Lieberman, if you make that bond, the court will hold a hearing to determine the source of the funds."

Thank you and goodnight bail.

I thank Goldberg. He gathers up his papers, both of them and does a smart two-step towards the door and lunch.

The big U.S. Marshal gently takes my arm and propels me back out of the court.

It wouldn't have been any good if the bail were a dollar. Not with a Scotland Yard 'hold' on me.

Back to square one.

Maybe Jack will invite me up for some more Gravad Lax and Once Upon A Time In America.

I need a bedtime story right now.

CIA HEADQUARTERS
LANGLEY
VIRGINIA
SEPTEMBER

"MEXICO CITY." James Benedict Ampleforth II slammed his fist onto the desk. His wife and two daughters jumped inside their silver frame.

"We have the most sophisticated surveillance systems in the world, thousands of field agents, FBI men and border guards. This one girl slips past everything and everybody, drives for nearly two days in a car she rented in her own name, calmly boards an airplane using her own passport, and we don't hear of it until twenty-four hours later."

Senior Co-ordinator Patrick Garrity stared up at the fire sprinkler on the ceiling. The Deputy Director was in one of his Hiroshima moods, and Garrity recalled the words of his dear departed Irish grandmother. 'Least said, soonest mended'.

Ampleforth erupted again.

"And Mexico City, for God's sake. We spend enough money down there. Did she visit the Soviet Embassy in Mexico City, or don't we know that yet, Patrick?"

Garrity winced. There was more than sarcasm in his boss's voice. The Deputy Director of the Central Intelligence Agency was certainly aware that the Soviet Embassy was subject to round-the-clock photographic surveillance. The Embassy provided cover for the largest KGB station in the Western

World. Every face approaching the Russian compound was photographed and flashed by satellite to Langley. Garrity had put a team of men on scanning the 'flashes'.

"No one remotely resembling Dee Stone has approached the gates of the Soviet Compound, Sir."

"I hope not, Garrity, for your sake." The pain in Ampleforth's shoulder blades had increased. Perhaps he should cancel his fencing match this evening, lighten up on himself a little.

He looked out through the vibration-proof plate glass windows at the well manicured lawns of Langley. The neatness and order reassured him.

"And where, pray, did the young woman go from there?"

"We've traced her to Madrid in Spain."

"Is she still in Madrid, Garrity?"

"I don't know, Sir, there's no record of her having boarded a flight out of there, but she needn't have booked a ticket in her own name."

The Deputy Director glared at his Senior Coordinator.

"Oh, really, Garrity. Well, that's news to me after thirty years in this Agency. People don't have to use their own names."

The Senior Co-ordinator began to wish he'd gone into the lumber business like his brother-in-law. A fine clean life, chopping trees down.

"Spain," said the Deputy Director. "I don't like it at all. I hope to hell we're not going to hear about this in a four hour speech from Fidel Castro. Find that girl, Patrick. I don't care what resources you have to deploy, what assets you need to use, but find her." Ampleforth waved a dismissing arm.

Ampleforth watched the younger man's retreating back. Maybe it was time for someone to contact the Englishman. He must know where his girl had gone.

The Deputy Director of the CIA picked up the telephone.

FCI
MANHATTAN
SEPTEMBER

I was lying on my bed eating pretzels, drinking orange juice, listening to Red the 'Razor Blade's' radio and wishing there was some dope to smoke.

The hacks had held a big purge recently and the wing was dry of drugs. In the absence of those and sex, I settled for Rock and Roll.

A shadow fell across my face.

I found myself gazing into the rat-trap mouth and paranoid eyes of the most dangerous man on the wing. Chuck Maclean.

"Englishman. I want you to do me a favour."

I needed Chuck like I needed gelding. Even the Mafiosi avoided Chuck.

Long time bodyguard and enforcer to one of America's most notorious trade union leaders, he was now being held for questioning concerning his boss's disappearance. Apparently, the boss had gone swimming off Miami in an overcoat.

Concrete, not Burberry.

Maclean was finishing off the last of thirty years worth of Federal and State prison sentences. His crimes ranged from extortion to murder, and he was a one-man killing machine, adept with blade, artillery, explosive, the garotte and his bare hands.

"What kind of favour, Chuck?"

He stood there, an older Charles Bronson playing a mean part, shunned and feared by everyone in the prison. Chuck was about as useful to me as aids.

Yet here he was, lowering over me. I couldn't imagine what he wanted. It wouldn't be anything simple like the loan of a jar of coffee until canteen night.

Maybe he's run out of dum-dum bullets or needs a new grip for his baseball bat.

The killer jerked a thumb at the typewriter.

"I hear you're pretty good with that machine, son."

Now I understood.

"But I'm fed up with punching the buttons, Chuck. I'm fighting three cases as it is." Pretty feeble stuff to deter the terror of the teamsters.

He ignored my protests.

"I need some typing doing, confidential like."

"I don't do it for other people." I knew that this was a mistake as soon as I had said it. The killer bristled. A scorpion about to strike. Little cold driblets slid down my back.

"You done typing for at least three men on the wing."

"Yes, Chuck and it turned out to be such a pain that I don't do it for anyone now. It's nothing personal."

"I'll give you a hundred dollars." The enforcer dug into his pocket and produced a roll that would have choked a horse. If Maclean hadn't strangled the horse first.

A hundred dollars was a fortune in prison terms. I'd seen people get stabbed over a pack of cigarettes. I wondered how confidential his typing was. It might be the kind where the typist would get eliminated at the end. Along with the used ribbon.

"Thanks, but no thanks," I said. "I have money."

This was true. I had four dollars in dimes for the telephone. The poker games had taken a distastrous turn recently and I'd wiped our little syndicate funds out in a battle with an Italian, who was serving serving ten years for selling pizzas with heroin where the mozzarella usually goes.

Typing out Chuck Maclean's 'mortuary' memoirs of life in the Teamsters was not the safest way of rebuilding a stake for the poker school.

The killer's eyes bored into my soul briefly then he turned and stormed out of the cell.

I'd made another friend.

Now I couldn't settle back to the radio.

I was dying for a smoke. I had asked around but even the Colombians who always had grass were dry.

I went to the kitchen and warmed up a plate of chow. The food here was not too bad, better than the cages. One time the kitchens had broken down and the whole jail had eaten Kentucky Fried chicken.

I ate, watched the seven o'clock news and returned to my cell.

Wearily I reeled a sheet in and began banging the keys.

After about ten minutes, I felt a rustle of movement and a shadow fell across the machine. An arm reached over me and something dropped onto the typewriter.

It was a huge bag of high quality marijuana. I looked up into the grinning face of Maclean.

"Okay, Chuck. What is it you want me to type?"

"Just my life story," said the hitman. "That's all!"

VIENNA
AUSTRIA
SEPTEMBER

The porter at the Imperial Hotel held the door of the Mercedes limousine open for Dee Stone. It was a warm sunny day in Vienna, and the map had shown her that Schottengasse was within walking distance from her hotel. But Dee was taking no chances. The flight from Mexico City to Madrid had been uneventful. At the newsstand in Madrid airport she was happily able to replenish her supply of puzzle books, and she had waited quietly in the restaurant for her connection to Austria.

Daniel had told her not to phone Benny again until she had completed her task in Austria.

Leaving Vienna airport, Dee had passed through customs without challenge and had taken a taxi to the Imperial. At this elegant hostelry she checked in, showing her real passport and paying a cash deposit. In her suite she breathed a sigh of relief.

She couldn't be extradited to Britain or America from Austria. She had asked the concierge to provide her with a chauffer driven car with black windows. She didn't want to be spotted by any blue pointed-head persons from Interpol, extradition treaty or no. From her oak panelled hotel suite, Dee telephoned the number Daniel had given her, making an appointment for within the hour.

Then she had stripped, jumped gratefully into the bathroom and had taken a swift shower. Now, refreshed with a cup of hot Austrian chocolate, and wearing the blue silk suit that Daniel had bought for her so long ago in Hong Kong, she sped along the Kaisering in the back of the Mercedes, clutching the crocodile satchel that held the packages.

Daniel had told her that these were their 'ace in the hole'.

She hoped he was right.

Daniel Mordecai Lieberman usually was.

FCI
MANHATTAN
SEPTEMBER

"I have thought about your situation long and hard, Daniel. You and the girl are in great danger. You have unwittingly compromised the National Security of our nation." Jack Heim reflectively applied flame to his cigar.

I perched uneasily on the edge of his bunk. Jack's fridge, photos and Mondrian had survived the transfer to the skyscraper jail. My coffee nestled untouched on my lap.

"How can I put matters right, Jack?"

"By yourself, you can't, Daniel." The old millionaire paused. "There's only one man in the world who can help you now."

"Who's that?"

The old man stared at me, his eyes flashing like pebbles in the sea behind his glasses as he spoke:

"The President of the United States of America."

BROWARD COUNTY JAIL
FLORIDA
SEPTEMBER

The cell in Broward County Jail, Florida, was gloomy. I regretted my decision to agree to extradition from New York. I had attempted to enliven the cell walls with some colour photographs of a Cotswold village which I had found in an old National Geographic Magazine. I used toothpaste for glue. The photos turned out to be not such a good idea, making me nostalgic for my father.

I daydreamed of speeding with him on Jaguar rides across the heart of England. Burford, Lechlade, Swindon, Marlborough, the names were tattered banners from a fading childhood dream. It was a good thing my father hadn't lived to see me slumped in this filthy prison.

So far I hadn't heard a word from the CIA, the FBI or the Mickey Mouse Fan Club. I knew Dee would get back in touch with Benny the bookie as soon as she'd finished the Austrian business. I was due to come up for trial soon and all the indications were that I would get ten years.

I realised now that the coin shop had been a CIA front. The boxes I had watched being unloaded in the garage at the back of the store were weapons destined for Cuba. The CIA had never given up on the idea of overthrowing Castro. I wondered if Congress knew about it. I wondered if they'd believe me.

As long as I had the packages I had evidence of

the destabilization plan. Hard evidence. I didn't want to blow the whistle. Hell, they could play their little games as far as I was concerned. I just wanted my freedom.

I looked at Dee's picture, also toothpasted to the wall. How long before I caressed her again, clean on clean sheets, on a fresh bed in a feminine room?

Across the cell, Bust Out Eddie held the poker cards literally close to his chest. Seymour, who was perched on the top bunk, had a habit left over from his Las Vegas days of peering over his glasses and reading your cards. Eddie reached under his bunk, and extracted a carton of Marlboro. In his Louisiana drawl the hold-up man said, "C'mawn Daniel, let's see if you have that third king."

From my vantage point on the bottom bunk, I sighed. The highest stakes in the whole jail were played right here. It was not for nothing that our cramped quarters were known to the top floor prisoners as the 'millionaires' club'.

Steaks and salads were served, and late at night when the rest of the cell was asleep, the whiff of fine sipping Bourbon could be discerned. Eddie had discovered the Hollywood Ocean Mile jewellery store two years before and had marked it on his list of "places I would most like to rob." The shop was a favourite spending hole of Boca Raton's wealthy. On his return to Florida, Bust Out had decided to take it.

The tall thief had told me that he studied staff habits, layout, routines and anti-intruder systems. He came to the reluctant conclusion that there was no way to burgle the place at night. Too many sophisticated alarms.

With a stunning blonde on his arm, Eddie had

appeared at the store, looking like a young Clark Gable. With the girl twittering and cooing, Eddie had paid cash for an eight thousand dollar ring, charming the staff and thus becoming an accepted customer.

Eddie bided his time. On his first visit he had noted the bulges in the carpet that indicated alarms. Returning to the store, Eddie paid a further six thousand for some tiny diamond chip earrings. He had gently pumped the staff and discovered that lunch time would be the best moment to hit the store. Only the owner and his assistant would be on the premises.

Eddie's careful reconnaissance had led him to discover a flight of emergency service stairs leading out to the back of the mall and to the electrical power cables that served the shop.

One lunch time, having primed the shop staff that he and his fiancee were going to a friend's wedding, Eddie appeared in morning suit, orchid in buttonhole reverently carrying a ladies' hatbox festooned with silk ribbons.

Once inside the store he accepted an offer of coffee, and choosing a moment when the owner and salesgirl were well away from the bulges in the carpet, he had opened the hatbox.

From the round candy-striped container he withdrew a Colt Python pistol, ·375 calibre, with a Parker Hale silencer.

Pointing this discreet cannon at the shocked jeweller and assistant, he ordered them to fill the hatbox up.

One and a half million dollars later, Eddie then handcuffed them and made his way down the service stairs. Pausing only to sever the power cable which he had exposed on his way in, Eddie had slipped outside into the back parking lot.

His rental car was exactly where he had left it seven minutes earlier, blocking the mall with its yellow emergency lights faithfully blinking. Placing the hatbox in the back, Eddie slid behind the wheel, killed the hazard lights and pulled away.

He was caught later, in a setup. Now Eddie was my cell mate. With fourteen escapes on his record, he had earned the name Bust Out. Facing forty years, he planned to escape one more time.

I was going with him.

His first plan was dangerous but simple.

On Eddie's next appearance in court, tough friends of his would come to the court holding cells, dressed in suits and ties and briefcases pretending to be his lawyers. Once inside the holding pound they would produce machine guns from their briefcases, and extract Eddie.

Me too, if I wished to go. A fine invitation. Why not? I had nothing to lose. Maybe once I was out I could find a way to get into my safe deposit in the Chemical Bank. The snag to that was the key, locked up downstairs with my clothes. And my identity.

Wait. My property travelled with me to court each time.

I told Eddie the situation. Eddie said his friends would help me take my property off the marshal so that I could escape with my passport and key.

That's what I call sensible. I began to warm to the whole plot, escaping at machine gun point from the FBI and marshals. Dee would love it. Benny would think it hilarious. I dressed in my court clothes and lay awake all night imagining men with machine guns springing me. It was like a movie. We'd be the talk of the jail, of Miami, the world.

It was a great offer.

I was going to do it.

In the morning my name was called for the court list. But not Eddie's. I was nervous. Downstairs I looked at the prisoners for the court bus. Eddie was not among them. For some reason the thief's case had been cancelled that morning. Had the plan leaked? Or was it mere bureaucracy?

I was very disappointed. I had really wanted the buzz of busting out at machine gun point.

There didn't look like any other way.

VIENNA
AUSTRIA
SEPTEMBER

Dee Stone left the limousine at the entrance to the camera shop, went inside and made her purchases. She used the back exit to leave, explaining to the proprietor that a man in the street was annoying her. Herr Müller would do anything to assist a beautiful young lady, especially one who had just spent three thousand U.S. dollars buying a Rolleiflex.

Wrapping a scarf around her face, Dee slipped down the narrow alleyway, turned right and found herself facing the headquarters of the Creditanstalt Bankverein, Austria's leading banking house.

The helpful porter standing in the elegant marble foyer directed her to both the ladies' lavatory, where she spent a few minutes, and then to the Foreign Accounts Section, where she now sat with the Senior Manageress, a charming grey-haired Viennese with twinkling eyes, Frau Held.

Frau Held had the air of one who has seen it all before, and at better rates of exchange.

She greeted Dee with warmth, remembering Miss Stone from her visits with Daniel.

"And how is Herr Lieberman?" enquired Frau Held.

"Oh, he's very well. He's in the United States."

"Wonderful," said the lady banker. "And how may I help you?"

"Is your secrecy total or optional like Switzerland's?" asked Dee.

Frau Held looked shocked.

"Austria really does have banking secrecy, unlike Switzerland. If the Swiss authorities decide that your money was obtained through criminal activities, your account can be frozen, then opened."

"Who makes that decision?" asked Dee.

"Only the Swiss Federal Banking Commission may decide what constitutes criminal activity, and their hearings are held in secret. You'll never know." The banker looked at Dee. "There are no such hearings in Austria, there is no such body! No one has the authority to order an account open on any pretext! You are concerned about the United States?"

"Daniel told me the United States Government opens up more of its citizens' Swiss accounts than a cat home opens sardine tins!"

Frau Held laughed. "Not so with Austria! Here we have true secrecy."

Dee explained exactly what she wanted, and handed over the remaining package.

"Well, Miss Stone, your first request is straightforward, and I see no difficulty in arranging that, but the second request - well, that is unusual."

"Can it be done?"

"Oh yes, we could treat it in exactly the same way as a renewable deposit, except that it is a package, not cash funds..." Her voice trailed away.

"Herr Lieberman anticipated that, and asked me to offer the bank a fee, as for a guarantee." Dee produced the last of Mickey the Buyer's money. "There's five thousand dollars there to cover bank charges."

"Oh, I am sure that the charges wouldn't be that much, but it's not just a question of the money."

282

"Herr Lieberman says that it's a matter of life or death to him."

The grey-haired Austrian woman laughed. "Oh, he is so dramatic, your Herr Lieberman. That's all right, I am sure that we can accept the package." She laughed again. "He is so dramatic. Has he finished his novel yet?"

"He's working on it," said Dee. "He's working on it."

"You will choose a secret word," said Frau Held. "A code word for the second package."

She handed Dee a printed form.

"Please write the word here."

In her clear handwriting Dee wrote RAINBOW.

BROWARD COUNTY JAIL
FLORIDA
SEPTEMBER

Eddie handed me the photographs and letters. A still moment held us. It was dawn, and everyone else in the cells was asleep.

"Watch TV," whispered Eddie. "When you know I've escaped, destroy these. They'll be in here looking for them. If I make it, okay. I'll get you lifted out at court—just like the first plan."

Bust Out Eddie had arranged to show the FBI where he had hidden over one million dollars' worth of jewels. The marshals were coming to collect him and fly him to Atlanta. There, somehow, he would make his getaway. I was sceptical, but if anyone could do it, it would be Eddie.

If he made it, he'd help me for friendship, not money.

We sat for a moment, sharing the last joint, and sipping sweet coffee. The lights came on in the outer corridor and a metal door banged loudly. Some sleeping figures stirred. A rattle of keys broke the peace, harsh light flooded the cell.

Eddie flicked the roach into the toilet bowl. Groans and curses came from a number of disturbed prisoners. While you're asleep and dreaming, you're not in jail.

Two marshals and a hack appeared at the entrance and rattled back the grille. I wondered for the thousandth time why they didn't oil it. Probably to aggravate us more.

The marshals were plump and well-groomed against the squalor of the cell. Their appearance spoke of warm houses, hot showers, fresh linen, caring families.

"Juniper," called the hack. Eddie stood. I touched his arm lightly.

"Take care, old son," I said.

"I will," whispered Eddie. "Just you watch TV."

The day passed as usual. Cards, a trip to the library, some mail, showering, eating rubbish, sleeping. Eddie had sent his salad up to me. He would be eating in-flight.

The TV rested on a ledge outside the cage. It was on most of the day. If you wanted to change the channel, there was a stick that could be poked through the bars. I watched the lunchtime news. Africa, Asia, senate hearings, drug busts, and a dog that had chased a crocodile in Hialeah County.

I thought of Juliette Dahl. I hoped that she had received the money Dee had mailed for the broken down Chevrolet.

No news of Eddie. The afternoon passed; a nap, checkers with Seymour, more gruel for tea. No special food for Bust Out Eddie from the kitchen. Someone had purloined it as it travelled up the three floors to the 'penthouse'. The kitchen orderly looked blank when questioned. I settled down to watch the seven o'clock news.

There it was. Third story, an awful mugshot of Eddie. The whole cell snapped to attention. The man holding the stick poked it through the bars to increase the sound. There he was, Eddie Juniper. One or two men called out to me, but I was already riveted to the screen.

The news item ran a brief replay of the Hollywood Ocean Mile Robbery. The story was that Eddie had escaped from the custody of the U.S. marshals and FBI men in Atlanta, Georgia, and was now the subject of a massive air and land police search.

I was ecstatic. The whole cage let out a whoop. Men were slapping each other on the back and shouting. I made my way back to the cell.

"Your buddy did it," someone yelled, thumping me on the shoulder.

"He sure did," I replied.

I returned to the 'time machine', and took out Eddie's letters and photos. I knew how much the dashing thief had treasured them. Piece by piece I tore them up and flushed them into the toilet bowl. Seymour appeared at the cell door and watched without comment as I flushed the last pieces away.

I kept back one photograph. Eddie's wife and kid. Now Eddie wouldn't have to wait forty years to be with them.

I slipped the photo amongst my own and tucked the package back in my cardboard box.

"You knew." From Seymour it was a statement, not a question.

"Now now, Seymour." I eased myself onto my bunk, lay back and closed my eyes. I hoped to Christ that Bust Out Eddie made it.

It was from a guard that I first heard that Eddie had been recaptured. I was collecting a letter at the bars of the cage, when the hack said to me:

"Lieberman. Your pal was caught in Atlanta."

I was stunned and sick. Was this for real? Eddie had only been free for two days. How had he been caught? His plans surely included getting out of Atlanta - indeed, he planned to be out of the State of Georgia in a specially arranged helicopter. Eddie's wife was a chopper pilot. A useful occupation if your spouse is in jail.

Was this a rumour put around by the prison authorities?

But no. The hack's next sentence dispelled that idea.

"They'll be bringing him back here tomorrow. He'll be right back in this cage."

The guard chuckled and moved off down the corridor with the letters.

THE PENTAGON
WASHINGTON D.C.
SEPTEMBER

"Vienna, Austria is a hotbed of spooks, pinkos, fellow travellers, pill freaks and Nazis." James Benedict Ampleforth II rubbed a tired hand over thinning grey hair. His Phi Beta Kappa fraternity ring twinkled under the neon lighting of the Pentagon corridor.

He waved the flimsy hand at Patrick Garrity.

"You know her hotel?"

"Yes, sir," said the big Irishman. "We have her under close observation. Two teams."

"Arrest her now."

The Senior Co-ordinator drew a deep breath. "Er, we can't just do that, sir. She's a British citizen, and it is Austria. The Austrian Government wouldn't like it."

"Damnation, Garrity, I de-Nazified most of those bastards personally in 1947. We made that country." The Irishman said nothing. He knew to quit while he was ahead.

Earlier, when the message had arrived at Langley, a delighted Garrity had torn the sheet off the teleprinter, and had driven directly to the Pentagon, telephoning orders to Vienna Station from the CIA staff car en route.

Now he was regretting the impulse that had made him interrupt the DDI at his meeting with the Joint Chiefs of Staff. His boss was boiling.

"What the hell is that dame doing in Austria,

Patrick? Meeting Sovbloc people?"

"There's no evidence to indicate that, sir. The Hotel say that she booked a chauffer driven car which took her to a camera store, waited an hour and brought her back to the Imperial. Of course all this happened before we located her, sir."

"A camera store, Patrick? Could she use photographics with ..." the DDI lowered his voice, the walls in the Pentagon corridors have ears. Electronic ones. "With those things?"

"I checked that with our lab boys, sir, they say that only specialist equipment would be of use, nothing that someone could rig up in an hour."

"Supposing she phoned ahead from Madrid, or Mexico?" The DDI gave the younger man a basilisk stare.

Garrity hadn't thought of that. He supposed that was why Ampleforth was the Deputy Director (Intelligence) of the United States Central Intelligence Agency, and he, Patrick Xavier Garrity, was about to talk to his brother-in-law about joining the lumber business.

Garrity's mind came back to the present. The DDI was speaking.

"We can't pussyfoot around any longer."

Pussyfooting was a favourite expression of the DDI. Patrick Garrity would have liked a dollar for everytime he heard his Chief use it. He decided to make a small protest.

"If I just have a little more time, sir."

"Time is the one thing we don't have, Patrick. I'm under pressure from the director and the Old Man himself. It's almost election year. We're lucky that the Englishman and the girl haven't approached the Soviets."

"We have the girl under day and night observation, and it's a certainty that our goods are with her."

"It's a certainty she's put them in a bank, Patrick. I've seen the reports from Vienna station. That girl has visited more orphanages and handicapped children's homes than a bikathon full of do-gooding Royalty. She knows we're on her trail, Patrick. That little lady is smart."

"I could pull the girl in, sir, secretly in Vienna. Have her taken to a safe house and interrogate her."

"Torturing the girl will do no good, Patrick." A vision of the Director's wife and daughters materialised in his mind. "If I'd thought it would, I would have authorised it by now. No, she's lodged our goods in an Austrian bank. Austria is not Switzerland. We don't have the same leverage. Austrian banking is the last bastion of secrecy on earth." The DDI looked wistful. Garrity spoke.

"Maybe we should buy an Austrian bank, sir?"

"Great idea, Patrick," snarled Ampleforth," but right now I want you to find out what this English girl did in that store, how long she was really in there for and where else she went." Ampleforth was in his stride now, spewing out orders. "Search her room. Check the hotel safe deposit," Ampleforth paused.

His voice became soft and dangerous. "Two more things, Patrick."

"Yes, sir?" The Senior Co-ordinator knew what was coming.

"Don't lose her, Patrick, and find our goods. She's too close to the East for comfort."

James Benedict Ampleforth II nodded to his aide

and strode through the double doors to the Joint Chiefs' meeting. Thank God he would only have to deal with straightforward problems for the next hours.

Like why three billion dollars had been wasted building a tank that was as effective as a baby's perambulator.

BROWARD COUNTY JAIL
FLORIDA
SEPTEMBER

The evening was humid. There had been a desultory fight earlier, and the mood in the big cell was tense. Around eight o'clock in the evening, the cage opened. I glanced up from Robert Ruark's *Poor No More* to see a familiar silhouette being pushed into the cell. Bust Out Eddie was back.

The tall thief was in a high fever. Somewhere en route he had contracted a mild form of jaundice.

Seymour and I took turns to nurse him over the next few days.

Piece by piece the story emerged. Eddie had arrived at Atlanta, Georgia, aboard a Delta airlines flight, accompanied by two U.S. marshals, and one FBI man from the Miami office. At Atlanta they had been met by two more FBI men and another marshal. In the airport Eddie was handcuffed, bellychained, and fitted with leg irons.

"These guys were taking no chances," grinned Bust Out, as we propped him up against the pillows.

"We set off in a convoy of two cars. I directed them to a woodland area just outside Atlanta. I guided them boys as deep into the woods as you can get. They were on the radio to their headquarters, both teams. We got to the point where you can't drive no further - you have to walk."

"'Course," Eddie continued, "both my wife and myself had played in those woods since childhood.

Here I was with all these guys, I told them that they'd have to bring picks and shovels, 'cos I'd buried the jewels pretty deep. Their minds wasn't on nothing but finding that treasure."

"I jollied them along, joshing, soon everyone was joking and laughing. I even told them I was trying to negotiate a reward with Lloyds of London and this would help. They knew I couldn't claim it, but my wife and kids could. They was real relaxed. I told them that I insisted on going out there with them, 'cos if I just told them the location, they could claim they found it themselves and that I hadn't co-operated. They understood that. Lawmen always understand suspicion and mistrust. We got out of the cars. I asked them to take off my leg irons, make it easier for me to walk. Six of them. All armed to the teeth, and they refused me! I stumbled along and kept halting and bending over from time to time, adjusting my ankle chains, like they was bothering me. Soon we was deep into the forest. They didn't know where they was. Up we came to a big old bush, the one me and Lou Ann used to canoodle under."

"Well, right there I reached down again to straighten my ankle irons, no one taking much notice of me. I said we was nearly there. I leaned down and fished around and sure enough my fingers touched cold steel. Right there. My little Lou Ann had left me a big Colt Python Magnum 450, more like a goddamn cannon than a handgun. I whipped that piece up and yelled 'FREEZE!'"

"Jesus. It felt good to be holding that gun after all those months in jail. You should have seen their faces. Big Cecil, he was the nearest, you know him."

293

I nodded. Big Cecil was a flashily dressed marshal in charge of the Miami cage. He had flown to Atlanta as one of Eddie's escorts.

"He wanted to be in the glory," said Eddie. "He finished up in the shit. I stuck that gun right in Big Cecil's ear and yelled out for everyone to freeze or Cecil gets his head ventilated. Cecil he was in charge, he told everyone to do as I said. I made them all throw their guns down. One didn't want to, he was a black guy, a nigrah marshal. He made a move. I just cocked the gun in Cecil's ear. Cecil was fair screaming out, 'He means it. Put the gun down.' He was kind of reluctant, that nigrah, but Cecil was the Boss Marshal. Jesus, I never seen six guys look so sick and angry all at once. Keeping Cecil next to me, I got him to unlock me, then I made them all lie down on the ground spread out. Shit! Those guys woulda killed me if they had the chance. I frisked them all on the ground. One or two were carrying small pistols. Illegal, I told them. They could get into real trouble for carrying them pistols on duty.

"The black guy even had dum-dum bullets, little crosses at the top to make them splay out. 'Shooting kinda mean, son?' I told him. 'That's a criminal offence, using dums-dums. As a citizen I should turn you in.' I was laughing fit to bust. That black marshal never said a word. Just laid there on the ground shaking. Fear or fury, I don't rightly know which. There was some cursing and muttering from the other cops but nobody said nothing out loud.

"I made Cecil get everyone's wallets out of their pockets and threw them down in a heap, then I told him to get everybody's handcuffs. I made Cecil lock them all together with their own cuffs, then I made them all walk around a tree and sit facing it in a big circle. Then I cuffed them together like a ring-a-roses round that tree." Eddie lay in the cell grinning at the memory.

"After that I walked back to the two cars. I had emptied all the money out of their wallets. They wasn't carrying more than ninety dollars cash money between the six of them. I kept some of the ID and credit cards, threw the rest in a stream. When I got to the cars, I ripped the radio out of the first vehicle and blew out the tyre. I just pointed that Python at the rear wheel and BOOM. Blew the sonofabitch out. It sure felt good, firing that gun. I took the second vehicle, switched the radio onto their frequency and high-tailed it out of there. Jesus, I felt good. Like a king with a million dollars."

Eddie sipped at the fruit juice I held out for him. There was sweat on his face and his eyes were glistening, pupils narrowed to pinpricks.

"What happened then, Eddie?" I asked.

"I headed for North DeKalb, a suburb of Atlanta. Lou Ann had left a Chevrolet with money and a change of clothing in the supermarket car park. There's around five thousand cars in that lot. Well, I criss-crossed that bastard for two hours. Lou Ann had left the car there alright, like I told her with the keys hidden under the mat. Someone musta found the keys or hotwired it, because that Chevy just wasn't there. I was hungry and still in my old clothes. I headed for the supermarket, and loaded me up a trolley, eating the food as I walked around. There was clothes there. I made like I was trying them on, then I slipped out and across the car park. No one even saw me.

"I headed for a motel in North DeKalb, I figured

295

I'd lie up there till the heat was off. I was gonna use the FBI man's Mastercharge till I noticed that the damn thing was out of date." Eddie laughed.

"I paid cash for one night and bought a bottle of Chivas Regal. Shit, I was on the television evening news, Special Flash. They was touring the streets with hailer cars. I was on the radio. I stayed in that motel room. A helicopter toured around overhead. Middle of the night I was real thirsty. I slipped out of the room to get some ice. Two guys saw me. They was drunk, but not drunk enough. I woke up with more artillery in my face than General Lee at Pottomac.

"FBI was madder'n hell. They never did put out the story how I overpowered them all. Too much damage to the image of the marshals and themselves.

"The FBI guy chained me to a goddamn radiator, that's how I got these burns. They had to keep that nigrah off me physically. Funny thing, Cecil couldn't stop laughing. Relief I suppose. He came up to me afterwards and said, 'Eddie, would you have shot me?'

VIENNA
AUSTRIA
SEPTEMBER

Dee Stone left the Creditanstalt and dodged back through the shopping centre. Pausing at the corner of the Maria Theresien Strasse, she could see the hotel Mercedes clearly. Parked a few yards behind it she spotted a green Opel Saloon, two men inside. She ran across the Schotten Ring against the lights and skipped up the steps into the Telegraphenamt.

The cable office was deserted.

The helpful clerk took the details of the cables Dee wanted to send. The English girl glanced around the telegraph office while the woman worked out the charges.

A figure in motorcycle leathers squinted at the fine print of the regulations pinned to the wall.

Dee Stone paid the hundred and thirty schillings charge and strolled out of the building.

At the waiting limousine, the driver sprang out and opened the rear door. Dee eased gratefully into the seat. Across the Schotten Ring the young man in leather kick-started a big BMW motorcycle.

"Where to, Fraulein?" Dee looked into the mirror. Was it her imagination or did the driver's eyes seem piercing? More than casually interested?

"I'd like to do some shopping," she said.

"What sort of shopping do you wish, Fraulein?"

"I would like to buy some clothes."

"There are very fine shops near the hotel, Fraulein."

"Very well," said Dee. "You may take me back to the hotel and drop me there."

The driver pulled the limousine smoothly out into the traffic of the Dr. Karl Lueger Ring past the university and the Rathaus, Austria's parliament. Magnificent buildings, adorned with statues flashed past her windows. The car seemed still, the city was moving. The Mercedes sped past the baroque confusion of Vienna's Natural History Museum and the open Volksgarten. In the rearview mirror she caught sight again of the piercing eyes of the driver.

Vibes, girl, she thought.

"Maybe we won't go to the hotel, just for a moment. I'd like to see more of the city."

"Certainly Fraulein. And where would you like to go?"

Dee stared thoughtfully at the chauffeur's stolid neck.

"I'd like to see the Belvedere Palace," she said. "Please take me there at once."

"Jawohl, Fraulein," said the driver as he accelerated the big Mercedes down the Schubert Ring.

Dee knew the CIA were on her trail, but the spooks didn't know who else was in town. Daniel's friend Kim had passed on the message in the ladies loo at the bank. She had nearly burst out laughing at the sight of the slim Londoner in drag. She had handed him the Rolleiflex with the first plate inside and accepted a heavy brown paper bag in return.

Dee took out her powder compact, opened it and began to dab unnecessary make-up onto her nose. In the mirror of the compact she saw that the green Opel was still behind them, and the motorcyclist on the BMW trailing the Opel.

Ooh lovely, she thought. It's really happening to me. Spies in Vienna. It's like a dream come true.

Dee took a deep breath and surreptitiously slid her hand under the flap of her crocodile bag. This was the big moment. Kim had told her that everything was arranged, and that she shouldn't be frightened. Well, she wasn't frightened, she was exhilarated. High on the moment. This was the adventure she had craved. Her fingers found the paper wrapping of Kim's parcel.

A roll of red flesh bulged over the back of the chauffeur's collar. The big BMW bike moved alongside the car, just as Kim said it would. This was the signal. The girl tried to keep her voice calm as she spoke.

"Take me out to Schwechat please. I want to make some enquiries."

Dee watched the chauffeur's eyes narrow in the mirror.

"But the airport is 18 kilometers, Fraulein. You can make travel enquiries from the hotel." The driver's hand moved toward the carphone.

Dee Stone pulled the big pistol out of her handbag and rammed it into the chauffeur's neck.

"Be a good little CIA man," grinned the Englishwoman. "Take me to the airport, please."

BROWARD COUNTY JAIL
FLORIDA
SEPTEMBER

"You gonna lie there playing with yourself all day, Daniel, or do you wanna play some cards?"

My interrogator was Seymour. Valium freak, Las Vegas gambler and bad cheque artist. Seymour was also one of my three cell mates in the 'chicken shack'.

"You already beat me out of four cartons of cigarettes, Seymour. What do you want? Blood?"

The tall, silver-haired con artist smiled down at me.

"I want to give you a chance to get even, Daniel."

"It's easy to see how you charm blue-rinse widows out of their money."

"Romance and a dud cheque, Daniel. Works every time."

Our chicken shack was a cage within a cage. Out in the communal area seated at an iron table were our other two cell mates, Bust Out Eddie Juniper, the jewel thief, and Spanish Eddie Sanchez, the heroin smuggler. We were all guests of Sheriff Tom Mighty of Broward County Florida.

The United States Federal Government didn't have room for all the people it had in custody down in sunny Florida and the Feds were paying Sheriff Tom seventy-five dollars a day per head to keep us in the penthouse suite of the hoosegow at Broward County.

There were a hundred federal prisoners kept in

four cages. I shared my cage with twenty-three
gentlemen including communist agitators, illegal
immigrants, coke smugglers, hijackers and a couple
of silent Paraguayan Mafioso.

Despite Sheriff Tom receiving fifty thousand green
soldiers every week for holding us there (we'd
have given him more than that to let us out!) our
conditions were primitive. We were locked up
twenty-four hours a day. No fresh air, no exercise,
no privacy, no religious services and, the final
insult in Florida, we never saw a scrap of fresh
fruit.

Twenty-three of us shared the same open toilet
which was conveniently near to the dining table.
This was useful because it was hard to hold down
the food that Sheriff Tom served. In fact food would
be an over-generous term to describe the mess of
black beans and filthy vegetable remains that the
good citizens of Broward County dished up for us.

Actually, Sheriff Tom didn't need to serve the
food. It would have crawled up by itself.

I joined my room-mates at the card table. Spanish Eddie was dealing.

"My partners were all New York Drug Squad
Officers," he said rubbing a swarthy jowl. "They're
driving around in Lincolns and I'm stuck here in
jail."

"Maybe you should have joined the police," said
Bust Out Eddie.

A man on the television was walking between
lines of gleaming motor-cars.

"I'll take two hearts," said Seymour.

"With or without the blue-rinse?" I asked. The
television told us that now was the time to visit
Dade Cadillac.

301

Spanish Eddie led a small club. "They took my drugs and three hundred thousand dollars cash."

We had all heard the story before.

"Clubs is trumps," Bust Out Eddie called.

"The biggest smack dealers are the CIA," said Seymour. "When I was in Nam those spooks flew tons of drugs to the States on Air America."

Bust Out Eddie nodded. "Sounds like a high flying line. I need a diamond."

"I got a packet of them in Switzerland," Spanish Eddie said as he tossed him two cards. Out of the corner of my eye I saw a hack appear at the bars of the cage consulting a list, two burly U.S. marshals behind him.

"Mail the diamonds to Sheriff Tom," said Seymour. "Maybe he'd send up a steak and salad."

We all groaned. Food subjects were taboo. I held the six of clubs ready to throw. The hack rattled his keys in the lock. The marshals scanned the cage.

"Play the eight, play the eight," said Spanish Eddie.

"He doesn't have the eight. I have it," Seymour said.

My mind wasn't on the game. The mention of Switzerland and diamonds had made me wonder how Dee was getting on.

"Which one of you guys is Lieberman?" called out the hack. The cage went quiet. You could have heard a warrant drop.

I played the seven of clubs.

Spanish Eddie banged the table delightedly. "I was *sure* you had the eight."

"Hey you, Lieberman," yelled the hack.

"I have the nine," I told Eddie.

"I wondered who had the nine," said Seymour.

"Hey you, Englishman. I'm talking to you."

"Who, me?" I looked up.

"You Daniel Mordecai Lieberman?"

"That's what my mother told me."

"Get your things. You're coming with us."

The whole cage was very still now. It was unusual to see marshals up on this floor. If they had to escort you somewhere they would wait in reception while the hack brought you down.

"Where am I going?"

"Just get your things."

"I'm not going anywhere unless I know where I'm going."

"You going to get your things or are we going to come in and get you?" said one of the marshals.

Bust Out Eddie and Seymour stood up. One or two of the other men in the cage got to their feet. Others began to swing their legs off their bunks and put their newspapers down. It was a pretty solid cell. On the television a voice was saying, "...and they're all available on easy payment terms." The marshals looked uneasy. Maybe their credit ratings were poor.

"You coming out or we coming in to get you?"

"I'll come out if you tell me where I'm going."

"I'm giving you one last warning," said the marshal.

"You better understand something here." It was Bust Out Eddie. "You're going to have to come through every man in this cage to get the Englishman, if he don't want to come with you."

CIA HEADQUARTERS
LANGLEY
VIRGINIA
SEPTEMBER

The Deputy Director gaped at his subordinate. "She did what?"

"The woman hijacked the driver and forced him to take her to Vienna Airport." Patrick Garrity covered the mouthpiece of the telephone. "At the airport the limousine was surrounded by armed men, two of whom held our man in broad daylight, whilst the others walked her through the VIP entrance straight out onto the runway. The men then identified themselves to the chauffeur as U.S. Secret Service Agents."

James Benedict Ampleforth II stared in horror at the younger man. His throat felt dry and his next question came out as a croak:

"What plane did she catch, Patrick?"

The Senior Co-Ordinator felt as if he was tumbling down a mineshaft as he replied:

"Air Force One, sir."

DADE COUNTY JAIL
FLORIDA
SEPTEMBER

The cell on the eighth floor of Dade County Jail was cool, comfortable and bathed in pale green light. The U.S. marshals had avoided starting a riot in Broward County, by breaking regulations to tell me that I was being moved here to Dade.

Sheriff Tom Mighty had discovered that I had presented a petition on behalf of sixty inmates. I had entered a class action claiming violation of human rights and violation of our rights under the United States Constitution. Three of the jail house lawyers helped me draft the petition and more than sixty federal inmates signed it. We had smuggled it out to a judge by giving it to a young man who was appearing in the District Federal Court.

From the defendant's box the youngster had whipped the petition out of his trousers and handed it to the judge.

We claimed that Sheriff Tom had subjected us to cruel and unusual punishments by:

1. Denying us the right to religious worship.

2. Keeping us locked up twenty-four hours a day with no fresh air.

3. Denying us the right to exercise.

4. Making men go to the toilet in front of thirty other prisoners.

5. Feeding us the same food every day except Sundays.

6. Suppressing the previous petitions we had attempted to bring before the court.

When that document reached the judge, the excrement hit the air-conditioning.

The other guys in the cell had persuaded me to present the petition in my own name because I was a British citizen. The wonderful thing about the American constitution is that it applies to everybody on American soil. The first direct result of the action was that Sheriff Tom refused to have me in his jail any longer.

Once the U.S. marshals explained the position, I calmed Bust Out Eddie and the rest of the boys in the penthouse suite as I collected my things, gave away my cigarettes, said my goodbyes and joined the marshals for the forty minute ride to Dade County Jail.

Many people have been thrown into Broward County Jail. I became the first man in its history to be thrown out.

CALIFORNIA
SEPTEMBER

The generous log fire crackled warmly in the stone grate, casting a glow over the faces of the five men studying the young Englishwoman as she finished speaking.

"That's quite a story, young lady," said the President of the United States of America. "When did your young man first discover this?"

Dee looked thoughtful for a moment. "When Daniel found the high pressure roller presses, he realised that they must be printing currency of some kind. Originally he thought it was American money, and that they were forgers."

"What was the gelatin used for?" The Attorney General was puzzled.

"Glue for sizing," the President grinned. "It stops the ink running into the paper. They make the gelatin from unwanted parts of slaughtered cattle," the old rancher smiled. "Hooves and ears mostly."

Dee Stone was impressed out of her mind. She had switched off her normal faculties some time ago. Perhaps after the third gin and tonic aboard Air Force One. The only other passenger had been the U.S. Ambassador to Austria, ostensibly "recalled for urgent talks" as an excuse for sending the Presidential plane. The diplomat had nodded frostily to her but had not spoken a word during the entire flight, sitting several seats away going through his papers. The Secret Servicemen couldn't have been kinder, but they explained that they were under orders to see that she spoke with no one, not even themselves. The cabin staff had served her a excellent lunch of filet mignon, smoked salmon, strawberries and cream.

She had travelled by helicopter to the President's Californian ranch, and had been given a very swift tour by the First Lady herself, while the President had been in conference with his Chief of Staff, the Directors of the National Security Agency, the CIA and the Attorney General.

The President's Lady, charming and genuinely friendly, had shown her the communications room, the stables, the swimming pool, the President's own superbly equipped gymnasium, and the luxuriously fitted cinema.

"Of course we keep our own movies in the library, but the President rarely looks at them. He sees video briefings here, and of course the latest adventure films." The First Lady sighed. "He likes action, I prefer romance."

"I know how you feel, ma'am," said Dee. She hoped 'ma'am' was the correct form of address for a First Lady. It did for the Queen, so it must be okay. Now sitting by the fireside sipping Earl Grey tea - "Your Prime Minister loved it" - and nibbling at one of the First Lady's home made cookies, Dee faced the high powered battery of officials with equanimity.

"But it wasn't U.S. currency that was being printed?" This from the NSA Chief.

"Daniel never saw any forged currency at all, but at the Airport," Dee lowered her eyes, "in the men's room, he opened the packages and found that they contained printing plates for Cuban pesos, and uncut diamonds."

"So Operation Reis was to have flooded the Cuban economy with false money, loosening the grip of the Government there, and then to have instigated a wave of armed uprisings in the unrest that followed?" asked the Attorney General. Dee didn't feel competent to answer.

The President looked at the CIA chief. "I know that you inherited this situation, Arthur, but I thought we had put paid to all those shenanigans years ago? We're dealing with the Soviet Bloc through trade and arms control, not revolution. The last Cuban nonsense nearly started off World War III. This business of forging currency would have done irreparable damage to us internationally. It's fortunate this young lady was sent to us. What is the Agency playing at?"

"I was told that these operations were aimed at supporting the Contras, Sir, not overthrowing Castro."

"So was I," glowered the Chief Executive, "but I didn't know what they entailed."

The NSA Chief looked at the young Englishwoman. "Where are the plates now?"

"They are in a bank in Austria," replied Dee. "The first plate can only be released by myself or Daniel going to Vienna in person, the second plate to be released by me appearing at the London Branch of the bank, within seven days. In both instances I must be unaccompanied." Dee looked at the CIA man. "This was a precaution against my being kidnapped. If the plates are not claimed within a certain period of time, then photographs of them, together with details of the whole story will be sent to a number of media agencies."

There was a sharp intake of breath, and Dee continued hurriedly. "It's not that Daniel wanted to be disloyal or anti-Western, but he feared that someone would try to murder us to keep the whole thing secret."

There was a long silence in the room, broken only by the snapping of the logs in the fireplace. Dee could hear her own heartbeat.

The President frowned sternly at her. "Are you prepared to return these plates to the U.S. Government?"

"Yes, sir," said Dee

"Unconditionally?" asked the Attorney General.

"I would like to trade them for our release."

The President of the United States shook his head. "We cannot bargain with criminals, nor be blackmailed."

"That's what Daniel said you'd say, sir, so he offers you the plates back unconditionally, and asks to be thrown on your Presidential Mercy, sir."

The old Californian smiled. Dee looked very vulnerable and appealing in the firelight. "I accept your young man's offer. I cannot and will not grant any form of clemency. In this matter, however the justice department is empowered to inform the judge of your co-operation, and such a recommendation goes a long way. I cannot order judges about, my dear, despite what people think."

Dee nodded. "We both accept that. Thank you."

The President of the United States stood up. Dee noticed that he was surprisingly tall, and very fit for his age. The Chief Executive turned to the Attorney General. "I don't want my Administration tainted with this sort of a scandal. See to this, Murray, and co-ordinate everything with the Agency. Operation Reis is terminated as of now.

That's a Presidential order. Return this young lady, and our Ambassador, to Austria, and make sure those plates are destroyed. "

The President of the United States offered Dee his arm. "Allow me to walk you back to your helicopter, young woman." The old Californian looked down at the girl. "Do you know, you are very pretty. You should be in the movies, my dear."

DADE COUNTY JAIL
FLORIDA
SEPTEMBER

After seven days and nights in the holding tank at Dade, with the lights on twenty-four hours a day and blood spattered, pill-crazed, insane and violent men surrounding me, I wished to Christ I was back in Broward County.

The door opened and slammed round the clock, preventing sleep. There was vomit everywhere. Foam blocks on iron bunks served as mattresses. The sheets were filthy rags. Graffiti covered the walls. The drains were blocked, toilet didn't work.

Apart from that, the place was a model institution.

I was quite pleased. I managed to lose twenty pounds in weight. Every day, prisoners came and went. I was the only permanent inhabitant of the part of Florida that never saw the sunshine.

Eventually God came to my assistance.

I persuaded a sympathetic hack to let me make a telephone call. I rang the first rabbi in the phone book and told him what was happening to me, begging for help. The good gentleman arrived to visit me, friendly but cautious. He brought a prayer book, promised to phone my family in England, recommended another lawyer and said he would speak to the jail authorities about getting me moved to another cell. Within hours of the rabbi's visit I was lying showered and in fresh clothes on the fifth floor of the jail.

I gave up a prayer of thanksgiving.

The silence was a benison.

Cool breezes from an invisible Gulf of Florida blew in through the bars. Now I had a comfortable mattress, a knife, fork, spoon and plate. There were other men in the spacious cell, who gave me books to read and lent me a radio with headphones.

Someone passed me a joint of Colombian grass. I was in paradise. It was the most relaxed place I'd been in since I came to America.

Paradise ended on the eighth day.

I had breakfasted that morning like a prince. Eggs, apples, Florida orange juice and fresh bread. I was lying on my bunk reading the Miami Herald when I heard several sets of footsteps echoing down the corridor outside.

This was out of synch with the morning's routine.

The feet shuffled to a halt outside my cell with a muffled murmur of voices.

I knew they'd come for me.

A rattle of keys sounded in the lock and the steel door swung open. The uniformed figure of a Dade sheriff's officer loomed. Behind him hovered two men in civilian clothes, burly and middle-aged. I recognised the no-nonsense look of U.S. marshals.

The sheriff spoke, eyes narrowed as he looked around at the prisoners in the cell.

Before he spoke, I knew.

"Which one of you guys is Lieberman?"

There was silence. Here we go again, I thought.

Looking forward to a quiet day in cell 219, lying on my mattress, I said wearily:

"I am."

"Get your things, son, you're coming with us."

"Where to?" I asked. This time I had no Bust Out Eddie and the A Team to back me up.

There was no discussion with these men.

"You're coming with or without your things." The sheriff and the marshals advanced into the cell.

"Get your things." Loud and heavy.

Go with the flow. I knew this jail was too good to last.

"Okay." I stood up and began packing my items into a cardboard box.

I gave away books, food and some wet clothing.

I was not moving fast enough.

The sheriff grabbed my elbow.

"Okay." I shrugged free. "Okay," I said, "I'm coming."

I managed to say "Goodbye, gentlemen" before being hustled out of the door. So far I've never seen cell 219 again.

They were a nice quiet bunch.

As I stepped through the door, one marshal took my cardboard box, my arms were seized violently from behind and I felt steel handcuffs being snapped onto my wrists.

These guys weren't fooling.

I was frog-marched down the corridor.

By the elevator door stood a third man, tan suit, sun-glasses, speaking into the walkie-talkie in his hand.

Was this the CIA at last? They'd taken their time.

The party came to a halt at the elevator.

"Where am I being taken to?" I asked the assembled company.

No reply.

Oh well, we hadn't been socially introduced.

Maybe they don't know. These men must come from the land of the Jolly Green Giant. They dwarfed me. The elevator whined.

"Gentlemen—what gives?"

"Someone wants to talk to you, son," said the sheriff's man.

"Who?" The lift doors opened.

We all crammed into the elevator. My arms pinioned behind my back, I was thrust face to face with Walkie-Talkie.

He chewed a mint.

"Got one to spare?" I asked.

No one spoke.

Walkie-Talkie popped a mint into my mouth.

Maybe it's full of lovely CIA drugs.

The elevator disgorged us into reception, into the milling bustle of police, lawyers, visitors and handcuffed men. No one paid us any attention.

My captors urged me through the bustle to an open door. In front stood two uniformed deputies holding shotguns, their barrels pointing upward.

I was being kidnapped in broad daylight from an American jail. If it wasn't the CIA, they were doing a good impersonation.

The sun was shining outside.

"Can I call my lawyer?"

Silence.

"For God's sake, what about my clothes?" I was wearing a T-shirt and undershorts.

"His clothes are at reception," said a marshal.

The men hesitated. First Walkie-Talkie nodded and spoke into the radio. There was a static filled reply. We all trooped back down the corridor and into an office. The man behind the desk never looked up. He tapped a large brown bag and pushed a form forward.

"Sign for this," he said.

"In handcuffs?" I queried. "I only do underwater escapes. Not signing."

"Release him," ordered Walkie-Talkie man.

I noticed the marshals were taking orders from the man with the mint.

"Which hand do you write with, son?" asked the marshal.

"Both," I replied.

The marshal uncuffed me and I rubbed my wrists. Everybody was strangely silent. The usual banter and barrage of insults was missing. Inside the bag on the desk I found the clothes I had worn to court weeks ago.

"Get dressed," said Walkie-Talkie, "and hurry."

"Can I call my lawyer?"

"No calls," said a marshal.

I dressed. I'd lost weight. My clothes flopped around me.

I found my paperback, Robert Ruark's Poor no More. I split my pocket forcing it in.

"Right. Let's go," Walkie-Talkie urged.

The marshal held up the handcuffs.

"Not so tight, please," I pleaded.

He recuffed me, a fraction more gently.

We trooped down the corridor again. Marshals, shotgun toters, walkie-talkie men. I was beginning to enjoy this. If I'd had a hat and a badge we could have re-stormed the Alamo.

The street was full of walkie-talkie clones holding guns. They must buy them wholesale, I thought. At the foot of the steps three cars were parked. Men behind the wheel. Clones waving hand-guns. It was like a sunglass salesman's convention.

316

I wondered who was looking after the President today.

We hustled down the stairs like an armed gay wedding with the groom in handcuffs. I was bundled into the second car, clones crowded in after me.

We pulled away with a jerk. Or should I say a carful of them.

"Can you tell me where we're going now, please." I was polite. The driver muttered into the car-phone. Walkie-Talkie was sitting on my right. He looked at me, opened his mouth and cracked chewing gum.

"You're going to the airport, Mr. Lieberman. We're catching a plane."

"Wonderful," I said. "Overseas or domestic? First or second class? Smoking or non-smoking?"

"You think you're quite a wiseguy, don't you?"

"I'm obviously not alone in that opinion. Unless the fifteen of you have got nothing better to do this morning." I hardened my voice. "Where am I going?"

The chewing gum cracked again beneath the dark glasses.

"Someone wants to talk to you."

What a conversation line these guys have.

"Who?"

Walkie-Talkie addressed me as if I were a child. "You'll find out soon enough."

Unfamiliar Miami streets flashed by the windows. We were heading inland, away from the ocean. Downtown buildings gave way to palm fronted parks. The convoy kept a good pace.

We swept up onto the West Dade Expressway, heading north towards the airport, and pulled off onto a perimeter road, beside a stretch of electrified fencing.

Through the wire I could see the control tower of Miami International. Maybe I could get some sense out of Walkie-Talkie now.

"My family and lawyers think I'm in Dade County. Where am I going?"

"Somebody wants to talk to you."

Who writes their scripts? The I-Speak-Your-Weight machine?

"Doesn't he have a phone?"

We came to a halt at a reinforced wire barrier.

A sign said, Security Gate #3.

The barrier lifted and we sped past a glass booth full of guards out onto the runway .

No boring check-in desks for these guys.

A DC9 stood on the tarmac, waiting for take-off. Surely not just for me?

The convoy came to a halt at the front of the plane. Portable steps led up to the open cabin door.

This must be how the President travels.

Men tumbled out of the other cars. Guns drawn.

A walkie-talkie man bounded up the steps and disappeared inside, then re-emerged giving an 'all clear' signal. The car radio crackled.

Goons surrounded us and opened the doors.

One marshal reached behind to undo my hand-cuffs.

"Federal Air Regulations forbid you to be re-strained in flight, son."

"Very sensible," I said, silently thanking Federal Air Regulations.

"Where am I going?" I asked rubbing my wrists. Might as well try one more time.

The marshal looked at Walkie-Talkie who nodded grudgingly as if the effort cost him blood.

"New York," he said.

"Now you're not going to give us any trouble here, son?" asked Walkie-Talkie.

I was reminded of Rod Steiger in Heat of the Night.

"No," I said. "No trouble. What about my lawyer? My family?"

"They'll be informed," said the marshal. He didn't look as if he believed what he was saying.

I didn't believe what he was saying either.

Climbing out of the car, I straightened my tie and mounted the aircraft steps. This is quite a day.

Then came the shock.

At the top of the stairway I was greeted by a pretty hostess in uniform. I could smell her perfume.

I hadn't been close to a woman in some time.

My clothes felt loose and heavy. I followed her into the interior of the cabin. The plane wasn't just for me alone. The three hundred passengers who had been kept waiting stared at me with undisguised curiosity.

It was embarrassing. They've seen the way I came on the plane. No wonder they stare. I was either the Head of FBI or the Hackensack Mad Monster. Three hundred pairs of eyes followed my every move. The stewardess helped me into my seat. The aircraft seemed cramped, crowded and luxurious all at once. The two marshals settled in across the aisle and studiously ignored me.

The cabin doors closed. The no-smoking light came on.

I smelled the perfume again as the stewardess leant over me to click my seat belt into place.

I lay back and closed my eyes.

The idling jets burst into life as we moved along

319

the runway.

I opened my eyes and looked out of the window where I could see the retreating convoy of cars, then eased back enjoying the comfortable seat.

The jet engines screamed as we gathered momentum and the airport rushed past outside. The nose lifted and we were airborne.

A few thousand feet later I looked down.

Below my right shoulder through the porthole, the Gulf of Florida shone, azure and vast, splashed with generous gold from the morning's sun.

Beneath me, an architect's-model-size Miami ribboned out along the Straits of Florida, tiny white fringed breakers fell in slow motion on to blond beaches.

A thought struck me as I looked down at the toy hotels and the miniature turquoise pools.

Less than twenty minutes had passed since my cell door had opened.

On board, the stewardess smiled and asked what I wanted to drink. I wondered whether she knew I was a prisoner. Alcohol must be verboten. It certainly was in the jail.

The marshals across the aisle still ignored me.

I quietly ordered a large spicy Bloody Mary. The lawmen said nothing. If they had heard me, they weren't bothered.

The stewardess brought the drink and a menu.

She dropped two miniatures of vodka discreetly into my lap.

She knew.

I sipped the Bloody Mary and slipped the miniatures into my pocket.

I ate the fillet steak I had ordered and caught the occasional glimpse of America as it drifted by beneath me.

I looked around.

Now and then another passenger glanced at me and then hastily averted his gaze.

Do they all know?

Once I went to the toilet by myself. The marshals' eyes followed me, but neither made a move to rise.

In the toilet, I knocked back the vodkas.

Two hours later, well drunk, I landed at Newark, New Jersey, the only disembarking passenger. I had learned from the stewardess that the plane was bound for JFK, New York.

At New Jersey there were only two cars. I felt my status slipping.

Two drivers, two walkie-talkie men and two more marshals.

Happily, I tumbled into the back between two big officers.

It was quite a squeeze. A blur of a grey airport, out through a side exit and then on to the New Jersey Turnpike at high speed.

We drove across the bridge into the city.

I returned to New York handcuffed, a prisoner again amongst the skyscrapers and endless streets.

The convoy drove to Manhattan. I was hot and cramped inside the car. There was no air conditioning. The six of us could have used some.

We arrived at a modern building and the cars swung down a ramp to the basement entrance.

We halted before a huge steel door. A pair of eyes appearing at a narrow Perplex slit.

The steel door began to rise.

We drove in.

A cage barred our way.

In front of us was a glass walled booth. One marshal passed out an envelope. There was paperwork to be completed. I was motioned out of the car.

Everyone stood about. It felt cold after Miami.

Someone banged at the coffee machine just inside the door.

Closed circuit TV cameras scanned us from the walls. Cigarettes were lit.

Phones rang. Someone undid my handcuffs. I rubbed my wrists: one of the marshals handed me a styrofoam cup of black coffee, no sugar. Breath blew out in clouds. I shivered in my tropical clothes. The walls were plain black, the floor concrete. The neon light strips gave me a headache. Through the cage gates I could see two yellow steel doors with small eyeholes and no handles. Phones rang. Papers were signed. Coffee cups were crushed and discarded.

I was handed over.

The marshal who had been with me from Miami grinned and said, "So long."

A man in a blue shirt emerged from one of the doors beyoind the cage gate and compared me with the photograph he was holding.

This was a fine time to learn I was the wrong guy!

Blue shirt nodded at the marshal and the gate rattled upward.

The man in the blue shirt spoke. "Welcome back to Manhattan, Mr. Lieberman."

JUSTICE
DEPARTMENT BUILDING
MANHATTAN
NOVEMBER

I ran my finger around the gold crazy paving of the Beaume & Mercier strap. If the CIA really wanted to impress me they'd fix my watch, I thought. It made me feel they weren't infallible. Not that I'd met any Intelligence people yet. The whole thing was being handled by the Justice Department.

The United States Attorney, Edmond Harrow, seemed a nice Harvard WASP, in his Brooks Brothers clothing. He was a pale young man of earnest expression, a well meaning priest with political ambitions, Delta Sigma fraternity ring and a thatch of unruly straw-coloured hair which he brushed back off a high forehead with delicate white fingers.

In the corner of the room the FBI agent who had escorted me up here sat pretending to ignore us as he flipped through a copy of the Village Voice.

Harrow obviously had his eye on high political office. All Justice Department Attorneys do. He was thrilled to be handling this deal.

"You must return everything that you took from Miami. You must plead guilty to Interstate Transportation of stolen goods. The United States will sentence you to 'time served'. You will face a deportation hearing which you will not oppose and you will be returned to the United Kingdom."

"What about Dee?" I asked.

"Well, we would obviously like to question her."

"No deal," I said.

Harrow looked pained.

The door opened and a pretty black girl placed coffee and sandwiches on Harrow's desk. I noticed the Attorney didn't look at her as he muttered his thanks. He must be screwing the girl and feeling guilty about it.

"You're not in a position to say 'no deal'."

"Take me back to the jail. I'll do the ten years."

Harrow pushed a sandwich across to me. I peeled back the corner of the bread. Ham. Was this a put-on? They knew perfectly well I was Jewish.

"Why do you object to us questioning the girl?" asked the lawyer.

"I don't eat pork," I said. "Can you get me some other kind of sandwich?" The FBI man gave me a murderous glare. No one had offered him food.

"What would you prefer?" Harrow enquired politely, making a sterling effort to control his irritation

"Smoked salmon, salt beef on rye or chicken. I am in New York, aren't I?"

"I'll eat the ham," said the FBI man.

Harrow unfolded himself from his leather-backed chair and crossed the room, pulled the door open and spoke into the outer office.

My eyes wandered out of the window. The U.S. Attorney's office had a billion dollar view. I wondered what they were doing in all the other rooms in Manhattan.

Harrow was seated at the desk now sipping coffee.

"They've gone to a delicatessen for you, Daniel. Why don't you want us to talk to the girl?" He was too polite to touch his sandwich.

"I'll tell you everything you need to know myself. I don't want her brought back to the States, interrogated, charged or harassed in any way—it's not necessary."

"All right. Assuming that's possible," Harrow rested his chin on steepled fingers, "do you agree to the rest of the deal?"

"I can't. I don't have everything."

The FBI agent looked up from the Village Voice alarmed.

"What do you mean, you don't have everything?" said Harrow, his visions of pleasing the CIA evaporating.

"Well, I've sold some of the gold."

The lawyer looked relieved. The FBI man's eyes narrowed.

"Do you still have the packages?" asked the Attorney.

Now we were getting to it.

"They're in a safe place," I said. I wondered how long the sandwiches would take.

"In Austria, you mean," said Harrow.

That shocked me. But it also pleased me. It meant that they must have been following Dee. So the CIA were interested after all. These Justice Department people were fronting for them.

"Yes. They're in a safe place in Austria."

"In a bank?" asked Harrow.

"Yes. In a bank."

The door opened and the pretty girl came back and placed a wrapped parcel in front of me.

"We can apply to the bank to have the packages returned to us."

Not in Austria—even if you find out which bank, I thought.

I opened the parcel. One salt beef on rye with cucumber and mustard, one smoked salmon and cream cheese. They wanted to make a deal all right.

"Austria is not Switzerland," I said.

Both men knew what I meant. Swiss banks are as full of holes as Gruyère cheese.

The Austrians were tougher. They are still holding on to Nazi money forty years after the Holocaust, insisting that claimants identify every banknote and coin.

"You can tell us who you sold the gold to," said the FBI agent.

"No dice," I said. "I'm twenty-six. I want to reach twenty-seven."

I bit into the sandwich.

"You must return those packages to us as part of the deal," insisted Harrow.

"I'll tell you what I'll do," I said. "I'll give you the gold that's left. You can have the package that you want and I keep the other one."

"That's impossible," said Harrow. "The Government would not be a party to a deal where you kept stolen goods."

"You want to see the other stuff centrefold in Pravda?" I asked.

The Attorney glanced nervously at the FBI man

who was following the conversation intensely, the Village Voice forgotten on his knee.

It occurred to me that Harrow might not be a Justice Department Attorney after all. He could be a Langley lemming.

The lawyer turned to the FBI man. "Would it be in order if, with all due security, I took Mr. Lieberman out with me?"

FBI didn't like it. But Harrow was Boss. FBI nodded. I stuffed more sandwich in my mouth.

"Follow me," said Harrow, holding the door open.

I gulped down my coffee, picked up the salmon sandwich and followed.

We did the deal in the law library.

I would return the gold and the embarrassing package and plead guilty. Dee would not be further involved. I would keep the uncut diamonds. The U.S. would deport me to face the orchestras of Scotland Yard and Interpol. Harrow said no purpose would be served by the United States keeping me in jail. The gold returned meant a crime solved, citizens happy. I could go home. Time served.

No nasty prisons. I liked the deal. I began to like Harrow, but I didn't trust him.

"How do I know you'll keep to the deal?"

"We are the United States Government," said Harrow.

"That's exactly what I mean."

Back in the Attorney's office, I asked if I could call my lawyer in Florida, the one the rabbi found me. The phone was pushed towards me.

I dialled the Florida law office. My attorney was

out in his Cadillac. I was patched through to his carphone.

"Where the hell are you?" The lawyer's face appeared in my mind. Sandy haired, glasses, Jewish, not too bright, but honest.

"Hello Louis, I'm in New York."

"For a guy in jail, you sure get around a lot, Daniel."

"I'm sitting here with U.S. Attorney Harrow from the Justice Department. He's offering me no time if I return the gold. Or else they'll push for the ten year max."

"Well! Grab the deal with both hands. Ten year max is a mean momser!"

"I agree, Louis, but I don't want to give the gold back and get fucked."

I glanced back at Harrow. The Attorney's pink cheeks were masticating his ham sandwich. He frowned and made a 'No Way' sign deprecatingly with his hands.

"Get it in writing, Daniel."

I looked across at the Attorney. "Can I have it in writing?"

"Sure." The Attorney spat crumbs onto his polished desk.

"He says I can, Louis."

"You're doing good. How're they treating you?"

"Fine, Louis. I'm a political prisoner."

The Florida lawyer laughed uncertainly over the patch: we both knew every word was being taped. "Where are they holding you, Daniel?"

"At the Federal Correctional Facility in Manhattan, eleventh floor."

"Okay. Have them send me the letter and call

me."

"I will do, Louis, and thanks."

"Anytime, my boy. Want me to fly to New York?"

"Not at your prices, Louis."

My lawyer laughed. "Okay Daniel, enjoy New York, catch a show or two for me."

"Thanks, wiseguy. All I see are the bars."

There was a hiss as the connection broke and I replaced the receiver.

"Now then," said the Attorney. "That's all settled?" He raised a patrician eyebrow at me. The FBI man had sat silently throughout the call, pretending to concentrate on the grey Manhattan skyline beyond. Overhead the fluorescent striplight whined. I leant forward, confident in my own clothes.

"Nothing is settled. I need a letter from you on U.S. Government paper. My attorney needs a copy in Florida. I need to speak to him and confirm that it's all okay. Then you can have my guilty plea."

"And.. er.. the gold and the package." The Attorney looked away as if mention of the filthy stuff was tainting. "The FBI must be satisfied that you have returned all the gold."

The FBI would be mad if they realised I'd got to keep the other package. I kept the thought to myself.

"I'll tell you in advance how much I will return. You can have all that I have left. That's the bulk of it," I said. "Seven hundred and fifty thousand at retail prices. Give or take a St. Gaudens Gold Eagle or two."

The U.S. Attorney glanced at the FBI man.

"Would that satisfy the Bureau?"

FBI jerked a thumb at me. "How do we know he is telling the truth?"

"I'll take a lie detector about it," I said. "Listen. You guys will let me go in exchange for me returning the gold. Fine. I'll co-operate with you. I'll return all the gold that I have."

The FBI Agent moved restively.

"What about the stuff that you have sold? Will you tell us the name of the fence you sold it to? You have to. It's part of the deal."

"It's not part of the deal," I said. The FBI man looked at Harrow.

"But the Bureau would insist."

"Not for me," I said. "If that's the case put me back in the pen. I'll do the ten years."

Harrow said, "It would demonstrate your full co-operation."

I started humming the Volga Boatman song.

Harrow turned to the FBI man. "I think in this case the Justice Department will be satisfied with the return of the stolen goods."

"Well, I'm not satisfied," said FBI. "I want the name of the buyer."

I held out my hands, wrists together as if for handcuffs. "I don't go in for that stuff. Not quite cricket, as we would say at my prep school."

"Listen, Lieberman. That kind of crap went out with Humphrey Bogart. These days everyone informs." FBI leaned forward earnestly. "We are the United States Government. You are a thief. You want to go home scot-free. This man," he gestured at the Justice Department lawyer, "this guy wants to let you go, naughty boy, slap on the wrists, give

330

back the gold that you didn't cash in and stuff up your nose or pass to your fancy girlfriend and we'll set you free." He minced grotesquely, leaning close to me, our faces almost touching.

I could see where the FBI man had missed shaving that morning. He had blotched skin, uneven yellow teeth.

"Me, I'd sooner you were in the jail with the rest of the fucking scumbags."

I smiled serenely at the FBI man.

"Fuck you," I said.

"Okay, fellas." This from the Justice Department man who could see his orchestrated deal going out the window along with his political career.

He turned to FBI. "I'll talk to your superior in Florida. If he is satisfied with the amount of gold returned, we have a deal. And Daniel, I'll call you back from the facility to approve it."

"Thank you," I said. I turned to the FBI man. "If you haven't mislaid the empty boxes from the airport, I can show you where all the coins fit. And as for scumbags, I didn't kill anyone, I don't push drugs, carry a gun or use violence."

"What do you want, Englishman? A fucking medal?"

I leaned forward. "I've already got a big boxful of those." Both men winced and I continued. "Mr. G-Man, I want Dee to go free in the U.K. She mustn't be brought back and tried for this either." I turned to the U.S. Attorney.

"Okay?"

The pink faced lawyer frowned. "I should think so."

"Put me back in the jail now please," I said.

"When you've sorted out all the ifs and buts, I'll give you the gold. There's less tension in prison." I stood up.

The FBI man seemed near to violence.

The day hadn't turned out so badly after all.

AMSTERDAM
HOLLAND
DECEMBER

At one a.m., long after the diners and staff have departed, the Lido Restaurant leans back from the Singel, Stadhouderskade's canal, as if disdaining to give away even its reflection without a cover charge. The sharp Zuiyder wind lacerated my cheeks, and I shivered despite the thermal underwear that the CIA had given me.

The gazebo was floodlit, it's wrought iron striking a sadly discordant note; a deckchair in a snowstorm. The Lido's Christmas Tree bulbs sparkled red, green and yellow in the cold canal. I squinted, and the neon blurred obligingly. In the black water the tree and its inverted doppleganger became a technicolor Rorschach blot. I closed my eyes, the colours remained.

As I trudged over packed and treacherous ice, trams rocketed past me, their passengers swaying, illuminated wax dummies. My watch said one fifteen a.m. Early. I brushed snow from a bench and sat down, the iron chilling my legs. I wished the CIA had bugged a longer sheepskin for me.

The night streets were alive. Bicycle bells rang, couples strolled around me arm in arm. I waited. The twelve dollar digital watch from the Florida prison canteen told me that it wasn't yet time to make the call. I studied the New Year revellers in the Leidseplien. It was quiet here. Most of Amsterdam was celebrating down in Chinatown. The Chinese will use any excuse to dress up as dragons and let off a few firecrackers.

The gazebo was the meeting place.

I had been too keyed up to rest aboard the Royal Dutch Airlines jet from JFK to Schipol.

The change from prison was exhilarating. The stewardess had served me a plastic dish of airline food decorated with artificial mistletoe. My 'handler' had refused to let me drink anything stronger than coffee, but I had swiped two miniatures of schnapps from the trolley, and swigged them gleefully in the aircraft toilet (my usual location).

At Schipol we cleared customs without a challenge. The CIA man handed me my passport, long enough for me to show Control. The young immigration officer returned it without a glance. Past the barrier I slapped the passport back into the Agent's waiting hand.

He led me hrough the terminal to where a biscuit-coloured Mercedes 600 with civilian plates waited illegally at the kerb. A tall, fit looking spook, whose tinted glasses matched the car windows, held the door open for me.

Two leather jacketed Dutch cops stamped their feet and banged their gloves together like they weren't watching. A nearby civilian nodded at my handler. I nodded at the civilian, just to confuse the issue, then bent my head and clambered into the back seat. Dark glasses closed me in and slid beside the driver. I noticed that there were no lock releases on the rear doors.

The big Mercedes pulled smoothly away from

the kerb.

I watched the police through darkened windows as they observed our departure, their breath escaping in clouds. They knew that this was CIA Amsterdam Station doing a pick up.

Who else could afford a Merc 600?

The three spooks took me to the Hotel Krasnopolsky, the fin de siècle slab of Dutch comfort within staggering distance of the red light district. We bounced past the glass boxes in the lobby, nothing as gauche as checking in.

Upstairs in the suite, a fourth man was waiting like an embalmer. I hoped I wasn't the corpse.

He was young, clean cut, cold eyed and like the others, he wore a suit designed by the CIA's tailor with a bulge in the breast pocket. I took off my thin raincoat and settled into one of the armchairs. Charlie, my handler, spoke.

"Would you like some food?"

Dark Glasses passed me a room service menu. I didn't feel hungry. I'd spent the flight snacking. I ordered hot chocolate and smoked salmon sandwiches on principle. The Agents all seemed relieved at this and when Charlie called room service the order had expanded to include steaks, fries and salads for the Americans.

"You can have a drink now, Daniel. What would you like?"

Butter up the punter time. My turn to put the hook in.

"I don't want any alcohol," I replied, "but I'd like some dope."

"Some what?" said Charlie.

"Dope," I said. "You know, weed, khif, bang,

pot, marijuana, grass, smoke. You know? Dope."

"We don't have any." The Embalmer spoke for the first time.

"Don't worry," I said. "I'll slip out along to the Bulldog Cafe and score some. Only take me ten minutes."

"I don't think taking drugs is a good idea, Daniel."

This from the Embalmer. The only thing he looked like he got pickled with was formaldhyde.

"Listen gentlemen." Time for the hook. "I'm giving you a million dollars in gold and no embarrassment with Cuba. Are you telling me that's not worth a smoke? Let me go to the Bulldog."

"No dice," said Charlie. "You can't leave the hotel until it's time for the rendevous. Have a drink."

"I don't want a drink. I want some smoke. We're two hundred yards away from where they sell it legally in little bags. I want some. So please can you arrange it?"

Charlie looked pained. Dark Glasses looked like he wanted to hit me. In the end it was the Embalmer who went to the Bulldog Cafe. He got sent out by the handler to score me a twenty-five guilder bag of Sensimilia and a packet of papers.

So I drank hot chocolate and puffed a joint. As I watched the smoke curl up towards the ceiling I wondered who else got the CIA to score their dope for them.

Probably everyone.

The meet was set for two o'clock. At midnight the room stirred. Charlie switched off the television, pleased. Three hours of rock video by satellite from London was enough for anyone.

Someone produced a sheepskin coat in a polythene bag. Brand new and my size. It felt heavy as I put it on. Probably bugged. I hoped that I would get to keep it: it was a beautiful coat. I found gloves and a woolly hat in the pockets. They obviously didn't want me to die of cold.

Well, not just yet.

Crossing streets in Amsterdam is the most dangerous act in Europe. Rapidly moving yellow trams attack from every direction, alternating with murderous assaults from taxi drivers whose indifference to Amsterdam pedestrians is as legendary as their hatred of passengers. Speeding vehicles appear from nowhere, like a three dimensional video game. The streets are a dodgem dance on ice, with death or injury as the pay off. I hoped I hadn't survived the Mafia, Cubans and the CIA just to be killed by a tram.

I decided I'd been in jail too long.

Seizing a lull in the onslaught, I skipped awkwardly across the cobblework. The angry little red electric man on the traffic lights was against me. So join the club. I needed a *telefoon*. I peered into the middle distance searching for a green booth.

I paused by the small statue of Arthur Van Schendel, whoever he was. Three girls giggled by me clutching together, swaying, their leather boots slipping on the ice. Above me from a street light hung the silhouette of a naked woman, advertising an escort service.

The snow around me turned blue and I heard the long ghostly whistle of an ambulance as it slid by, fat and white with a thick red blood sign down its side. The canals echoed its flashing light, and probably held its customer. In Amsterdam, if the heroin or trams don't get you, the canals will.

The sharp northern wind swirled lost snowflakes around my head. I was grateful for the woolly hat. I wondered if it was bugged like the coat.

A peal of laughter that was not quite a scream startled the night. Across the road some students were snowballing each other at the entrance to the park. To my left, the Marriott Hotel proclaimed itself ready for festivities, its brick front dressed in little white neon Christmas trees. Headlights picked me out as late revellers swished home through the frosted boulevards. Comfortable Dutch bourgeoisie ensconced in their Mercedes, Audis and BMW's. Mobile insulation against the nasty, cold streets.

I fought down the urge to turn round and look behind me. My fan club would still be there. I wondered how many agents were being deployed. The Americans didn't need them—I wasn't going to run. I hoped they'd be quick enough if trouble resurfaced.

My deal had been simple. Dee and I would meet alone and she would hand over the package. That way no one could claim later that I hadn't co-operated fully. Dee was to be allowed to leave unmolested. Except by me.

I wanted a night with my lady.

I squinted across at the gazebo, still deserted. Inside the telephone booth I fumbled in my pocket for one guilder and kwatjes coins. I supposed that I was being extra-paranoid in insisting on making the call from the box. The CIA had probably bugged every booth in the vicinity, but maybe they hadn't. At the hotel, they'd had to send downstairs for change: some hotshots.

They had let me out of the Krasnapolsky, following at a discreet distance. I had told them that I must meet Dee alone. They agreed to take me on trust. If you call trust bugging my overcoat and filling the Leidseplein with secret agents.

I breathed on the phone booth window, and cleared a little space with my glove. I couldn't spot anyone I knew. The Hotel Kabul switchboard took it's time about answering.

I asked for Herr Green's room and heard some clicks, and a slow beep beep. I hoped the microphones in the sheepskin were relaying all this back to the Agents. After a minute the operator told me there was no reply. Good.

Kim had got the message.

The CIA weren't the only ones with people out here on the streets this morning.

"My coat's bugged."

"You can get moth remover, Daniel." We kissed again, her mouth hot and hungry, cheeks cold and salty from the tears. Her familiar perfume triggered me off.

I held her in my arms, a vibrant figurine, her face framed in a silver fox hood, like Lara in Dr. Zhivago. I could feel her warmth beneath all the fur and sheepskin.

"If the coat's not bugged, then they're listening to us with parabolic microphones."

"Para what?" asked Dee, grinning up at me.

"Bolic."

"Sounds wonderful and speaking of bolics..."

339

She reached her hand down and tried to unzip my fly.

"Don't, my God. It'll get frostbite." I grabbed her arm.

"I hope that you haven't been doing anything naughty in that jail." Snowflakes swirled around us. Dee's eyes glistened, reflecting from the Christmas tree and her silver coat flashed multicolours as she moved. Below us on the canal, a moored barge rocked suddenly, sending ripples across the still water.

It was quieter here by the Lido.

"I made sure all my lovers had the aids test, dearie," I said.

"And you only screwed them if they were positive?"

"I'm not on a suicide mission."

The word mission broke the spell.

"Daniel, I've been followed since Austria."

"Good. There must be more CIA men out here tonight than snowflakes." A noise leapt from the moored barge. A thin stream of light speared the blackness, vanishing as the hatch re-closed.

"Why do they think you chose Amsterdam?" she asked. I walked her to the edge of the gazebo, her scent flooding my memory. Across the street a large pale coloured Mercedes had stopped at the edge of the pavement.

"I told them it was because I was crazy about hot chocolate and space cake."

"Speaking of space cake, I've got something for you." Dee pressed a packet into my hand. I slipped it in my pocket quickly. We kissed again and hugged tightly, our eyes closed. It had been a long time.

A large panel van pulled up behind the Mercedes. No one emerged from either vehicle.

"Whats next on your Magic Agenda, Daniel?"

"Come back to my hotel with me, spend the night."

"You don't mess about."

"We don't have time to, Dee."

"What about all the spooks?"

"They can watch each other, kid."

"As long as they're not watching us," she laughed. I looked across the street. The snowballing students were walking arm in arm singing, their voices carrying between hissing tyres.

"I told them it made sense if we were together tonight. They can give half their people the night off," I said.

"Or all their people half the night off," said Dee.

The rear doors of the panel van opened. Dark figures tumbled out. Below me the barge rocked again. Tell-tale ripples eddied across the surface of the canal .

"Daniel, you know that I was searched at customs and my hotel room has been hurricaned?"

I had expected that.

I thought I could see the tall man from the airport amongst the figures now, but I couldn't be sure.

I kissed her.

"Did they find anything, darling?" Her head lay on my shoulder. We rocked together in a mother and child reunion.

"Only the naughty underwear I bought in Vienna for my mum." Dee squeezed my arm, I turned around.

We were no longer alone.

A dozen men had materialised around us. They stood silent Easter Island figures, long coats flapping, faces in shadow. A shiver ran down my spine, not just from the cold.

Amsterdam is full of deep canals.

The barge was still in darkness. T held Dee close. I recognised my handler, holding his walkie talkie.

The Easter Island figures began to close in.

"They've been watching too many movies," said Dee

"I hope they're the kind where the hero's still alive in the last reel," I replied.

.....

"MARIJUANA?" exploded James Benedict Ampleforth the Second. "She handed him a package of marijuana?" His expression was incredulous.

"Not a very big one, sir."

"I don't give a fuck what size it is." The Deputy Director of the Central Intelligence Agency felt damp, cramped and cold in the barge, and his back ached. Operations were not his field. He was an Intelligence man, more at home with reports, digest, analysis, code traffic. He was out of condition for this schoolboy stuff.

The duty officer played with his communications equipment as the tapes rewound. They had heard Dee's voice clearly as she told Daniel that she had 'something' for him.

Ampleforth had given the order to move in.

The Agents had taken Dee and Daniel to the panel van, and strip-searched them. The DDI could now hear the English couple's angry protests relayed from the van. He heard Daniel insisting that they be taken back to the hotel and that they had no right to hold Dee.

"Goddamn, it isn't even a criminal offence to possess dope in this country," moaned the Deputy Director.

"What do we do, sir? Garrity is waiting for orders." Ampleforth removed a chased silver hip flask from the pocket of his cashmere overcoat, and disdaining the little silver cup, he swallowed a good belt of schnapps. The hot spirit only fuelled his anger. Damn those anti-Castro freaks. Why did he have to clear up their mess? He wished he were back in Langley studying NSA reconnaissance photos. The pain in his back was getting worse. He stretched out a leg and a spasm erupted in the base of his spine.

"Take them back to their fucking honeymoon suite at the Krasnapolsky," he snarled. The Englishman had outsmarted them. They had already raided the Hotel Kabul, the low budget rabbit warren next to the police station. His men had torn apart the room of 'Herr Green', the man whom the Englishman had phoned. Herr Green had left only a hardback edition of The Man Who Stole Portugal and the latest copy of the Vienna Kurier. Both were messages whose nuance was not lost on the CIA Chief. The Vienna Kurier stood ready to print damaging stories about Western intelligence agencies, and the book, a true story, ran uncomfortably close to the destabilisation plans the Agency had for Cuba. Had, until this Lieberman had intervened.

The Englishman had promised them the package

in the morning. He, Ampleforth, had jumped the gun.

Now they had to play this the Englishman's way. Everyone had assumed that the girl would bring the package from Austria.

Ampleforth sipped brandy. He should have figured on an accomplice. Herr Green's registration form was missing from the Hotel Kabul's reception. No one seemed to remember Herr Green or his nationality. Probably a few hundred guilders had changed hands. Ampleforth knew a blind alley when he saw one. The Englishman was good.

He had blown a truly clandestine operation.

The President had only found out about it when the Englishman had lifted a corner. Somehow the English girl had met the President and warned him, making a deal for the return of the plates. The Soviets and the Cubans would have a field day if 'Operation Reis' leaked. The Chief wouldn't be happy if Ampleforth muffed this one. There'd be dead jelly beans all over the Oval Office floor. His twenty-five year career in Intelligence lay on the brink of ruin. The DDI took another swig of brandy and stared at the blue and white 'Dutch Boy' scenes on the barge curtain.

A crackle of static came over the loudspeaker and he recognised Garrity's Bostonian tones. "Magpie wants his dope back." Magpie was their code name for the Englishman. Ampleforth nearly choked on his schnapps. He grabbed the microphone, losing his balance as he did so, causing the barge to rock violently. The Deputy Director of the Central Intelligence Agency was red faced as he screamed into the transmitter. "Give him his fucking marijuana back, Garrity, and tell him I hope it fucking well sends him loopy."

I open the bedroom doors. Dark Glasses and the Embalmer are seated at the dining table, cards scattered between them, guilder coins stacked in little piles. Embalmer's eyes widen as he sees my street clothes. "Going out?"

"If that's okay with you?"

"It's four o'clock in the morning."

"What are you, a spook or the speaking clock?" I ask. He doesn't smile. In my mind I sing childishly, 'Embalmer doesn't l-i-ike me. Embalmer could become a problem.' "I want to go for a walk." Dark Glasses sighs and stands up. "I'm going to have to come with you, Daniel."

"I'm leaving Dee here as a deposit."

"No matter," says Dark Glasses. "Do you want me to wake Charlie?" asks the Embalmer. "No need," replies the tall man. "Let him sleep." Confident bastard.

.....

The snow storm had stopped now and I walked down a narrow busy alley, Dark Glasses trailing me like an Asian wife. The clubs were still open and the streets were crowded with the mostly young. The establishments here had names like De Brit, Miami, Casino de Mer, Sam Sam. I pretended to pause and look at them all. It was into one called The Champ that I strolled. I worked my way around the boisterous drunks at the door and fell into the high noise level of a live jazz band. A black man who looked like the head of the UNESCO, but probably played better sax, accompanied a young girl pianist in a purple jumper. The music was north of Brazil/south of Texas.

It was a party atmosphere. Joints and drinks were flowing and the conversation was animated. By the musician sat a pale lady in a perfect Twenties outfit. The cellist resembled a landed lord on his night off.

I worked my way through the crowd and found an empty beer barrel serving as a bar stool. Squeezing in between a black woman in leather and a gaunt, thin faced young man wearing steel rimmed spectacles, I tried in vain to attract the barman's attention. After a few moments the thin faced man slid a glass in front of me.

"Cognac," he said.

"Cheers," I replied, picking up the glass and draining it.

"Nice schmutter," said the man, feeling my coat.

"Bugged," I said.

"That's handy," said the thin man. "Mind you, par for the course from the firm you're working with."

I eased the sheepskin off and passed him the coat, which he folded and put next to a loudspeaker.

Kim Reilly had been a friend of mine since school. Once one of the ablest and most sought-after cat burglars in London, he had retired after a particularly spectacular silver theft from a stately home. He'd come out for me as a favour. It was Kim who had met Dee in the Austrian bank, collected the currency plates from her in the ladies toilet whilst dressed in drag and had smuggled them to Holland inside the Rolleiflex camera, dressed as a man. Kim was loving every minute.

The barman brought us two more cognacs. Kim's spectacles flashed as he scanned the club.

He raised his glass and muttered out of the side of his mouth;

"Is the moody ice-cream in the dark bins yours?"

"I'm afraid so, old son," I replied.

I love Kim's slang, it's what we used years ago.

Recently we'd seen a very learned exchange of opinions in the 'Letters' column of the London Times, with various bods pontificating as to the origin of the expression 'Old Bill' as slang for the police amongst the criminal classes.

When the London CID first got plainclothed Q-cars Kim noticed they had sequential BYL registration numbers.

I remember Kim saying 'Here's Old Bill again' whenever a Q-car appeared. That's how the expression was born. Kim invented it.

"Where do they get these people from?" asked Kim eyeing Dark Glasses. "Central Casting?"

"You should see the rest of the team."

"I'd love to, Dan. Beats sitting at home watching the tropical fish."

AMSTERDAM
HOLLAND
JANUARY

It took me a few moments to realize that the molten gold pouring under the curtains was Dutch sunshine. I touched the sweet softness of Dee; scented, warm and asleep. There was a discreet tap on the door and a not so discreet head peered round like a coconut at a carnival.

Charlie, my CIA handler.

"There's a messenger downstairs at reception."

"Send him up," I said.

"He won't come up," said Charlie. "He says his instructions are to meet you in the lobby in public." Charlie grinned.

I stumbled out of the bed, dizzy from sex, drugs and cognac. The room tilted. I staggered into the bathroom.

Zombie moments later, showered and dressed, I stood amongst the jewellery displays and scattered spooks adorning Hotel Krasnapolsky's lobby.

I platzed by Reception whilst two elderly Americans in new raincoats obtained canal ride tickets from the concierge.

"Ah, Mijnheer Lieberman. There is one koerier waiting for you, sir."

"So I've been told. Where is he, please?" I'm always polite. I was having a wonderful time in Holland, such a change from the nick.

"But he was here one moment ago."

I began to feel disturbed. Was this a ruse to get my body down into the lobby? To get me out of my well guarded room into a public place? Where was the mysterious messenger?

Charlie and the CIA boys were looking at each other blankly. Embalmer gripped my arm and began to back me towards the lift. Everyone started reaching inside their jackets. Except me.

I was wearing a pullover.

The concierge was at a loss to explain the vanishing messenger. Charlie punched lift buttons. The ladies' room door next to us opened suddenly and a figure in motorcycle leathers emerged, the face obscured by the tinted visor of a crash helmet.

Embalmer drew his gun. The figure in the visor ignored him and kept moving towards me, Charlie and the lift were behind me. My back against the wall. There was nowhere for me to go. I started to say the 'Shema' silently. The Jewish prayer for when your life is in danger. A muffled voice came from within the helmet.

"Mijnheer Lieberman?" A hand went up to the visor and struggled with the strap. The lobby was very still. I wished I had been kinder to my mother. I was conscious of Embalmer's drawn gun. I'm going to get shot here, I thought. This'll teach me to play spooks, when I could have been safely tucked up in jail.

Why didn't Embalmer shoot?

The helmet came off and a pretty freckled face appeared shaking loose a bundle of auburn curls.

"Ah, yes. You are Heer Lieberman. I have seen your photograph."

Had she? This must be Kim the thief's work.

"And who might you be, my dear?" I said.

"My name is Elsa. I am motorcycle koerier. I am sorry I must to use the toilet. I have a package to deliver to you. Do you have identification?"

I turned to Charlie, who had been following the whole conversation. "My passport please."

Charlie reached into his inside pocket and passed me the document. Elsa examined it scrupulously. She would have made a good immigration inspector.

"Ah yes. Please will you sign here, Heer Lieberman." She held out a pad and pen.

"But I haven't received anything yet." I took the pad.

"Of course not," she smiled, one black glove came off revealing a slim hand. Fascinated, I watched the scarlet fingernails unzip a pouch on her leather trousers. The fingers extracted a brown wrapped packet. I signed the courier company pad. She passed me the packet. I thanked her and gave her fifty guilders. CIA expenses, what the hell. She smiled. She was a lovely, young, healthy thing with a wonderful smile.

As Charlie and the Embalmer moved me towards the lift I saw Dark Glasses questioning her. Much change would they get from her. Charlie relieved me of the package in the lift.

Up in the room I watched Charlie the Handler rip it open. He turned on me accusingly.

"There's only one plate in here." His face was furious.

"Don't shout at me, Charlie. That one plate does two things," I said. "It shows my good faith and it

350

stops anybody from printing the Cuban currency. You can have the other plate and the location of the gold as soon as I know Dee is free in England."

Embalmer made as if to speak. Charlie silenced him with a wave of his hand.

"She's going to be charged by the English police."

"And bailed, Charlie. I don't want you people interfering with that." The CIA man would have thrown his hands up in the air if he hadn't been holding the plate.

"You don't have to play these games with us, Daniel. You have the letter. You've made your deal with the U.S. Government."

That's what worries me, I thought. But I said nothing.

"And I'm sticking to it, Charlie. You get the rest when Dee is home free."

I noticed no one had mentioned the uncut diamonds.

FEDERAL COURTHOUSE
MIAMI
FLORIDA
FEBRUARY

"Can I believe this?"

Louis the Lawyer looks tanned and prosperous. He stops shuffling papers and taps the document I am holding.

"In that letter, the United States Government states that they'll let you go. No one else is to be charged. You're a lucky guy, Dan. Excuse me now. I have to talk to the prosecutor."

The court is bright, oak panelled and full of people. There's a rolled Stars and Stripes and a golden Federal Seal. All very kosher. The neon lights make me squint. A marshal gently takes my arm, and leads me to a wooden corral that would not restrain a lethargic sheep.

Court officials, lawyers from other cases and witnesses mill about. Louis is deep in conversation with an earnest young man.

Suddenly I catch sight of Stuart doing a boiling kettle act. He's obviously heard about my deal. Kathy rests a hand on his arm, and whispers urgently into his ear.

What are they doing here?

Louis the Lawyer approaches with the earnest one who sticks out a hand.

"Ed Brewer," says Ed Brewer.

"Ed is from the U.S. Attorney's office," says Louis. "He's the prosecutor." I bid him good morning.

"What happens today?" I ask Louis.

He turns to the prosecutor who says, "You will plead guilty, Mr. Lieberman. The judge will know that you have co-operated fully with the highest levels of the United States Government and returned the gold."

"And everything else?" Across the room Falkman and Kathy are talking to a man in a loud check suit.

"No mention will be made of the other matters," the prosecutor continues. "You will be sentenced to time served and deportation."

Louis nods. He likes a secret deal.

The check suit man has moved away from Falkman and is talking to the clerk of the court.

The clerk nods at Check Suit like a back-of-the-car window dog. I decided to give Brewer some stick. The prosecutor is full of shit. They all are.

"Nothing you've told me sets me free." He doesn't like that.

"You have your letter from the Government, Mr. Lieberman."

"Everyone keeps on about the bloody letter—it's a piece of paper," I say.

"Now, Daniel, now," says Louis.

Check Suit is really blowing down the clerk's ear now.

I must have looked worried because Louis the Lawyer told me not to worry.

"Okay," I said. "I won't fight the programme."

Louis nods, and moves away in conversation

353

with Brewer.

I watch as the clerk disappears through the oak panelling, a cheap demon at the pantomime. No smoke.

Someone pokes me sharply in the back. I turn and find myself face to face with Falkman. Bailiff's man or the back half of a panto horse?

This is going to be boring.

"I'm going to see you get ten years in jail," hisses the jeweller, "and then another ten on the alligator swamps." My God. The CIA Theatre School Road Show. He's boiling.

"Don't overdo the act, Stuart," I say loudly.

Heads turn. The cop stirs uneasily, but does nothing. My lawyer moves next to me. Much good may that do.

"There's no need for this, Mr. Falkman," says Louis.

"I hope you ROT in that jail, you thief," Stuart yelling now. My God. He's going for a clandestine Oscar here today.

"I may go to jail," I say. "If I do, I'll exercise, lose bundles of weight, get fit and read. I'll see you in there after your insurance company do you for swindling them. The FBI want to talk to you now, you clown, for claiming double." That'll show him.

The jeweller looks like he's going to take a swing at me, his arm giving thirty-one days' notice by registered post. I move nearer to Louis.

"Where's the rest of my gold, you sonofabitch," he yells as he lunges at me. One of the U.S. marshals moves up to us.

I step hastily behind my lawyer. I wonder whose

benefit all this is for.

Check Suit is still lurking in the well of the court talking to Kathy. Who the hell is he?

The marshal leads me back to the defendant's bench. Why does Falkman think that I'm going to jail? Haven't his Agency bosses told him the deal? Surely it's all an act.

Above the hubbub a voice sings;

"All rise."

We rise in a hush. Kathy, pretty in pink, is dabbing at Falkman's sweating face with a handkerchief. A door opens behind the empty dais.

The clerk scurries out pursued by a little wizened old man. A suntanned turtle in black robes.

His Honour the Judge.

Everybody gonna do time today.

The old judge seats himself. The clerk says, "The Federal Court of the Florida District of the United States of America is now in session." I hope the judge will rap his gavel.

He doesn't.

The clerk sings out:

"Case of the United States of America versus Daniel Lieberman.

An uneven match. I don't have a submarine, missiles or billions of dollars. Why pick on me to fight, USA? Get someone your own size!

Red Admirals dive bomb my stomach. Clerk and Check Suit are head to head. Clerk reassures Check Suit. On the bench the judge takes out a gold pencil and marks papers. Maybe he's moonlighting as a teacher. Check Suit shakes hands with the clerk as he leaves.

Who the hell was he?

My name is called, the marshal leads me to the defendant's box where I stand and face the judge.

The old turtle is now wearing half moon spectacles, over the top of which two watery marbles pinion me.

My head feels funny. I don't like the vibes. Come on Turtle-judge. Get on with the charade. I touch the government letter in my pocket for reassurance, a paper talisman. The tension in court has tripwire quality.

The stenographer's machine clatters as the clerk reads the charges and asks how I plead.

Concentrate, son. This is your line.

I look straight into the Turtle's reptile eyes with sincerity. Just the right theatre school catch in my voice, as I tell him (breathe):

"Guilty," (pause) "Your Honour." I cast my eyes downward. No applause. A general murmur breaks out, rhubarb rhubarb. I risk a glance back up the dais. The judge is staring at me. He hasn't moved. I'm a specimen being examined under an x-ray microscope. My feet ache. Surely the old Turtle must let me sit down. He can see the size of me.

I glance at Falkman. Falkman glares back.

My lawyer finishes speaking and sits.

Suddenly, Turtle acknowledges me. "Sit down."

I sit in relief.

Turtle is reading the clerk's paper now and mutters to Clerk. Clerk says:

"The defendant will now rise."

I rise. The backs of the judge's hands are mottled with liver spots. He must be eighty years old, if he's a day. Frail spider fingers toy with a slim gold pencil. The court is very still.

"Daniel Mordecai Lieberman." I look the old Turtle straight in the eye. "You cannot come over here, rob our citizens, and then think you may simply return your ill gotten gains and go free. You will go to the Federal Penitentiary for two years."

My head reels.

Turtle raps his gavel, stands up and moves off stage.

"All RISE," calls the clerk.

The old Turtle sweeps through the door. Black robes like verminous beetle wings billow behind him. Dazed, I feel handcuffs closing on me.

I look for Louis in the spinning carousel that the court has become.

Across the court, Falkman's face is twisted in a triumphal grin. I'm falling in an out of control elevator. I've been shafted by the government, the CIA, by Falkman, the Justice Department, the FBI, my own lawyer, everyone. If I were Julius Caesar, there wouldn't have been room for all the knives.

Louis the Lawyer puts his hand on my shoulder. "I'm sorry, Daniel. This shouldn't have happened. We'll appeal. I'll see you downstairs." Still in shock I am taken down to the pit by an iron barred flight of steps. Back in jail where the hack locks me in a cell. Three black men stare into space waiting for Godot. They get me. "How long, man?" One looks at me, a flicker of interest for a moment. My parched lips find the words. It's difficult to get my mouth around them. "Two years." The black man spits on the cell floor, his interest dying. "Shit and a shave, man. I got thirty." There's no reply to

357

that. Still, two years is a long shit and shave.

STATE COURTHOUSE
FLORIDA
FEBRUARY
SAME DAY

I've returned a million dollars on the strength of a letter from the American Government, saved the CIA and the President from the biggest embarrassment since the Bay of Pigs and Watergate and they've screwed me. Two years! I could die in prison.

Maybe that's the idea.

A rattle of keys at the door. A guard appears consulting a clipboard. I know it's for me. A flicker of hope that the judge is calling me back soon dies. Some ESP. Here I am. Kafka out of a cornflakes packet, the poor man's Solzhenitsyn. Back in the world of guards and keys. The hack wants me.

"Which one of you guys is Lieberman?"

The old script. No one moves. The Tell the Truth game. I stand up.

"I have to wait to see my lawyer," I say to this bastard.

"You can see him in court."

"What's going on? I've just been to court. This must be a mistake."

Famous last words.

The guard consults his clipboard. "You're down here for an appearance right now in State Court. Come with me."

"This can't be right."

"They all say that, son."

The State Court? What the hell is this?

I follow the man down the corridor. At the end another guard motions me through an open steel door. The bastard hack undoes the cuffs. Three grey suited guards surround me in a tiny iron walled chamber. I rub my wrists. Do I get beaten up here or what?

The room starts moving. We are in a steel elevator! No one speaks as we descend. I try again.

"My lawyer was coming down to see me back there!"

A silver-haired hack gives me an interested look. My accent.

"Most likely he'll be in court, son," his voice not unkind.

I don't fancy this at all.

"Court? What court?"

The steel room stops. Silver Hair opens the door.

"State Court."

I step into a tunnel of shock. Thirty men are chained together with cuffs and leg irons. Like extras for Spartacus. I didn't know they had galley slaves in Florida. In the tunnel's gloom, we are surrounded by armed police.

I've died and gone to hell.

I'm asleep and dreaming; this is a nightmare and tomorrow I'll wake up in England like the CIA promised me.

It's no dream.

The shackles are real.

They handcuff and belly chain me and run a lead chain through my arms. The doomed battalion, we shuffle down the black tube.

I just don't believe it. Where's Dante?

We are denizens of another world. Far above us, laughing citizens drive convertibles in sunlight. Below, in the part of Florida the tourist never sees, shackled slaves shuffle through a warren of tunnels designed for security, not style. As we clank along, we stop occasionally, unshackling a slave here and there. All disappear through barred gates.

Talk about culture shock.

One minute I'm in a lounge suit in the civilised atmosphere of court, chatting to my lawyer, perfumed women bustling about. Then I'm stumbling in irons among subterranean sewers.

What will they do to me in the next court? Alligator swamps?

The column stops. My original hack miraculously appears and I am unchained. I follow him through doors. Someone's made a fortune down here from the riveting contract on the ironwork.

Up we go in the elevator. A door opens with a searing burst of light and I find myself in another court.

This one has a high green ceiling. The flag of the State of Florida furled next to the Stars and Stripes. I am led into the prisoner's box. This court is packed. A young man in black robes sits on the judge's bench. White face, rat-trap mouth, horn-rimmed spectacles. I catch the flash of a pink dress high up in the public balcony. A recognisable snatch of Falkman's gruff voice drifts down. No sign of Louis the Lawyer. Same B picture. Same lousy script. Different actors. Same star. Me. Clerks, stenographer, prosecutors and policemen.

Everyone but my bloody lawyer. I don't have my copy of the script or any friends in this room. "The defendant will rise." Here we go. The clerk says, "State of Florida versus Daniel Lieberman. You are charged with Grand Larceny contrary to the laws of this state." Another even bout. "Surely this is double jeopardy? I can't be tried twice for the same crime." I have spoken out loud. The young judge looks at me. "Are you Daniel Mordecai Lieberman?" "Yes, Sir." "Then there's no double jeopardy." Oh. I rattle on. "But my lawyer is not here." "No matter," says the judge frowning. "This hearing will proceed." This is America? The judge speaks. "Your guilty plea in the Federal Court today is accepted by the State of Florida and is sufficient for verdict of guilty to be brought in this court. That verdict is so brought." Is this a trial or a horror show? No jury? No defence lawyer? Rat Trap continues: "Daniel Mordecai Lieberman, I sentence you to serve the maximum term of five years in the state penitentiary. This sentence to run consecutively to the two years term passed upon you this morning in the Federal Court." I am numb with shock.

I feel like crying. I see Falkman in the public gallery bursting with triumph. Seven years in prison. If they let me live that long.

CIA HEADQUARTERS
LANGLEY
VIRGINIA
FEBRUARY

"Democracy has to be defended in the jungles of Nicaragua, in the high passes of the Khyber, the gates of West Berlin and right here in Langley, Garrity."

James Benedict Ampleforth the Second bent his elegantly clad patrician frame to the machine and placed his eye in the scanner beside the Intelligence Section's door.

"I was at the White House dinner with Mrs. Ampleforth last night, and I don't mind telling you, Garrity, I partook of more than one glass of the President's Californian Cabernet. I just hope this half million dollar eye scanner can handle blood-shot."

Garrity, who had sunk a fair amount of Bushmills whiskey himself the previous evening, although in the less august surroundings of Betty's Bar in downtown D.C., shared his chief's hope that the machine was intelligent about such human failings.

Ampleforth straightened up and punched his personal code number into the concealed box. There was a pause, then a green light shone while electronic locks released themselves. Garrity waited on the far side of the pressure pad until his chief had passed through the first door, before bending forward to apply his own eye to the scanner.

The Deputy Director (Intelligence) paced up and down on the (Aubusson) carpet, a gift from his wife, and spoke whilst chewing on his (American) cigar.

"The Englishman has made a fool out of the CIA." Ampleforth counted points off on his fingers. "He penetrated a clandestine network, ruined a key de-stabilization operation, set back our anti-Castro programme by years. He has gained knowledge of our most closely held Contra secrets. And last but not least, he attempted to blackmail this Agency."

His boss thundered on as if addressing a Daughters of the American Revolution Meeting. Garrity wished he'd taken painkillers. Ampleforth's gung ho mood always made his temples throb.

The DDI continued. "Thanks to the fortitude and patriotism of a Federal Judge, this criminal is in the penitentiary where he belongs!"

Ampleforth paused by the giant picture window to gaze at the rolling greenery. His hands, immaculately cuffed in white linen, rested lightly on the sill. Small clouds of breath discoloured the green armour plate glass as he spoke. The DDI raised his voice as he drew back from the window.

"That English swindler possesses knowledge which is a danger to our glorious free country." The Director gestured through the bulletproof glass at the Doberman patrolled CIA forests beyond.

"Prisons are dangerous places, Garrity. Accidents can happen to a man in the penitentiary. An inmate can die in a fight, or slip on a bar of soap in the shower and crack his skull." The Intelligence Chief paused and fixed his Senior Co-ordinator with a penetrating stare.

Garrity had been with the CIA long enough to recognise the Henry the Second approach to murder. No direct instruction would be given. This execution came under the 'Will no one revenge me of the injuries I have sustained from one turbulent priest?' Act of 1170. The 'Thomas à Becket' System.

However, Patrick Xavier Garrity had also been long enough in the Service to recognise the type of blood that may not wash off. Especially that spilled in the DDI's electronically sensitive office.

"Forgive me for mentioning this, Sir, but didn't the President forbid erasure in the matter of the Englishman?"

"Don't pussyfoot around with ME, Garrity" Ampleforth shouted, slamming his hand down on the teak desk. "We're here to carry out the President's wishes as well as his orders. The Commander-in-Chief did not want a problem with the Englishman whilst he was free and those...." The DDI paused, also aware of whirling unreachable tapes. "Those things were in his hands."

Garrity sat silent as the Deputy Director pursued his point.

"Now that they have been safely returned to the Agency and destroyed, our only danger comes from the Englishman's tongue. Thanks to that fat criminal, a brilliantly conceived operation costing millions of dollars has been aborted. There's a lot of anger among our Cuban friends. They have their own people in the prison system. A small bureaucratic detail could transfer one of them. We need not be directly involved. We must encourage them to satisfy their Latin need for la revenga."

The Spanish word slipped surprisingly easily from Ampleforth's aristocratic lips.

"Our Cubans must not lose faith in us, Patrick."

Garrity shifted uncomfortably in the leather armchair and drew a deep breath, anticipating the older man's explosive response to his next request.

"I would need a direct written order from you, sir."

The eruption never came, With calm deliberation the Deputy Director extracted a slim silver pen from his pocket and turning the Englishman's purple file to the last page, he wrote, RECOMMENDED ACTION: ERASURE then signed his name and rank. The DDI closed the file and held it out to his Senior Co-ordinator.

"No problems please, Patrick. This is election year after all."

IN LIMBO TO TEXAS
MARCH

"Don't do the crime, if you can't do the time."

The black man chained to me shakes his head as he hangs it downward.

The jail on wheels rumbles through the night.

This is all a mistake. We centipede our way across Alabama. The nineteen-fifties single decker seems like it was last cleaned when Eisenhower was on the throne.

Its cargo? Human. Chained wrist and ankle. Dress? Scraps of army surplus clothing. Destination? The penitentiary.

There are forty of us on board the prison bus, smoking, cursing and coughing. Most too tired or subdued to talk. All of us hungry, thirsty, ill, filthy. American government prisoners on the move. All colours, shapes and sizes. The black guy sticks a cigarette in my mouth, and deftly lights us up, juggling his shackles.

We are the enemies of the Regime. The dispossessed, the weary. Chicanoes, Blacks, Italians. Homoeopathic doctors, illegal immigrants, mafioso, communists, horse race fixers. Drug dealers, murderers, thieves. Sex offenders, disgraced politicians, crooked lawyers. The profitable enemies of Uncle Sam. Necessary opponents of a perfect regime. The black man I am chained to tells me that the U.S. keeps an average of 2,500 men in transit at anytime. A whole industry, employing guards, coaches, planes, trains, marshals and stop-over jails.

This is all a mistake.

It's not happening.

But it is.

I should be on a jumbo jet heading for England. My lawyer told me I was going to be free and clear. The U.S. Government promised freedom.

Not chains.

So what the fuck am I doing chained up heading for prison in Texas, for God's sake?

Seven years. That's what I'm doing.

How could it happen to me? I never felt so low or depressed in my life.

Five days earlier, I am stripped and finger-printed, deloused, medically examined, my hair has been cropped, I have my photograph taken holding a number under my chin. Don't ask me the number.

My clothes are taken from me, even my under-wear. I am dressed in ragged, torn army surplus. My too-small trousers are bursting open, my bare feet are crammed in shoes made of black plastic. A belly chain is slung around my waist and ankle chains hold my legs, my hands are cuffed.

Apart from that little lot, I'm as free as a bird.

Save for what my mother used to call 'catlick washes', I haven't been able to clean myself in five days. The man I am chained to stinks. I can't smell much better myself.

What will prison be like? Not the George V in Paris.

I have lapsed into bouts of feverish sleep. Now I awake on the last stage of the trek from Talahassee, Florida, to Texarkana, Texas. I have no idea what to expect from an American penitentiary. I remember snatches of old Jimmy Cagney movies watched snug in my parents' house years before.

As we lurch through Alabama, my dreams return once more to family Sunday afternoons in the English suburbs. Billy Cotton Bandshow on the radio. Round the Horne. Roast beef, fresh green peas, roast potatoes and Yorkshire pudding. Watching Robert Mitchum win the war or Jimmy Cagney on the prison yard.

I am lost in dreams, riding across the Salisbury Plain. My father beside me at the wheel of his Jaguar. I am in Jamaica swimming with Dee and she is laughing, splashing water at my face. We will dive among the corals.

The bus jerks me back to reality.

I wake up.

Seven years.

Christ, it's a lifetime.

It can't be real.

But it is.

There comes a murmuring, a subtle awareness of destination arrived at. I have settled into a weary acceptance. I want to prolong the journey believing that, 'It is better to travel hopefully than to arrive.'

My limbo ends as the penitentiary looms out of the darkness.

Belsen.

Texas style.

Eerily lit in that cruel neon and sodium that institutions adore, the prison brings on the horrors.

Blood, bars, bullets. An ice-wave of fear knifes

me. This is really happening. How did a nice Jewish boy like me wake up to this? My generation had escaped the Holocaust.

I've found my own concentration camp.

A harsh cold penal settlement set in nowhere. The architecture? Hell in 'thirties bleak.

Beyond the barbed wire, I see silhouettes of dogs and men. Searchlights rake the bus, dazzling us. Figures holding rifles stand at the perimeter fence. Up in the towers, the guards wear halos of neon rain on their hoods and capes, their faces hidden in shadow, breath coming out in clouds.

The penitentiary is on 'alert'. This is an arrival. A security problem. Prisoners moving at night. Open gates. Risk.

The prison gate closes behind us. Immobile guards monitor our progress, their straining Alsations slaver beneath flickering searchlights.

My God. This is not a prison from Universal Studios. No Hollywood happy-Sunday-afternoon-cheap-thrill this. This is the real thing. Accept no substitute. High walls, shotguns, searchlights. Like the movies, except for one thing.

Me. I'm here. It's real. I could die in here.

The bus rolls into a sodium lit courtyard glistening from the night rain. More guards stand around cradling weapons. Beside them Dobermans and Alsations bark and leap viciously to the limit of their leashes. I hope I'm not the dog's breakfast. I feel like one. The bus stops. Two guards amble to the steps and point shotguns at the open door.

We stumble out.

My ankle chains snag at the doorway as I shuffle forward doing my Marley number. I lose my footing and fall down the steps. I throw my shackled hands forward to protect myself, but I hit the concrete heavily and lie dazed. I am bleeding and soaked. My shirt rucks up, exposing my bare skin to the gravel. Dogs lurch forward barking angrily. Guards stand around. No one helps me.

A torch in my eyes dazzles me. I struggle back up and follow the others.

Who has a choice? My knee is in agony. Blood, trickling from my cut face and oozing out of my badly grazed elbow, seeps through my mud soaked shirt.

A light dazzles me again. I make out a huge belly stuffed into a belt and trousers.

"You're one sorry sonofabitch!" The belly turns. "Send this one through to Medical. He fell off the goddamn bus!" I glimpse the name Smith on a plastic badge. "Thank you," I mutter.

The shoulders of the open cape are soaked. He's been out here for some time.

I am led away to the Medical Wing.

It's warmer here. A young white coated man sits me down by a table and examines me. An eye chart is tacked up next to a notice about AIDS in six languages. Taking scissors he begins to cut away at my rags.

"SMILEY!" he yells.

"Yeah, Doc." A prisoner appears in a crisp shirt, a knife-edge crease to his trousers and shining shoes.

"Get this man some pants and a shirt from Reception."

"Yessir."

The doctor turns to look at me.

"Relax, son," he says. "Just relax."

Patched up, I am returned to the others in the holding room. We are given plastic coffee cups and the ubiquitous federal Bologna sandwiches.

There is a toilet at one end of the room and the forty of us queue.

This place isn't quite as uncivilized as I imagined.

It's worse.

Evil, cold strangers mill around me.

How the hell can I stand seven years here?

I was putting up my few possessions by my bedspace. A parcel had been forwarded from Broward County Jail. Inside was an old photo of Dee in London, poised in mink on the bonnet of my Rolls Royce. I had made a small wooden frame for the picture. As I propped the photo on the locker beside the bed, a black man detached himself from a group of card players. He was young, fit and alert. He perched on the end of my bed and picked up Dee's picture. "Some lady, some wheels. That your lady, man?" "Yeah, she's coming here tonight." The young black man chuckled. "That your car, man? What kind is that?"

"It's a Rolls Royce."

"Shit, man. I never met nobody with a Rolls Royce before."

"Well you ain't met one now. The cops took it." He laughed again. "Shit, man. I can tell you gonna get another. Where you from, man?"

"London."

"London, England?"

"Yes."

"Shit." The black man stuck out his hand. "Makepeace. Friends call me R.D. I never met anyone from England." I introduced myself. He crossed the big cell and returned carrying cold orange juice and a pack of smokes. We talked for a while.

R.D. Makepeace was a 23 year old gunslinger from Fort Worth, Texas, doing eight years for armed robbery. He told me that he had been in and out of jails since he was fourteen.

"Everyone uses guns in my family. My daddy shot me, I shot my daddy and my mama shot both of us."

"Well, I've never used a gun, R.D."

"Shit, man. How you steal any money?"

"Conversation."

The black Texan let out a whoop.

"You one bad motherfucker, man. Con-ver-sa-tion." He quadrupled the word. "Say, man. You gotta a running partner?"

"A what?" I said. Vague memories of an identical question in New York, a lifetime ago jarred at the back of mind.

"A running partner, man. Someone to watch your ass. You can't survive in the penitentiary on your own, man. Someone gonna rob you, shank you or fuck you."

"Nobody's done those three things to me so far," I said. He smiled as he replaced the photo gently on the locker top.

"Daniel, I like the way you are. You want me to be your running partner?" He gave me a searching look from two clear brown eyes.

"That's very kind of you, R.D. Yes, please."

"Partner," said R.D.

"Partner," I replied, gripping his hand.

It was a good job I did accept R.D.'s offer. Later

on that handshake saved my life.

I put the phone down after talking to Dee. It was the first proper conversation I'd been able to have with her since I was sentenced. She was shocked at what had happened to me. At the same time she was nervous. Whilst staying at her ex-husband's cottage on the Earlswood Lakes, she had noticed that two men were following her. I told her to contact Kim so he could follow them and find out who they were. Her voice was soft as she said good-bye.

Her husband had stood bail and hired top defence lawyers for her on one condition.

Dee must have nothing more to do with me.

FCI
TEXARKANA
MARCH

"Our government shafted you, Daniel," Jack Heim told me under the brooding eyes of the armed guards in the watch towers. As we walked to the exercise yard the old man slid open his leather cigar case and offered me a huge Havanah.

"As soon as I heard, I asked for you be sent out here to Texas with me. Someone has to look after you."

So Jack had had me transferred. It didn't surprise me. The man had more power than government departments.

The whole scene still felt unreal. The barbed wire, walls, dogs, searchlights. This was no dream but a waking nightmare.

There were around a thousand men in FCI Texarkana. Say three hundred Blacks, three hundred Chicanos, three hundred hillbillies, ninety-eight Italians and since I had joined Jack, two Jews.

We walked round and round the yard in our U.S. Army fatigues. About us men played chess, jogged or lifted weights in the crowded area. The old man puffed on a Partagas Lusitania. Despite the U.S. ban on Cuban Imports, it was typical of Jack Heim to have a box of Havanas here in jail.

I nipped the end off my cigar and tapped my pockets for a light. Jack passed me his lighter as he spoke.

"Your attorney tried, Daniel. It seems to me that the anti-Castro people were pretty pissed off with you. They got a sympathetic judge and your deal fell through the ice."

"But surely the government letter should have bound the judge."

"It should have done, Daniel. But under the checks and balances of our constitution, judges don't take orders from the government.

Voices exploded ahead of us.

A fight had broken out on the yard, but it was over before it had begun, the combatants pulled apart by onlookers.

"Will my appeal have any chance, Jack?"

The old man stared beyond the wire. I cupped my hands around his lighter, a gold and Laque de Chine Dupont. Everyone else in the jail used matches. The cigar singed as my godfather replied.

"Yes, Daniel. I believe the appeal can succeed. You put your neck on the line for our government, returned the plates to the CIA, and saved the States a lot of embarrassment with the Soviet Union and Cuba." We paused by the wire. A Texan cornfield stretched away, dotted with little yellow markers. They said the guard couldn't shoot at you if you made it beyond the yellow marker—but no one had ever made it.

"And they fucked me." I had the cigar well alight now.

"The Agency were yammering in the prosecutor's ear, they were pissed off with you—once you gave up the plates you had no leverage, and you kept the diamonds. Plus, you know about the white business."

Jack tapped his nose and replaced the Dupont back in his pocket. I didn't need to ask him how the trials had been fixed. The CIA had reached the judges. Heim's lawyers in Florida and Washington had been tracking the progress of the case, and Jack had had me shipped out to Texas through connections in the prison department. The old man had promised to help my appeal. His people couldn't appear officially, so we were doing everything through Lazy Louis.

My lawyer didn't know who was pulling his strings.

"I'll take you down to the library, Daniel. There's a charming attorney there. Serving five years for faking evidence! He's just the man to help you with your affidavit."

Suddenly, Jack's eyes shut, and his face became bright red. He doubled over and emitted a sound like two gorillas strangling each other.

I realised Jack was laughing.

A Texas bee was doing an electric shaver impersonation around my head as I woke up. Today I
was due for O and I. Orientation and Induction.
R.D. had elected to be my guide, and as I stood
under the hot showers, I felt that maybe this prison
wasn't so bad after all. At least I would stay in one
place; there were clean clothes here, decent food,
they let you use the telephone if someone would
accept the charges. There were law library facilities to fight my appeal. And most important of all,
my 'godfather' Jack Heim was here. I was due to
see him later. Right now I showered.

"You are one fat sucker!" R.D.'s voice echoed
against the washroom tiles.

"Listen. This stomach cost me thousands of dollars, R.D."

"Well, you gonna get rid of it. We gonna get you
weightlifting, exercising and running." The black
man bounced around the shower room, leaping in
the air making short jabbing punches, doing a Mohammed Ali.

"First we got to get you some duds, sucker." This
was true. I was so fat that the night I had arrived
they couldn't find a pair of trousers big enough to
go around my waist.

"Goddamn," the reception man had said. "We

got six thousand pairs of pants here from the U.S. Army and I can't find any to fit you."

R.D. was taking me to the tailor shop this morning, where for two packs of cigarettes I would be kitted out with decent shirts, handmade trousers, fresh socks, shoes. If you didn't pay the two packs you were a bum and finished up in rags.

Somehow I'd been adopted by R.D. and Jack. Two men at the opposite ends of the American dream spectrum. Jack, the sophisticated industrialist, serving time for nine million dollars' worth of tax evasion: R.D., the black gunslinger, doing his stretch for armed robbery.

From the tailor's shop, shaved, showered, crisply dressed and smoking a five cent White Owl cigar, I walked tall down to the Education Room.

Here, in common with the thirty or so intake, I sat down to fill in the personality indicator and general intelligence tests. There were endless forms and they gave you a pencil. You simply put a dot against your chosen answers. The U.S. Government then takes the forms and runs them under a scanner. The location of the dots is supposed to indicate if you are psychotic or whatever.

One question posed, "Are you a messenger from God?"

Of course, I dotted the 'yes' box.

Afterwards when I told R.D. what I had done, he said they would classify me as mad.

As I finished my general intelligence test ahead of the rest of the class, I was allowed out early to join my black friend waiting in the corridor.

R.D. was a cleaner, he told me: "That's the best job, man. You can wander anywhere on the compound and you get to carry things and shit like that, so you can hide things. If a hack ask me what I'm doing anywhere, I say I'm the cleaner, man."

I decided to become a cleaner.

"It's tough to get on the cleaners," said R.D. "Everybody got their name down. You're going to have to start off in the laundry, sorting socks with the other suckers. But right now I'm going to show you the rest of the joint, man."

I followed R.D. down endless corridors, my new shoes squeaking on the immaculate linoleum. The young Texan opened a huge double door. A cacophony of sound assaulted my eardrums.

"These are the rehabilitation workshops, man," R.D yelled. "They repair trucks here, teach you how to fix engines." We walked through the huge workshop as inmates toiled busily on several old vehicles. My new friend stopped by a red Ford truck where a pair of legs and a back disappeared under the hood. R.D. slapped the man's bottom, yelling, "Git your head out of there, sucker. I want you to meet someone."

A tall, young black man emerged. There was an awful lot of him. The anger on his face changed to a wide grin as he recognised R.D.

"Say, R.D. Makepeace. What you doin' here man?"

"Zoots. I want you to meet Daniel, from London, England.

The tall mechanic grinned, holding out an oily hand apologetically. I shook it in the soul brother grip.

Oil squelched through my fingers.

"Delighted to meet you, Mr. Zoots," I said.

"Hot dog," said Zoots, "don't he talk funny."
The young man was powerfully built and towered
above us both.

"That's how they talk in London, England," said
R.D.

"Well, shit," said Zoots. "You're the first Englishman I ever met."

"I'm the best one you'll meet as well, Zoots."

"Hot shit," said Zoots.

"Get me high, brother," murmured R.D.

The black mechanic's eyes darted around the
workshop.

"It's cool, man, it's cool," R.D. assured him.
Zoots leant a shoulder forward.

"There's a jay in my shirt pocket man. I can't
take it out 'cos my hands is all greasy."

In the hot sunlit yard behind the workshop, we
smoked our joint sitting in an ancient Ford Edsel
that would never cruise the Texas highways again.
Zoots behind the wheel.

"Shit, man," exploded Zoots. "I got two more
years to do in this place. This ain't as bad as some
prisons, Englishman. We got movie houses, video
education centres, a gymnasium, baseball pitch
and if you can read, a big library." He passed me
the smoke.

"What are you going to do when you get out,
Zoots?" I asked.

"Shit, man. I'm the fastest wheelman in Fort
Worth."

"What's a wheelman?" I was puzzled.

Zoots jiggled the Edsel steering wheel around.
"I'm a getaway driver, Englishman. You know,
BLAM BLAM, EECH EECH." Zoots made tire-

squealing getaway noises. R.D. leant out the back window yelling, "rat-a-tat-a-tat" and firing an imaginary machinegun. I banged the dashboard in front of the passenger seat, ducked my head to avoid the bullets and shouted, "Faster, Zoots, FASTER!"

We played like three children. Less than two hundred yards away were the shotguns, towers and guards at the penitentiary perimeter fence. Zoots turned a violent corner.

"What did you do, Englishman?"

"I robbed a gold store," I said.

"You kill anybody?"

"No, Zoots. I don't even carry a gun."

"Shit, man. How you rob the store?"

"Conversation, Zoots. Just conversation."

FCI
TEXARKANA
APRIL

"Hey, Englishman, you want some smack?"

"Hey, Englishman, I got good pills, man."

"Hey, Englishman, you want some grass?"

I threaded my way through the street bazaar that was the exercise yard of the penitentiary, Texarkana, Texas.

I was broke and seven thousand miles away from home, serving seven unexpected years. The U.S. Government had broken its word. Lawyers, friends and family had proved powerless to help me. Even Scotland Yard couldn't get me back.

I was on my way to meet Jack Heim.

Now my godfather, himself a prisoner in this Texan outback, had promised to help me. We were pushing the case to the Supreme Court.

By the phone booth Jack was on my case. I hung around ferrying him coffee, cookies and cigars. A big thug I christened Fred Flintstone kept prospective phone users away while Jack talked with various people, pushing his power buttons.

I was thrilled.

I had broken through to real help.

I'd found my rabbi—but could he work miracles?

If a man breaks the prison code, he finds himself with a problem.

If he considers being stabbed a problem.

Trouble had been brewing for me for sometime.

One good old boy confronted me in a deserted part of the prison. I had been delivering cash wrapped in plastic in my dirty bucket of water from one part of the jail to another, doing a favour for a Sicilian bookmaker.

Being a cleaner, I wandered unsupervised all over the compound. Now my path was blocked by these five goons. Was this a robbery?

Has someone set me up?

What will the Mafioso do to me if I don't show up with his cash?

The nastiest one spoke. He was a pale rat-faced creature doing three hundred years for homosexual murders. A nice genuine kind of a fellow.

"Don't you know you are a white man, even if you are all a Limey Jew?"

Oh, now I've got it. I must have put their little minds on 'tilt'. A Jew with black friends. My hand gripped the icy handle of the shank in my pocket.

"Eat with your own kind, son," sneered another. "You think you're a nigger."

"Yeah, he thinks he's a nigger, he hangs round

them niggers so much," from a third.

They move around me in a semi-circle, pinched faces, heroin eyes.

Weird rats, too long behind the wire, or depending on your point of view, not long enough.

"One of them niggers fucking you, son?" said the gay murderer. I think of R.D. and laugh inwardly. Is he jealous? Is this his fantasy?

"Reckon they all are," said another.

Not happy.

I touch the shank in my pocket again. This is where I increase my time. If I stab a couple of these poisonous half-formed deviants it won't look good on my behaviour sheet. If I don't, it'll be me who doesn't look so good.

I give them my best Oxford: "Things are different where I come from." A bit lame, I know but I'm not inspired conversationally.

"Gonna be different up your ass if you get shanked, boy," says Rat One, his hand moving to his jacket.

I know what is coming before he produces the wicked knife, with its serrated arrowhead. A craftsman's shank. I see every detail of the blade. There is a stopped clock quality to the moment. Motes of dust in sunbeams, Adam's apples bobbing; every spot, pimple and mole on their faces is magnified. I watch my reflection in cold eyes. What do they see? Am I going to die? How much will it hurt? Should I stab first?

Rat One's breath quickens in sexual anticipation of violence. He is a lunatic. They all are. I imagine the blade slipping into me, gouts of blood splattering them as they laugh. I see their rotten gums and yellow teeth, smell their hunger for thirst and violence.

Which one do I stab first?

There are no words to deflect the coming onslaught. No slick remarks.

This is high noon in Texarkana.

Thirteen hundred dollars wrapped in plastic at the bottom of the bucket. Uncut diamonds in Austria. Dee in some lover's arms across the Atlantic. Should I give them the money in the pail and take my chances with the Mafioso later?

The evil polished blade looks like my immediate problem.

Suddenly just like in all the best movies, I am saved. Two guards appear, less than forty feet away. The white trash break up their ring of hate.

The pervert murderer turns as he walks away.

"Eat with the white men, son."

FCI
TEXARKANA
MAY

I am lying in bed in the part they call the West Wing.

An elegant country house it isn't.

The Frog has been pouring me home-made wine all morning on top of the acid tab, and I'm not sure exactly where I am. I thought I was on the Riviera at the Carlton Hotel in Cannes, with Joe waiting on the jetty by the boat.

I remember standing on the balcony watching the white-jacketed waiter loading my picnic. Dee must still be asleep. We had a big night at Jimmy's in Monte Carlo, discoing the dawn away.

Surely all I need to do is hop off the bed, slip on shirt and shorts and stroll down the corridor, through the lobby, and run the normal gauntlet of 'Bonjour M'sieu's from the reception staff. Then out into the sunshine, tell Franco on the door that I don't need the Rolls till this evening, across the Croisette with its palms and roses and out along the jetty to the Riva.

Polished wooden decks gleaming and Joe's weatherbeaten face smiling at me in the sparkling sunshine.

Ah, the Cote d'Azur. There's nowhere like it.

There's chilled Blanc de Blanc in the silver bucket and a couple of pots of caviar nestling on beds of ice. I can feel the depth of the soft towels lying on the powerboat's seats. The white leather burns my bare legs.

We have a routine, Joe and I. No water-skiing. Since the embarrassing incident when I couldn't even lift myself out of the water onto the skis, let alone do anything adventurous like falling off.

Joe fires up and casts off; I open the champagne and sit facing the stern, watching the white Rococo facade of the Carlton and the rich sprawl of Cannes shrink as we pull away, a wave of boiling turquoise behind us. I pour a glass of Tattinger for myself, but nothing for Joe who clinically died six times on the operating table at the American Hospital, Nice. He leaves the champagne out these days.

I look forward to my swim off the Isle Marguerite and perhaps a quiet salad Niçoise at the pretty harbourside restaurant....

The acid tab that the Frog gave me must have been a belter, for I never noticed the five black men around my bunk holding knives.

"Say man," said R.D. "There's trouble in the chow hall. You got to carry a shank."

I look at him, returning from the Riviera to reality. The barred windows, the cracked linoleum, the tense faces. The timewarp of real time in the penitentiary.

R.D. is holding out something towards me. A sharpened steel bayonet fashioned in the prison workshops, handle wrapped in masking tape. Not much thicker than a knitting needle, this slim weapon is invariably lethal when plunged between the ribs or into the stomach and pulled upwards. I blink up at my friend. I am a long way from the Carlton.

"If there's trouble in the chow hall, R.D., I'm not hungry."

"Listen mister comedy man, Mr. Jerry Lewis, you are the damn trouble. You don't go down to the chow hall, those trash gonna come find you. A hundred men are carrying shanks for you, sucker, they ain't gonna help you if you chicken out and lie up here like some fatass acid-head. Smashjaw been giving you so many tabs you don't know what's happening."

The Frog winked at me.

One sunny day a Vietcong landmine had blown away the lower half of his face. Suffocating on his own blood, the soldier had wrested his bayonet from his M16 and cut his own throat, performing a self-tracheotomy like they'd taught him at Fort Bragg. He recalled later that it was the one lecture he'd taken any notice of.

The Frog had survived his own ministrations and the poor repair job in a field hospital, which left him resembling his nickname.

The young soldier had collected a Congressional Medal of Honour and a Reader's Digest first person award of $10,000 with which he had scored a kilo of cocaine and five years' federal imprisonment for dealing it.

The Frog reached silently under his mattress to produce his own shank. Go with the flow. I hauled myself off the bunk, collected my eating kit, took the shank from R.D. and pushed it into my trouser pocket. The sharp point pierced the lining with a sigh and cold steel chilled my thigh. The six men

390

stood waiting for me to speak. "What is for lunch anyhow?" I enquired.

"The CIA kept yammering in all the judges' ears, Daniel. That's why you got seven years. My people in Washington believe that your appeal must succeed. The Federal Judge was wrong to break the Government's word to you. The State Judge was wrong because he was an asshole that wouldn't be spoken to. You're coming up before a new judge, one with political ambitions. He's much more reasonable."

It was the day after the chow hall shank-carrying which had turned into a heavily armed non-event. The tension had been thicker than the soup. No one had been stabbed and I had suffered only indigestion. Now I sat with Jack in the deserted baseball diamond as the Texas summer evening faded beyond the wire.

"But won't the CIA block me again, Jack?"

"Daniel, I'm going to show you that there is justice in America and that it's beyond the reach of clandestine coldhearts skulking beneath slimy stones. The United States is a lionhearted and enlightened country and our justice system is unjealous and honourable." The old godfather paused. "Besides which, Daniel, I've got the finest and most expensive legal minds in the nation masterminding your case. You'll get your hearing. You will have your day in court."

I thought I had one too many days in court already, but it would have been churlish of me to voice this to Jack.

FCI
TEXARKANA
JUNE

The head phones were lifted away, and R.D.'s voice boomed into my ear.

"Say, man. You got problems!"

"Tell me something new, R.D. I'm doing seven years."

A stubby black finger poked my chest.

"You don't need to worry about doing no seven years. You gonna be lucky if you do one more week."

I could see he was unsettled. I turned down the easy loving black Texas music I had been listening to.

"Come on. What are you talking about, R.D.?"

"Well, man. I don't know what this shit is, but there's some Spanish dudes don't like you. Talkin' about gitting you."

"Aw, come on, R.D. You hear that conversation fifty times a day in jail."

"Man, this ain't no conversation. These dudes are serious with a capital C."

"What Spanish dudes? What are they bullfighters or bullshitters?"

R.D. ran his hand up and down the steel rail of the bunk in a nervous gesture.

"Shit, man. You don't take nothing nobody tells you serious. I'm telling you, sucker. These Chica-

394

nos gonna get your ass."

"R.D. We're going around in circles. Who are they? What are they? "

"1 told you man. They Spanish."

There was a loose thread at the end of my bed blanket and the black man twisted at it agitatedly.

"Everybody South of Mexico is Spanish to you, R.D. Are they Puerto Ricans?"

"Shit, man. I don't know. But I'll find out for you."

It was about an hour later, I was pushing a broom about the Education Wing trying to look busy, when R.D.'s head popped around the corridor.

"Say man, say. Come in the storeroom."

The storeroom was our den; we took drugs, drank coffee, hid money and stayed out of the way in there.

I opened the cupboard door and we squeezed inside. I passed my friend the joint that I had been saving all morning and he lit it, closing his eyes as he inhaled. After a moment he spoke.

"Say man. Those dudes." A cloud of marijuana blew in my face. "They not Puerto Rican." R.D. was obviously bursting with his important news. I played along.

"So what are they? Chinamen? Eskimos? Come on. What are they?"

In the close confined space of the broom cupboard, amongst the toilet rolls, cleaning fluid and reams of useless printed forms, I felt the black man's raw magnetism hum like a dynamo.

"They not Eskimos, sucker. They Cubans."

R.D. pronounced it 'Q-Bahns'.

Now I took the threat seriously.

"What do they want?"

The Texan sucked the joint vigorously. "They want your ass on the silver platter, sucker. They wanna waste you. They don't care who knows."

"Why?"

"The word is that you done stole some money from their friends, some kind of freedom fighters, down in Florida. They ask them to shank you."

I got the message. The Agency had decided I was too much of a nuisance. Or maybe this had been their plan all along. Promise me my freedom, get what they wanted, sling me in jail and have me murdered. Who cares about a man in jail? It's just another prison death. Thousands of people die in jail. I've seen men die over a pack of cigarettes or imagined insults in the penitentiary.

My face must have reflected my thoughts because R.D. put his hand on my shoulder.

"Shit, man. Don't look so worried. They only a bunch of greased-assed Chicanos." He passed me the joint.

"So what are we, R.D.?"

"We're a Texas nigger and an English Jew. That's a bad motherfucking combination. Besides, you fat sucker, I'm gonna look after you. You promised me you was gonna show me London. I ain't gonna let no greased-assed Cuban shank you before I had me some of that English pussy. I'm going to go down there and tell them."

"Whoa, R.D." I interrupted. "What are you going to tell to who? You're gonna march up to the Cubans and say that you're going to fuck with them? They'll just wipe you too."

"Listen, you crazy English sucker. There's better'n three hundred black men in this jail. Them Cubans are going to be decorating the perimeter fence if they start that kind of shit."

"R.D., there may be three hundred black men in here, but they're not going to go to war for me."

"Man, sometimes I think you so dumb for a guy that supposed to be so smart. There ain't another white guy in jail that has the same kind of respect from the blacks as you do."

"Bullshit, R.D. You're just trying to make me feel better."

"It ain't no bullshit, man. You the only white that sit down and eat with the black men. You down tight with a lot of black dudes, man. You give respect and you get respect. I already done told some of my people about what them grease-balls said about you. Everyone remembers the time when them cracker trash wanted to shank you."

It was true. I had been threatened with stabbing if I continued eating with the black men. The trouble had come from some of the Jew hating, anti-black hillbillies. The dining hall was segregated unofficially. As you walked in, there was a broad corridor down the middle between the races. On the left a sea of black faces. On the right, the white.

Despite threats, I continued to eat with the black men.

I had even addressed a black Muslim meeting on the need for understanding Zionism.

As conspicuous as a reindeer at a racetrack.

So far no one had stabbed me. But I was racking up enemies in the pen at an alarming rate of knots.

It was good to have someone on my side.

In the dining hall, the table you ate at conferred and confirmed your power and social status. The Mafiosos and the Italians ate together and occasionally I was invited to join them. The Chicanos ate in their part of the hall. I had always been able to move freely to anybody's table I chose. In jail terms I had become a 'politician'. In the crowded dining hall with a thousand men streaming in for their meals, space was at a premium, yet I could always find a seat. There were two godfathers who held court and empty chairs were always respectfully left at their tables.

One godfather was a Sicilian Don who ran his empire of loan-sharking, trucking, prostitution and policy rackets from his comfortable cell and lunch table.

The other godfather with the empty chairs was Jack Heim. There was always a place for me at Jack's table and the day of R.D.'s warning about the Cubans I sat with Jack.

Three thousand knives, forks and spoons clattered around us against a thousand trays. Jack, elegant in his well pressed khaki shirt, picked at his specially made omelette.

"You know, Daniel. The Cubans have always been a difficult people. It wasn't like this in the days of Batista. He was a man you could do business with." The old millionaire sighed. "Myer had everything organized with Batista; hotels, casinos, tourism, cigar exports. But the Marxists wanted a Caribbean base, the Soviets a missile site ninety miles off the coast of Florida. After Truman died and Castro came to power, the so-called Liberals in Washington, many of them secret communists, tied the hands of Eisenhower and John Kennedy. They made a big thing about human rights under Batista, and an even bigger thing about Myer Lansky, with stories about the Mafia ruining the economy of the country. Hell!" Jack munched a forkful of egg. "Till Castro came along, Cuba was a paradise. We were importing over fifty million dollars worth of Havana cigars a year into the States and our tourists were spending better than two hundred million dollars each year. Far from ruining the country, we were propping it up!" Jack sighed. "If the U.S. was to start trading with Cuba again it would be worth billions in today's money to the Cuban economy." Jack sighed.

I was always fascinated by the old man's discourses, but I had an immediate problem.

"Meanwhile I still have Cubans wanting kill me, Jack."

The old man shook his head. "And you made a deal with our government. I'm sure the President wouldn't have sanctioned this, Daniel. The anti-Castro people see you as a saboteur. You upset Cuban Intelligence, because as far as they know you were working with the anti-Castro people in Florida."

"But I was only there to rob them, Jack."

The old godfather chuckled. "And rob them you did, Daniel. Because of it the anti-Castro people are angry with you for stealing the sinews of war, my boy. The Agency are furious with you for exposing their plot and trying to blackmail them. The guy you robbed is mad because you made a fool out of him. The FBI don't like you because you went over their heads to make a deal with the CIA." Jack chuckled. "You're a popular man, Daniel."

I toyed glumly with my salad. I had really made a mess out of my life and Dee was in danger in England. CIA men, Cubans, Mafioso. What a circus! But there was no point in brooding over it. How was I going to cope? In fear every second of being stabbed? Worried about Dee being abducted?

Prison is such a confined area that ther's no escape from your enemy; you see him everyday. You pass him in the corridor. You see him in the washroom. He stares at you across the dininghall, he broods with his cronies in groups on the exercise yard. You line up with him at the doctor's and dentist's. The defence in a penitentiary is to choose a running partner. A friend who will stand with you back to back against all comers. You're lucky if you can find someone to help shoulder your aggravations.

R.D. was mine. Being someone's running partner is a very serious commitment indeed. You are totally responsible for the others' debts and problems. As the knife is sunk in, the last words you hear may be, "That's for your running partner."

I waited in line by the glass phone booths on E. Wing. For days I had been calling up the U.S. Justice Department and getting the runaround. At the CIA contact number in Langley, I had been met with evasions and a stone wall of silence. Louis the Lawyer assured me my appeal was in hand and Jack Heim's attorneys in Washington and Florida were working on the case, but so far to no avail.

It was Kim I needed to talk to now. Whoever was following Dee in England was playing on my territory.

I might be a long way from home, but my friends weren't.

KEY LARGO
FLORIDA
JUNE

"The Agency people have their plates back, my niece has lost a husband, I'm out a whole heap of money in expenses and the Englishman still has a parcel of uncut diamonds."

Arturo Jaconelli rolled Tagliatelli Alfredo around his fork and waved it at his guest;

"Now I'm told that he looks like winning his freedom in the Court of Appeal." The Mafioso stuffed the pasta inelegantly into his mouth and chewed, his tanned cheeks bulging. "It's not right and it's not fair."

"Mohammed Ali's left leg," stated his companion.

"What?" asked Jaconelli through a mouthful of food.

"Mohammed Ali's left leg. It's not right and it's not fair," repeated his guest.

The cocaine king grunted. He wasn't in a mood to joke. Normally he wouldn't take that kind of shit from anyone. His preferred humour was of the scatological genre, but he respected his lunch companion. Here was a man of honour, a man of death.

"So what do you want?" asked the visitor. "To hit the Englishman?"

"First I want the uncut diamonds he stole, then he gets hit."

"He won't have them in the pen with him."

402

"No, but he could be persuaded to let me know where they are."

"But he's bound to have stuck them away in a safe place. Didn't he put the CIA stuff in some bank?"

"His lady friend did."

"Where is she now?"

"In England. I have some people there sitting on her ass."

"From the photos I've seen, that's a nice position," said his guest as his guest reached for the pasta bowl. "What's your idea?"

"We pick her up, and get her to speak to him on the phone in jail. I know he has to authorise the bank in some way to release the packages, that much my friends at Langley learned. She could be the pressure point, she could be taken to the bank to draw them out, with his authority."

"Are they worth that much?" asked the visitor.

Jaconelli told him.

They lunched beneath the shade of a silk parasol, at the edge of Jaconelli's oval swimming pool, secluded behind the white walls of the oceanfront villa.

As his grizzled companion heaped more pasta on his lunchplate, Jaconelli commented;

"My Aunt Sophie makes this for me, in Firenze. Then I have it deep frozen and flown across in my Gulfstream."

"Do you send the jet just for the pasta?" asked the other.

"No, I'm not that crazy," the Italian laughed. "My suits come too when they're ready, from Brioni in Rome. The Grumman also brings my shirts from Turnbull & Asser in London and -"

"Your smack from Pakistan?"

"Not in my personal plane, goddamn it, I was going to say my wife's shopping, which usually fills up the aircraft."

His guest nodded appreciatively. Jaconelli had style, balls and money, a terrific combination.

"Now, about this Englishman." Jaconelli pushed his plate away.

"He's still in Texarkana?"

"Yes. When is your home leave over?" The Italian toothpicked his teeth.

"I'm due to report back to Allenwood on Thursday. I have two months left to serve."

"How would you like a transfer?"

"Not much. Allenwood's a nice easy joint, full of senators and crooked government contractors. There's no restriction like at Texarkana."

"Would a hundred thousand dollars change your mind?"

"It just did," said Chuck Maclean.

FCI
TEXARKANA
JUNE

Something about the new guy in the next bunk bothered me. The previous occupant had been a mellow old soul known as Cadillac, serving time for moonshining. But Cadillac had been transferred back to the Federal Medical Facility at Butner, North Carolina. The eerie 'Cuckoo's Nest' from which men never emerged in quite the same state as they had entered. Butner had performed a frontal lobotomy on Cadillac and the old distiller had been recalled for tests, leaving the bunk next to me empty. My friend R.D. had tried every connection to get himself moved into the space but to no avail.

The new arrival, a black Spanish speaker named Guiterrez, had been transferred from Leavenworth, a notoriously violent penitentiary. My new neighbour was a surly individual of uncertain temper who rarely spoke but followed my movements grimly through rattlesnake eyes. I felt distinctly uneasy with him sleeping next to me.

I went over to the carpentry workshop to look for Guido Pirezza, a Sicilian serving five years for doping racehorses. He had done time at Leavenworth and I wanted to find out if he knew the new arrival.

I found Pirezza planing wood.

"Sure, I know him. He's a fucking animal. A lot of those black Cubans are animals." The Sicilian's arms swayed as he concentrated on his carpentry.

"Cuban?" I questioned. "I thought he was Puerto Rican?"

"He's a 'marielita' reject from Cuba. Castro threw him out with the rest of the scum from his prisons."

"Wow," I said.

"Is he bothering you, Daniel?"

"Not yet, Guido. But he's in the next bed space."

"Well, watch him, Englishman. Watch him. He's a faggot murderer. And very handy with the blade."

"Jesus Christ," I said.

The Sicilian looked up from his woodwork and smiled at me.

"Now isn't that typical of you Jews," he said. "The moment you got a problem you call on Jesus."

"Well, Guido. Jesus was a nice Jewish boy until you Italians nailed him up."

The horse doper laughed.

"Mama mia, I took too much off this wood."

"What are you making, Guido? A coffin?"

The Sicilian straightened up and looked me in the eye.

"With Guiterrez in the next bed you may need one."

That night I stayed awake clutching a sharpened shank, the slim blade cold as the grave. Lying with my face towards the Cuban's bed, I was determined that the moment he moved, I would stab him. I'd never stabbed anybody in my life but I was surer than sure that this creep had been sent here to kill me. If he got up to take a piss in the night, it would be his last.

The interminable hours passed and the Cuban snored peacefully. I ached for sleep, but I never allowed myself to close my eyes for a second. I debated whether to get up and stab him anyway, while he slept, just to make sure. But some code deep within me forbade the pre-emptive strike. The Cuban would have to make a move against me. I longed to turn over and move my position but there was no way I was going to offer this murderer my back.

I have never been so grateful to see the dawn. I dressed and shaved before everyone and found R.D. in the chow hall.

Over Texas eggs and Mexican hot spice I told him my problem.

"I can't live like this, I can't sleep and I'm terrified of the guy."

"He's a mean motherfucker, Daniel. I checked him out when they moved him into your next bedspace. No dude like him, no dude talk to him, no dude walk with him. He's a killer fairy doing one hundred years for cutting up little boys."

I pushed my eggs away moodily.

"So what do I do, R.D.?"

The black man spoke through a mouthful of toast.

"You don't do nothing, sucker. That's what you got a running partner for. You got to keep your ass clean. Beat your case and get on home to that blond pussy in London."

"But R.D., I can't spend another night like this. I'm exhausted. I thought of getting out of bed and stabbing him just to get some sleep."

"You ain't gonna spend another night that way, sucker."

That afternoon I was waiting for my turn at the telephone booth when a commotion erupted from the direction of the toilet. I heard screaming, a striking noise and then silence. The hack at the desk hit his alarm button and ran toward the washroom. Klaxons began to wail all over the prison. In less than a minute, hacks in riot gear were pouring onto the wing from all directions.

Nobody around the phone booth had the faintest idea what was happening.

A few moments later I was shocked to see R.D., blood pouring from his head, being marched out between two baton toting guards. Suddenly, para-medical orderlies from the hospital ran towards the washroom carrying a stretcher.

Shortly afterwards, they emerged bearing an unconscious figure, arms hanging off the stretcher's sides.

I leant forward to take a look. The head was a battered mass of blood and hair. I barely recognized the black Cuban child murderer from the next bedspace.

Two days later I managed to get down to the punishment 'hole' by swapping duty with the regular cleaner. I pressed my face by the hinge of R.D.'s cell.

"What did you hit him with, R.D.?"

"A sock full of padlocks."

"Are you hurt?"

"Shit, no. I cut myself over the eye with a razor to make it look like the faggot attacked me. I told the guard captain that he was trying to fuck me. I was just defending myself. What happened to him anyhow?"

"They flew him out to a hospital, R.D. He nearly died."

"Shit. I thought I'd killed the motherfucker. Anyhow, they won't put him back here no more. Anybody say anything to you?"

"Not a word."

"Good, sucker. I told Zoots to take care of you. The captain sentenced me to one week down here and sixty days loss of good time. Just don't smoke all the grass."

That night, whilst R.D. lay in the solitary confinement wing, the prison was seething with tension. A violent argument was raging amongst certain members of the black community regarding me. They thought I must be an evil white man to cause bad blood between black brothers. There was talk of men finding me in my cell and stabbing me.

Fortunately, for me, wiser councils prevailed, for Guiterrez' reputation was well-known.

The event died down after a few days. We heard on the grapevine that the Cuban had been shipped back to Leavenworth. I was alive and unharmed. I was determined to see the warden to get R.D.'s punishment rescinded.

R.D. sent a message out to me saying he'd break my head too if I did any such thing.

"You know who came in on the new intake?"

I lowered the Financial Times. "No Frog, who?" I asked.

The Vietnam vet grinned his horror smile. "Chuck Maclean, the Terror of the Teamsters."

"Maclean's here, Frog? I heard he was in Allenwood, finishing his time, a reformed man."

"Well he ain't too reformed, seems like he had a fight with some con in Allenwood and they shipped him down here to finish his sentence."

I rolled off the bed, my newspaper forgotten. Chuck Maclean was no hothead to ruin his chances of going home with some stupid pen-fight. I remembered some of his memoirs from my typing session in Manhattan. This was a man who did nothing by chance. He was a calculating killer. I wondered why he had been shipped out to Texas instead of back to New York.

Was this more of the Agency's doing?

"Didn't you say that you knew him, Dan?" asked the Frog.

"Yes, Frog, we did time together up in Manhattan."

"Well, he's over on B wing, if you want to see him."

"Do you know, Frog, that's not a bad idea."

410

CIA HEADQUARTERS
LANGLEY
VIRGINIA
JULY

"Patrick, I have a million and one problems on my desk and this business of the Englishman is like a cancer that won't go away. Tell me what happened to the marielita that the Cubans sent in."

"He was injured in a fight with a black inmate, sir."

"This whole affair is dogged by bad luck and missed opportunities.

"It has now become imperative to kill this man and it must be done..." the Deputy director paused and looked at the piece of paper in his hand, "by October."

"Why October, Sir?" Garrity was puzzled.

The Director waved the flimsy. "I have just been notified that the Englishman has a hearing in the Court of Appeal in October. Whilst no one in jail may believe his story, the last thing this Agency needs is some uncontrollable Federal Justice asking awkward questions about Operation Reis just before the election."

"Do we talk to the Cubans again, Sir?"

"Since the Cubans have failed, we must take up the matter ourselves."

The Deputy Director inserted his hand into the fingerprint analysis machine outside the Operations

Room door. He then inserted his personal code number, rolled his finger backwards and forwards to enable the scanner to read his prints and stood back while the computer decided whether his security clearance was sufficient for him to enter. Lights blinked, there was a whirring noise and the outer door sprang open. The DDI passed through and nodded to the armed security guard.

James Benedict Ampleforth II stood for a moment strumming his fingers on the guard's desk while Patrick Garrity repeated the fingerprint process outside.

The Operations Section had made a secure room available for the DDI, but there was little love lost between Intelligence and Operations and Ampleforth loathed having to seek the assistance of his brother officers on such a delicate matter. A number of high security files were waiting stacked on the desk.

"I want you to study these, Patrick, and find the most suitable operative. These men are all employees of the Federal Bureau of Prisons who are retained by the Agency to carry out tasks from time to time. I suggest you find a man with a rank of Guard and have him transferred to Texarkana. Make sure that he's a good marksman and is assigned to Tower Duty."

"And what then, Sir?"

"The Englishman wouldn't be the first prisoner in the world to be 'shot whilst attempting to escape'."

"Very well, Sir. Anything else?"

The Deputy Director paused at the door. "Remember the calendar, Patrick."

"How much did they offer you, Chuck?"

"A hundred thousand dollars, Daniel."

"What have you got to do? Kill me?"

"After you give up the diamonds."

"Who contacted you, the spooks?"

"No Daniel, the spooks have their own people. I've never been one of them."

"So it must be the Mob?"

"You said it, I didn't."

"What's the deal, Chuck?"

"What do I get if I tell you?"

"You get their hundred grand, and the same from me."

"You'll have to go through some kind of a pantomime, Daniel, they're following your girl in England."

"I already know. That's my territory, Chuck, they're playing an away match. Now you and I are pals, and I've just doubled your going home money, so what's their plan?"

"They pick up your girl in England. I put you on the phone to her from this end, and you make her give up the stones. Simple. Then they waste her and I'm supposed to do you the same favour."

I sat silent for a while. "Okay," I decided at last. "This is what we do."

Chuck listened to me patiently, then his old scarred face lit up.

"You're a fucking genius, Daniel."

"No, Chuck," I replied. "Just Jewish."

"Say, man."

I opened my eyes. It was my friend, messenger, running partner, aggravator, nuisance.

R.D. Makepeace. The man who saved my life.

Five foot six inches of black whip-spring energy, a coiled cobra in U.S. Army fatigues disturbing my stolen slumbers in the blanket store.

"Say, man. There's a dude looking for you."

"What is he this time, R.D.? Cuban assassin, Mafia hitman or an aggravated victim?"

"He says he's a friend of yours, man. He say he done time with you in Broward County, Florida."

I sat up. "What's his name?"

"Shit, man. I don't know his name. He a white dude from Louisiana." R.D.'s voice was filled the contempt that black Texans reserve for 'southern gentlemen'.

"What's this friend of mine look like, R.D.?"

"He a long tall cracker, man. He just arrived. They got him on death row."

There is no death row at Texarkana.

R.D. was using jail slang for the hospital.

I bent over and scrubbed the floor vigorously, my hands blistered and raw from the carbolic soap. R.D. crouched about fifty feet away scrubbing the other end of the corridor.

415

"This is a damn fool idea," I said softly.

"Man," he whispered. "You can't go visiting death row with a bunch of motherfucking flowers like you was at Mount Sinai. I had to give the dude on the cleaning detail half a carton of Marlboro to get us in this wing, man. We ain't even supposed to *be* here."

So far we had scrubbed the hospital cleaner than it had been since the jail was built. I hadn't recognised anyone from Broward and R.D. hadn't seen the 'long tall cracker'. I was tired and the carbolic was hurting my eyes.

"How much more to do, R.D.?"

"There's only the seg wing left, man."

"Shit, R.D. I'd give two cartons <u>not</u> to go in the seg wing."

"We got to do it, man. I promised the dude we'd do the cleaning duty and the seg wing is the only place that your sucker can be."

"If he's in the seg wing he is no friend of mine. They've all got aids in there."

"Shit, man. He don't have to be sick to be on the seg wing. That's what it means. Seg-re-ga-tion. Keep a dude's ass away from the rest of the joint."

"Especially if he's got aids."

"Every mother is worried about aids. You can die from lead poisoning, mercury poison, or radiation from atomics. In here you can get shanked, cut or shot. If I was a faggot I would reckon aids was a pleasurable way to go." R.D. laughed into his cleaning bucket, the sound echoing in the still corridor.

We reached the seg wing still on our hands and knees. R.D. kept scout at the top of the corridor while I ran down lifting metal flaps and peering through little spyholes set in iron doors.

In the last cell on the left I found a face I recognized. The sleeping occupant was Bust Out Eddie.

I tapped gently on the door.

"Eddie, Eddie," I called softly.

The tall jewel thief came awake.

"Who's there?"

"It's me. The Englishman." Eddie leapt off the bunk and stood close by the door, pushing his eye up to the tiny peephole.

"Daniel! That you?"

"Yeah. I've been looking for you. What's happening?"

"They just transferred me here. I'd be out in the main joint but they found a map and a wire in my shoes. Plus I got jaundice, so they stuck me in seg."

"Do you need anything?"

"They took my cigarettes away."

"I'll get you some sent in with your food. Anything else I can do for you, Eddie?"

"Could you call up Lou Ann?"

"Sure thing."

I fumbled a pencil and paper out of my pocket and took down the number. Eddie told me what he wanted to say to her.

I had spoken to Eddie's wife before from the priest's phone in Broward County Jail, Florida, to pass the last innocuous seeming message. Eddie now had fifteen escape attempts on his record.

I hoped his sixteenth would be successful.

I wanted out as well!

R.D. was signalling me frantically.

"See you later, Eddie," I murmured, and began

to turn away.

"Daniel," came Eddie's voice.

I pressed my ear against the cold iron again.

"When they asked me where I wanted to do my time I chose Texarkana," Eddie whispered, "cos I knew you were here. Those spooks really fucked you over. Did you give them their money back?"

"Yeah," I said.

"And the packages?"

R.D. was becoming agitated now. "Yeah, those too," I muttered dully.

I heard a rattle of keys and hacks' footsteps.

Eddie's voice came softly from the cell.

"You wanna come with me, Daniel?"

At the end of the passage, R.D. had dropped down and begun kneading the brush into the floor.

I thought of all the bullshit lawyers, the appeals, the crap, people wanting to kill me, the years stretching ahead of me in a foreign jail. Eddie whispered again.

"Lou Ann will lift us out."

I breathed into the cold metal.

It was time I threw a wild card instead of waiting for the dealer. "Yes, I'll come with you, Eddie." I was already on my knees scrubbing vigorously when the hack turned into the seg corridor, swinging his key chain.

OLD RHODES KEY
FLORIDA
AUGUST

"They were picked up with smack?" Jaconelli exploded into the phone. "What the fuck were they doing with that?"

"They say that it was planted on them, at their room in the Stratford-on-Avon Hilton." The English solicitor's voice crackled over the Atlantic. "Your friends say that the British police burst in and headed straight for the bathroom, where they found half a kilo of high quality Pakistani heroin. Your friends swear they hadn't seen it."

"They're no friends of mine," screamed the Crime lord. "Stupid moonlighting bastards."

"They begged me to tell you that they had no knowledge of the drug, they swear that the whole thing is a set up."

Jaconelli's eyes narrowed, was it possible? Had the Englishman framed his people? Had they been spotted tailing the girl, or had Maclean sold him out? This whole business was one mess after another.

"So what happens now?" he asked.

"They have been remanded in custody." The lawyer paused. "They are likely to serve a jail term and then be deported. The British police have their records from the FBI, not very savoury I'm afraid."

"Okay, hire the best people to defend them."

"I have already retained leading counsel, but I shall of course require," the solicitor coughed delicately, "further remuneration."

Jaconelli sighed. This whole damn business was getting expensive. "Okay, I'll have my bank send you a draft. What are the guys' chances?"

"Of an acquittal? Pretty slim," said the lawyer. "They were found in possession."

"So how long will they get?"

"Between three to five years each. I'm afraid that the British courts do not look favourably on foreigners smuggling drugs into the country."

"Well, do your best," sighed the Mafia chief as he broke the connection.

Arturo Jaconelli stared sightlessly at a priceless Poussin, realisation dawning in his mind like the opening of a grave.

His people had been set up!

The Sicilian's face darkened in fury.

Who did the Englishman think he was fucking with?

FCI
TEXARKANA
SEPTEMBER

Eddie shakes my shoulder, startling me. I'm here on the volleyball pitch like he insisted. It's eleven o'clock. My twelve dollar watch tells me so.

The day is bright and crystal skied. The effects of the Frog's latest homemade acid tab are wearing off, but I still experience traces of awareness. Bust Out Eddie is excited. His lean face flushed, his manner urgent. He is saying something to me. I can't understand him. I hear only the cries from the figures frozen in the distance on the baseball diamond. A spirited game is in progress.

Turning my head toward the field I watch the weightlifters; exercising insects on a cloth of green, Seymour amongst them.

Scarborough Fair in Texas and I am high and tripping.

Sharp against the cornflower sky, a black speck materialises.

Lazily I look up at a mechanical dragonfly.

Eddie shakes me again. "Daniel! That's my chopper. I'm going, Daniel! Are you coming?"

I squint skywards, the speck expands into a helicopter, straying away from the Fort Worth-Dallas flight path. I remember discussing this latest escape plot with Eddie. I had taken it for fantasy. With Bust Out I should have known better.

"Daniel, come with me." Eddie's hold becomes tighter. His voice insists, "Come with me!"

The helicopter drifts nearer. Heads crane upward. It's all so clear and treacle-slow. The acid is heavy upon me.

I trip.

You trip.

We trip.

The figures on the recreation fields move in slow motion.

Thawing from a frozen replay.

I have never really noticed Eddie's eyes before. They are a bluey-grey. The machine crosses the perimeter towards us, angry and dangerous.

A madness comes over me. I will escape with Eddie!

On the baseball diamond the play has stopped. Men gape skywards.

I realise that Eddie and I are standing in the middle of the white circle drawn on the volleyball pitch. The whirlybird chatters, a great white locust hovering above us. The word POLICE painted large on its side.

The trip vanishes and I am here. There are reasons why I must not go.

"The supreme court hears my appeal tomorrow, Eddie."

"My chopper's here now, Daniel!"

It was too.

The helicopter filled the sky as it descended. It's rotor buffeting the exercise yard with violent gusts of wind. Up in the guard towers, the hacks' body language radioed nervous puzzlement and rifles were unslung. I caught the flash of binoculars helioing briefly towards us.

It looked like Jacques the assistant warden up there, but I was too far away to be sure. The chopper was landing now less than twenty yards away. Up in the tower Jacques was on the telephone.

Eddie pulled my arm. We bent double and broke into stumbling runs toward the machine. The cabin door swung open as we dashed beneath the beating blades.

The distinct crack of a rifle spoke above the rotor noise. I heard an angry whine as bullets whipped between us. Eddie let go of my arm. We were almost at the cabin door. For a moment I thought we'd made it.

Eddie was in front of me and in slow motion I watched his jacket burst redly and his spine arch backwards, viciously. He half turned, mouth open, hands flopping as a crimson mushroom spread across his neck and shoulders. Then he righted himself. I grabbed his elbow half propping, half pushing him towards the door. A gloved hand reached out grabbed the front of Eddie's jacket, pulling him into the chopper cabin.

Gunfire again. Bullets ricochetted against the hull. I stumbled and the hand reached out for me. Decision time. Go—or stay.

I've read Rupert Brooke and the Cabalah. I know I'm not delirious.

They say that I'm delirious but that's ridiculous. I know the bullet went into the back of my neck because I heard the doctor say so. I knew he was a doctor even though I couldn't see him. He was gentle, he told me I had been shot. They say that I'm delirious. Well I know that Jack is here. Jack's okay.

The Pygmies thought Jack was OK. Jack's here. Jack's with me in the hospital. I know what happened. I'm not delirious. I wasn't going to get in the helicopter with Eddie, anyway. I was just trying to help Eddie. I know who shot me. I don't know who shot Eddie, but I know who shot me.

"The Government shot me, Jack."

"It's always the Government, Daniel."

This is a hell of a system they've got in this country. You think those industrialists don't take what they want? They sit in their mansions and they shoot workers. I've seen the newsreels. They shot the students on Kent State University and they shot the prisoners in Attica. I must have spoken out loud for Jack answers me.

"Sure, Daniel. They shot them in Kent and Attica. It was a bad day for this country when they shot the students on the campus at Kent."

"Was it the Government, Jack?"

"It's always the Government, Daniel."

"What about the people they sent to die in Vietnam, Jack?"

"What about the people who died on the Jewish Lake, Daniel?"

It was Smitty up in the tower. I remember last week I stood against the perimeter wire of the jail and looked out. I spread my arms out and hung onto the fence limply. The Frog had given me another acid tab. I was tripping.

Smitty fired a round at me. A warning, he said. Don't stand next to the fence. There were other inmates near me, he couldn't make another clear shot.

Smitty works for the Federal Bureau of Prisons and probably the Agency. But the sunshine. About the Pygmies.

"If I can see sunshine does that mean I'm going to live, Jack?"

"Yes. You're going to live, Daniel."

"You lived with the Pygmies?"

"It was the only way, Daniel."

"That's how you got the emeralds, right Jack?"

"Yes. I was twenty-three years of age. You had to live with the Pygmies in their huts. Go blowpipe hunting with them for monkeys. They would shoot the creatures down from the treetops, and carry them home to the village hanging from bamboo poles. The women would cut the monkeys up and the whole tribe would eat them."

"What did it look like in the jungle?"

"It was beautiful, Daniel. It was like being in a fluorescent green cave with ultraviolet flowers. The scents and sounds tropic and alive. It was another world, Daniel. If the Pygmies liked you they gave you emeralds."

"And if they didn't like you, what happened, Jack?"

"You never came out of the jungle."

CIA HEADQUARTERS
LANGLEY
VIRGINIA
SEPTEMBER

"Just tell me this very slowly, Patrick. And tell me how the President knew. I've been seventy-two hours around the capitals of Europe explaining our Middle Eastern bombing policy to our allies. A day at Gleneagles for Bilderberg, boosting SDI following space disasters and I come back here to find you telling me that this Agency is incapable of carrying out a simple erasure inside our own federal prison system?"

"Well, sir."

"Don't 'well sir' me, Garrity. I heard a story once about military cadets that paid two dollars for a good 'well sir' excuse when they were late back into camp. So don't 'well sir' me."

The Senior Co-ordinator snapped awake. There would be blood on the wire if this went wrong.

"The facts are these, sir. At 1100 hours yesterday a Bell helicopter with blue and white Texas State police markings flew into restricted airspace over the Federal Correctional Institution at Texarkana and landed on the volleyball pitch."

The Deputy Director closed his eyes in anticipation of pain.

"Carry on, Patrick," he murmured and leant back in the big chair, jetlagged from his trans-Atlantic trip in Air Force Two. He had a throbbing headache from the noise of the Hughes that had choppered him here from Andrews Air Base.

"Two men attempted to escape, Sir. They were Daniel Mordicai Lieberman, age twenty-six, serving two years for Interstate Transportation of Stolen Goods, and Edward Gable Juniper, age thirty-eight, serving forty years for armed robbery, kidnapping, etc. The whirlybird lifted off with Juniper and the whole thing has been on coast-to-coast television."

"And the Englishman was shot? He didn't escape, Garrity?"

"That's correct, Sir."

"How badly was he shot, Garrity?"

"Well, our man in the tower hit him a few times while he was on the ground. He's now in hospital in a serious and unstable condition."

The DDI opened his eyes. "That's the first good news I've heard all day, Patrick. It's a short step from the hospital to the mortuary."

Patrick Xavier Garrity groaned inwardly. He knew this was going to be one of those days. Today the DDI was more Borgia than gung ho. The Co-ordinator could never make up his mind which of his boss's moods was worse for his liver or career.

"There are complications at the hospital, Sir."

"Medical complications, Garrity?"

"No, Sir. Another inmate."

The DDI rubbed a hand over his eyes.

"Patrick, you're talking in riddles. Maybe I'm tired. What complications can another inmate in Federal Prison present to us here at the Central

428

Intelligence Agency, Garrity? Either I'm going soft or you are."

"The other inmate had his bed moved into the hospital and is staying next to the Englishman. The man's name is Jack Heim."

"Jack Heim?" The DDI's eyes widened. "Lansky's consigliori?" Ampleforth prided himself on being 'hip'. He'd seen the Godfather.

"Yes, sir."

"The man we negotiated with when we bought into Nevada through Howard Hughes."

"Yes, sir."

Ampleforth remembered Jack Heim now. The Agency, and indeed the United States Government, had had close dealings with Jack Heim over the years.

James Benedict Ampleforth the Second was well aware of the long standing triangular links between the Central Intelligence Agency, the Syndicate, and Howard Hughes. The CIA had traded directly with organised crime for years.

Prior to the invasion of Sicily in 1943 it had been President Roosevelt who had negotiated with Salvatore 'Lucky' Luciano in order that American boys would not have to spill blood for every yard of the island taken. Luciano had been in prison in Danbury, Conneticut, the DDI remembered. Still with silk underwear. Roosevelt had given Luciano his freedom in exchange for an opposition-free invasion of Sicily.

The go-between had been Jack Heim.

The Deputy Director brought his mind back to the present. "I don't like any of this, Patrick," he said. "The appeal is due to be heard shortly, and

Heim is involved." The DDI shook his head sadly. "I think the Englishman needs medical attention."

"But he is in hospital, sir."

James Benedict Ampleforth the Second closed his eyes and sighed, suffering his fool ungladly.

"Yes, Patrick. So send for The Doctor."

Jack is sitting with me now. I've been very sick but I'm going to get better. I feel it. Jack told me Eddie got away in the helicopter. If I close my eyes I can still see the blood spreading across Eddie's jacket.

Jack has been telling me about Las Vegas and Bugsy Segal and Meyer Lansky and 'Lucky' Luciano and how they all smuggled whisky distilled in Canada across Lake Erie, the 'Jewish Lake' and how when Prohibition ended, they were searching around for the new move, and how Bugsy Segal discovered gambling and Las Vegas. I'm not delirious.

And then the War came and Bugsy wanted to hit Hitler and Meyer wouldn't let him.

The doctors keep coming. They think I'm going to die. But I'm not going to die.

"But after the War, Jack," I asked. "What happened then?"

"Segal's energy and foresight founded the American gambling industry as it is today. He put a lot of passion into starting Las Vegas but the Sicilians were unhappy with the slow returns, and we found Benjamin splattered across the wallpaper in his Thunderbird Hotel suite. Benjamin Segal

431

sleeps with the Nevada armadillos. I picked up the pieces of Las Vegas."

Jack mopped my face with a flannel. He needn't make such a fuss.

"Go on, Jack."

"When I took over the running of the New Frontier and The Silver Slipper there had been a lot of problems. I cleaned them up and soon we were handling six million dollars a month. A lot of money in the early Fifties. A lot of money. I was just one of the people responsible for building and cleaning up the industry. When Hughes came to town he checked into one of the hotels. He took the top two floors with his entourage and the medical machines. We didn't want him there. He didn't gamble. We didn't want Hughes there."

The old man polished his glasses. His hair white in the sunlight that streamed through the blinds and bars to the prison hospital.

I know where I am. I am in Texas. I was shot trying to get into Eddie's helicopter. Yes, I would have gone with Eddie, but suddenly I decided not to. I pushed Eddie into the chopper. I can remember that. But I'm not delirious. Jack continues.

"So Hughes was asked to leave. He was taking up suites that were reserved for the high rollers, the big gamblers. Instead of leaving he asked us how much we wanted for the casinos. All of them. Thirty-five million dollars he paid us, Daniel, and I never met him face to face."

"How did you do the deal?" I asked.

"Hughes, well, I suppose it was Hughes, was in the room above me. He had one of those old-fashioned gadgets with two pads and two pencils.

Whatever is written on one pad is reproduced on the second. One pad in each room. Deal took six hours. Back and forth. A strange disembodied scrawl; a poltergeist's handwriting. My people thought he was crazy, but he paid the thirty-five million dollars easy enough. By draft. I knew Hughes wasn't crazy, Daniel. City's worth a hundred times that today."

FCI
TEXARKANA
SEPTEMBER

The silver Porsche Turbo 911 rumbled throatily into the car park of the Federal Correctional Institution at Texarkana, Texas.

The guards were used to the sight of the obscene bulbous sausage amongst their sedans and station wagons. One or two of the officers ran Lincolns or Cadillacs, which they claimed they could afford from overtime pay. Nobody else had a car like the doctor's Porsche.

Doctor Jan Scucek was a child of Polish immigrants who had come to Texas to work the oil fields. Father Scucek had been successful with his last wildcat. This strike had not made the family rich by Texas standards, but had given them the means to live in a good suburb of Houston, and provide their only son with the medical education that he had desired.

Young Jan had inherited his father's fierce anti-communism and had willingly responded to the CIA recruiter on campus, when the Agency had advertised for Polish speaking candidates. The young man had been recruited, tested and inducted into the CIA.

In defiance of the United States Constitution and the Central Intelligence Agency's charter forbidding domestic activity, the CIA maintains a secret

434

national network of agents who carry out clandestine operations on U.S. soil.

Doctor Jan Scucek was an inhabitant of this twilight world.

Outwardly a successful consultant to Houston's most prestigious hospital, the young doctor was ideally placed for carrying out the secret tasks which he did with a venomous precision. The CIA had discovered in Jan Scucek a young man with an extraordinary aptitude for one evil activity.

Assassination.

The cold, calculating fanatic had carried out more than one erasure for the Agency, his position as a doctor affording him an unrivalled range of pretexts for travel and entry into restricted areas.

Today he had been called out for one such task, assisting in the demise of an English prisoner who had been injured in an escape attempt.

In this instance it was relatively easy for Scucek to gain admission to the hospital since he was also the Consultant Medical Inspector (Texas) to the Federal Bureau of Prisons. An astute observer may have been puzzled as to why the doctor's hands were clad in thin unseasonal black leather gloves.

But there was no observer to remark the fact.

The Pole was being paid thirty thousand dollars by the Agency for this hit, money that he would donate to so-called freedom groups in Poland.

The doctor was a fanatic.

But he was not a fool.

The Englishman could not die on the first visit.

The doctor was well versed in the various ways of killing an unconscious patient in hospital, and he wanted to judge for himself the least detectable method for the circumstances.

Jan Scucek, Doctor of Medicine, picked his bag up from the hood of the car, locked the doors, and strode towards the prison hospital.

FCI
TEXARKANA
PRISON HOSPITAL
SEPTEMBER

I'm getting better. I'm feeling stronger. Jack fed me some soup. He told me stories how he and his cousin Meyer fled a pogrom across Poland. How the Cossacks came and murdered their family in the village. How he and Meyer walked by day and night to Cracow.

Jack feeds me soup. I can taste the chicken soup from Poland sixty years ago. I can taste the chaloh and the lokshen. I feel the salt in my face and the machine gun in my hand and the night winds of Lake Erie and I hear the whisky bottles rattling in their crates. I feel the ticker tape welcome in New York after Howard Hughes broke the world speed record. I'm in the RKO studio making movies. Little Caesar, Hell's Angels and The Outlaw.

Ava Gardner hit me over the head with a statue but I'm not delirious. I'm with Jack and Bugsy Siegel and Howard Hughes and Lucky Luciano and Grandfather Heim.

The old shammes smiles and takes us inside the shul, the synagogue in Cracow. The shammes leads us to our cousin Meyer who we find deep in prayer. His eyes are closed, his hands hold his tallis, his prayershawl up to his face, his body sways in the ancient ways that remind the Jews of their travels from the Holy Lands in Bible times, when prayers had to be recited on the backs of camels as we fled our pursuers.

As Meyer and Jack fled to America.

I know where I am. I'm in Texarkana. Eddie escaped in a helicopter. I hope he didn't die. If he did that was how he would have wanted to go.

SEAQUARIUM
MIAMI
FLORIDA
SEPTEMBER

The thirty foot black and white killer whale arched up, bounced the giant rubber ball decorated with Stars and Stripes, seized a fish from its trainer's hand and crashed back into the topaz water sending fountains of spray cascading over the audience.

James Benedict Ampleforth II, Deputy Director (Intelligence) of the CIA was soaked.

"Wasn't that great, Uncle Bendy?" The DDI winced at his four year old nephew's use of the family nickname in front of his Agency colleagues.

Patrick Garrity suppressed a giggle. The whole day had been crazy since he had touched down at Miami International and followed the circled shark signs along US 1 beyond the Rickenbacker Causeway to the Seaquarium. In the company of his boss and two hard-eyed Agency bodyguards sporting dark glasses, bulging jackets and lapel microphones, he had stood with the crowds for the show in the porpoise tank, been drenched by the penguins, soaked by the seals and amused by the pelicans, and was now seated in front of the grandstand watching the establishment's biggest captive earn its lunch.

Ampleforth's precocious four year old nephew,

Eric, sported a bright yellow Just-Us-Kids T-shirt and seemed to have a unquenchable appetite for the Whippy Cones which dripped over the dark sleeves of the DDI's bodyguards as they wearily schlepped back and forth to the ice-cream parlour.

Finally, Ampleforth turned to his Senior Co-ordinator and raised a patrician eyebrow, a signal for the briefing that Garrity had travelled fifteen hundred miles to give.

"We have the hospital room bugged, sir. The Englishman is delirious and near death. "

"That's very good, Patrick. And what about the old man?"

"Heim is still at his bedside, sir, telling him stories."

"What kind of stories, Patrick?"

"Oh, stories of his youth in Russia, Poland and Brazil, his life among the Pygmies, the early days of the Bugs and Meyer gang, tales about Howard Hughes. Stuff like that."

"Of course, Patrick, Heim knew Hughes as well as any man. I never met the old billionaire myself although he worked with the Agency since the days of 'Wild Bill' Donovan."

The killer whale roared across the aquarium towing his keeper on special skis as Garrity spoke: "Hughes was a little before my time, sir. He was just a legend to me."

Ampleforth's face took on a wistful mien. "Do you realise, Patrick, that in the thirty years following the Second World War, the United States fought in Korea, Vietnam and a dozen other places around the globe. We sent rockets around Mars and Venus, put a man on the moon, had one President assassinated and another resign in disgrace. But we could not get Howard Robard Hughes inside a Federal courtroom." The Director was lost in thought for a moment and then turned to Garrity.

"How near death is the Englishman?"

"He's not expected to last the night."

"The sharks are on in ten minutes, Uncle Bendy."

"Yes, Eric. And we're going to see them. I promised your mother you'd see everything." Ampleforth smiled indulgently and patted the little boy on the head.

Garrity thought that the DDI had a touch of the basking shark about him, himself.

Ampleforth touched Garrity's arm. "So we've wasted our thirty thousand dollars on the Polish doctor?"

"Well it does seem like we don't need him now, sir."

"Maybe he'll give us credit for one, Patrick?"

Patrick Xavier Garrity realised his boss was making a joke.

FCI
TEXARKANA
PRISON HOSPITAL
SEPTEMBER

I know what happened to me. I crashed the XF-ll into some lady's roof in Beverley Hills.

Jack is sitting beside me now talking to me. I'm an old man. I inject codeine into my legs to dull the pain from the airplane crash. I take heroin, but I'm not delirious.

I like double pumping. I inject half the fluid, then I draw it back up into the syringe with my blood. I let the needle dangle for a moment then I shoot the full load back into my system.

Now I can relax.

Hey bop-a-ree-bop. Hey bop-a-ree-bop.

I know what was wrong with the plane. I designed her and built her, and I'll damn well test fly her. If anyone's going to fall out of the sky, it'll be me, I said. Well, I did. I know what went wrong and I told Noah. It was the ailerons. They pulled the opposite way. Some stupid bastard fitted them wrong. I wouldn't be paranoid if I - but that's what they say about me. That I'm paranoid. I'm Howard Robard Hughes.

The courts forced me to take five hundred and thirty five million dollars for my shareholding in TWA. I ask you. Is it a free country when they can do things like that to you?

TELEPHONE CONVERSATION BETWEEN LANGLEY AND WASHINGTON D.C.
DIRECT LINK
OCTOBER

"The doctor called, sir."

"And how is the patient?"

"Deteriorating and delirious, sir."

"Let me know when he's reached the next alliterative."

"Pardon, sir?"

"Dead, Patrick. Let me know when he's dead."

FCI
TEXARKANA
OCTOBER

"That real estate is Government owned, Jack." The attorney's voice echoed hollowly down the line.

Jack Heim and his Washington lawyer knew of at least six agencies that would be tapping this call, so they chose their words with care.

"What's the condition of the property, Irving?"

"Not good, Jack. There's a lot of subsidence there."

"Is the structure safe?"

"No, Jack. It's in a very dangerous condition indeed."

"Thank you, Irving. There's no need for you to pursue the matter."

"Alright, Jack. Is there anything else I can do?"

"No, thank you. Goodbye, Irving."

"Goodbye Jack."

The old man stepped out of the telephone box. So the Polish doctor was a CIA hitman, was he? Jack Heim decided to pay a visit to the woodwork shop on his way back to the hospital.

CIA HEADQUARTERS
OFFICE OF THE DEPUTY
DIRECTOR (INTELLIGENCE)
LANGLEY
VIRGINIA
OCTOBER

"The latest prognosis from the hospital is that the Englishman is not going to die, sir," said the Senior Co-ordinator.

"Oh yes, he is, Patrick. Oh, yes he is."

FCI
TEXARKANA
PRISON HOSPITAL
OCTOBER

Light filtered through the Venetian blinds into the dark ward where the white coated figure of Doctor Jan Scucek crouched tensely over the unconscious Englishman.

Scucek kept his movements as silent as possible to avoid disturbing both the patient and the old man snoring gently in the soft armchair across the room.

Turning his back on the old man, the doctor held the syringe up to the light and pushed the plunger, squirting out a small quantity of liquid.

As he did so he felt a sharp prickling pain in the back of his neck and his arms and legs became heavy.

The doctor froze, eyes fixed on the needle in his hand. He became numb and motionless. His brain alive but unable to transfer messages to his limbs. Paralysis spread down his neck across his shoulders and then through his body. His knees buckled and Doctor Jan Scucek collapsed against the hospital bed, before falling heavily onto the floor.

Across the room Jack Heim lowered the wooden blowpipe from his lips. A second dart was not neccessary. The old man's aim was as good today as it had been when he had lived with the Pygmies

more than fifty years earlier.

"It's a triumph of justice, Daniel. The Federal Judge overturned himself. The new State Judge has sentenced you to time served. You're free to go."

Jack's eyes were twinkling sapphires behind his pebble glasses as he beamed at me.

"I don't know how to thank you, Jack."

"Your freedom is thanks enough for me, Daniel. You didn't do anything against the U.S. You could have exchanged those printing plates for a lot of money and the ticket East at anytime. But you didn't. You made a deal with the U.S. Government and they broke their word. Well, they've mended it again now. There is justice in America."

"How about you, Jack?"

"Oh, don't worry about me. I'll be completely free within a few months. They never did get the nine million," the old man laughed.

"I suppose they'll turn me over to Scotland Yard?"

"Only if you want them to, Daniel. You have the Right of Return to Israel, and you can't be extradited. I've spoken to my people. If you want to stroll down the Dizengoff in Tel Aviv, you can."

My mind revolved. The thought that I wouldn't automatically be deported to England never occurred to me. Should I go to Israel and still have problems hanging over me? No. I don't want to keep on running. My family and friends are in London.

"Thank you, Jack, but I'll go home."

FCI
TEXARKANA
NOVEMBER

"Man, you not free, not if you're going to Dallas Jail."

I admired myself in the brown suit again. I'd lost a heap of weight and although the clothes from reception were not to my taste, they would do to go home in. Even if they were a little on the light-weight side for an English winter.

R.D. prised the cap off a Coke bottle and inserted a straw. I hunched a shoulder up in the suit. The sleeves were too long. The nylon material felt odd, but there was no doubt that I looked well. I was tanned and the time exercising had been well spent. I hadn't looked or felt this good in years. I pirouetted in front of the mirror.

R.D. sucked his Coke, making exasperated noises.

"Are these sleeves too long?" I pulled at a cuff.

"Shit, man. You just don't understand. Dallas Jail is one mean place," he paused. "They're bad moth-erfuckers there. I'm from Dallas."

"I'll tell them I'm a preacher," I said. "It's only for one night before Immigration collect me."

"Preacher shit!" R.D. was plainly disgusted. "Dallas Jail ain't safe for Jesus. I'm worried about you, sucker." R.D. finished the bottle, and banged it down on the table. I had never seen my pal so uptight. Was he joking? Trying to scare me?

"I'll be alright, R.D." The young Texan crossed the room and gripped my arms the same way as Eddie had done on the volleyball pitch.

A voodoo shiver seized me.

I backflashed to the gunfire. I was under the helicopter blades. The crimson blood patch mushrooming across Eddie's back again.

R.D. shook me and I snapped to the present. The young Texan looked at me tormentedly, as if I were embarking upon a dangerous voyage through uncharted waters.

"I'll be safe in Dallas, R.D."

The black man shook his head. "Man, they killed the President in Dallas."

TEXAS
NOVEMBER

I found the car small and strange, the motion an unstable sensation after all those months in prison. An uncertain claustrophobia enveloped me in the dark interior as we sped across dusty Texas.

The wide highway rolled through endless fields of mechanical donkeys nodding black gold out of the Texan soil. Nod, nod, nod. The marshals were polite enough. We stopped for a hamburger in one of the fast food cafes that dotted US 30. We flashed through Sulphur Springs and Greenville toward the dreaded Dallas.

I was heading for what? Deportation?

I still had to face London.

England. What would the Yard do to me? Would they oppose bail? I had an English trial to face, wigs and gowns, suppressed evidence, less rights for the accused awaiting trial. No private letters, no telephones in the jails, no practical access to judges for relief from mistreatment.

I had been impressed with many aspects of the American justice system, despite my Kafkaesque experiences of multifarious courts, jails and police forces.

I would be less able to defend my case from inside Brixton Prison.

If I ever reached London alive.

I remembered the prisoner I'd met one day in the punishment cells. He was serving a hundred and four years.

I enquired of him what he liked to do best.

"Heroin," said the Lifer.

"How do you cope with your sentence? I had asked.

"One day at a time."

"We are running early," said a marshal. "You'll be in Dallas jail soon."

"Do we go through the centre of town?"

"Sure," replied the Texan. "Why?"

"I'd like to see the book repository and the Grassy Knoll."

The other marshal turned around and grinned at me. "Are you an assassination freak?"

"No," I replied. "It's just that, well, I've never been in Dallas and I'm being deported. So if you don't take me to see where they shot Kennedy, no one else will."

"Okay, Huey. Head for Dealey Plaza." The big sedan accelerated. I relaxed in my seat enjoying myself. This was like the movies.

The two marshals drove me around downtown Dallas, pointing out all the places made infamous in endless newsreels and documentaries. The younger marshal turned to me.

"What do you think of the Kennedy killing?"

"A scar on the American psyche like Vietnam and Watergate."

"Well, I guess it's a scar that will never heal." The marshal shook his head.

I had seen the outlines of those scars under the surface of modern American life. The United States seemed to me to be in the grip of racism, violence, drugs and over-policing. I was glad to be leaving.

Only there was still Dallas jail to be faced.
The marshals headed downtown.
The tourist trip was over.
Only a miracle could save me now.

OVAL OFFICE
WHITE HOUSE
WASHINGTON D.C.
NOVEMBER

The President of the United States popped another jelly bean into his mouth and smiled into the telephone.

"Thank you, Jack. You and the committee have been a tremendous support to me throughout this whole campaign."

The Chief Executive's eyes narrowed as he listened to the authoritative voice on the other end of the line. When the voice stopped the President spoke.

"No problem at all, Jack."

Across the room, James Benedict Ampleforth II felt another spasm of back pain and shifted his weight nervously to the other leg. The President had not invited him to sit nor had addressed a single word to him in the ten minutes that the Deputy Director (Intelligence) had stood on the Oval Office carpet. From time to time during the phone call from Jack Heim the President had looked up at Ampleforth, his expression grim.

The suntanned Californian face lightened now as he exchanged parting pleasantries.

"Why, thank you, Jack. I'll pass those fine wishes onto the First Lady, and please give our warmest regards to...." The old politician glanced at the briefing paper in front of him, "- your lovely wife, Julie."

The President of the United States replaced the telephone receiver and affixed the CIA man with an Argus eye.

"Whose side are you on, Ampleforth? The Soviet Union's? Your response to every difficulty is kill, eliminate, erase. You have alienated the most powerful lobby in Washington. You've upset one of our party's biggest fund raisers. You have damn near single handedly embroiled this administration in a scandal involving the Cubans, the Mafia, cocaine for Contra arms, anti-Castro freaks and the British Government. And all this, just before an election. You have disobeyed a direct instruction given to you in this room by your Commander-in-Chief. I have nothing more to say to you. You may leave your resignation with my Chief-of-Staff on your way out."

James Benedict Ampleforth II stood erect, fighting down bitter tears. Only his West Point training enabled him to take his leave in dignified silence.

As the (ex) Deputy Director (Intelligence) left the Oval Office, he heard the President say:

"I'm ready for my call to Texas now."

TEXAS
NOVEMBER

The miracle came in a crackle of radio static.

Our car number was called. I listened to an exchange between the marshals and their base. I made out the words 'airport' and 'immigration'.

The young marshal in the front seat turned round to look at me.

"You ain't going to Dallas Jail, son. We're taking you direct to the airport. You're flying to Miami, you lucky son of a bitch." He slapped his colleague on the shoulder.

"Make a 180, Huey."

FEDERAL COURTHOUSE
IMMIGRATION SECTION
MIAMl
FLORIDA
NOVEMBER

The immigration hearing passed in a blur, for I was high on freedom. Louis the Lawyer led me into a tiny wood panelled courtroom. I've been in bigger phone boxes.

Despite my weight loss there still wasn't room for me, and I was made to stand at the door like a naughty boy, which I suppose I was, since the United States of America was deporting me. It was another Alice in Wonderland number. The Immigration Service Agent whom I had told to 'fuck off' when he had banged on the bars of my cage at four o'clock in the morning, handed my passport to the judge. I glanced at my watch, still stopped, but the circle of diamonds reassured me.

I thought about some other diamonds in a little leather bag in the Austrian bank. I brought my mind back to the present.

The judge wrote in my passport and handed it to Louis the Lawyer, who bowed and gathered up his papers. The three minute hearing was over. In the corridor Louis returned my passport to me. The judge had written across the U.S. visa 'MIAMI D' followed by the date.

It was all very discreet.

Whoever held the strings was pulling them very gently indeed.

KEY LARGO
FLORIDA
NOVEMBER

Arturo Jaconelli slammed the telephone receiver back into its cradle. His contact in the CIA had been explicit. The Englishman was being deported and the Agency were under orders to take no further action.

But he, Arturo Jaconelli, was not under anybody's orders. The young Mafioso was driven purely by his own manic sense of retaliation. His face was dark with fury as he barked his instructions at the intercom.

"Fuel the Gulfstream for Europe."

LONGITUDE 77
LATITUDE 27
MID-AIR
NOVEMBER

"Hello, would you like to join us?"

The lobster faced sergeant smiled at me awkwardly. When I didn't reply, he continued.

"We don't have to talk business."

England was here already.

Inflight.

There were two of them. I recalled the inspector from years ago. He had been a TDC, a Temporary Detective Constable on 'my manor' when all this had begun. I smiled at him as the stewardess opened the Möet. He had risen rapidly to high rank. He was probably super bright or a freemason.

Or both.

"We've had a wonderful week in Miami," the inspector said, "and we want to thank you for it. We've got no axe to grind, no animosity."

"Well, cheers." I raised my glass.

"Cheers."

A well drilled happy little chorus drinking my champagne at twenty-six thousand feet. Now for the biscuit. I wanted to start work on getting bail straight away. I needed to hit the streets in London, not the dank overcrowded rat hole of Brixton Prison.

461

The sergeant got up from the seat and patted his stomach. There was plenty to pat.

As he moved down the aisle I leant closer to his boss.

"Can I get any help?"

This was the key question. The phrase meant, Will You Take Money To Help Me?

"Oh, I should think so." The Inspector nodded. "You know someone, I understand."

My turn to nod.

In order to bribe a British policeman one needs a 'vicar' to vouch for you. In this case it was Benny's man, a south London Detective Sergeant. All the crooked business is done through a D.S.. That's the ambitious rank. The lower ones don't have the power, and the higher ranks don't want to get their hands dirty. This inspector had just been 'made-up' from Sergeant. He would probably do the business himself. "Can I get bail?"

The policeman twirled his glass, staring into it. "I don't see why not."

After that, the flight was a breeze.

"I brought you some Danish from the pastry cook at Caesar's Palace. I kept them in the chiller on the way down here."

"Thank you, Harry," said the prisoner.

The dapper little visitor looked around the meeting area. Inmates were sitting with their families and friends. Some cuddling children on their knees, others kissing sweethearts, arguing with wives.

The business-like little man in the dark airweight suit felt out of place.

Jack Heim munched appreciatively on the pastry, licking the white icing sugar from his fingers.

"How are things on The Strip, Harry?"

"They're good, Jack, they're good. All the houses are doing fine, but I didn't need to fly all the way down just to tell you that."

"I appreciate you coming, Harry. This couldn't be handled over the phone. Tell me, are those Florida Italians still trying to get in to Atlantic City?"

The little man paused before answering. Now they were coming to it.

"They're busting a gut to do so."

"Well, maybe it wouldn't be a bad idea to let them in," said the old Godfather as he moved a hand back toward the pastry bag.

His visitor eyed him shrewdly. "You think they should be let in?"

"There's room for everybody, Harry." Jack Heim fished around amongst the tissue paper and chose another Danish. "I wouldn't have any objections, but the Italians are being difficult with a young friend of mine."

"How difficult?"

"They don't want him to see another Yom Kippur, Harry."

"So how can I help?"

Jack Heim told him.

PADDINGTON GREEN
POLICE STATION
NOVEMBER

Paddington Green Police Station, the Met's anti-terrorist centre, knew me well. This station had been my local nick for years. They were always bashing my front door down looking for dope, or hovering about outside moaning about the Rolls being double-parked on the pavements. It was from here that the four year hunt for me had been co-ordinated. But time is a great diluter of police passions and only the ghosts of the detectives who had started the chase now remained.

Lobster Face led me into a sparse office which boasted a wonderful view of the rain drenched station yard below, with its assortment of police cars, impounded vehicles, high walls, security cameras and dustbins.

Paddington Green is a fortress with underground bunkers, bombproof living accommodation, radio and TV control centres, communication rooms and weapon stores.

It's a long way from Dixon of Dock Green.

Many British policemen have acquired a callous arrogance when dealing with members of the public. Their elitism is rooted in the custom that British policemen are rarely if ever brought to justice for assault or murder. More than three hundred people die in British police cells every year, allegedly of natural causes.

I hoped I wasn't going to be one of them.

The killers of Blair Peach, Jimmy Kelly, et al are still out there smiling in their crisp blue uniforms as they courteously assist elderly ladies across the road.

The police demonstrate the same even-handedness towards the public whether they are bashing up pregnant hippies at pop festivals, shooting five year old children to death or unleashing fusillades of gunfire at innocent members of the populace who vaguely resemble someone they're after.

None of this happened to me.

I was given a cup of tea and biscuits.

Good old Britain.

DEAUVILLE
FRANCE
NOVEMBER

Arturo Jaconelli strolled along the windswept beach, shoulders hunched, head bent, the better to hear the softly spoken little man walking by his side.

"Arturo, this request has nothing to do with business. It's personal."

"It's very personal to me," said the Mafioso. "I have some dear friends in an English jail and my niece is still a widow."

"I understand how you feel, but you did invite yourself to the party. If you ease up you'll be doing us a great favour, Arturo, which my people won't forget."

"You say this is personal."

"Someone who commands a lot of respect amongst your people and ours, wants the Englishman to have no more trouble." The dapper man cast a quizzical eye up at Jaconelli.

"I've had a great deal of expense," complained the cocaine king.

The other nodded. "I understand that you have problems with your licence applications in Atlantic City."

"Everyone says *your* people," Jaconelli jabbed an emphasising finger, "have been doing all the objecting. I heard that the Jews don't want to share

467

anymore."

"Now Arturo, that simply isn't true." The little man shook his head sadly. "There's enough pain in this world without our quarrelling with each other. You'll find no more obstacles in the way of your licences."

The two men turned back toward the distant black Citroen Prestige waiting solemnly on the deserted seafront. Jaconelli broke the silence.

"And the Englishman?"

"He lives."

"My father always respected your people."

"Thank you, Arturo."

IN THE CELLS BELOW PADDINGTON STATION NOVEMBER LATER THE SAME DAY

I heard the rattle of keys first then the heavy door swung open to reveal the lobster faced sergeant smiling at me.

"Visitor for you."

Benny bounced into the cell, wearing a cashmere overcoat and a watermelon smile.

"A nice to-do this, old son."

My friend looked around the gloomy chamber. Despite the brand new police station the architect had managed to retain some of the original charm of the Victorian era by tastefully using broken white toilet tiles, a smashed lightbulb in a rusty cage, iron studded doors, a bell that didn't work and fine old horse hair police blankets (1928 issue).

"Do you want a colour television and a four poster sent in? Why don't you have a phone? I told them to get you a phone."

I burst out laughing. Benny's superconfidence was irrepressible. The lobster policeman withdrew leaving the door discreetly open.

"Here." Benny handed me a carrier bag. "There's smoked salmon, orange juice, clean shirts, underwear and a spy-less thriller. Oh yes, and socks. They're not silk but I know you won't mind."

469

"Thank you."

"Never mind 'thank you'. You mother's upstairs in a mink coat and diamonds looking very angry, waiting to sign you out. Dee's been on the phone; she loves you and wants to see you. Your 'Daily Mail' is all fixed and you owe me another two grand."

"Well done, Benny. How much bail do they want?"

"I'm not the fucking magistrate, I don't know. There's a hearing at Westminster this afternoon." Benny dug into his pocket.

"Here." Benny held out a small silver compact and a little silver spoon. I opened the compact. Glistening crystals of cocaine shone back at me as I dug the spoon into the snow white pile.

"Hurry up," said Benny. "Or the whole fucking police station will want a line."

TEWKESBURY
GLOUCESTERSHIRE
ENGLAND
DECEMBER

A fine glitterdust of frost had turned the garden into a winter fairyland and caused the white Silver Spirit to glimmer in the moonlight. Somewhere an owl hooted. I stood at the door of the old hunting lodge and looked out at the starlit night.

These grounds were an animal sanctuary now, something of an irony in the heart of the Cotswolds, where hunting is a way of life. I had been feeding a hare with carrots and chopped apple and I could see from his tracks across the snow covered lawn that he had enjoyed his supper.

In my drive, alongside the Rolls Royce, stood a new Mercedes Coupé. The sports car's mud spattered flanks spoke eloquently of the high speed dash back from London, loaded with turkeys, cigars, champagne and other plunder from Fortnum's.

Incongruous between the two luxury beasts nestled a little yellow Mini. I turned back inside closing the centuries old door behind me.

In the great hall, logs roared in a fireplace that could have roasted an ox, casting a glow of fire about the hall. The music of the Eagles, Hotel California, wafted thirty-six feet up to the polished oak beams of the mediaeval ceiling.

On a rare Bakhan rug, Kim sat Pasha-like, stuffing a bronze pipe with hashish. From the kitchen came the gentle clatter of coffee cups, and I caught a glimpse of Dee's pink dressing-gown as she fiddled with the percolator.

In front of the fire, Jade, the Great Dane puppy, sprawled contentedly, eyes closed, power latent in the muscles beneath his golden back.

The computer phone beeped insistently, and I hunted beneath the pile of court affidavits for the instrument.

I gave my usual brilliant telephone opening line. "Hello."

An American operator identified herself and asked if I would accept a collect call from a Mr. R.D. Makepeace in Texarkana, Texas.

I said I would.

"Say, sucker." R.D.'s voice echoed down the line. "What's happening?"

"Oh, ain't nothing much, R.D. How are things on the wing?"

"Say, sucker. They 'bout the same as ever, man. How you doing?"

"I'm keeping off the streets." I placed the receiver close to the Eagles and blasted them back across to the States.

"Say man." R.D.'s voice was heavy with emotion. "Thanks for your letter. I got some good news too. I'm coming out. I got three days' homeleave next week, then I'll be free for good in a few months."

"That's fantastic, R.D." I was thrilled for him.

Dee came out of the kitchen. "Is that R.D.?"

I nodded.

472

"Give him my love."

"R.D., my woman sends you her love."

"Just wait till I get there, man. She can have it in person."

I sensed that something was troubling my friend.

"Anything I can do for you, R.D.?"

"Say man. I ain't been home in four years. I don't have no clothes, no money."

"I got my pen and paper here, R.D. Tell me what you need, I'll get it and freight it out to you."

"I go home Friday, man. Today's Tuesday."

"No problem, my man. It'll be there. My pleasure. What do you need?"

"I want a green suit, a green shirt, and a green tie."

"Right on," I said. "Anything else?"

"Yeah man, shoes."

"Colour?"

"Green." We both said it in unison. I took down sizes. "Dee will go up to London, to the Kings Road tomorrow, R.D. She'll go shopping for you. In a white Rolls Royce." I knew my friend would like that. "Say sucker. There's something else." "You need money. I'll send some."

"Say, sucker."

"Man, you're a real nuisance, R.D. Save my life just so you can drive me crazy." A glowing silence crossed the airwaves powerful enough to heat the chilly Atlantic itself. "It'll be done, R.D., and airfreighted."

"Say, man."

"Don't say nothing, man."

A few days later, I was idly watching the nine o'clock news when the phone rang. It was the operator from America. I grinned in anticipation. The trip to the Kings Road and the airfreight had cost the best part of a thousand pounds. Not to mention the ten one hundred dollars bills built into the heel of one of the green Bally shoes. Just where he used to keep our stash in the penitentiary.

Except that our prison footwear hadn't been soft Swiss leather.

R.D.'s voice came on the line.

"Say, sucker." For once the garrulous black Texan gangster was lost for words.

"Say ....."

THE END?

THE HOLE IN ONE GANG.

PAUL SIMONS & JOHN CARTER.

TRUE STORY

Being keen golf fans they were amazed at the number of times "Yellow Disc" – denoting a hole-in-one – would appear on the scoreboard.

They started betting on holes-in-one wherever and whenever they could. There were astonishing financial rewards. The duo discussed the possibility of a major hole-in-one assault and were soon convinced 1991 would be a year the bookies would never forget.

Once accepted each successful hole in one bet would create a tidal wave of money running onto the year's final tournament for a potential payday of all time.

The mind blowing betting revelations are at last revealed to the world in this controversial true life comedy/ adventure about two shrewd gamblers who land!!!

"ONE OF THE BIGGEST COUPS IN GAMBLING HISTORY"
The Sun
"THE BIGGEST GOLF KILLING OF ALL TIME"
The Sporting Life

Paperback price £4.95 net U.K.

YELLOW BRICK PUBLISHERS. 2, Lonsdale Road, Queens Park, London. NW6 6RD.

AUTOBIOGRAPHY

GANGSTERS LADY.

ELLEN CANNON.

The story of ELLEN CANNON'S life tells what it's like being a member of one of Notting Dale's largest families. This Book is packed with incidents. As her man rose through the ranks of villainy and became a major gangland figure, she was introduced into the society of London's top Jollies of the underworld.
She learned to play the game of the gangsters lady in strict accordance with the rules. Whatever knowledge she had of the secrets of gangland she kept to herself. Now for the first time she's telling all.
She pulls no punches and gives a documented account of the violent life with her husband.
She is a remarkable lady.

Paperback price £4.95 net U.K.

CARDBOARD CITY.

JOE CANNON.

What turned a happy family man with an infant daughter to drink? When his money ran out, he found refuge among London's homeless beneath the arches of Waterloo Bridge. Living amongst a community of the homeless and the hopeless where society's outcasts sleep in cardboard boxes. This is a harrowing story marked by scenes of violence.
This book tells the story of Tommy Hutton? Who is he?

Paperback price £4.95 net U.K.

YELLOW BRICK PUBLISHERS. 2, Lonsdale Road, Queens Park, London. NW6 6RD.